Songbird

Laci Barry Post

Copyright © 2013 by Laci Post

ISBN-10: 061592669X
ISBN-13: 978-0615926698

For My Grandparents –
James and Joyce Barry
Paul and Gwen Green

Chapter 1

May 29, 1943 - Ava's hands trembled as she gripped the wheel with one and turned the key with the other. The car roared, and so did her heart.

"Come on, Ava. Give her some gas and let out the clutch. James will be out here any second!" Carson, her older brother, shouted over the loud motor.

"I'm a' hurrying," Ava yelled back.

She scooted up as far as she could in the seat and pushed the gas pedal and let go of the clutch at the same time. The car jolted, threw them forward, and stopped.

"Slower on the clutch."

Ava inhaled and tried a second time. This time it worked, and they went whisking through the open field.

"Whew!" Carson watched the dirt fly up in the air all around them. "Take her to the right."

Ava turned the wheel sharply, the car whinnied to the side, and the two laughed at their endeavor. Her confidence was rising and so was their speed.

"Circle her up!"

One circle, two circles, three circles -- Ava obeyed. She couldn't believe she was actually behind the wheel of a car, much less driving. Her mother would find it scandalous, but she didn't care at the moment.

"Boy, what a ride!" Carson hung on for another lap.

Ava widened her circle and was about to give the vehicle yet more gas when the running and waving figure of her oldest brother, James, stopped her. Either the noise of their adventure or the missing key had given them away. Ava let go of the gas pedal, the car lurched to a stop, and they bounced back in the seat with unremorseful grins covering their faces.

"Out! Out! Out!" James hollered when he had reached them and flung open Ava's door. "Ava, if it wasn't your birthday, I'd tell mother on you, and Carson, I guess you're off the hook too, but if I ever...."

Victoria Stilwell rotated the multi-layered cake, dripping with sugary chocolate icing, as she lit each of her daughter's birthday candles.

"You better blow them all out before I beat you to it," her father Sheffield said and leaned his puckered lips in toward the now seventeen glowing candles.

Carson mimicked his father and also leaned his sunburned face in toward the cake.

"I'll get ya both if you blow this girl's birthday candles out." Victoria pushed away their faces with the palms of her hands. "Now, Ava, make a wish, and it better not be about any young men."

Ava laughed, tilted her head, and smiled as if thinking of a wish her mother would not approve of.

"And, it better not be about driving any Fords, either," James said and received a sly smile from his sister.

He owned the first car in their family, and he didn't let anyone forget it.

"Enough nonsense. Let's sing to Ava and let her blow out her candles." Victoria quieted the family, placed a hand on Ava's slender back, and began the birthday melody.

Ava's luminous face hovered over the awaiting candles, and her lips parted in a radiant smile as she accepted her moment of grandeur. Her parents, her brothers, her new sister-in-law Estelle, and her grandpa, Chester Carson, serenaded her, but it was her grandpa's bombastic voice that ended the song with a raspy howl. Ava pushed back her dark-brown hair and blew out the candles with three successive puffs. Everyone clapped, and Chester Carson gave his granddaughter a kiss on the cheek.

"Happy Birthday, little Annie."

"Can't you call her by her rightful name now that she's a young lady?" Victoria sighed.

"I would if you wouldn't have named her after that despicable aunt of yours."

"Ava gets the first piece." Victoria slapped away Carson's reaching hand and set before Ava a large slice of chocolate cake.

Ava selected a sizeable bite with her fork and let it melt in her mouth, relishing the moistness and richness of the cake. Her mother made delicious pound cakes and chocolate pies throughout the year, but she would only make her celebrated chocolate cakes for family birthdays.

"Ava, Estelle and I have a little present for you." James revealed a long, neatly wrapped package from underneath the table.

"We hope you like it," Estelle said.

When Ava had slipped off the bow and opened the box, her gray eyes widened.

3

"It's the Marian Martin dress pattern I saw in dad's newspaper!" She held up a cream-colored dress with a fitted bodice, capped short sleeves, and full, knee-length skirt for everyone to see.

"We thought a working girl might need some new clothes to go to town in," James explained, and Victoria sighed at the mention of her daughter working outside the home.

"You'll look lovely in it, Ava. Your mother showed me the pattern and told me how much you liked it; so we ordered it, and I made it for you. It doesn't have your mom's expert handy work, but I think it turned out well, considering." Estelle helped Ava hold the dress up to her 5'4" frame. "If it's a little long, I can take up the hem."

"Oh, it's perfect, Estelle. I'm sure that I'll look swanky walking around Anniston now." Ava altered her voice to sound like a sultry radio actress and hugged her sister-in-law and then her brother.

James and Estelle married in early December and lived in a small house on an adjacent three-acre plot of land that Grandpa Chester had given them as a wedding present. As long as Ava could remember, though, Estelle had been a part of their family, and she loved her as much as her brothers.

When Ava finally returned the dress to its box, Carson dropped a smaller package wrapped in newspaper in her lap. She unwrapped the gift and found it to be a box of scented stationary.

"Thanks, Car," she said without an embrace, holding the pages of stationary up to her nose.

"Yea," he shrugged as he left the table and stretched out his long legs on the living room floor.

Her last gift was from her parents, her grandpa, and her grandparents Jack and Lavenia Stilwell in Birmingham. Her father handed her a square-shaped package, and Ava moved it from side to side and ran her fingers over it.

"Don't guess at your presents like your brother. Open it," Victoria said.

At her mother's prodding, Ava unwrapped the package to find an ornate silver music box decorated with roses. She lifted the lid of the box, and an airy song that the engraving identified as *Midnight Serenade* met her ear. There was an inscription inside that read, "To Ava on your 17th birthday. Love, Mom, Dad, Grandpa, Grandma, and Granddaddy."

"So, whatcha think?" her father asked.

"It's beautiful. Where did you get it?"

"Your grandparents and I conspired to have it shipped from Birmingham." Sheffield leaned over his daughter and turned the small handle protruding from the side of the box to make the music continue. "We know how you love music, and we wanted to give you something you would always remember us by."

In response, Ava embraced her parents and grandpa.

Ava helped her mother and Estelle clean up cake crumbs, plates, and forks. The men were already seated around the radio listening to the "News from Europe" radio hour.

"With the recent surrender of German and Italian troops in North Africa, it is suspected that the war will move to a European arena now," a clear, intuitive voice announced.

Estelle always got quiet when the war was mentioned, and Ava watched as she methodically wiped the table with a damp cloth. Her amber eyes looked beyond the table, however, and her pink cheeks paled in apprehension. She was terrified that her husband's 3-A military classification due to his marriage status and defense work at the Ordnance Depot

5

would be re-classified to 1-A at any moment and that she would lose the only man she had ever loved.

"Estelle, you'll have to come to Wakefield's and visit me. I could help you pick out a new hat," Ava said.

"Of course I'll come see you, and you can help me spend all of James's money."

They laughed, put up their dish clothes, and went to sit with the men. Estelle sat down next to her husband, and he wrapped his arm around her and began whispering nonsense in her ear.

Beside them was Sheffield, who sat listening to the radio with his long legs stretched out, his hands behind his graying dark head, and his sapphire eyes fastened on the ceiling.

"Welp, I think I'll go lie down a bit," Grandpa Chester said and disappeared.

No one answered; they were all accustomed to his evening ritual of sleeping off his full stomach.

Victoria emerged from the kitchen and stood with her back against the wall, wiping her hands on a cloth and only half listening to the war reports.

"I still don't see how come we had to tramp off to Africa first. We could've just whooped them in Germany and been done with the whole mess."

"I told you, blossom, the Allied forces aren't strong enough for a European attack yet," Sheffield explained.

"Well, they didn't have a problem in Africa."

"It's a lucky thing for President Roosevelt that he doesn't have you on his war committee." Sheffield hid a grin from his wife.

"Umph" was her only response, and she looked over at her son Carson and told herself that he would never have to go to North Africa. James had already obtained military exemption for defense work, and she firmly believed and prayed that Carson would be exempted for farm work when he turned eighteen in September.

Carson was still lying on the floor, but now propped himself up on his elbows with a half-hidden look of excitement written on his face. Ava sat beside him, sharing his feelings about the war. She had heard him talking to his friends and wasn't as sure as her parents that he would seek deferment from the draft. While the world experienced peril, it was something new and exciting for them both, even in their small southern town of Jacksonville, Alabama. She now knew the names of countries she had never heard about in school, and she had an ineffable feeling emerging within her that her life was about to change. Her thoughts and the war news came to an end when the voice of Gene Autry filled the room.

"James, let's go get Brother Whatley." Sheffield stood up from his chair and nudged his son's leg with his work boot. "The bus from Gadsden will be in soon, and he'll need his rest before church and the revival singing tomorrow."

"I guess I could beat you at checkers again," Carson said to Ava when James and Sheffield left, and Estelle and Victoria went outside to sit on the porch swing.

"We'll see about that."

Her father and brother soon returned with Brother Whatley, and the redheaded preacher with risible green eyes and a freckled face stooped down and gave them both a small bag of assorted candies and a hearty hug.

"Hello, my favorite youngsters, and happy birthday, Ava."

Ava saw her mother's eyebrows arch up, and she knew that after the munificent pastor left, they would all hear about how their teeth were going to fall out from too much sugar.

The traveling preacher kicked off his shoes and made himself comfortable. Grandpa Chester reemerged from his nap, and they all sat up with the pastor talking, laughing, and singing every song her mother could think of to play on the piano. James and Estelle finally left, and Ava went to bed. Carson had to give up his bed for the preacher every Saturday night, and he had already found a pillow and was fast asleep on the floor.

It was a sticky Alabama evening, and Ava lay on top of her quilt fanning herself with a Brown's Funeral Home courtesy fan. She gave up sleeping several minutes ago and alternated her attention between the storm that bellowed outside her window and the voices of her parents and Brother Whatley on the other side of the door. She was accustomed to them staying up discussing the Bible and singing into the early hours of the morning. So much for the pastor needing his rest before their own church service and the special revival and singing they were accompanying him to tomorrow. Her mother's rich voice won her attention over the storm, and she listened to her speculate on the height of King David's Goliath.

"They say people are taller now-a-days. So, any man over six foot tall might have been considered a giant in David's time." Victoria accented the word "giant" to express her opinion.

"He was a great deal taller than six foot, blossom," Sheffield said. "I read in the *Jacksonville News* just the other day where some experts speculate that Goliath was probably over nine foot tall."

"That's impossible."

After a momentary silence, Brother Whatley gave his authoritative word.

"It may not be impossible. Just like men lived to be hundreds of years old in the Old Testament, they also might have rivaled the bears in size back then."

Ava could picture the pastor squinting his penny-sized eyes and pointing his finger in her parents' faces to make his point. When she was younger, she was scared of his vindictive finger, but she had learned since to lower her eyes as if in prayer when she saw it coming her way.

"Regardless of how tall he actually was," Brother Whatley continued. "He had to be a very large man to test and strengthen the faith of the stubborn Israelites."

Just then a crack of lightning diverted Ava's attention back to what was going on outside her window. It got her parents' attention as well, and she heard her father shut the front door. She watched the branches of the oak tree next to her window sway back and forth with the angry wind.

Another flash of lightning brought Victoria to the door, and Ava saw her mother quietly enter the room. She tiptoed across the wooden floor and made sure that the window was closed tightly.

Ava believed her mother to be the most beautiful and strongest woman alive. She had an unblemished olive complexion and long black hair, which she always pinned up in the back. Both of these features were attributed to the Creek Indian side of her ancestry. The western features of her family softened her, however. As a Carson, she had pale blue eyes, an oval-shaped face, and a full, short figure.

She was the youngest of her parents' six children, each named by Ava's deceased grandmother after a royal member of the English or French court. Evie Belle wanted her children to be royalty, and in Ava's mind, her mother was as grand as any true queen.

Ava also believed her parents' love story to be the most romantic one she had ever heard, and she wondered if her mother was even prettier when her father fell in love with her. When her mother was her same age, a tall, affable young man from Birmingham, Alabama visited his aunt in Jacksonville and was smitten by the town beauty, who could play the piano and sing like an angel. Aware of Victoria's two great passions, music and flowers, Sheffield James Stilwell charmed her with bouquets from his aunt's garden and with his violin and smooth tenor voice. After four months of courting, he left his father's prosperous grocery business in Birmingham, dropped out of Howard College, and married his young bride.

As Victoria left the room, Ava hoped she would be as beautiful in both person and spirit and as fortunate in love as her mother. With these thoughts, she finally fell asleep, despite the Alabama heat and the ongoing biblical debate on the other side of the door.

Chapter 2

Ava sat between her mother and her cousin Rosemary in the back seat of James's Ford Tudor as her brother drove down dirt roads to Four Mile Baptist Church, where Brother Whatley would be preaching and her family would provide the music. Estelle and Brother Whatley shared the front seat with James. Rosemary's father, Jude Bonds, drove his farm truck behind them, and her mother, Myrtle, and her sister, Judith, rode along with him in the front seat while Sheffield and Carson shared the bed of the truck. Grandpa Chester stayed behind complaining of a stomach ache, but Ava knew he didn't want to listen to Brother Whatley preach the same sermon twice in one day. She looked back and could see Carson's long legs swinging over the side of the truck as it bumped along. Victoria had made the mistake of commending the pastor's morning sermon, and Brother Whatley was already blessing them with a second rendition.

The ground became more sloping as they drew closer to the foothills of the Choccolocco Mountains, and Ava looked ahead at the lofty pine trees and farms that spotted the horizon. Unable to listen to Brother Whatley any longer, she began a private conversation with her cousin in hopes the preacher wouldn't notice her muffled voice and that her mother wouldn't pinch her for being rude.

11

"Want to meet out in front of your house tomorrow morning?" Ava turned her head to Rosemary and whispered.

Beginning her new job and her new life was all she could think about, and she was ready for the day to be over and for tomorrow to arrive.

"Sure," Rosemary whispered back without turning her eyes from the preacher to discourage any further conversation.

Ava sighed and looked back out the window. She couldn't understand how her cousin wasn't as excited as she was about starting their new jobs. It wasn't easy to persuade both of their parents that they should work rather than help out on the farm during the summer months.

Rosemary was Ava's second cousin and best friend. Her father Jude was the son of Victoria's oldest sister, Marie Antoinette, and, because of the sixteen-year age difference between Marie Antoinette and Victoria, Victoria and Jude were more like siblings than Victoria and Marie Antoinette. Their children were also closer in age; Rosemary was only two months older than Ava.

The car turned and stopped at the outskirts of an open field by a narrow white church with an even narrower steeple. In the distance, they could see a large tent and several long tables of covered dishes with a crowd of people surrounding them. Once they were out of the car, Rosemary pulled Ava back.

"I didn't forget your birthday," she said and reached inside her purse. "It's not wrapped, but I reckoned it would make it more noticeable if it was."

She pulled out a little black tube of red lipstick and put it in Ava's hand.

"I never saw how a little paint didn't improve a barn," Ava lowered her voice and pointed her finger to mimic their

12

beloved pastor's response to her mother's concern over young girls wearing make-up. They both laughed.

Even if her hair wasn't brushed or she wasn't wearing any other make-up, Ava always wore a deep shade of red lipstick. She felt naked without it, and in her mind, it somehow made her into the attractive, mature woman she longed to be.

"Come on, Ava! Hurry up, Rosemary!" Victoria and Myrtle shouted back to their daughters.

James and Estelle were already hand-in-hand at the tent area. Carson was carrying Judith on his shoulders some distance ahead of them, and Sheffield, Brother Whatley, and Jude were conversing with some of the Four Mile Baptist Church members.

When they were almost at the tent, a stout, blond young man began making his way to them.

"I didn't know Jake Green went to this church," Ava said, and her cousin's tanned face turned as pink as her sundress. "I guess he knew he would find you here."

Jake Green was two years older, the son of the town doctor, and the only boy around who Ava had ever thought was worth considering for a husband.

"I might have mentioned to him that we would be here," Rosemary replied without looking at the approaching young man.

"Ava, I can't wait to hear you sing," Jake addressed Ava first.

"I hope I don't disappoint you. Are you really leaving for the Navy in a week?"

"It looks that way. Hi, Rosemary," he said, resting his green eyes on her.

"Hello, Jake." She watched some kids playing chase in the distance instead of returning his gaze.

"Have they started eating yet?" Ava asked.

They were eating lunch later than normal, and she was famished.

"Not yet, they're waiting for more people to arrive."

"Ava!" Victoria called from underneath the tent, and Ava left Rosemary and Jake and joined her mother.

Carson and James took out their banjos and strummed the strings in preparation, and Victoria instructed them about the order of songs they would be singing.

"We're going to start singing right after the blessing," she said, now straightening the collar of Ava's flowery summer dress.

"We don't get to eat first?" Ava could smell fried chicken, and her hunger was growing.

Her mother started to answer, but hearing Brother Penny, another local pastor, instruct everyone to bow their heads for prayer, she only shook her head at her daughter. Ava closed her eyes and felt her pulse quicken. She was well experienced at singing before crowds, but she still got nervous right before a performance.

Brother Penny said "Amen," and her family and cousin Jude began to assemble themselves at the front of the tent. Sheffield motioned for his sons to begin playing, and Ava began to sing.

"When I come to the river at ending of day, when the last winds of sorrow have blown," she sang out by herself.

It was *I Won't Have to Cross Jordan Alone*, her mother's favorite song about heaven, and she was always careful not to get any of the words wrong. Just then a commotion occurred outside the tent. Mrs. Valencia Boozer was approaching the food tables with three young soldiers, and everyone was greeting them like rich relatives.

"There'll be somebody waiting to show me the way, and I won't have to cross Jordan alone," she sang the words mechanically now, watching the older men and women make a place in the front of the picnic line for the strange men.

They must be from Fort McClellan. The first verse was over, and her family joined in on the chorus.

She remembered reading stories in the newspapers of street dances, driving tours, and special suppers for the soldiers, but she had only caught glimpses of the uniformed men on their family trip to Anniston in the late fall. Apparently, the city swarmed with them now as men from all across the country came to the fort for basic training before being shipped overseas. Her dad was right; the community did treat them like heroes.

She studied the backs of the three young men as they selected various southern dishes. The lanky soldier in the front of the line had copper hair and skin that glistened in the heat. The middle soldier had close-cropped auburn hair and was larger and taller than the first, but neither of them was as tall as Carson or her father. The last of the three soldiers was not much taller than she was and had a freshly shaved head that shone in the sunlight. Ava momentarily forgot the words to the song as she saw the first soldier in line turn his head and look at her and then motion for the soldier directly behind him to do the same. Knowing they were watching and listening to her made her cheeks flush to the color of her lips, and she quickly looked in the other direction. When the song neared its end, she dared to look at them again. They were eating their lunch on a blanket next to Valencia Boozer's family. She almost turned her eyes away when the lanky soldier grinned at her. The song ended, Ava looked at the dirt floor, and her father and cousin Jude began their next song.

"Who's the singer?" The lanky soldier paused between bites of fried okra and pointed at Ava with his fork.

"Her name is Ava Stilwell." Valencia Boozer turned her head toward the tent and shielded her eyes from the sun. "Her family is the most musical family I have ever met. Everyone of them sings and plays some kind of instrument."

"She sure can sing like a canary," the short soldier said.

They all listened a little while longer as they ate, and the lanky soldier resumed the conversation.

"It would be nice to have her sing at the next U.S.O dance."

"We could probably arrange that." Their hostess smiled and shielded her eyes again to get a better look at Ava's performance.

"What a friend we have in Jesus, all our sins and grief to bear." Ava's precocious voice began another song and deftly glided over the musical scale.

"She's also a looker," the lanky soldier said when their hostess left them for a piece of pecan pie.

"Not as beautiful as my Marg, but pretty." The short soldier softened his voice at the mention of Marg.

"Oh, no woman could be as lovely as Marg."

"So, what do you think of her?" The short soldier elbowed his silent friend sitting next to him.

"All you two think about is food and women."

Mrs. Boozer returned with her husband, and the lanky soldier began conversing with them about the dishes he had never eaten before back in Kansas.

"I've never seen a bean this color." He pushed a purple hull pea into his mouth.

"Me neither, but I sure wish Catholics ate like this," the short soldier said.

The quiet soldier took a gulp of water and studied Ava's confident character. Her shoulder-length hair was an enormity of dark-brown, wavy curls that leapt and fell about her oval face and petite shoulders when she sang. He could tell that she possessed a passionate and vivacious spirit by the way her voice escalated over the verses and by the brilliancy of her gray eyes. They were large for her face and were light-colored pools of emotion. As he looked into them with the rest of the picnickers, they conveyed that she was young, expectant, and believed in life, love, and God, all things that he himself had begun to question.

The song ended, and the audience clapped. Ava rejoined Rosemary, Jake, and Judith, who bounced up and down with her plate of food.

"That was some more beautiful singing," Jake said.

"Do you want a biscuit, Cousin Ava?" Judith held up a buttery biscuit with her chubby fingers. She still hadn't lost her baby fat, and she often reminded Ava of a plump cherub.

"Not right now." Ava ran her fingers through Judith's soft blond ringlets, and the little girl began to crumble up the rejected biscuit in her hands.

"Don't play with your food, Judith," Rosemary chided.

Ava winked at her younger cousin as Rosemary brushed the crumbs into the grass.

"Your hands are greasy now." Rosemary looked around the blanket for something to wipe her sister's hands on.

"I'll get another napkin," Jake said and hurried off.

"Did you see the soldiers from Fort McClellan with the Boozers?" Ava asked and dared to look in their direction now that Jake was gone.

The men had finished their meal, and Mr. and Mrs. Boozer introduced them to a group of churchmen in their Sunday's best overalls.

"Yes, I saw them. Ernie Ingram told us that Mrs. Boozer is the new hospitality director of the Red Cross and is always feeding and entertaining them."

"The one with the sandy hair smiled at me while I was singing."

"Maybe, he likes more than your singing," Rosemary said, and Jake reappeared with the much-needed napkin. "Thanks, Jake."

She took the napkin from him and scrubbed Judith's hands, which were now also covered in coconut cream.

"Are you not going to eat, Ava?"

"I'm not that hungry any more, but I guess I'll get something."

She made her way toward one of the food tables and selected small spoonfuls of string beans, squash, and black-eyed peas. Before she could finish filling her plate, she was taken aback to see Valencia Boozer coming straight toward her with the three men.

"Hi, Ava," Mrs. Boozer called out.

Ava bit her lower lip to keep it from trembling as the round, older woman with tight brown curls approached with the soldiers behind her.

"These men would like to meet Jacksonville's talented young singer." She put a hand on Ava's shoulder without giving her a chance to respond and turned toward them.

"Fellows, this is Miss Ava Stilwell."

18

Ava stood up a little straighter and smiled as confidently as possible.

"It's a pleasure to meet someone with such an angelic voice." The lanky soldier put forth his hand, and Ava secured her plate in one hand and shook his hand with the other.

"It's nice to meet you too."

Phil Boozer approached them with a crying two-year-old.

"Goodness, what's wrong with you?" Mrs. Boozer took her red-faced grandson from his grandfather's extended arms. "You'll have to excuse me for a moment, folks."

"I'm Sydney Saunders from Kansas." The lanky soldier leaned over her once his hostess had left and smiled as he had done earlier.

Ava stepped back, both uncomfortable and pleased with his close presence.

"I'm Barry Roosevelt from New York, no relation to the president," the bald, short soldier stepped forward and introduced himself in a northern nasal accent that was new to Ava.

"Nice to meet you."

Barry pulled out a wallet from his back pocket.

"You're lucky. You get to meet Mrs. Roosevelt too," Sydney explained as his friend located a picture in the middle of his wallet.

He handed a worn photograph to Ava.

"My wife Marg says I can only talk to other women if I show them a picture of her first."

"You have a smart wife," Ava said and studied the picture of an exceptionally thin woman in a plaid dress. "You also have a lovely wife."

"Thank you. There's not another one like her."

19

They all three laughed. Ava laughed too, not understanding what she was laughing at.

"Winn, don't be rude. Tell her your name." Sydney stepped back from Ava and pushed him toward her.

Ava's cheeks grew warm as his clear blue eyes first avoided her face and then swept over her.

"Hi, I'm Edwin Livingston." He looked away as quickly as he had said his name.

"Our man Winn is a Tennessee boy and the best shot in the Army," Sydney said, and Edwin smiled in embarrassment, but Ava noticed that it was not entirely without gratification.

"He could shoot a bottle top off a wire fence a mile away."

"I imagine that's a good thing for a soldier," she said, not knowing what else to say.

"Oh, these two clowns are just such bad shots that they make mine look good."

"Hey now!" Barry punched his friend in the arm.

"Mrs. Boozer said that you're from Jacksonville. Do you ever come to Anniston?" Sydney changed the subject and moved close to Ava once again.

"As a matter of fact, my cousin and I are starting jobs there tomorrow at Wakefield's Department Store." She tried to sound as comfortable with him as he was with her.

"So, we're talking to a working girl."

"I think that it's good that women are doing their part and working on the home front. Marg just got a job as a welder. That girl can do anything," Barry said. "Maybe I could come see you at your store, and you could help me pick out something to send her."

"I would love to."

"We'd also like to hear you sing again," Sydney interjected.

"I think my family is finished singing for the day, so I don't know – "

"Excuse me, Ava. The church would like to honor you men before the service begins." Mrs. Boozer returned with Brother Penny and her clinging grandson.

"That's unnecessary," Sydney answered for the three of them.

"Fiddlesticks, if you could each tell Brother Penny a little about yourselves."

Ava excused herself and left them to the pastor.

Not wanting Jake to think that she was interested in meeting the soldiers too, Rosemary refrained from asking about Ava's conversation with them. Exchanging knowing glances, however, Ava sat down on the blanket and finally began to eat.

"Do you know those boys, Cousin Ava?" Judith looked up at her with her inquisitive brown eyes.

"I just met them." Ava tickled Judith's side, and the little girl let out a high-pitched squeal.

"Are they Yankees?" Jake asked. "Buster Welch works at the fort, and he said that most of 'em are from up north."

"Only one is."

Jake was about to speak again when Brother Penny's voice boomed from the open tent.

"On behalf of Four Mile Baptist Church, I would like to thank you all for coming to our special Sunday," he began and nodded his head in the direction of each group of people present. "Before Brother Whatley blesses us today, we would

21

like to introduce you to three men from Fort McClellan who have honored us with their presence."

He motioned for them to come forward, and Ava watched as Sydney, Barry, and Edwin joined Brother Penny at the front of the tent.

"Brethren, this is Private Edwin Livingston from Tennessee, Private Sydney Saunders from Kansas, and Private Barry Roosevelt from New York. Let's give them a round of applause for being here today and for serving our country in this Job-like time of trial and need."

Everyone clapped. Sydney smiled broadly, Barry nodded his baldhead, and Edwin acknowledged the audience and then turned his gaze back on the preacher.

"On their behalf, the men have asked that Miss Ava Stilwell come forward and lead us in our national anthem."

Ava's cheeks flushed at the mention of her name, and she felt a large lump grow in her throat as all eyes turned upon her. She stood up, attempted to smile, and made her way to the front of the tent. When she passed by her parents, her mother arched her dark eyebrows in a tacit question. Brother Penny made room for her between himself and Edwin, and Ava began to sing without looking at the men by her side. The congregation followed her lead, and the words of the national anthem filled the humid air. The current affairs of the country gave power and magnitude to the familiar song, and a moment of voluntary silence hung in the air when the last stanza ended.

"Thank you, Miss Ava, for that fine rendition, and thank you men for your service to our country," Brother Penny broke the silence.

Everyone clapped, and Ava and the soldiers made their way back to where they were sitting.

It was now time for Brother Whatley to preach. Mothers worked to quiet their children, teenagers stifled their contagious giggles, and everyone settled back on blankets to listen. Ava sat on her quilt with her legs crossed to one side. She was determined to listen to Brother Whatley's explanation of the parable about the farmer and his seed, which she had heard numerous times, and not think about her new acquaintances. Nevertheless, her mind began to wander, and her eyes followed close behind. When the sermon came to an end and the minister gave the closing prayer, she noticed Mr. and Mrs. Boozer leaving with the soldiers. She wondered if she would ever see them again, and she smiled as Judith's nodding head dropped in her lap.

Chapter 3

Ava and Rosemary sat upright and readied themselves to leave as their bus stop approached. Ava wore her new dress, and even though excitement exploded inside her, she strove to appear mature and collected for the other riders around them. Despite her efforts, her enthusiasm flashed in her eyes and seeped through the dimples of her controlled smile. Now that the day had arrived, Rosemary also looked excited, and Ava felt closer to her as a result. Rosemary wore a blue, cotton dress made from a simpler pattern, and she appeared warm and fresh as she chatted with her cousin about what they would be asked to do on their first day of work.

Ava pulled the cord, and the bell rang for the bus to stop at the corner of 10th Street and Noble Street. They left their seats and stepped onto the streets of Anniston. Even though they had been to the city several times with their families to buy farm supplies, their new independence made it a novel experience for them both, and they stopped to breathe it all in.

The city was abuzz as people woke up from their Sunday of leisure and worship and returned to their weekly duties. Cars lined the sides of the streets, and people moved in all directions around them. Street lamps marked every few feet of the road, and the American flags affixed to them fluttered in the spring breeze. Since the war, the town had become a fevered scene of patriotism and industry. It was a brilliant day, and Ava and Rosemary regained their purpose and walked to the door of Wakefield's Department Store, less than a block away.

Ava opened the door, and Rosemary followed her into the store. A bell announced their presence, and Lorraine Crockett, the store's manager, paused in her instructions to a fidgety adolescent boy with large ears who flicked a broom at her feet.

"Ladies," she greeted and peered at them as if they were a shoebox randomly misplaced by a shopper and needing order. "I'll be with you in a moment."

Ava and Rosemary moved away from the door and stood without talking as they awaited their own instructions. Employees were already busy preparing the store for its 9:30 opening. A girl their age was carrying an assortment of boxes from a back storage area to the front of the store, and they watched her as she walked their way, somewhat hidden by the load she carried.

"Do you mind taking the top boxes?" the girl asked.

Ava and Rosemary were happy to help, and they each took a box from the top of her pile. They followed her to the corner of the store window and placed the boxes on the floor where she indicated.

"Thank you. I always get more than I can handle to avoid making a hundred trips. I'm Alta Tyler."

Ava and Rosemary started to introduce themselves, but she stopped them.

"Don't tell me. You're Ava, and you're Rosemary." She pointed at each one of them correctly as she said their names and then laughed out loud.

25

"Mrs. Crockett told me we were getting an Ava and a Rosemary from Jacksonville."

"You guessed us right," Ava said, and she and Rosemary laughed too, but not so boldly as their new acquaintance as their manager was still close by.

"My father always says that country girls are better workers than us town gals, so I'm anxious to see if he's right." Alta untied a tape measure that was wrapped around her waist.

Ava felt like she was looking at a movie star. Alta had short blond hair that neatly curled away from her temples and a perfectly proportioned face and figure. She wasn't skinny, like Ava, or plump, but had a healthy, hourglass figure. Her most attractive feature, however, were her expressive eyes. They were a soft blue, but what made them stand out were the thick, dark eyelashes and smoky eye shadow that surrounded them. Ava and Rosemary wore powder and lipstick, but neither of them knew any girls their age who wore eye make-up. It was flattering on their new co-worker and made one look her straight in the eyes.

Mrs. Crockett was finished instructing her young employee on how to sweep the store inside and out and was now ready for them.

"Girls, welcome to Wakefield's. We're glad to have you."

"We're happy to be here," Rosemary answered for them.

"Well, let's get you started." Mrs. Crockett put her hands on her hips and looked about the store for their proper place.

Ava and Rosemary followed her darting gaze from the front to the sides to the back of the store.

"Rosemary, let's start you off in the dressing room. Florence!" she called to an unseen woman.

An older woman with a heap of gray and dark speckled hair appeared from the back of the store.

"Rosemary Bonds will be working with you today in the dressing area. If you would please show her how everything is done." Mrs. Crockett waved for Rosemary to follow Florence and then turned her attention toward Ava.

Ava felt scrutinized as her meticulous eyes swept over her.

"And, let's put you with Alta. She's redoing our window display today. Alta, make sure you place the war bond posters where they are more visible this time. Mr. Wakefield wasn't happy last week when S.H. Kress & Co. appeared more patriotic than us," she went on without a pause. "I'll be walking around the premises if either of you need me."

"Yes, ma'am," Alta replied, and Mrs. Crocket left them to reprimand the boy who was now twirling his broom like a baton.

"If he wasn't related to Mr. Wakefield, he wouldn't be here," Alta whispered to Ava and then laughed.

"What can I do?" Ava asked, kneeling beside Alta as she opened a box of gloves.

"First of all, let me tell you about the importance of the window display." Alta stopped searching through the box and placed a hand on Ava's arm to emphasize her wry explanation. "In Mrs. Crockett's and Mr. Wakefield's words, the window display is the pride of the store. It's the first thing people notice about the store and often the reason they come in or keep walking down the street." Alta laughed more quietly this time, and Ava smiled in understanding.

They worked on the window display the rest of the morning. All of the old items had to be taken down and the new items arranged. They fastidiously hung dresses with all the right creases, placed and replaced men's hats, and displayed the most fashionable shoes. They also hung miniature flags and various war bond and "Support Our Troops" signs throughout the display.

Ava felt satisfied with their creation and her new friend as the morning passed. By her first impression, Alta, who was only a year older than she and Rosemary, was the epitome of what it meant to be modern and glamorous, and Ava was eager to discover everything about her. When lunchtime came, she, Alta, and Rosemary went to the Palace Drug Store to eat. Rosemary became as open with Alta as Ava was by the middle of the lunch and even confessed her feelings for Jake Green.

"He sounds like a dream," Alta said. "I guess there will be no local uniformed men for you, then."

Rosemary blushed, and Alta laughed.

"How did you meet Charlie?" Ava asked.

"Because my last name's Tyler, and I'm supposed to know everything about this city, I got asked to be a city hostess for a group of soldiers, and that's how I met him."

"Are you seeing him Friday night?"

"I'm going to Oxford Lake with another soldier named Jon on Friday night, but I'm going to see a picture show with Charlie on Saturday."

Ava and Rosemary both looked at her in amazement. The thought of seeing two boys at one time was inconceivable to them.

"With the war, there are too many nice-looking men in Anniston to see just one," Alta said, and they all laughed.

"You'll see what I mean soon enough, Ava, if your soldiers from the revival come looking you up."

Ava smiled, but she couldn't imagine any man trying to seek her out. Barry did, however, ask her to help him shop for his wife and maybe Sydney would come with him.

After lunch, Ava and Alta finished the window display, and Ava was asked to sort through a new shipment of women's stockings. Rosemary spent the remainder of the day helping out in the dressing area.

When the workday was over, they walked to the bus station to catch the 6:00 bus leaving for Jacksonville. The streets of Anniston were becoming quieter as people moved about at a more leisurely pace. Ava and Rosemary both glowed with self-satisfaction from their successful first day of work and from the feeling that they were now a part of the life that surrounded them.

Chapter 4

Wakefield's, along with almost all other Anniston establishments, closed early on Wednesday afternoons. Ava and Rosemary caught the mid-afternoon bus for Jacksonville, and Ava walked with her cousin to her house, which was closer to the bus stop, before continuing home. They had laughed all the way about a lady Ava had helped that morning who was so large that she burst a seam in one of the store's new summer dresses. The lady's perplexed expression still caused Ava to laugh when she approached the red wooden fence and dirt driveway that lead to her house.

No sooner had she spotted her mother and Estelle in the distance, than her mother's movements told her something was wrong, and her smile faded. Victoria was vigorously uprooting the day lilies that thrived and spread across the front of the flowerbeds. She had been complaining for over a week that the multiplying flowers choked her azalea and hydrangea bushes. It wasn't the work that she did, but rather the manner in which she did it that alarmed Ava. Incapable of fretting or crying, her mother worked out her frustrations with physical exertion. Ava now watched her mother's rigid and furious motions as she thrust her shovel deep into the ground and flung discarded roots and green leaves several feet behind her.

Estelle sat helplessly beside her on the bottom step of the front porch, watching a butterfly as it chased and alighted on the freshly dug-up plants. When she noticed Ava, she sat up and cautioned her with her eyes.

Ava forced herself to speak.

"Mom, is everything all right?"

"On the table," Victoria said, without looking at her daughter and without a pause in momentum, as the shovel continued to strike the ground and push upward in a furious motion.

Ava stood staring at her mother for a moment and then walked into the house afraid of what she would find. A million different fears presented themselves to her imagination as she approached the kitchen table. *Has something happened to Grandma and Granddaddy in Birmingham? Has Daddy or Grandpa hurt himself in the fields?*

A short letter lay in the center of the table, and Ava recognized Carson's long, careless handwriting. Her heart relaxed, as she wondered what mischief he was up to now. She picked up the letter and read.

Dear Mom and Dad,

I have gone with Pete and Jimmy to join up with the Army. I am almost 18, and I need to serve my country. Try not to worry about me.

Your son respectfully,
Carson

The letter did not have the same effect on Ava as it did on her mother. While she would be concerned for her brother, her eyes gleamed with romantic pride of what she considered a noble act. She was still naïve to the gravity of war or the pain of being apart from someone she loved. Estelle had followed her into the house and now put a comforting arm around her. When Ava suddenly realized that Carson, who was not quite a year older than she, would have to lie about his age to enter the Army before his birthday next month, she bit her lip hard to suppress a giggle. It just seemed like another joke he pulled and she was privy to.

"When did Carson leave?" she asked, catching sight of her mother outside the kitchen window.

"Sometime early this morning. Your mother thought he was out working in the fields with your father until your father came in asking where his lazy son was. Then, they discovered this note lying on Carson's bed. Willis Ponder came out about an hour ago and said that he saw the three of them in one of those military trucks Fort McClellan keeps sending out to recruit boys for the Army," Estelle explained as she too looked out the window at her mother-in-law, who now slung the uprooted day lilies into a wheelbarrow.

For the rest of the afternoon, the whole family waited for news of Carson. Sheffield and Grandpa Chester came in from the fields every so often to get a drink of water and casually ask if anyone had heard anything. Sheffield appeared calmly upset, and Grandpa Chester was more fidgety than usual. Ava read fear in both men's eyes, but she could also detect traces of pride. James was still at work and knew nothing about the ordeal, and Estelle stayed with them the rest of the afternoon trying to help out in anyway she could. Ava noticed tears welling in her eyes, and she knew that Estelle was not thinking about Carson but rather about the possibility of James doing the same thing.

Unable to sit idly by or work with her mother any longer, Ava decided to take a walk around the farm. She strolled around the back of their property and pictured Carson in a uniform somewhere overseas reading the long letters she would send him on the stationary he had given her for her birthday. He would want to keep up with all of the family and community gossip.

She neared the back barn and thought of Dixie. Dixie was her father's oldest mule and her favorite pet. When she was young, she would often ride the now feeble mule around the farm pretending that she was a princess on a unicorn. She went through the open door of the big barn and approached Dixie, who stood relishing a dry piece of hay. The mule turned his big, chocolate-colored eyes toward her, and she stretched out her hand over the fence to pet him. As her hand met his dark brown mane, she noticed a movement on the other side of the barn, and she drew back her fingers and looked in its direction. Her face paled, as she saw Carson lying on his back in a pile of hay with his hands over his face sobbing. She had never seen him like this, and she didn't know whether to go to him or leave and pretend that she hadn't seen him. She knew he would be embarrassed at her finding him crying. Unable to decide, she just stood and stared at him. Dixie grunted for her to pet him again, and Carson unfolded his arms and looked at her. His face, which was already red from crying, crimsoned deeper when he saw his sister.

"Go on. Tell 'em I'm back," he shouted and turned his face away from her.

"What happened, Car?" she asked, walking toward him whether he wanted her to or not.

He ignored her question.

"Carson, please tell me what's wrong. I won't say anything if you don't-"

"They didn't take me, all right," he answered with his face still hidden.

"How come?" She was determined to make him talk to her despite their inability to be serious with one another.

"I'm 4-F on account of my stupid eyes."

She sat down next to him and dared to touch his arm. At her touch, he turned his rejected eyes toward her. The hostility in them faded and gave way to raw remorse. They sat without speaking for sometime, and then Ava ventured to say something more.

"Carson, it's not shameful that they didn't take you."

"Yeah it is. The whole town will think that I'm a coward. Pete and Jimmy are leaving in two weeks." He put his hands back over his face.

"I'm sure that everyone already knows you tried, and that's all that matters. They can't accuse you of being scared. Besides, I'm the only one who knows about your fear of rolly pollys." She laughed and hoped he would, too.

When Carson was a boy, he accidentally ate a rolly polly that found its way into his glass of milk, and, ever since then, he had been disgusted by the minuscule bugs. To tease him, Ava would collect them from all over the yard and put them on him while he was sleeping. His mouth, which was slightly perceptible from below the palms of his hands, smiled faintly at her joke and then disappeared.

"Ava, would you go tell 'em what happened for me and that I'll be home for supper?"   "If you want me to. Mom is so worried about you that she has almost dug up the whole front yard."

Carson began to laugh at this, and Ava was glad that she accidentally found him. She got up and started to leave but then spun back around.

"I'm glad you're not leaving," she said, and then without giving him a chance to respond, she ran out to accomplish his request.

When Ava returned to the house, James was back from work, and he and Sheffield were smoking cigars on the front porch, still in their dirty work clothes, while Grandpa Chester generously massaged his thin elbows and knees with red liniment. Normally, they all washed and changed clothes before supper, but she knew that they were each afraid of missing news of Carson. Estelle and Victoria were busy starting supper in the kitchen. No one suspected that she would be the bearer of the news they waited for, and, when she returned, the three men, each absorbed in his own thoughts, didn't even look at her as she passed.

Unsure of how to approach the subject, but feeling her new importance, she paused with a hand upon the screen door and said, "Dad, Grandpa, James, if you would all come in the living room, I have something to tell you."

They all three just stared at her, and she knew that at that moment they cared little about anything other than her brother.

"It's about Carson," she added and walked inside the door.

There was a quick shuffle of feet behind her.

"Ava, could you start the biscuits," her mother said with eyes that accused her of being idle while they worked.

"Mom, Estelle, if you'll come to the living room, I have news of Carson."

Forgetting the green beans and fat back she was stirring, Victoria looked dubiously at her daughter and followed her and Estelle into the adjoining room. Ava stood in the center of them, and as they all penetrated her with eager stares, she couldn't help but enjoy her position.

"Well, what have you heard and who told you?" Victoria demanded, wringing her hands on her apron.

"I haven't heard anything from anyone."

Victoria sighed in exasperation.

"I saw Carson."

"When? Where?" her father and mother asked, moving closer as if they could lay their hands on their son through her.

"I found him in the back barn."

"Did he not really go then? Halleujah!" Victoria lifted up her hands in joyful relief.

"Yes, he went, but they didn't take him because of his eyesight."

Victoria sighed and sank down in a chair. Estelle also let out a deep breath and put her arms around her husband. If Carson was not allowed to go, maybe James wouldn't be allowed either. Sheffield began pacing the room, and Ava could tell that he was torn between sharing his wife's happiness that their son wasn't leaving and feeling anger at his rejection. Grandpa Chester now sat with his hands supporting his chin and with a vexed expression on his face. He couldn't help but interpret Carson's rejection as an insult to the virility of their family.

"What on God's green earth is wrong with my grandson's cotton-pickin eyes?" he grumbled, first looking at Ava and then around the room for an explanation.

"You should just be thankful that he isn't going." Victoria put a peremptory end to his question.

No one would dare answer him now. Ava hadn't thought about it before, but, since the question had been

36

asked, she remembered catching Carson several times with their grandpa's bifocals doing his homework, and she recalled how he often asked to see her and Rosemary's notes from the chalkboard, which he never took down himself. She and Rosemary had often blackmailed him into doing their chores for the notes, and she suddenly felt guilty.

"So, where's Carson now?" James interrupted her culpable thoughts.

"He said he'll be home for supper."

At the word "supper," her mother remembered their dinner.

"My goodness, the beans!" She rushed into the kitchen before her beans burned on the wood stove.

Estelle also went back to the kitchen, and Ava began to follow. Her moment of importance was over. As she passed her grandpa, he caught her by the wrist and pulled her close.

"Annie, is your brother all right?"

"He's just upset, that's all."

She could feel her father gazing at the back of her head, and she knew that he had heard what she said. Before leaving them, she glanced around and saw him running his fingers through his coarse hair, deliberating as to how to relate to his son when he returned. As women crave affection, men crave respect, and Sheffield wanted to treat his son with sensitive dignity.

When supper was ready, Carson still wasn't home, and everyone kept glancing at his empty chair as they sat down for the blessing. Sheffield said "Amen," the screen door opened, and Carson walked in. He avoided their eyes and hung his hat on the wall. His face was red and rough from splashing it with cold water to hide his emotion.

"Carson!" Victoria ran to him and flung her arms around him.

His mother's devotion moved him, and fresh tears began to moisten his hard-set eyes. Their supper turned out to be an awkward blend of Victoria's elation, Carson's dejection, and everyone else's attempts to be mindful of both. Victoria had anticipated her son's return and fixed all of his favorite dishes, but Carson just pushed his food from one side of the plate to the other. Ava watched him from across the table, and a new feeling of love for him overcame her. For the first time, she saw him as a man and not just as her brother.

Chapter 5

Francis Green spared little of her husband's expense for her son's "Send-off to the Navy" party. Everyone in Jacksonville had been invited to the soiree in the town square, and everyone had gladly accepted. Red, white, and blue balloons flew above every tree branch and building, and a large banner reading "We will miss you Jake" stretched from the top of one massive oak tree to another and over the stone head of the gallant Civil War hero John Pelham in the center of the square. Platters upon platters of pork barbecue and bowls upon bowls of potato salad, baked beans, and biscuits sat upon checkered-clothed tables. The Greens also furnished Coca-Cola from the local drug store fountain and a few select bottles of wine for Mrs. Green and her more intimate Presbyterian friends. Finally, for dessert, Mrs. Green had arranged for The Creamery to provide rich vanilla ice cream with fresh strawberries.

Ever since Jake arrived at his party, a faint hint of embarrassment remained on his healthy cheeks. Other boys who had left for the service were given going away parties, but nothing as lavish or absurd as his mother's doings. He felt both annoyed and grateful to her and tried to avoid answering direct questions about how well he liked every detail. More than the party, however, Rosemary lay heavily on his mind, and he went to her the moment she arrived with her family. He was determined to talk to her about his feelings before leaving in the morning. All day he had been putting his thoughts together in the most intelligible sentences possible to impress her and convey his love for her. As he looked into her hazel eyes, which still sought and then ran from his gaze, all the sentences he had formed in his head grew muddled.

They stood with a group of friends eating ice cream and both pretending to be amused at a joke Pete Gunter told with vivid animation.

"Then that crazy fool just fell over his own two feet with his drawers over his head!" Pete reached the end of his story.

Rosemary laughed and again dodged Jake's gaze. She was honored by his persistent affection but also conscious of his mother's disapproval. Despite his mother's cool cordiality, Rosemary knew that she didn't care for all the attention her son gave her. She couldn't help but wish that he leave her for just a few moments and mingle with all the other guests. All night, Frances Green had been calling to her son and trying to engage him in conversations with other people. Rosemary looked in the distance at Ava, Aggie Whorley, and Floraline Dempsey, who were all three laughing and dancing wildly when no one was watching them. Several of the local men brought their banjos and guitars, and an on-going assortment of music filled the night air. She would like to be carefree and out from under Mrs. Green's invidious watch, but she also wanted to be close to Jake before he left. She knew that she would miss him terribly and dreaded his departure.

Ava was giddy and red-faced from dancing with her school friends, but she watched her brother's every movement. Since Wednesday night, Carson had been moody and petulant with everyone, and she feared that Jake's party would throw him into an even greater depression. Just then, he finished up a card game with Edgar Gunter, Winston Green, and Jimmy Johnson, who had been accepted into the Army. They patted him on the back, signifying him as the winner, but his face reflected little of the triumphal glow it normally did after any kind of personal victory. She watched as he collected the cards and smiled at his friends' jokes. They all four stood, Winston went in search of his young bride, and the other three began walking in their direction toward the ice cream tables. She whispered to Aggie, and, as Carson passed, they each grabbed one of his arms and spun him around to the fast tempo of the music.

"Don't you two make me look as silly as you do," Carson said and twirled Ava out away from him before picking up Aggie like a sack of potatoes over his broad shoulders and then pretending to almost drop her.

"It doesn't take much to make you look foolish," Aggie joked.

Ava observed them with a smile. She believed if anyone could cheer her brother up, it would be Aggie. Even though he would never admit it, Ava knew that her brother liked Aggie. She and Rosemary had laughed about the way he looked and flirted with her all year at school. Aggie wasn't necessarily pretty as much as she was adorable, and Carson was charmed by her curly, strawberry-blonde hair, freckles, diminutive figure, and witty confidence. She was barely five feet tall, and Carson's long body towered over her as she laughed and pushed him away.

"Hey, you and Ava are the ones that started this." He lifted up his hands in a non-guilty gesture.

"Aren't you going to ask us to come eat ice cream with you?"

Carson gave in, and they all followed him to the ice cream tables. Ava smiled at her clandestine accomplishment.

"Why did you have to bring them with you?" Jimmy said when Carson approached with Aggie, Ava, and Floraline.

"They made me bring 'em." He grinned down at Aggie.

"We're eating ice cream with Carson, not you," Floraline said.

Because she liked Jimmy, she couldn't respond kindly to him. Floraline was one of Estelle's younger sisters, and, like Estelle, she had russet hair, amber eyes, high cheekbones, and a soft smile. Unlike her sister, however, her feather-thin, undeveloped figure caused her much private anguish and often affected the way she viewed herself and related to men.

"What's wrong, bean pole?" Pete Gunter teased and put an arm around her.

Pete had a nickname for all the girls, which his friends quickly adopted. While Floraline liked Jimmy, she despised Pete, partly because of the nickname he gave her and partly because of his propensity to annoy her. She shrugged off his arm and shuddered to show how he repulsed her. She, Ava, Aggie, and Carson now stood with Pete, Rosemary, Jake, and Edgar.

"Ava, I want to warn you now that my mom is going to ask you to sing before the night is over. It was my only request of her," Jake said.

"Oh, we get to hear from the Siren tonight!" Pete covered his ears with his hands and grimaced.

"If I could make you crash into a heap of stones, I would." Ava knocked the back of his blond head with her hand.

"Can we sing with you?" Jimmy asked, and they all laughed remembering last year's graduation ceremony when Ava was singing the school anthem, and Jimmy, Carson, and Pete jumped up on stage with her and howled like werewolves before Principal Synder pulled them down and paddled them, even though they were all almost twice his size.

Pete puckered up his thick lips and howled, and Ava pinched them together with her fingers until his howling gave way to laughter.

"So, Jake, your mother is giving you a fantastic party," Aggie said to shift the attention away from her friend.

"Yeah, it's great," Jake answered, as his cheeks reddened with fresh awareness of the event in his honor.

"Maybe your mother could throw us a party in a couple of weeks," Pete said, "My mother will probably just be thankful that she has one less mouth to feed."

"Not to mention that you eat enough for all of our sisters put together," Edgar, Pete's older brother by two years, added.

Pete, who was plumper than his brother and his friends, answered by eating another heaping spoonful of ice cream.

"The Army will take care of that gut." Edgar punched Pete in the stomach just as he swallowed his ice cream.

"Now, I can picture Jake in a uniform, but I can't picture you two clowns in one." Aggie placed her small hands on her hips and looked from Pete to Jimmy.

"Aggie, you know that me in a uniform would melt your heart," Jimmy said and stood up taller in his boots.

43

"We'll see about that."

Ava's face grew warm with indignation, as she listened to Aggie now flirting with Jimmy about him and Pete leaving for the service. She wanted to slap her freckles off. Even though Carson was smiling, his eyes had grown sullen and remained fastened to the bowl of ice cream in his hands. Ava looked desperately at Rosemary, who also watched Carson, and tried to think of a way to change the subject. Rosemary had a thought first.

"Carson, why didn't you bring your banjo? Mrs. Green asked if you would be playing tonight."

"Aw, I'm not really in the mood for it, that's all."

"That's one thing I'm going to miss," Pete said, "If you were going with us, I would demand that you bring your banjo."

"I reckon I'll be playing for just the cows now," Carson joked, but his face reflected little mirth.

"I'll be working alongside of you this summer," Edgar said. "I wouldn't leave Pa during the harvest, like my good brother Pete, but, in the fall, I'm going to follow you guys and enlist."

Carson winced. Edgar had been promising to change his deferment status and enlist for the past year and a half, but he always used his crippled father as a reason for delaying. Everyone knew he really didn't want to go, and Carson hated the thought of being classified with his friend's older brother.

"Every man should at least attempt to serve his country, like you, Carson, even if they can't," Edgar continued. "What burns me up is these guys working in the defense plant making all this money while everyone else gets next to nothing on the farm or in the Army."

Ava's face turned white. Edgar had forgotten that James was one of the guys he referred to. Carson's face, which had been withdrawn and grim, suddenly ignited, and Ava shrieked as he clenched his fists and barreled into Edgar. Carson tackled him to the ground and punched him in the ribs. Edgar was surprised by the attack at first, but he quickly regained his senses and began fighting back. He was thickset and big-boned, and he rapidly evened the score. Ava and Rosemary screamed for Jimmy, Pete, and Jake to intervene, and when the cloud of dirt swirling about them subsided, they all three attempted to break up the fight.

Everyone at the party soon knew there was a fight, even though the perpetrators were still in question, and a crowd began to form around Carson and Edgar. Sheffield and James recognized Carson's long legs and dark head, and they both pushed their way to the center of the spectators and began to help pull Carson and Edgar apart. In a few minutes, Sheffield and James held Carson back, and Jimmy and Jake held Edgar back. Pete stood in the center of the two parties with a blank expression, trying to understand what had just happened. Carson's face was still red with rage and his nose bled profusely on one side. Even though Edgar tried to appear unhurt, his hands unconsciously grasped his aching ribs.

"James, take your brother home," Sheffield ordered and released his son's arm.

James let go of Carson's other arm and began to walk to the car, which was parked just a short distance away in a patch of tall grass.

"We'll talk about this later," Sheffield said without turning his eyes toward his son.

Carson also refused to look at his father or anyone else for that matter, and becoming conscious of the blood that

45

trickled down to his lips and chin, he followed his brother to the car.

James and Carson rode in silence until the house came to view in the headlights.

"What were you letting Edgar have it for?" James tried not to sound as curious as he actually was.

He had far outdone his brother in the category of school fights, and Carson had the reputation of being even-tempered, like their father. He couldn't imagine what would make Carson go after his friend's brother with his fists.

"I'd rather not talk about it," Carson said and opened the passenger side door just as the car came to a stop.

After Carson and James left, Victoria and Sheffield demanded that Ava tell them what the fight was about, and Ava told them, without Estelle, the conversation that preceded Carson's outburst. Her explanation extinguished their anger, and she could tell by their silence that they both somewhat approved of Carson's impulsive actions. He wouldn't be seriously reprimanded, but he wouldn't be praised either. Shortly after, Sheffield, Victoria, Grandpa Chester, and Estelle left to see about Carson, and Ava stayed behind. Mrs. Green asked her to sing just as Jake promised, and even though the fight had left her disinterested in anything at the party, she agreed to sing the national anthem and a couple of hymns.

She had just finished *The Star Spangled Banner* and had begun *Amazing Grace*, when Jake, noticing that his mother and father were preoccupied with Mayor Ponder, took Rosemary by the hand and pulled her away from the crowd. Rosemary's heart quickened, and she blushed as Jake led her out of the town square. She glanced behind her to ensure that no one had noticed their departure and was both happy and afraid of what was about to take place between them. She could feel the sweat of his palm and knew that he was nervous. Somehow this made her want to laugh and gave her confidence. Jake stopped, turned toward her, and kissed her. Rosemary kissed him back and felt her new confidence waver. It was the first time during the past three months he had been courting her that they had really kissed each other. When he finally pulled away, she forgot her reserve and looked him directly in the eyes.

"I don't want to leave you," Jake whispered even though they were alone.

"I don't want you to leave me." Rosemary pressed both of his hands with her own.

"I was thinking that," he stopped, trying to remember how he had decided to word his declaration earlier that day, "I was thinking that, if it's all right with you, that we could write to each other while I'm gone and then when I come back, maybe … you would consider a future with me." He blurted out the last part of his sentence and looked into her face for signs of her true feelings toward him.

"I'll write you every day, and I'll be waiting for you when you return," she whispered back, tears filling her eyes and throat.

Jake kissed her again and again, and they were both reluctant to return to the party. Even though he always tried to do the right thing, at that moment, he wanted to run away with Rosemary and leave behind the war, his mom, his decision to be a doctor, and every other responsibility. He smiled down at her just before they rejoined the party, and Rosemary felt in her heart that if he would have asked her to marry him that night, before he left, she would not have hesitated.

Chapter 6

On the following morning, Ava almost went to Wakefield's alone. Rosemary's malleable emotions often affected her physically, and Jake's departure nauseated her stomach. Her heart was elated after their intimate conversation, but, when she tried to go to sleep that night, her mind drifted from his kiss and the words he had so genuinely spoken to thoughts of his leaving and the possibility of never seeing him again. On telling her mother how she felt, Myrtle filled her daughter's stomach with Black Draught and sent her disconsolate and pale-faced to meet Ava for work. At Wakefield's, however, there was no time to be sick. The store was brimming with Saturday shoppers, all oblivious of her personal pain and anxious to gape at the new summer fashions and spend the little cash jingling in their pockets. Rosemary and Ava had never seen so many people inside or outside the store. On the weekends, people from the surrounding countryside poured into Anniston, and the city turned khaki-colored from all of the Fort McClellan soldiers that swarmed the populated streets. Even though her nerves were frazzled, Rosemary begin to feel stronger and her tanned face regained its healthy glow as she helped customer after customer find the right-sized skirt, a matching handkerchief, and the perfect tie to coordinate with a suit.

While Ava was careful not to ignore her customers, she peered past the extravagant window displays of the store's large windows at every chance she got. Alta seemed to know everyone who walked through the door, and she listened to her countless conversations throughout the morning.

"Did your little Fannie recuperate from the croup?" Ava could hear Alta asking a fashionable young woman who was trying on a new hat.

"She's finally up to playing with the other children, but…," the young woman began to answer as she positioned the delicate hat at just the right spot on her head.

Ava didn't hear the rest of little Fannie's condition as an elderly woman asked her to look at a pair of nylon stockings. She carefully removed the stockings from their box and placed them on the counter for her customer to touch.

"Everyone says that they are very comfortable to wear," she repeated a line that she had heard Mrs. Crockett use the day before.

"Are they not unbearable in the summer, though?" the older woman with rings on every finger asked, scrutinizing the novel material with her aged hands.

"I'm not sure," Ava admitted, unable to recall anything else she had heard Mrs. Crockett say about the stockings.

"Hey, everybody! Mr. Lloyd is flying his big plane again!" Leo Wakefield, the adolescent boy who Ava and Rosemary witnessed being lectured their first day of work, screamed at the top of his lungs.

He dropped his inactive broom and raced out of the store with a throng of customers at his heels. Ava fell in with the crowd and pushed her way through the front door. People lining both sides of the streets squinted their eyes up into the bright sky at Mr. Lloyd's compact, red plane as it zig-zagged in

49

and out of lumpy clouds. A banner reading "Eat Lloyd's Bread" and tailing from the plane disappeared and reappeared as it whipped its message in the spring wind.

E. C. Lloyd owned a bakery and a cafe in town, and he loved to dazzle his potential customers with his airplane maneuvers as much as he loved to fill their stomachs with his baked goods. He deftly flipped, turned, and circled the plane directly over the heart of Anniston and above hundreds of excited eyes. His airplane spectacular far outperformed the wild and clumsy crop dusting planes that Ava watched growing up, and she followed the plane with her gray eyes as it buzzed and somersaulted through the air.

On the other side of the street, Edwin Livingston and his friends also watched the aerial advertisement. Edwin gazed at it with amused interest, but, after a few minutes of watching the same flying pattern and reading the same message, he turned his attention to the other spectators. He scanned the rows of upturned faces and found Ava among the crowd. Without meaning to, he stared as her incandescent face appeared fascinated with the plane, and he was moved again by her palpable passion. She looked up into the sky with the same rapture with which she sang, and he again felt her love for life. She was still gazing up at the sky when the young woman he had seen her with at the picnic tugged on her arm and pointed toward a middle-aged woman with a severe face who was motioning for them to come back inside the store. Ava dared to glance once more at the plane and followed her friend.

Even though Sydney had praised her voice and pleasing features all the way back to the fort, and Barry had said several times what a nice girl she was, they had not discussed Ava again. Edwin had dismissed the impression she made on him, but the sight of her left him feeling restless and agitated. He was attracted to her against his will and for reasons unlike any other girl he had been attracted to before. Like Sydney, he liked her voice and fresh, pleasant appearance, but there was something else, something he didn't understand that was drawing him to her. He wanted to talk to her, and he deliberated as to how to see her without his friends discerning his romantic motives. Barry, Sydney, and Percy continued to laugh at Lloyd's daring techniques.

He lived with Barry and Sydney in the same barracks, and the three of them became fast friends their first week of Branch Immaterial Replacement Training at Fort McClellan four weeks ago. Even though they were from different parts of the country, the subjects of fishing, shooting, and their feelings toward the war brought them together. Barry and Sydney also took turns reviewing and rewriting Edwin's few letters back home as his reading and writing were painfully elementary. He was embarrassed to ask them at first, but many of the men from rural areas had the same difficulties. His superiority in rifle marksmanship, which gained their respect, also evened them up in his mind. They were astounded by his shooting precision and by his ability to take apart and reassemble a gun in the dark, a trick his father had taught him on hunting trips when he was just a boy.

Percy was from Savannah, Georgia and the lieutenant over their squad. Even though he could be arrogant at times, he was also generally amicable and made everyone under his leadership feel like a peer within good reason. Sydney was particularly fond of him and invited him to join them on their trip to Anniston.

"I think that the Air Force could use ole Lloyd here," Sydney said, as the plane completed its marketing mission and headed back to its hanger.

"And our mess hall could use some of his donuts," Barry agreed, putting the last bite of a donut from the self-acclaimed Lloyd's Bakery in his mouth.

They were so physically active training during the week that they were always hungry.

"I should've got one of those. Let's go back," Percy suggested to Edwin, who had also refrained from buying one.

"Hey guys, I need to see a girl first," Sydney said, looking in the direction of Wakefield's.

Edwin's face fell, realizing that Sydney had also not forgotten about Ava.

"Remember that girl I told you about that can sing like Jo Stafford." Sydney turned to Percy. "She works in that store."

He pointed to the door of Wakefield's, and Edwin wondered if Sydney had noticed her gazing at the plane as well.

"Let's go." Barry rubbed the sugary remains of the donut off his hands and onto his pants. "She promised to help me pick out something for Marg."

"Oh, no, we're going in there to look at dames, not shop for them." Sydney laughed, as they crossed the street toward Wakefield's.

When they entered the store, Edwin's eyes immediately found Ava. He watched her pensive profile as she rearranged a pile of women's hosiery. Sydney and Barry had not noticed her as quickly as he had. Barry was looking at a tall mannequin modeling a sundress, and Sydney and Percy were both concentrated on the blonde woman approaching them.

"Can I help you boys?" Alta asked with a bright smile.

"We're not boys, miss. We're men of the service," Sydney corrected her.

"That's what they all say." She laughed and began to play with the ends of the tape measure that always accented her waist whenever she was working.

"Actually, we're looking for Ava Stilwell."

"Well, men of the service, Ava is working in women's accessories right now." Alta motioned in Ava's direction with a flip of her long, manicured hand.

"Thank you, Miss …," Sydney said as they followed her direction.

"Alta," she finished for him and then greeted another customer who rattled the bells of Wakefield's front door.

Ava was turned away from them, and Sydney approached her first and dropped to one knee just behind her.

"Ava, please sing for us again," he begged with clasped hands.

She was so intent to win back Mrs. Crockett's approval for abandoning the store that she hadn't noticed their entrance. Startled, she almost dropped the pile of nylon stockings in her hands.

"Sydney!" she exclaimed, recognizing his rakish grin and friendly brown eyes.

"We must hear you sing again," he urged, still on his knees.

Ava's face reddened, remembering Mrs. Crockett, and her anxious eyes surveyed the store for her boss, who was conversing with a customer by the front counter. Seeing her nervousness, Sydney laughed and stood up.

"So, are you not going to sing for us?" he asked, leaning over her.

"I don't think my manager would like that." She looked uneasily in Mrs. Crockett's direction, and he followed her eyes to the feared woman.

"Barry, didn't you need Ava's help to buy something for Marg?" He looked back at Barry with a smirk.

"Yes, I do. How are you, Ava?" Barry moved toward her enthusiastically.

"Oh hi, Barry. I would love to help you," she said, noticing him, Edwin, and Percy for the first time.

Ava looked at Edwin next. His eyes were already on her, and she flushed as she did the day she met him. There was something feral and searching in his gaze, which made her unsure if he liked her.

"Do you like your new job?" he asked.

"Yes, I love working," she answered, and the way her eyes sparked told him that she loved people and being in the center of something moving and active.

"Ava, this is Lieutenant Percy Bledsoe." Sydney waved his unknown friend forward.

"I'm looking forward to hearing you sing," Percy said, tipping his military hat down at her.

"Thank you." Ava's heart quickened at the thought of Sydney talking about her.

Percy's smooth, lean face, commanding posture, and surly brown eyes communicated to her that he was older and refined, and she felt slightly intimidated by his powerful presence. He was one of the most handsome men she had ever seen.

"Actually, Ava, we want you to sing next Saturday night at our U.S.O. dance," Sydney broke in.

Her eyes darted to his face, trying to absorb his sudden invitation. He really was serious about wanting to hear her sing again.

"Say yes," Percy coaxed. "We all want to hear the voice that has won Sydney's heart."

54

She didn't know what to say. Her whole face felt hot, and she knew that she couldn't agree to anything without speaking to her parents first.

"Ava, does this dress come in a smaller size?" Edwin pushed his way in between them with a woman's suit in his hands just as an obstinate Mrs. Crockett approached them.

Ava looked from Edwin's urgent eyes to the dress and then to Mrs. Crockett behind him. Remembering her place, she hastily took the garment from his hands.

"Yes, it does," she said loudly for Mrs. Crockett to overhear. "Let me just look in our petite section for you."

"Is everything o.k. here?" Mrs. Crockett interrupted with a stern smile.

They had been warned about fraternizing with soldiers while at work.

"Your attendant is just helping us pick something out for one our wives back home," Sydney answered, giving Mrs. Crockett a wide, winsome smile.

"Lovely. I just wanted to make sure you were all being helped."

Sydney's efficacious charm even worked on Lorraine Crockett. She smiled more naturally at all of them and walked away. Ava let out a deep breath. She would have been crushed to anger Mrs. Crockett twice in one day.

"She seems like a regular sergeant." Barry whistled.

"Thank you," Ava looked up at Edwin.

"No problem," he shrugged.

Despite himself, he was moved by her attention, and, as his rugged cheeks began to warm, the softness in his eyes changed back to aloof hostility.

"You picked out this dress for Marg?" Barry asked, taking the garment and holding it up away from him as if picturing his wife in the suit.

"It was the first one on the rack," Edwin admitted, embarrassed to be picking out women's clothing in front of his friends.

His ears, which stood out from his face, reddened.

"Edwin has good taste," Ava said, observing his embarrassment. "This is one of our most popular fashions right now."

"Hey, Winn, maybe you could start helping all of the boys pick out dresses for their sweethearts," Sydney joked, and he, Percy, and Barry all laughed.

"So what if I know how to please women."

He knew that if he showed his displeasure at being teased, they would laugh at him all the more.

"Ava, you didn't answer my question," Sydney said. "Will you come grace us with your presence next Saturday, or do I have to get on my knees and beg again?"

Ava flushed from the flattery of his persistent invitation and because she wouldn't be able to tell him yes or no without speaking to her mother. Her father rarely opposed her mother on these types of issues. She noticed Alta out of the corner of her eye and was envious that her co-worker was her own person and would not have to even think about her mother if the question were posed to her.

"I'll have to talk to my parents first," she answered, and, thinking of her mother's almost certain reaction, her cheeks began to burn.

"Don't ask questions. Just leave your parents to me." Sydney winked. "We'll see you next weekend."

Ava was confused by his confidence. He didn't know her mother's disdain for dancing and revelry, and she was at a loss as to how and what he could possibly do to alter her mother's impervious mind. He didn't even know her parents, did he?

"You can bring your friends with you. Isn't that the girl you were with at the picnic?" Sydney pointed at Rosemary who was filling out a ticket for a customer.

"She's my cousin Rosemary."

"Bring her and your other work friends." He glanced at Alta across the store.

Sydney promised to get in touch with her before Saturday night, and she helped Barry actually purchase the suit that Edwin had selected. They all left before Mrs. Crockett revisited her again, and Ava worked distractedly the rest of the afternoon. She no longer looked outside the store's windows for excitement but reflected within her own heart. She wanted so desperately to go but had tessellated emotions about everything. She was thrilled about dancing and music and young men, nervous about singing in front of so many strangers, and perplexed about what to do about her mother.

Victoria was just about to open the June meeting of the Four Mile Community Garden Club when the front door opened and in walked Valencia Boozer patting sweat beads off her broad forehead and pug nose with a handkerchief. Knowing she was late, she had almost run the distance between their two houses.

"What is she doing here?" Victoria said where only Myrtle could hear.

Valencia hadn't attended one of their garden club meetings in at least a year.

"Hello, Valencia," Victoria greeted, but her eyes questioned her intentions.

She had never been good at hiding her true feelings.

"Don't mind me, Toria. I just decided to come at the last moment, and I can see that you're about to go ahead with your meeting," Valencia said, finding an empty kitchen chair.

It always bothered Victoria how Valencia talked so fast that she never could spit out her full name.

"Won't you have some fresh lemonade?" she asked, looking at Estelle.

Now that Ava was working, Estelle had been promoted to her untitled assistant. Estelle carefully put down the piece of paper that Victoria had labeled in bold capital letters "FOUR MILE GARDEN CLUB ROLE – JUNE 1943" and began to rise from her chair.

"Don't get up sweetie. I'll get it," Valencia jumped up and beat Estelle to the table where the cups and pitcher sat carefully arranged. "Isn't it a hot but lovely day? What a fine day to talk about flowers."

"That's just what I was saying to Maris as we walked over here," Alice Fitzpatrick, a short woman with a large, heart-shaped face, agreed as she sipped her own crystal cup of sour lemonade.

Victoria waited impatiently as Valencia poured her drink.

"A little rain would be good for my roses, though," the mentioned Maris added, nodding her thick shock of marigold-colored hair.

Valencia returned to her seat, crossed her legs, and looked up at Victoria like a dutiful schoolgirl.

What does she want? Victoria asked herself, resuming her garden club president demeanor.

"We will begin with the roll, which Estelle will take down," she announced, "and in honor of this month's theme, 'Plants that Thrive in the Household,' when Estelle calls your name, if you could each respond with the name of a plant that does well indoors."

Even though Estelle personally knew every woman present, the formal roll calling was a standard procedure that could not be done without. The names that she marked would appear in the Tuesday edition of the *Jacksonville News*. All of the twelve ladies present began to travel mentally room by room through their homes contemplating their indoor plants.

"Myrtle Bonds," Estelle called out alphabetically.

"Mother-in-law Tongues," Myrtle answered, and Estelle placed a tiny black check mark next to her name.

"Ingrid Carson."

"Ivy," Ingrid, the excessively overweight wife of Victoria's brother Louie, spoke up.

Victoria looked at her dubiously. Ivy had never thrived in her house, and, in her opinion, her sister-in-law only knew how to properly cultivate weeds and dandelions.

"Abigail Dempsey," Estelle looked up at her aunt whose eyes were closed as she mulled over the perfect indoor plant.

"Um… Christmas Cactus," Abigail said, smiling that she had mentioned what she believed was the apotheosis of household plants.

When the roll taking was finished, Maris Ingram, the acting secretary, read the minutes of their last meeting in which they had participated in a rose bud contest. Delores Waters who had been declared the undeniable winner smiled humbly as her achievement was remembered, and all of the ladies re-congratulated her with friendly pats and courteous remarks.

59

When Victoria had quieted them once again, she spoke about the suitability of peace lilies in the house and called on Opal Gunter to display one of her flourishing peace lilies, which she had brought early and hid on the back porch until the opportune moment. Everyone awed and complimented Opal's potted masterpiece, and she readily explained her watering and cow manure fertilizing cycles. Afterward, Victoria and Estelle brought out a plate full of sugar cookies and more lemonade, and the garden talk turned to the social news of Jacksonville. Some of the women were not in love with flowers like Victoria, and this part of the meeting was the genuine reason for their regular monthly attendance.

"Did everyone hear that Winston Green's young wife from Huntsville, Elsie, is having a baby?" Alice asked with a maternal flutter of eyelids and a softness of the voice as if she were the mother in waiting.

"Yes, I did. Frances mentioned that at Jake's party." Ingrid nodded her baggy chin. "The whole family is beside themselves with excitement."

"Speaking of Jake's party, what a fine, good-looking young man he's become," Valencia added, putting the first bite of a buttery sugar cookie in her mouth. "He'll make some lucky lady a nice husband when he returns from the war."

Estelle blushed for Rosemary. Everyone in town must have noticed how attached to one another they were last night.

"If my eyes aren't deceiving me, I would say that he intends to make your Rosemary that lucky lady." Alice turned to Myrtle.

"Don't you go getting my daughter hitched before she's ready," Myrtle, who was usually demure like her daughter, warned with a look of her green eyes and a curt giggle, which sounded both friendly and stern.

She never knew whether it was nervousness or habit that made that giggle always follow any comment of importance she tried to make. She had watched Jake and Rosemary for the past several months during their budding romance and particularly last night and was certain that their relationship had taken a more serious turn, but she wouldn't admit it to anyone until Rosemary told her first. Secretly, she was ecstatic over Rosemary's match making. Jake Green was indeed the finest boy in town, and she was proud that her daughter might become his wife.

"Estelle, when are we going to get a little James, Jr.?" Valencia changed the subject.

Estelle's brown eyes widened, and she now blushed for herself. She would love a family more than anything, but talking to older women about these types of matters was not something she was accustomed to.

"I guess when God is willing," she smiled with pleasure at the thought of having a son like her husband.

Victoria put a hand on her daughter-in-law's shoulder.

"That's right. When God decides to bless, he will," Victoria sermonized, thinking warmly of the possibility, despite herself.

"These cookies are simply delicious, Toria," Valencia praised, holding up the last bite of a cookie as if inspecting it for a secret ingredient before placing it deliberately in her mouth.

"Thank you," Victoria said, sharpening her gaze.

She was now convinced that Valencia was setting her up for something unpleasant.

They all sat and continued to chat for sometime until household duties and the thoughts of children began to turn their minds homeward. One by one they each excused

61

themselves for a different obligation and promised to come back next month to discuss how to keep weeds out of flowerbeds. The only ones left now were Myrtle and Estelle, who always helped her tidy up, and Valencia. Victoria continued to search Valencia's face for answers. She was growing more and more impatient with her loquaciousness.

"Well, Victoria, there is another reason I came today," Valencia said at last with an unnatural hesitation. "Even though I do always love your garden parties."

Victoria sighed.

"Your daughter was simply stunning last week when she sang the national anthem at my church, and I have a direct request from Fort McClellan that she sing it next Saturday night at their U.S.O…event." She intentionally substituted the word "event" for "dance," knowing Victoria's rigid Baptist viewpoints on dancing.

She personally liked to think of herself as a more modern Baptist.

Estelle and Myrtle both turned their eyes to Victoria. She folded her hands in her lap. This is not what she had expected. She had guessed that the purpose of Valencia's visit was to enlist her in some endless charity work, not sweep her daughter away to a host of unknown men. She was both flattered and frustrated by the proposal.

"It will be an enjoyable, well-chaperoned event, hosted jointly by members of the Salvation Army and the Red Cross. Phil and I would personally look after her," she worked to keep her voice steady under Victoria's intense gaze. "We would also love for Rosemary to come and give Ava company." Valencia now looked at Myrtle, relieved to focus her attention elsewhere.

Myrtle looked back at her with noticeable surprise and bit her bottom lip to control the nervous giggle she felt emerging.

"We could pick the girls up in Phil's car and then bring them home afterward," Valencia finished and then sat patiently waiting for a response.

"I'll have to think on this, Valencia," Victoria finally spoke. "I have heard about the behavior of some of the local soldiers and am not sure if that would be good for my daughter to be...."

"I can assure you that there are many moral and nice young men at Fort McClellan who it would be an honor for both of your daughters to know," Valencia curtailed Victoria's unreasonable objection.

"You may be right, but I'll have to speak with Sheffield before coming to any decisions. However, I do appreciate their admiration of Ava's singing." Victoria stood up to signal an end to the conversation.

"Oh, they were amazed by Ava's voice." Valencia also stood up. "And we have a wonderful local band that she would be performing with."

"Please thank them for the invitation, but I will still have to talk this over with my husband," Victoria stated with unflinching resolve.

"On behalf of our men in the service, thank you for considering it." Valencia smiled as cheerfully as possible, appealing to her old friend's patriotism and guilt.

Anxious to leave, she now walked as fast as she talked toward the door. "I hope to make next month's meeting," she promised uncertainly. "Good-bye, Estelle. Good-bye. Myrtle."

Estelle and Myrtle waved and wished her well as the front door shut behind her, and Victoria looked hotly after her.

Chapter 7

The evening had not gone as Ava had planned. She was angry with Rosemary, confused by her parents' strange behavior, and stuck in a cramped closet between Carson's knobby knees and a box of her mother's Christmas decorations. Jacksonville had a new air raid warden, and Victoria was adamant that they participate in Clyde Ponder's inaugural drill. Ever since a report came out in the *Anniston News* that Birmingham, Alabama was a suspected German target, as well as any city within 300 miles of the coastline, Jacksonville began performing its own regular air raid alerts.

Ava pushed against Carson's leg as hard as possible, but she could not budge him, and her cheeks flamed with anger at his smirking face in the candlelight. His only source of amusement during these hour-long interludes was torturing her, and his dampened spirits did little to hinder the diversion. At the present, he was determined to keep her wedged tightly to the box on her side. He was also enjoying the curious behavior she was receiving from their parents and looked at her with mocking empathy as if she had done some misdeed and was about to be severely punished. He was pleased that the unfavorable attention he had been receiving from their parents over the fight might be shifting elsewhere.

Ava was more than perplexed by the way her parents had spoken to and looked at her all night, and of all nights, the night she most needed their kindness, as she was waiting for the right moment to talk to them about the dance. Ever since she had come home from work, her mother had ignored her and given her hard stares as if she was displeased about something, and she had caught her father looking at her several times as if he was about to decide some grave question of which she was the unwilling subject.

Grandpa Chester always refused to participate in the community drills, and she could hear the radio interlaced with his grumbling snore from where he sat in the dark just outside the closet door. He referred to the drills as "pure nonsense" and said that if Hitler wanted him, he dared him to come and get him. At that moment, he was missing out on Brother Whatley trying to retell a Methodist joke he had heard on the bus.

"Once there was this man up in Heflin selling a litter of puppies. Well, another feller came along wanting to buy one, and he noticed that the puppies were in two separate boxes, and the box nearest him was selling for more. He asked, 'What's the difference between those puppies in that box and these puppies in this box?' The man selling them looked at him kinda funny." Brother Whatley's voice rose as he reached the climax of his joke. "He said, 'Well sir, the ones in this box are Baptist puppies, and the ones in that box are Methodist puppies, because they ain't got their eyes open yet.'"

Brother Whatley leaned back his red head and roared. Victoria and Sheffield also laughed from their roomier side of the closet, and Carson breathed in, where only she could hear, as if to say that was the stupidest joke he had ever heard. Ava laughed too, even though she was out of humor. She knew that once she asked her parents about the dance, they would consult Brother Whatley for advice. To her mother, Brother

Whatley's opinion was almost as good as the Bible. She hoped that if she could win over the preacher's graces on red lipstick, she could also win his approval for her unexpected invitation. He had never married or had any children of his own, and he treated her, Carson, and James as the children he never had. Ava had also counted on Rosemary's help, and her cheeks glowed in the pale light again at the thought of her cousin's stark refusal to attend the event with her next weekend, even if their parents did agree. Rosemary wouldn't say it, but Ava knew that she would think of it as a reproach to Jake, and, because of this, they argued all the way home.

"How was your first week at Wakefield's?" Brother Whatley peered at her from his place in the middle of the closet.

"It was wonderful. Rosemary and I've almost learned everything already." Ava stole a look at her mother and tried to sound enthusiastic, wishing to impress her parents as much as the pastor.

She wanted to ask them about singing for the soldiers without Carson, but, needing Brother Whatley's support, she decided that now was the best time.

"Good, good." The preacher nodded. "The Proverbs says a virtuous woman worketh willingly with her hands."

"She takes being a hard worker after her mother," Sheffield said, squeezing his wife's shoulders.

"You won't believe what happened at work today," Ava said as brightly as possible to dispel the nervousness she felt from her voice.

She looked from her father to Brother Whatley with the warmest smile possible, knowing that her looks would be powerless on her mother.

"I was invited," she began, as the anxiety she worked to abate begin creeping into her voice, "to sing for the Fort McClellan soldiers next Saturday."

"We already know all about it," Victoria informed her.

Ava's eyes grew wide as she looked at her mother's impregnable face in amazement.

"Valencia Boozer came to the garden club meeting today and asked if you could go."

Her eyes and tone were stern, but not without promise, and Ava read from her expression that her parents were undecided on the matter. Carson sat up from his reclining position, eager to watch the altercation. Ava ignored his repeated nudges to her side.

"Well, well, what an invitation." Brother Whatley chuckled, not wanting to express any definite opinions until asked.

"Yes, it is," Sheffield agreed, unable to keep the pride he felt from his voice. "However, we're concerned about the type of influences Ava would be around were she to go. The Boozers have offered to take and look after her, but we haven't made up our minds yet."

He could be firm with James and Carson but not with his only daughter.

"If the Boozers would be with me, then I am sure I would be fine," Ava said with caution, not wanting to alienate her mother with her boldness.

She knew that arguing with her would only make matters worse.

"What do you think about this, Brother Whatley? Sheffield and I have always respected your spiritual guidance." Victoria looked to the pastor without acknowledging her daughter's comment.

Brother Whatley licked his thin lips and blinked his beady eyes reverently.

"I understand your concern. I've heard about some of the local soldiers' foolishness in Anniston too, but the ones that came to the Four Mile revival were very nice young men." He remembered how intently they appeared to listen to his sermon.

"Well," he continued after another moment of reflection, "I guess I don't see anything harmful with her singing for them. Maybe she could lead some of them to repent with her voice. If anybody can sing a song, it's Ava, but you're her God-given parents, so you'll have to decide."

Even though her heart was jumping, Ava kept her expression relaxed, not wanting to appear too victorious in front of her mother just yet. If Brother Whatley thought it was all right, how could she go against a man of God?

"Suppose there should be dancing?" Victoria almost whispered the word "dancing" as if it were morally shocking.

"I think you've raised your daughter well, and I'm sure that Ava wouldn't do anything to disappoint you," the pastor vouched for her behavior, giving Ava a sharp look of warning.

She winced as his green eyes took on a ghastly admonition.

"You trust me, don't you, Mom?" Ava asked, sensing that her mother was beginning to soften to the idea.

"Of course, Ava."

"Are you sure?" Carson couldn't resist saying. Ava punched him in the ribs.

"We certainly do trust your sister," Sheffield answered with the firmness he lacked with his daughter.

Three short, horn-like blasts signaled the end of the drill, and Ava emerged from the closet with an elated face, believing that she had won. Grandpa Chester leaped up from his chair and smoothed back the wild hair that was always combed over his baldhead.

"Are we safe from the Germans?" he said and then laughed, moving his hands across his body as if checking to make sure that all his limbs were still attached.

That night, just after Ava went to bed, the door to her room opened, and she heard her father's familiar heavy footsteps on the wood floor, followed by her mother's more gentle ones. She opened her eyes to see her father sitting beside her on the bed and the outline of her mother behind him.

"Ava, we've talked it over till we're blue in the face and have decided to let you go sing for the soldiers," Sheffield spoke.

Ava smiled at him in the dark. She knew by him being the one to tell her that her mother had consented but was still unsure of the situation.

"We expect you to be on your best behavior, Ava Lillian Stilwell." Victoria now moved closer to the bed until her light eyes were discernible in the dark.

"I will," Ava promised, glad that her face was half-covered by the quilt.

"We know you will." Sheffield patted her unseen shoulder. "Well, goodnight."

He stood up tall over her bed.

"Goodnight, Daddy."

She was amazed sometimes at just how tall he and Carson actually were. He left the room while Victoria lingered behind.

"Sweet dreams. I love you," Victoria said with all the motherly tenderness that had been absent from her voice a moment before.

"I love you, too," Ava said back, as her mother left her alone in her triumph.

Chapter 8

Ava kept touching the back and sides of her hair. She couldn't get accustomed to her now bare neck. She and Estelle had gone to Aunt Elizabeth's house Wednesday afternoon for a hair cutting. Her aunt could cut straighter than a sewing needle and was in charge of all the family haircuts. She had been flabbergasted with Ava's request to cut her hair short and argued with her sometime before putting her scissors to the task. Ava's hair had always been long and thick, but she wanted a more contemporary, older look like Alta and other girls her age in Anniston. She dared not cut it as short as Alta's, but it was shorter than she had ever worn her hair before. She studied her wavy, dark tresses in the mirror and sighed. It wasn't quite the mature look she had hoped for.

"How do you like it?" Alta called from the other side of the dressing curtain.

Ava looked down at the dress she was wearing and smiled. Her hair still might not be perfect, but the dress was exquisite. It was a maroon, sleeveless garment with a jacket that accented her red cheeks and lips. It was covered in a delicate outer layer of the same color, and Ava ran her fingers over the transparent material on both sides of her slender hips, as she turned in front of the mirror, contemplating her profile. She felt romantic and light.

"Well, are you going to come out or not?" Alta called again. "We're anxious for a look."

Ava pushed aside the curtain and emerged in the dress.

"Oooh!" Alta motioned with her finger for Ava to turn around. "It's beautiful!"

Rosemary nodded coolly in agreement. She would not forgive Ava for having to go to the dance tomorrow night. Her parents were demanding that she accompany her cousin. Ava turned as requested and smiled at her sympathetically.

"It's very pretty," Rosemary finally admitted, angry with herself for giving in to Ava's ruefulness.

"You have to buy it for tomorrow night," Alta persuaded, already beginning to fill out a sales ticket for her.

Wakefield's had just closed, and the three of them were shopping for themselves in the empty store. Ava couldn't help but feel guilty. She was raised to be resourceful and frugal and wasn't comfortable with buying things for herself. Grandpa Chester always chirped that if you couldn't wear it or eat it, you shouldn't waste your money on it. Well, she could wear this dress, but should she buy it? Her clothes had always been home sewn. Still, it was the finest dress she had ever put on.

"All right," she gave in, but in order to justify her purchase, she also bought some of their nylon hosiery for her mother and Estelle, the skinny tie that reminded her of her father, a pair of socks for each of her brothers, and a new bottle of Watkin's Liniment for Grandpa Chester.

She would be spending almost all of her first $20.00 earnings.

"Rosemary, are you going to buy anything?" she asked.

72

If Rosemary also bought something, she would feel better about her purchases.

"Not today," Rosemary answered almost spitefully Ava thought, and, as she walked back into the dressing room, she gave her cousin an unseen look of exasperation.

Jake suddenly defined everything Rosemary did and thought, and she was annoyed with her constant moroseness.

"I haven't decided what I'm going to wear yet. Jon likes my two-piece, taupe dress, but we will see what I'm in the mood for." Alta talked as much to herself as to Rosemary and Ava as she returned two dresses that Ava had also tried on back to their rack.

"Hey, did I tell you two that Jon is a movie star of sorts?" Alta asked. "He played a night club owner in a Cary Grant movie and a butler for Humphrey Bogart."

Ava slipped the suit back on that Estelle had made her and rejoined them. They finished balancing their books, and she paid for her new things. She couldn't wait to take her family their gifts, and she imagined their astonished, appreciative faces all the way home. Looking out the bus window, for she and Rosemary were unusually quiet due to Rosemary's sullenness, Ava decided that she liked having her own money. She felt almost powerful with all of the neatly wrapped things she had bought in her lap.

When she got home, she could hardly repress her excitement before stashing away her new dress. She wanted to present them all with their gifts before revealing what she had bought for herself. Her family didn't disappoint her. They were all delighted with the gifts, but her mother and father both warned her about the deceitfulness of money and the shame and ignorance of not saving. When she finally disclosed the dress, her mother's only response was a wide arching of the eyebrows, but Estelle fawned over it, and James planned to buy his wife a similar one.

Rosemary stood alone and watched Ava begin to sing the *Star Spangled Banner*. As she sang the national anthem, all the soldiers stood upright and in unison all over the spacious room with right hands reverently over the hearts they had pledged to their country. The sight of them brought Jake to her mind, and she smiled to herself as she pictured him standing in the same posture. She could tell by the heightened color of Ava's face that her cousin was alive in the moment, which only made her voice soar even more effortlessly from note to note. The uneasy sensation of observance pulled Rosemary's attention away from the stage, and she glanced about her, finding two haughty, brown eyes looking at her. The stranger smiled, but she refused to return his greeting. She turned away. It was the older man with Ava's friends at the store last week. She tried to refocus her attention on Ava's performance, but the feeling of being watched continued to disturb her, and she wished more than anything that she hadn't come. She sensed him walking toward her, and she crossed her arms over her chest.

"You're Ava's friend, right?" he said when he reached her.

Her uninviting stance only made her all the more attractive to him. Something about her light-colored hair and golden skin reminded him of lemonade and sunshine and effused a soft warmness that her attitude toward him could not conceal.

"I'm her cousin," she answered, refusing to look at him.

74

"Do you sing like your cousin?" he continued, smiling at the way his questions agitated her, and he guessed that she was playing faithful to an absent lover.

"No." She pretended to be completely immersed in the activity around them.

The song ended, Ava was clapped for, and the band quickly took over. Percy stood in silence beside her as the band began to play a brassy ballad.

"You must have a boyfriend in the service." A slight chuckle escaped his lips when a look of frightful surprise and annoyance overcome her composed expression.

"I do. He's in the Navy."

"I have a fiancée back home in Georgia myself."

Rosemary had nothing else to say him, and, seeing Ava exiting the stage, she started to leave him until he caught her arm.

"Since we're both spoken for, will you dance one song with a lonely soldier?"

She pulled her arm away but looked up briefly at him, and the directedness of his gaze startled her. He wasn't accustomed to being refused.

"I wouldn't even ask you if I didn't know you also had someone," he said, regaining her arm, and before Rosemary had time to think, he had pulled her to him, and she was dancing with him.

"I'm Percy Bledsoe."

She could feel his breath hitting her cheek, and her head felt hot and dizzy. She said nothing as her mind mulled over her situation, and she remembered Ava not saying his name but referring to him as "Mr. Clark Gable."

"Are you going to make me guess your name?"

"I'm…I'm Rosemary Bonds."

"Rosemary, that's a fitting name for you." His lips curved into an amused smile, revealing white, even teeth.

When she still wouldn't relax or return his smile, he laughed out loud.

"Don't worry, Rosemary. I'm not going to bite you. It's just nice to talk to a girl who isn't looking for a man in a uniform."

Ava's heart still beat furiously as she accepted the praise given her and walked away from the stage. She had promised to return to Rosemary immediately after her performance, and she looked toward the side of the room where her cousin had been standing. Not finding her, her eyes roamed the other sides of the wall and then the entire room, agitated that Rosemary might have left. Noticing Mrs. Boozer and her husband with another chaperoning couple, she began to go inquire about her cousin when she recognized Rosemary's straight white dress and long, curly hair on the dance floor. She was stunned. Rosemary was actually dancing with someone other than Jake and that someone was the incredibly handsome Percy. Her surprise quickly gave way to envy, as she realized that Rosemary, who didn't even want to come, was dancing before she was, and she was at a loss as to where to go or what to do with herself.

"Hey, you," a deep voice called behind her, and she turned in its direction.

"Do you dance as well as you sing?" a blusterous soldier asked as he extended his hand toward her.

Before she could answer, a familiar blonde head ducked in between them.

"Ava, you were wonderful," Alta screamed over the music, hugging Ava. "I just couldn't believe my ears. If Mr.

Wakefield could hear you, you would make more money than all of us put together."

"Thanks." She smiled. Seeing a man behind her, she asked, "Is this Jon?"

Alta tucked a small hand under her date's arm and pulled him forward, and the brazen soldier left to find another dance partner. She hadn't mentioned that Jon was Asian, and Ava looked up at the claimed movie star's olive-brown complexion and dark eyes with some surprise.

"Yes, this is Sergeant Jon Chong," Alta introduced, squeezing his arm.

Jon was about to speak when Sydney appeared next to Ava.

"I knew everyone would love you," he said, leaning close and putting a hand on her back.

She was growing to like his familiarity. He smelled like aftershave and mint.

"Decided to spend the night with the men of the service, did you, Alta?" He laughed, recognizing Ava's co-worker.

"I'm impressed that you remember my name, and I'm assuming that you're the one responsible for getting our Ava here."

"That's right, Private Sydney Saunders, pleased to be the guilty one."

"Meet Sergeant Jon Chong."

"Nice to meet you both." Jon was allowed to speak this time, and he shook Sydney's hand and smiled down at Ava.

Another song began, and Alta gasped and tugged on Jon's shoulder.

"It's the Jersey Bounce. We have to dance!"

"We'll join you." Sydney put a hand on each side of Ava's waist and pushed her forward onto the dance floor behind them.

Ava was nervous that she wouldn't be able to dance like the other young men and women, but Sydney moved her with smooth agility to the quick tempo of the small orchestra. Music always had an emotional power over her, and her blood coursed through her body and colored her face as she swayed to the resonating rhythm of the trumpet and trombones. She had never experienced such music first hand, and she was enamored with Sydney's dancing expertise. He smiled down at her just a few inches above her face, and she wondered if she was falling in love with him. He wasn't necessarily handsome like Percy or even Edwin. He was very thin and had a protruding nose, but he also had swarthy skin, an appealing smile, and irresistible charm with everyone. Still contemplating her feelings for him, he twirled her around until the room was a blur of colors and, peering over his shoulder breathlessly, she met Edwin's eyes for a fleeting second. He was sitting with a group of laughing men and watching her with the wild eyes that had first intimidated her. She knew that she affected him and that awareness along with his recent behavior at the store now made her comfortable with him. The song came to a loud, clashing end, and Sydney spun her around once more as the last note reverberated throughout the room.

"So, you can dance too," he complimented, but they were both aware that he was the reason for the success of their dance.

He still held one of her hands and led her to where Alta and Jon were now resting.

"Want to trade for a song?" he asked Jon to Ava's astonishment, but Alta seemed to have almost expected it.

"Ava, I must warn you that Jon might step on your feet." She laughed as the good-natured Jon turned scarlet in the face, and she patted his cheek before leaving him.

Jon and Ava looked at each other uncomfortably.

"I'll try not to hurt you," he said, putting his arm around her.

"Oh, I'm not worried." Ava smiled.

Dancing with Jon did not have the same invigorating effect on her as dancing with Sydney. He certainly wasn't light-footed, and, while Sydney overcame her weaknesses, Jon exacerbated them. She felt that they looked clumsy together and enviously watched Sydney and Alta over Jon's shoulder as they moved together to the music that she felt had become stale.

"I hear you've been in the movies," she said, trying to direct his attention away from his feet.

"I've been in a few pictures," he replied.

"I think that Alta looks like a movie star."

Jon looked regretfully at his date, and Ava wished she wouldn't have mentioned her co-worker.

"Yes, she does, but you know there are many famous brunettes, too."

The top of his foot grazed hers, and she pretended not to notice. The song finally finished, and they were both embarrassed when Sydney and Alta continued dancing. She couldn't bear to dance with Jon any longer, and she suddenly remembered Rosemary.

"Do you want to dance another song?" he asked, but he could tell by her dashing eyes that her attention had moved elsewhere.

She spotted Rosemary now standing alone where she had been when they first arrived.

"Actually, I need to go see my cousin. We came together, and I promised not to be gone too long."

"I'll see you around then."

She walked quickly to where Rosemary stood, just as Percy reappeared with two glasses of punch. Rosemary welcomed her with a bewildering look that she couldn't yet discern.

"Your performance was every bit as good as promised," Percy greeted.

"I was terrified," she half lied.

She had been nervous, but the thrill of performing elated her like nothing else. When she was on stage, she transformed into a greater person. It was the only place where she could completely forget herself.

"You sure couldn't tell it. Your cousin has been entertaining a lonely man whose fiancée is back home." He smiled down at Rosemary, who only partly returned the expression.

Rosemary was still unsure of his motives, and Ava understood her situation all at once. She gave her an empathizing look that told her so, and Rosemary looked gratefully back at her.

"Would you like something to drink?" Percy interrupted their thoughts.

"I'll be fine."

"You must be thirsty. I saw you heating up the dance floor with Sydney. I'll be right back."

"If you're not having a good time, we can leave after I'm finished singing. Mrs. Boozer said she would take us home whenever we wanted," Ava offered when he left, but not without a reluctance in her voice.

"No, we can stay. I know you're having fun, and I would hate to ask Mrs. Boozer to take us home early. Besides, Percy knows about Jake, and I know about his fiancée."

Reason told her it was all right to talk to Percy, but her heart told her it wasn't, and she was frustrated by her own ambivalence.

"You must admit that he has to be the most handsome man you have ever laid eyes on," Ava said as she watched Sydney spin Alta around the room just as he had her moments ago.

"He may be your type, but he isn't mine."

Rosemary recalled Jake the day of his going away party, and she smiled, remembering the way he had kissed her. Percy returned with Ava's drink, and she could tell by his broadening grin that he mistook her expression for Jake as for him, and blood rushed to her face in embarrassment. She purposely frowned at him and turned away as he laughed at her. He was completely unnerving, and her mortification was giving way to nervous anger. She would not dance with him again. Barry had come back with him and was already talking to Ava.

"I mailed the dress to Marg, and I can't wait to hear back from her."

"I'm positive that she will like it," Ava assured. "And, maybe she will even send you a picture of herself in it."

"I hope so!" He laughed, imaging the nonexistent picture.

Ava was beginning to like him more and more, because he reminded her of one of Carson's silly school friends.

"Did you see how the corporal is dancing with his wife?" he asked Percy, slyly pointing in the corporal's direction

81

for Ava and Rosemary to see. "He looks like an Alaskan Husky in pain."

They all watched and laughed at the unknowing man as he moved to the music with absurd and exaggerated movements. Even Rosemary was lightening up with Barry's jokes. Ava caught Edwin watching her again from his circle of non-dancing friends, and she smiled boldly at him out of her giddiness. He pretended not to see her and continued talking to the man sitting beside him.

"Why doesn't Edwin dance?" she asked Barry, as he followed her eyes to where his friend sat slouching in a corner.

"Edwin only likes and does two things, cards and shooting. He's kind of a loner."

"He needs to learn to dance."

"Why don't you make him," Percy suggested, taking a cigar out of his pocket.

Barry and Sydney might not have noticed it, but he had seen the way Edwin looked at Ava at the store last week.

"Hey, Edwin," he yelled across the room with the deep voice of a lieutenant and motioned with his now lighted cigar for him to come over.

Edwin looked in their direction as if he had seen them for the first time that night and casually walked to where they stood. Even though he refused to look at her, Ava felt that he observed her every movement, and his shyness both delighted and emboldened her.

"How's it going?" he asked as indifferently as possible.

He had convinced himself to go to Ava after her performance, but seeing her with her work friend and then Sydney had discouraged his plans. It was obvious that she liked Sydney, and he wouldn't get in the way.

"Percy thinks that I need to make you dance and not sit in a corner all night." Ava laughed, amazed by her own temerity.

His ears reddened to the color of what auburn hair he had left. He couldn't help but look at her now.

"What if I want to sit in a corner all night?"

"Oh, come on, Winn, you know you want to dance with her," Percy said.

"Tennessee boys know how to dance, don't they?" Ava challenged him, holding onto his gaze.

In reality, he had only danced briefly on two occasions and seeing her dance with Sydney had demolished any confidence he had in his own abilities.

"Not very well," he admitted.

"Let's see what you can do," she said, knowing that he wanted to dance with her.

He followed her out onto the open floor and lightly put his arm around the delicate part of her back as he had seen Sydney do.

"I won't break." She laughed up at him, still surprised by her frankness with him.

He grasped her more firmly, and they began to dance. Even though he was cleanly shaven, his face still possessed a manly roughness, and she knew without asking that he was a farmer. His broad shoulders and arm muscles, which she could feel as he held her, were like her father's and brothers' and told of arduous manual labor.

"You're a farmer, aren't you?" she asked.

"What makes you think so?" he replied, focusing on the movement of his feet.

"My grandpa and father are farmers, and I can just tell," she said, pleased with his swift feet and coordination.

He wasn't a polished dancer like Sydney, but he had a definite rhythm to his step.

"Oh, really, and what can you just tell about us?" He smiled, beginning to feel more at ease with her now that they had fallen into motion with the music.

She was embarrassed to tell him the truth, so she teased him instead.

"If you must know, it's the smell."

Not realizing that she was joking at first, his ears reddened again, but he relaxed when she started laughing and laughed too.

"I'm afraid I don't smell like anything now but dirt trenches and gun powder."

They talked until the end of the song, and Edwin was just about to ask her to dance again when Sydney found them.

"I was wondering where you disappeared to?" he addressed Ava and then noticed that she had been dancing with Edwin. "Do you mean to tell me that you actually got Winn here to dance with you?"

"Tennessee boys can dance." She smiled up at Edwin.

"I guess all things are possible. Hey, man, I hope you don't mind, but can I cut in? I have only got to dance with our little singer once so far."

"Oh, no, go ahead. I was just going back to smoke a cigar with Barry," he lied, but Ava was pleased with the look of disappointment which swept over his gruff face.

To validate his fib, he did smoke a cigar with Barry. He tried not to watch Ava dance with Sydney. All night, he had fought with himself to keep his eyes off her, and he was embarrassed that she might have noticed. She looked even more amazing in her fancy dress and with her new haircut. He saw her smile at him once from the dance floor, but he only looked away. If Sydney liked her, he wouldn't stand in the way of his friend. He put out his cigar and decided to head back early to the fort.

Chapter 9

Estelle glared down at the cold, black typing with glassy, disbelieving eyes. Her heart told her what was inside the envelope without even opening it, and she dropped the letter on the kitchen table in repulsion. Doubting her own clairvoyance, she picked it up again and held it up to the sunlight that cast its glow through the window. Nothing, she could see nothing. The paper was too thick.

"Mr. Sheffield James Stilwell, Jr.," she read again.

Who, but the government, would address her husband in such a ceremonial manner? She ran her finger along the sealed flap of the letter and contemplated opening it. Of course she wouldn't open it. She had never opened up anything addressed solely to her husband before. It would be disrespectful even if she was his wife. She dropped the letter back on the table and turned away from it, determined to be respectful.

"I've got to start supper," she told herself and tied an apron around her waist.

They were eating alone tonight, and she had promised him a meal as good as his mother's. She picked up a freshly washed potato that had been left to dry and dug through a shallow drawer to find her chopping knife. The knife sliced the potato long ways and then into thin cubes. Pleased with the pieces, she slid them into a bowl of water to keep them from turning pink. She reached for another potato, and her eyes caught sight of her husband's name on the strange envelope again. Fear flooded her thoughts, and the knife cut deep into her index finger instead of the vegetable. She screamed out in pain and reached for a white kitchen towel. Red blood soiled the towel as she pressed it firmly against her fresh wound.

"He can't leave me," she said aloud as she sobbed for her pain and the message she suspected.

She sank down on the kitchen floor and hung her head between her knees. Everything was too sweet for him to be taken away. She sat still in her morbid thoughts as the first pain from her wound began to subside and looked back up at the letter waiting patiently for James. Her will wavered, and she crawled to the foot of the table and reached with her healthy hand for the envelope addressed to her husband. Trembling, she held the letter between her knees and opened it with her free hand. Her face grew dim as she read what she knew it would say. Her husband's deferment was over. He was expected to report in just three weeks to a local reception center and then on to Texas.

Exactly how far west is Texas? Her brain screamed.

She had never traveled further than Atlanta, Georgia. Noticing the familiar crack in the wood floor next to the wall, she was tempted to destroy the letter and dispose of its remains in the hidden crevice. She read the letter's full content again.

"As a soldier you have new responsibilities. They are to yourself as a soldier, to the country, and to the men in service with whom you will soon serve," the same dismal typing explained.

"But what about his responsibilities as my husband!" she demanded out loud and flung the letter away from her.

She knew it was a selfish question, but she didn't care. How could she exist without him? She hung her head again between her knees and sat motionless in her distress for seconds and then minutes.

"Stelle, I'm home!" James shouted as he came barreling through their front door from work with his usual energy.

Finding it unusual that she didn't meet him at the door, he walked into the kitchen where he thought she must be busy cooking and found her sitting with her face still hidden in brown folds of apron between her knees. She raised her head and looked at him with catatonic eyes.

"What's wrong, sweetie?"

He dropped to his knees in front of her. Seeing the bloody towel wrapped tightly around her hand, he was alarmed and his fearful hands felt her hair, head, and shoulders.

"Don't leave me!" She gasped him, and her eyes spilled fresh tears.

"What do you mean don't leave you? What happened to your hand? Are you all right?"

He tried touching her hand, but she pulled it back and pointed at a crumpled letter on the floor. He looked from her distraught face to the letter and understood.

Ava gently closed her bedroom door, not wishing to attract her mother's unwanted attention, and sank down on her bed. She could bear nothing else today. Her brother was leaving for the war soon, but she couldn't think about that yet. What happened to her today was already too heavy on her mind to consider anything else for the moment. The last half of her workday had been miserable, and she had thought of nothing more than to go home and be left alone. When she finally did return home, she was inundated with the news of James. Estelle was out of her mind with worry, her mother was cross, her father reverted to silent reflection which upset her mother even more, her grandpa was asking questions that agitated everyone, Carson was pretending not to care, and James was saying anything he could think of to bring peace of mind to his family. He wouldn't be gone long. The war couldn't last much longer. All things that everyone knew weren't true. She had finally found an opportunity to slip away unnoticed, and she relished her dark room and the feel of the soft quilt touching her temple.

"What makes Alta so appealing to men?" she asked herself silently, and the memory of her lunch-time conversation with her co-worker drove out James and her family from her thoughts.

She was sure that Sydney liked her. He had danced with her with such energy and complimented her all night long. How could he ask Alta out on a date? Didn't he realize that she was dating every other soldier at Fort McClellan?

"Ava, I'm not sure what your feelings are about Sydney, but he asked me out," Alta had said in between bites of egg salad sandwich and in the middle of their discussion about the latest window display.

She had almost choked on her soda.

"If you like him, I won't go out with him. But if you don't have strong feelings for him, then I want to go," Alta told her with her usual frankness, and Ava managed a false smile that wore her out to maintain the rest of the afternoon.

She didn't want to smile again for the rest of the day, and, luckily, her family wouldn't expect it of her.

"Oh, he's just another out-of-town soldier." She had laughed unnaturally, as Rosemary scrutinized her profile and saw the real truth.

Ava closed her eyes and pictured Sydney with his likeable smile and recalled the familiar way he had touched her back even when they weren't dancing.

"It's his nature, the way he is with every girl," she admitted to herself.

She had noticed his same behavior with other women all night but had dismissed it. She was just another girl to him, even if he did like her voice. Feeling foolish, she buried her head deeper in the quilt. Alta wasn't just another girl, though.

"Don't worry. James will be all right." Her father touched her shoulder and sat down beside her.

She had been so absorbed in her own embarrassed and jealous thoughts that she didn't hear him open her door. Her absence had been found out.

"I'm fine, Dad." She sat up, feeling guilty for his misperception.

"He's a Stilwell, and we Stilwells always survive," he comforted, but Ava discerned a slight flicker of doubt in his kind eyes.

She smiled up at him and followed him back into the family room before her mother discovered they were both missing.

90

Chapter 10

Rosemary gently folded the glossy slip as Mrs. Crockett had demonstrated. Her careful hands tucked the bottom half of the delicate material directly underneath the top half and pulled the tiny straps upright.

Perfect. The slip lay folded just as instructed.

Going to work in Anniston was one of Ava's many ideas that she did not go along with at first, but now she was happy that her cousin had persuaded both her and her parents. While Ava enjoyed being in a moving atmosphere, Rosemary enjoyed the work itself. She liked caring for the merchandise and waiting on customers. Ava was always gazing outside the store windows and at the people coming in and out; Rosemary was always focused on her task. The job also took her mind off Jake's absence. When she was at home, her thoughts were constantly absorbed with receiving a new letter from him or what it would be like when he returned, but at Wakefield's, her mind was filled with the work at hand.

"Rosemary," a male voice called her name, and she looked up from the slip to Percy's smooth, grinning face.

She was surprised and not pleased to see him.

"You look busy," he said when she didn't greet him.

"I am." She moved away from him to a rack of dresses, embarrassed to be holding women's undergarments in front of him.

She began re-straightening the dresses that didn't need altering.

What is he doing away from the fort on a Friday afternoon? Normally, a soldier is not to be seen in Anniston until at least 5:00!

"Can I help you?" she asked, suddenly realizing that he may be approaching her as a customer and not as a young man.

"Actually, I want to ask you to supper tonight?" He smiled broadly as if his question were as natural as vinegar and cucumbers.

She gave the dress she was holding a baffled expression intended for him and continued her work.

"I don't think my boyfriend would like that," she answered without looking up again.

"I'm asking you as a friend, Rosemary." He laid a hand on her wrist as she reached for another dress.

"Don't you remember that I have a fiancée myself?" He laughed, and her face crimsoned.

He was making her into the inappropriate one which infuriated her.

"You're a sweet person to talk to, Rosemary, and that's what I need right now."

"I'm sorry, but I'm afraid that I still can't. I have plans tonight," she lied and was relieved to see an actual customer seeking a sales clerk. "Excuse me, I have a customer."

"Maybe another time, then," he spoke to her back as she hurried away from him.

"If they don't show soon, we're not going to get a good seat," Ava complained for the third time to Rosemary.

They were standing outside the Noble Theater watching for James and Estelle, and the line wrapping around the gazebo-like box office was growing a few persons longer every minute they waited.

"Hey, nigger, your theater is in Hobson City!" a pimply, adolescent boy shouted as Ava and Rosemary's eyes now sought the subject of his taunting.

Their search rapidly ended at a middle-aged Negro man in a wide-brimmed hat. He was with a young girl, and they were admiring the theater's extravagant name in lights. Ava held her breath. It appeared that he was about to answer the boy, who was now laughing at him with his friends and making other obscene comments. His mouth opened and then closed, and he walked off with the girl. Ava couldn't help but sympathize with the unknown man, even though blacks were not allowed in Anniston's theaters, and she was relieved that the confrontation was over.

"Ava! Rosemary!" James called from the opposite direction.

He held Estelle tightly by the arm and maneuvered them through the thick crowd. Ava stepped into the line and motioned for them to join her.

"I had to park almost a mile up the road," James said when he reached their place in line.

Estelle's cheeks were pink from running, and her brown hair fell in thin strands over her forehead and into her eyes.

"And your brother even drove faster than a tornado to get up here." She smiled up at her husband and smoothed back her rustled hair.

The singular smile arrested all of their attention. Estelle had been disconsolate and pallid since the letter arrived on Monday, and it was a relief to see her happy again. James couldn't help but lean down and kiss her now bare forehead.

93

"Do you have our money?" she asked, aware of the attention they were all giving her.

"Let me see?" he said, patting his pockets and pretending to find nothing.

He pulled out a piece of gray lint from his pants and smiled.

"James Stilwell, there better be more in those pockets," Estelle crossed her arms and declared.

"And just what would you do if I didn't have this?" He grinned, pulling out one silver coin and then another.

"I would just have to find another date, now wouldn't I."

She loved him best when he was flirting with her like he did before she was his wife, and her lustrous eyes told him so. Rosemary held her own money in her hand, and Ava dug for the admission price in her purse. She had been so busy worrying that she had forgotten that she would have to pay.

"Quit your fretting, Aves. I have three dates tonight." James shut his sister's purse over her fingers and took Rosemary by the arm.

"Fine, but you don't have to break my fingers off."

"You know that three girls can be expensive," Rosemary said.

"Oh hush, you can save your money for when I'm...." He started to say the word "gone," but checked himself thinking of his wife. "When I'm not at the movies with you," he paused and then finished.

Tickling Estelle's waist, he assured himself that he hadn't made a verbal mistake that would ruin their evening. It was their turn at the box office, and he paid for all of their admissions.

Life-size Hollywood advertisements surrounded the octagon-shaped box-office and greeted them as they walked down the lit aisle to the theater's ornate doors. Beautiful young men and women in romantic embraces, hero-making battle scenes, and in perilous situations told of more portentous and interesting lives and stirred their imaginations. Rosemary's eyes were drawn to a poster depicting a Navy officer tap dancing with a young starlit, and she substituted Jake's green eyes for the officer's brown ones and his short nose and dimpled smile for the officer's angular nose and comic smile. As she imagined him, she wondered if he was as happy as the man in the poster.

They entered the large double doors of the theater. Ava and Rosemary had never been to an indoor movie, and their eyes expanded at the grandeur of the opera house converted theater. Even though the building was long past its prime of live and infamous orators, songsters, and musicians, the old burgundy velvet, brass fixtures, and Italian frescos still regaled an austere richness that made one feel privileged to enter its vast milieu and relax in its leather chairs. The movie would begin in a few minutes, and they stood at the back of the auditorium trying to find the best four seats possible together. Rosemary scanned the rows and rows of seats until an increasingly familiar face caught her attention. Percy stood beside her with his hands in his pockets and a haughty smile.

"Rosemary Bonds, out and about?" he said more as a question than a fact.

"I'm watching a show with my cousins," she replied, realizing now that he wouldn't be ignored.

"Ava, how are ya?" He turned away from her to Ava.

"Good, and yourself?"

"Up middle way and to the left." James pointed out a group of seats.

Ava stopped him and Estelle and introduced them to Percy. The two men shook hands.

"I hope you all enjoy the picture," Percy said, leaving them without another personal word to Rosemary, which surprised her.

They found their seats just as the lights went out. The large screen flickered twice and then gave way to its black and white feature. The zealously patriotic Jean Renoir film starring Maureen O'Hara and Charles Laughton entertained them with a story of betrayal and love and strengthened everyone's rancor for the Germans. They were all immersed in the film, and when the bright lights met their cue to come back on, everyone had to squint to readjust to real life. James led them out of the auditorium, and they were almost out of the theater when Percy and another soldier overtook them.

"Ava, excuse me, but a friend of mine would like to meet you."

"Hi, Ernie Granberry." The soldier he was with took off his hat and smiled down at her rather sheepishly.

He was of average height and had a blonde crew cut, a fair boyish complexion, and thick eyelashes that drooped over two round, blue eyes.

"I heard you sing last weekend. You were amazing," he complimented, and Ava thanked him.

"Ernie knows about music. He plays the piano and trumpet and gives music lessons," Percy explained for him.

"Do you play any instruments?" Ernie asked.

"I play the piano a little," she confessed, partly ashamed.

She would be able to play the piano with much more precision if she had practiced and been able to concentrate on her mother's weekly piano lessons. Simply because her mother wanted her to play, she had worked hard not to learn.

James and Estelle had walked on ahead but were now retracing their steps back to them, and Rosemary waited to the side. Percy introduced his friend to everyone else and suggested that they go for coffee and dessert. James consented without even asking his three dates. He wanted to keep his wife in a cheerful mood, and he thought that it might be good for her to meet some soldiers. Rosemary suspected Percy of conspiring to be with her, but his continual efforts not to speak to her began to soften her negative impressions of him, and she wondered if he was respecting her feelings after all. They walked together to Vic's Café and pulled a couple of extra chairs up to a small table in the crowded restaurant.

"When Ava was a youngster, Mom used to wear her hide out for pounding the piano keys and trying to teach the cat how to play instead of practicing." James laughed.

He was affable like his father and at home with everyone. Ava tried to laugh along while casting upon her brother a series of stern looks, which seemed to bounce unseen off his risible face. He liked to tease her as a doting older brother while Carson liked to tease her out of spite.

"James will be stationed in Texas." Estelle dredged up the subject sore to her heart to intervene for her sister-in-law just as James was remembering another witty story about Ava's musical past.

"A buddy of mine is in Texas," Ernie followed the shift in conversation as he sipped the strong coffee that had just been brought to him.

"I think everyone in south Georgia was sent up north except for me," Percy said.

"I would much rather go to Texas for basic than up north." James played with a strand of Estelle's hair as he cautiously approached the subject himself.

"Are you going with him?" Ernie asked, looking across the table at Estelle's down-turned face.

At first, she didn't realize that he was talking to her, but the momentary silence at the table confirmed that he was, and her eyes widened in confusion.

"I'm not sure what you mean? I wish I could." She looked from Ernie to James for clarification.

"Lots of wives move to the town where their husbands are stationed," Ernie said.

"My brother's wife was with him in Pennsylvania before he got shipped out," Percy said, just as a large man in a stained apron interrupted their conversation with six pieces of pie.

Estelle's face was beginning to shine with a new and eager hope.

"Did they get to see each other much?" James dropped the strand of Estelle's hair he had been twisting between his fingers and leaned forward.

He too had never thought of the prospect before, and his mind was already calculating the possibilities but from a more realistic approach than his wife.

"On the weekends or when he managed to sneak away from the fort."

"Where did she stay?" Rosemary asked, aware that she was inviting him to speak to her again.

"Robert rented her an apartment just off the fort, which wasn't hard to get to unnoticed, if you know what I mean." Percy winked, addressing his answer more to James and Estelle than to Rosemary, which she didn't fail to notice.

"He never got caught?"

"Nope, he was too sly for the Army."

The new possibility of her following her husband was becoming almost certain to Estelle now, and she imagined herself in a quaint apartment worlds away with James doing all he could to get to her every night. She didn't even taste the chocolate pie that she put in her mouth or hear the rest of their conservation.

While James paid for their pie and drinks, Ernie invited Ava to go with him to a concert next Friday night, and she agreed to go. As they were leaving the restaurant, a group of soldiers was entering, and the last of them held the door open. Ava looked up at the soldier to thank him and was surprised to see Edwin. She could tell by the way his eyes seemed to question why she was there and then look to see who she was with that he too was not planning to see her. It was as if he expected her to be somewhere else. She would have spoken, but Ernie was behind her still talking about the concert. Edwin nodded at her and Ernie and hastily walked through the door behind them.

Chapter 11

No sooner had church concluded and Sunday lunch been digested than Sheffield left to take Brother Whatley back to town for the bus. An infrequent visitor then appeared. After seeing the paunchy figure of Mott Dempsey ascending the steps of their front porch, Carson jumped up from his Sunday nap and ran to his sister's room. The Stilwells took the Lord's Day of rest seriously by sleeping the afternoon away. Grandpa Chester had retired to his room directly after dessert, and Ava's daydreams had just given way to sleep when Carson came barreling in and began jostling her bed up and down with his fists.

"I told you old Mott wouldn't like the idea of Estelle running off to Texas with James and that Mom didn't really like it either!"

"What are you talking about?" Ava asked, rubbing her eyes open.

"She's here. She and mom are talking it out on the front porch," he explained over his shoulder as he ran out of her room.

Ava's curiosity overcame her sleepiness, and she left her bed and found it to be just as Carson reported. Mott and Victoria were rocking together on the porch swing and talking in animated whispers. Carson's head was already ducked under the familiar oval window in the family room, and Ava joined him in his detective work. It was the position they always took when anything of interest was to be overheard on the front porch.

Just the sight of Mott Dempsey promised that something of importance was indeed about to be said. She never appeared unless she disapproved of something concerning Estelle. After Estelle and her oldest daughter, Margaret, married, Mott Dempsey wished them well, having done her duty, and turned her attention to her two unmarried, younger daughters. However, she didn't fail to keep up with the news of her married daughters' lives, and she was the first to speak when something didn't suit her ideals for them.

Victoria was unusually quiet after James and Estelle announced their plans of being together in Texas, and Ava and Carson argued about her quietness. Ava hypothesized that it was due to her mother's sadness over James leaving, and Carson guessed that she wasn't sure about Estelle following him. It now appeared that Carson was right, and they both strained their ears to find out the truth.

"I've heard tales that people don't take kind to married women tramping across the country after their husbands." Mott shook her rotund face, which only matched Estelle's with its lofty cheekbones. "It takes men's minds off their duty to their country."

"I can assure you that James will have his mind where it needs to be," Victoria said, sitting up as straight as possible in the swing as it swung backward and forward underneath her dangling feet.

"I'm not questioning James, Victoria. I'm questioning the propriety of her going with him."

They both now mused silently, staring out at Sheffield's new rows of planted cotton.

"I just hate to see them waste everything they've saved for boarding in Texas," Victoria broke the tense silence.

"I perfectly agree." Mott nodded, and her agreement reestablished their common purpose.

They had never been close friends before their children married and even less after the marriage. It was only at times like this that they became intimate friends.

"And what if it's all for nothing? What if James rarely gets to even see her?" Victoria said, shrugging her petite shoulders in exasperation.

"It would break her heart, and she wouldn't have anyone else around to help her deal with it," Mott furthered the argument.

She was truly concerned about her daughter, even if she rarely revealed it.

"I'll speak to James," Victoria said with resolution.

"And I'll have a word with Estelle," Mott declared, just as a car motor interrupted their freshly developed plans.

Sheffield had returned, and both women took his arrival as a cue to end their discussion.

"Come visit again," Victoria called out loudly enough for her husband to hear when Mott carefully descended the steps which she had just a few moments ago tottered up.

"I certainly will," Mott answered.

She spoke to Sheffield in passing and breathed deeply to prepare herself for her walk home. Victoria slid her feet down to still the swing, and Sheffield sat down in the spot that Mott vacated. He stretched his much longer legs out before saying anything.

"What are you two women up to?" He looked down at his wife's tiny feet compared to his own.

"If you must know, Mott is not exactly thrilled about Estelle leaving with James either." Her tone was already defensive.

"Heck, I could have told you that. So what did you two meddlers decide to do about it?"

"Well...," Victoria hesitated, not wanting to hear her husband's criticism, "she is going to have a word with a Estelle, and I said that I'd have a talk with James."

"By having a word, you mean she will nag her daughter to an early grave," Sheffield said, bending his knees and giving the swing a big push.

"I think she will be reasonable." She tried to sound supportive, but there was evident uncertainty in her voice.

James often complained to them about his mother-in-law's overt opinions.

"And I don't think you should talk to James either." Sheffield folded his hands behind his head and peered down at the top of his wife's head.

Victoria turned hot eyes upon him.

"What do you mean?"

Her husband rarely forbade her anything.

"I mean just that," he said, returning her gaze with unflinching eyes. "James is a married man who doesn't live under our roof anymore, and he deserves some respect for his decisions. Right or wrong, he is allowed to make his own mistakes."

She broke the gaze and inhaled the humid air. She knew he was right, and it made her angry to feel impotent.

"Besides, James asked what I thought this afternoon, and I voiced our concerns."

Victoria's anger lessened and she grasped her husband's arm.

"What did he say?"

"He promised to think about everything long and hard." Sheffield dropped an arm around his wife and pulled her toward him.

There was now a long silence, and Ava tried to ignore Carson's gloating smile. The conversation appeared to be over.

"Should we warn Estelle that she's about to be pestered to death?" he whispered from under the window.

"I'm staying out of it," Ava whispered back and stood up from her crouching position.

"Always a goodie-two-shoes!"

Creaking steps on the porch halted their raillery, and Ava ran back to her room as Carson dove for the floor and assumed a sleeping position.

Chapter 12

Sydney, Barry, and Edwin usually enjoyed a game of cards in the evenings, but there would be no card playing tonight. The entire company had been assigned disciplinary kitchen duty. The weary soldiers carried the partially nude reason for their punishment in their arms. A muscular soldier named Wayne held Private Reginald Acre in an unrelenting headlock. Another equally tough soldier named Ben held his right arm. Edwin carried his left arm, and Sydney, who could never be irascible with anyone, half-carried and half-dodged Reggie's kicking feet. An excited Barry followed close behind with another dozen soldiers who were all anxious to witness the fun and deserving humiliation.

"We'll show you why you better take your own baths!" Wayne shouted, tightening his grip around Reggie's head and at the same time muffling his pleas.

"Quit swinging your feet," Sydney said and re-circled his hands around their victim's jiggling ankles.

"You asked for it, Private Filth," Edwin joined in, recalling Sergeant Monroe's name calling with a wide smile across his strained face.

Reggie was heavier than a soldier in their intense training should be, and they each felt it as they carried their portion of his solid, struggling body. Their fellow soldier had not bathed in three days, and they were all being punished for his negligence. The Army was strict on personal hygiene, and the soldiers' appearance was inspected daily. They lugged him through the latrine doors, which continued to pound open as all of the eager soldiers crammed into the tight space.

"Please, please!" Reggie screamed when they approached the latrine and lifted his body to its height.

"A little too late for that," Wayne said, and they flung him into the latrine's trough.

Sydney squirted soap all over his bare skin. Ben and Edwin took G.I. brushes out of their back pockets and scrubbed him raw, and Wayne splashed water behind his ears and all over his grimacing face. A roar of laughter resonated off of the close walls.

They were still laughing over their incidence of vengeance as they scraped and scrubbed meat sauce and canned vegetables off of industrial-sized pots and pans. When the undeserved kitchen duty was completed, Edwin, Barry, and Sydney reclined outside their barracks during the few minutes they now had left before their 10:00 curfew. They were enjoying a box of cigars that Marg sent Barry.

"I think he almost cried," Barry said and puffed a cloud of smoke into the air surrounding them.

"He sure did." Edwin laughed.

"There won't be any dirt behind his ears for a long while." Sydney grinned, selecting a long cigar from the gift box and holding it up in the moonlight.

Joking and pranks were what made the Army livable.

"Hey, guys, mind if I join you?" Percy appeared and sat down beside them. "I heard about your act of revenge this afternoon. Well done, I must say."

"Just helping out Uncle Sam," Sydney greeted his more distinguished friend.

106

"You know Uncle Sam likes his men clean."

"Want a New York smoke?" Barry asked, tossing him the gift box.

"Don't mind if I do."

They smoked in silence for sometime, looking up into the Alabama night sky and relishing the moments of rest. Millions of obscure balls of light blinked down upon them.

"I ran into your friends Saturday night," Percy said with his eyes still fixed above.

"Which ones?" Barry asked.

"Ava and Rosemary," he replied, and Edwin's body stiffened. "They were at the movies with their brother. Nice guy, by the way, and, since you decided to ask Alta out instead, Sydney, I fixed her up with a friend of mine."

He observed the outline of Edwin's rigid profile in the faint light.

So, that's why he didn't ask her out, Edwin thought.

He had toyed with how to ask Sydney about his date ever since he saw Ava Saturday night.

"Who's the lucky fellow?" Sydney sat up and put out his half-finished cigar. He had never been able to smoke long.

"Ernie Granberry."

"Don't know him, but he better have his eye out for me."

"Thought you weren't interested anymore." Percy laughed behind his cigar.

"Oh, I'm always interested. There's just something fascinating about Alta that I have to investigate first. You guys should have seen the way she…."

"I'm turning in." Edwin stood up.

For the first time, he was angry with Sydney, and he wouldn't let it fester and be noticed.

"I've got a letter to read from home," he quickly added.

Barry and Sydney looked at each other when he walked away, knowing that they would be asked to reread the letter later to him in private.

"He's so hung up on her," Percy said as his friends tried to follow what he was saying. "You two haven't noticed the way he looks at Ava."

They sat in tacit surprise.

"Really?" Sydney said, looking toward the barracks in which his friend had just disappeared. "Then why in the world did you set her up with what's his name?"

"I wasn't sure until now, and besides, he hasn't done anything about it." Percy let out another carefree puff.

Edwin took the letter he had been avoiding all day off his pillow. Maybe, he would wait until tomorrow to open it. Letters from home depressed him more than cheered him, and he wasn't in the mood to be depressed. He flipped it over and contemplated breaking the seal and then flipped it back over and looked at his older sister's squashy, bold letters. All of his family mail came through her since his mother could not read or write. He sighed and decided that he had better open it and try to read it since he had used it as his reason to get away. His reading skills wouldn't be so underdeveloped if he had spent more of his school days at school with his sister rather than on the farm with his dad. He read slowly, trying to absorb the identity of each word. He made out the word "birthday" and that they wanted to know what to send him, and he remembered for the first time since he had arrived that he would be 19 next month. The words "new shed" stood out to him next, and he cringed with an old, nagging anger. His stepfather had talked about taking down their old shed and putting up a new one ever since he had married his mother eight months ago. Edwin had told him that a new shed was not necessary.

A familiar pain shot through his heart as he thought of the possibility. How could his mother let him do it? He had helped his father build that shed when he was just ten years old. He was beginning to wonder if his mother ever really loved his father. His face was now as red as the roots of his auburn hair, and he wadded up the letter and stuffed it back in its envelope. He was glad to be in the Army and away from home. He laid down and shut his eyes, imagining the old shed and all of the things that filled it. Even though it might look in disarray to an outsider, he knew where every rusty tool and contrivance hung, sat, and was piled upon other random things. Edwin gritted his teeth and shuddered thinking of the shed's destruction and the rearranging of all his father's beloved objects.

Ever since his father's sudden death two years ago, he had been gritting his teeth as his world was taken away from him. They were forced to sell a portion of their family land to pay for debt. Then, while he was trying to manage what was left, his mother began seeing Davis Mathers, an old bachelor who lived nearby. He would never forgive her for marrying him and giving that man everything that was theirs. She tried to explain that she did it for him, but he didn't believe her. At first, he refused to attend the wedding, but then went out of respect for his mother and stood at the back of the church with clenched fists buried deep in his pockets. Finally, when his sister also married and the draft came his way, he gladly took it as a chance to escape.

"Want me to read your letter for you?" Sydney asked, standing awkwardly over him and breaking through his dismal thoughts.

"No thanks, I made all I cared to make out of it."

"Bad news?" Sydney said, feeling guilty about Ava.

"Oh, nothing big." Edwin rolled over and shut his eyes.

He could hear Sydney walking away, and then he remembered that his mother and sister had also failed to send him the coat hangers and washrags he had asked for. It was some time before his fury would let him sleep, and, when it finally did, he suffered through another restless night.

Chapter 13

Rosemary boarded the bus for Jacksonville without Ava, and, for the first time since Jake's departure, she felt truly lonely. It was different from missing him. She could miss him and still be full of the presence of her family, co-workers, and friends, but now she was really lonely, and it was a heart sickening feeling. She looked out the window of the moving bus at a group of young couples walking into a diner, and she wondered where Ernie would take Ava for dinner.

The Sanitary Café? Vic's Café? Oh, I bet they'll eat at Lloyd's Sweet Shop and then go upstairs to the ballroom for the concert.

She then thought of her own Friday night meal. Her mother always cooked a roast with potatoes on Friday night, and she frowned for the first time at the mundane supper.

What can I write Jake about today?

She wrote him everyday as promised, and sometimes she wasn't sure what to write about. She was afraid that her daily routines bored him, and she had already written to him all the news about James and Estelle, Judith's tooth being knocked out, and Pete and Jimmy leaving for the war. Hopefully, there would be a letter from him, and she could just respond to all his news and questions. Even though his letters were always full of longings to be with her, she could tell that he was happy and succeeding in the Navy. He was stationed at the naval base in San Diego, California, a place that she could only vaguely imagine. In her mind, she pictured him sunburned and smiling amid movie sets and the beaches that he always wrote to her about. She had never seen the ocean. The bus came to a slow halt, and the driver beckoned to her that they were at her usual stop. She stepped down off the bus, and walked home alone.

The vigorous melody of the harmonizing big band instruments hushed the pre-show chatter and filled Lloyd's Crystal Ballroom and Banquet Hall. Ava sat beside Ernie with her hands folded in her lap, her legs crossed underneath her pleated yellow skirt, and her red lips upturned into an expectant smile. Even though the music was coming from the many instruments on the stage, it seemed to have absorbed into her skin and to be pounding out its rhythm on her heart. A young lady moving across the front of the room caught her attention. The girl met a man in the center of the stage and turned toward the audience just as he began to sing. She was tall and poised and wore a white dress that seemed to float about her figure. Her silky, brown hair was parted in the middle and curled away from her face and down to her shoulders, and her dark-brown eyes seemed to mirror her suppressed smile as they peered down at the audience. She dangled her hands, which were covered in long, white gloves, unclasped and assuredly by her side, and Ava marveled at her composure. The older, tuxedoed man finished his solo, and her white-gloved hands reached for the microphone standing in front of them.

"Who wouldn't love? Who wouldn't care?" her clear voice began to sing, and Ava was mesmerized by its fluidness and the unassuming way she accented each word and traveled over each note. "Who wouldn't buy the west side of heaven if you just winked your eye?"

"The trumpet player came all the way from South Carolina to play tonight," Ernie leaned over and whispered, and Ava became conscious of his presence again. "With the war going on," his voice rose, as the music escalated, "everybody is losing band members."

"You should offer to play with them," she said, wishing to turn her full attention back on the music.

"I'm afraid that the only playing I do now is for Uncle Sam." He chuckled as the music dipped, and his voice became audible to those sitting around them.

Ava glanced embarrassedly to each side of them. There was a small musical interlude, and the man and woman resumed singing.

"You're the answer to my every prayer, my darling. Who wouldn't love you? Who wouldn't care?" they sang in unison to end the song.

A maelstrom of musical notes accompanied them, and an enthusiastic applause broke out when the last note played itself out.

Ava and Ernie waited until the rows behind them filed out of the ballroom and it was their turn to do likewise. Ernie was rating the musical adeptness of all of the individual band members, and Ava was pretending to listen while she recalled the feel of the music and the young girl's performance.

"Excuse me, miss," a short, corpulent man dragging a rectangular black box behind him called out to her. "Aren't you the young lady who sang at the U.S.O. dance a couple of weeks ago?"

113

"Yes, I am," she answered in surprise, trying to mentally place his face in her memory.

"You probably don't remember me, but I play with The Willie Harold Band," he explained, licking his dry, thick lips, "the band you sang with that night."

"Of course, you do look familiar." Ava remembered being introduced to each band member right before they rushed to practice her songs and the dance began.

"We've all been trying to get in touch with you, and I was thrilled when I saw you in the audience. We're looking for a female lead singer to accompany us on a few numbers. Would you be interested?"

"Well, I don't know," she said, already picturing herself in the same white dress and long gloves as the girl on stage had worn.

"We only play once or twice a month, and we could practice…." He stopped, noticing Ernie and sticking out his hand. "Sorry to hold you up. Jonathan Cousins."

"Ernie Granberry. Nice to meet you. Enjoyed the concert." Ernie shook his hand.

"Thanks, but we were a little off tonight. Half of us, including myself, have never even played with the Birmingham Boys Band before."

"I didn't even notice," Ernie lied.

"Anyways, where was I?" he said, licking his lips again. "Oh, yes, we would practice in Anniston and wouldn't take up much of your time."

"I would love to," Ava accepted, her gray eyes shining with resolve.

It was the first time in her life that she had ever made a major decision without consulting her parents first, and it felt good.

"Great, where can we get in touch with you?"

"I live in Jacksonville, but I work at Wakefield's Department Store, so that would probably be the best place."

"Well, Miss...." He laughed, realizing he didn't even know her name.

"Ava Stilwell."

"You'll hear from us shortly, Ava. We're playing at the next U.S.O. dance. Pleasure to meet you both," he extended his hand to Ernie again, and the two men shook hands.

Ernie walked Ava to the bus stop and waited with her until the bus appeared. She was relieved when it arrived, and she could get away from him. She needed time to herself to think over the concert, the unexpected effect it had on her, and the invitation to sing with The Willie Harold Band. She leaned her head against the bus window and looked out at the trees that the night had made almost invisible. It didn't matter. All she could see was herself in the white dress singing, and singing, and singing, as her music saddened, engulfed, and lifted the hearts of her imaginary audience.

The events of her date had been more significant than the actual man she had been with, and she became aware of this walking up the steps of her house now. He had mentioned something about seeing her again next Saturday night, and she seemed to remember telling him yes. To make music like she had just heard, though, was the only passion her mind could presently entertain. She walked into the house and was called down from her fantasy stage.

"Did you have a good time?" Victoria looked up from her chair, where she sat sewing until her daughter returned.

Ava hadn't even noticed her mother, and the voice startled her.

115

"Oh, yes," she answered, pausing before her mother.

"Did he treat you to a nice supper?"

She was sewing a shirt for James to leave in. It didn't matter that he would only be wearing khaki uniforms soon.

"Yes, we ate at Lloyd's Sweet Shop."

"And?" Her mother now arched her full, black eyebrows and looked up into her face.

"And, what? We went to the concert."

"And? Was he a nice, considerate young man?" Victoria said with her eyebrows still high on her forehead.

Ava colored somewhat, realizing again that she had barely noticed him since the concert began.

"Of course."

She started to tell her mother about the man from the band wanting her to sing, but thought better of it. It was too soon and too fresh in her own mind at that moment. There would be too much desperation in her appeal, and, besides, she would rather have her father present. With these thoughts, Ava faked a yawn and said goodnight to her observant mother.

Chapter 14

There was no need for anxiety since Ava chose the day before James's departure to tell her parents about singing with The Willie Harold Band. Her father looked at her as if the question had already been resolved, his sapphire eyes questioning what was different about singing this time with the band than before. Her mother had just thrown up two floured hands that were busy baking a cake for James. She was more vexed with Ava about bringing up something else for her to consider in lieu of her son's leaving than she was about future performances with the band.

"You won't be dancing up on that stage, will you?" she asked, mixing the thick batter as strands of black hair began to escape from their pins.

The family was having her chocolate cake on a day other than a birthday, which signified an unusual allowance and gave a sacred seriousness to her cooking.

"Of course not," Ava said, at the same time picturing herself dancing in the white dress with a tall soldier.

"Pass me the sugar." Victoria ended the dance in her head and dismissed the inopportune discussion.

Ava slid the large bag of sugar to her mother, wondering how she had managed to acquire more sugar rations.

"Now, start frying the sausage for breakfast while I get this cake in the oven." She was determined to get her cake baked before leaving for church.

"Morning." Brother Whatley stepped into the kitchen. "Something sure smells good."

"We're a little behind this morning, Reverend," Victoria said.

She always fixed the preacher a large breakfast to fuel his Sunday morning sermon, but, this morning, even he was being somewhat neglected for James.

"No need to worry," he said as the smell of frying sausage accentuated his hunger, and his stomach growled.

The morning's church service was particularly solemn. Brother Whatley asked all the men in their small congregation to lay hands on James at the altar and pray for his health and safety in the service. Ava watched the top of her brother's disappearing and reappearing head as each man knelt over him on the sawdust floor and prayed in earnest whispers just audible over her mother's somber music. Ava observed her mother's fingers moving thoughtlessly over the familiar keys of the piano. She too was watching James's down-turned face. It was her grandfather's turn. His bony back heaved up and down as he prayed louder and more reverently than any before him, with the exception of Brother Whatley and her father, whose usually calm prayers turned into urgent supplications. She sighed, looking at the last three men preparing to pray over her brother. Why was it that the longest-winded ones always kept themselves to the back of the line? She glanced at Carson, who she was sure was thinking the same thing, but his face was fixed in a stoic expression that appeared to be staring beyond the church walls.

Maybe, I should be praying myself, she thought, noticing Estelle kneeling with clasped hands beside her.

She bowed her head and closed her eyes and for the first time, really thought about her brother leaving.

It was now very late, and the whole family, including Rosemary, her parents, and Judith, were all full of chocolate cake and dreading the end of the night. As the minutes passed, they all looked at each other to see who would signal the close of the evening and thought nervously how they would each say good-bye to James. It was finally James himself who broke the unspoken tension.

"Well, I need to get home. I have a big day tomorrow." He sighed with misty eyes and turned away. He wanted his wife.

She was right behind him, reaching out for his hand. There was a smile on his handsome face, but the rest of him looked suddenly like a frightened boy. Estelle was the tough one tonight, and her shining eyes strengthened him. The source of her strength was her role as his wife and her unwavering faith that she would be with him soon in Texas. The gentle pressure of her hand reminded him of their sanguine plans.

James did ask for his father's advice, but they had made up their minds to be together, no matter the cost. Hand in hand, they had informed their families of their plans and discouraged any further discussion of the matter. Estelle was also avoiding her often-absent mother with significant meaning, and Victoria had so far been reticent, at least publicly, on the subject, as she promised her husband. Their plan was that James would immediately begin searching for a place for her to live near the fort, and that she would join him as quickly as his search was successful.

Myrtle nudged her husband to be the first to act, and Jude reluctantly stepped forward and put a large hand on his cousin's shoulder.

"We're sure going to miss you around here," he said, casting his good brown eye on James as his glass green eye stared forward.

James looked back at the familiar eyes. He still remembered helping his cousin pick out the glass one from a catalog years ago after a hunting accident. To a young boy, the glass eye had been fascinating.

"You know you're all glad to get rid of me." James tried to laugh.

"Be sure to give your Mom your address, and we'll write you real soon," Myrtle said, embracing him with Judith tucked in between them hugging his knees.

James picked up the unusually cheerless toddler and swung her in the air. The trick worked. She giggled, and he sat her back down.

"Love you, James." Rosemary took her turn and embraced him.

Myrtle herded her husband and children out the back door to leave him to his immediate family. It was a sad ceremony. Victoria cried and fussed over what the Army would feed him. Sheffield went over every last minute detail to avoid the actual thing that was happening. Grandpa Chester warned James about Texas tarantulas. Carson was happily surprised when James gave him the keys to his car, and Estelle looked on, without tears, as her own goodbye would come privately later. Ava would always remember her own final words with her brother.

"Ava," he drew her to the side and leaned down over her as if he was about to tell her something amusing. "Keep Estelle happy until she gets to come to Texas. I'm afraid that it won't be as soon as she thinks."

She looked into his gray eyes, which were very much like her own, and nodded as she began to cry.

"Come on, Ava, don't be silly like Mom." He fought back his own tears with a laugh.

"Sorry."

"Keep me up on the real family news, o.k."

"You can count on it." Ava smiled, knowing she would relish her role as his informant.

He then hugged her, said goodbye to their parents, and rushed out the door with Estelle.

Chapter 15

The next morning, Ava ate her breakfast, met Rosemary, and rode the bus to work in silence. She was thinking about James, remembering what he had asked of her and considering when Estelle would be able to join him. If she thought that the rest of the day would have been spent in the same cogitation, though, she was greatly mistaken. Just as she and Rosemary approached the door of Wakefield's Department Store, Florence Burnham was marching out, muttering loudly as her tall, speckled hair shook high above her head in consternation.

"I quit!" she announced, stamping her foot.

"What's wrong?" Rosemary asked, at a loss as to what could have upset such an even-tempered lady.

"My husband told Mr. Wakefield that if he ever hired a Negro, his wife wouldn't work for him, and what did he do?" she said, looking at them as if they were Mr. Wakefield himself. "He went and hired one."

They both looked at her in astonishment, and her hands went to her hips.

"He says with the war going on that he can't find anyone for heavy lifting. Well, that's an excuse if I ever heard one!" She glared back at the door she had just exited. "He's just a softee, and thanks to people like him, Hobson City will run Anniston over one day I tell you. Good day, ladies."

Rosemary and Ava looked at each other and then at the door, unsure of whether to enter. When they did, they found an unusually discomposed Mrs. Crockett being interrogated by two of her best employees, an older, bearded man who worked in the shoe department and a lady, around Mrs. Crockett's age, who only worked part-time and who had obviously just come in that morning because of the rumors.

"I couldn't believe my ears, Lorraine, when the church women were talking yesterday in Sunday School about Mr. Wakefield giving a job to a colored man," her purple lips ranted. "I said they were telling lies in the house of God, but I see that I was the one speaking untruths."

"If Mr. Wakefield is only hiring this man because he can't find anyone else, will he be firing him then when someone more suitable is found?" Frank Marshall asked.

"That makes sense to me," Geraldine Dallas interjected without giving Mrs. Crockett time to answer.

"Perfect sense," Frank agreed.

"I'm not sure of Mr. Wakefield's long-term plans," Mrs. Crockett managed to say between their mutual complaining. "But whatever he does will be what he feels is best for the store and Anniston."

She was not only hard-working, but also loyal, putting aside whatever personal thoughts she might have in favor of Mr. Wakefield's decisions.

"We walked into a lion's den this morning, didn't we?" Alta came up and whispered between them.

"You're not kidding," Ava whispered back, without removing her eyes from the altercation before them.

123

Alta had apparently been there some time. She was carrying a stack of blouses to a nearby rack and already had a tight loop of tape measure about her waist.

"Old Florence stormed out just before you two got here."

"We know. We ran into her," Rosemary said.

"Did Mr. Wakefield hire a Negro man to work in the stock room?" Ava questioned.

"Sure did. He's back there working quietly by himself now. You should have seen the look of horror on old Florence's face when she saw Douglas!" Alta put her fingers to her lips and burst out laughing, and Ava and Rosemary both smiled at the humorous scenario.

It was clear that Alta found the situation more entertaining than scandalous. Her eyes still sparkled with amusement even when her laughter died down. She was racy and progressive, caring little for social rules. Suddenly, Ava thought that her mother wouldn't approve of her work friend if she knew more about her.

Ava and Rosemary went to work without a word to anyone else until Mrs. Crockett disengaged herself from her more troublesome employees and sought them out to tell them personally about the situation. She explained that Mr. Wakefield had tried to find other help, but was unable, and that the man hired knew how to act appropriately.

Geraldine Dallas finally left, vowing not to come back until "that man" was gone, and Frank Marshall went to work with an inexorable scowl plastered on his face. James was losing his place in Ava's thoughts as she and Rosemary both imagined what the controversial man in the stock room was like. They were also busier than normal with the shortage of regular employees.

Ava's chance to see him for herself finally came when Mrs. Crockett sent her to the back for another pin cushion. Walking into the store's well-organized stock room, she looked for him as she made her way to the basket of sewing supplies on its customary shelf. Catching sight of the broad back of a black man standing above her on a ladder, she stopped. He was whistling, and she watched him as he selected a box of men's apparel, held it firmly in one arm, and swaggered down the ladder with the other. He then turned toward her, and she was surprised to recognize the same man she had seen outside the Noble Theater. Remembering the pin cushion, she walked quickly to the basket when he became aware of her presence.

"Why, hello, miss." The man smiled, apparently either unaffected or unaware of the trouble he was causing.

"Hi." She smiled back, rummaging through the basket.

"Name's Douglas. You work here?"

"Yes, I do. I'm Ava." She pulled out the needed pin cushion and slid the basket back into its place.

"Very pleased to know you."

"Welcome to Wakefield's," she sincerely said and left with the pin cushion.

Recalling what she had witnessed at the theater softened her heart toward him. She heard his carefree whistling resume as she closed the door behind her. He certainly didn't seem like a dangerous man.

Ava, Rosemary, and Alta sat together in their usual booth at the Palace Drug Store, going over their impressions of Douglas and eating their lunch of chicken salad sandwiches.

"He was whistling when I went back there," Ava said as if there was something unusual in whistling.

"He was when I went back there for more clothes hangers too," Rosemary said.

"He's certainly not losing sleep over it." Alta began laughing to herself. "When old Florence screamed at finding him in the back, like he was some kind of ghost or something, he just grinned at her and asked if she was feeling all right!"

"I wish I could've seen it," Ava said, but thinking back to the malicious way that the young boys were taunting Douglas at the theater, she wasn't so sure.

"Oh, Ava, I almost forgot." Alta slapped her forehead. "Sydney and I have a blind double date for you Friday night."

"What?" Ava asked, recovering from the pang she always felt when Alta mentioned Sydney.

"He's a buddy of Sydney's and that's all I know."

Ava had never been on a blind date before, but it sounded exciting.

As if she were reading her mind, Rosemary tried to calm her enthusiasm by asking, "Don't you already have a date with Ernie this weekend?"

"That's not until Saturday," she replied, dismissing the question and ignoring the look of disapproval on Rosemary's face. "Sydney didn't tell you anything about him?"

"Nope, but you never know, he could be the man of your dreams." Alta smiled at her friend's curiosity.

Ava hadn't yet accepted, but she knew that she would go, and she listened to Alta go over the few details she knew of their date as they walked back to the store. She hid a slight frown, realizing her only reservation. It would be awkward being around Sydney and Alta together, and she was embarrassed that Sydney might think she liked him. She was still mulling over these less pleasant thoughts when a man's voice interrupted them just at the store door.

"Ava, excuse me," the voice called, and she looked up at the thin, suited man and recognized him as Willie Harold, the bandleader.

A broad smile replaced her frown.

"Good heavens, I'm glad we've found you." He sighed, shoving two disproportionately large hands in his pockets.

He was fair headed and as slender as a pencil with a serious face that always squinted as if he was reading a line of music.

"I know you're working, but I wanted to see if we could get together Wednesday afternoon at the Red Cross Building to practice for next Saturday. You'll only need to rehearse three or four numbers. You are off on Wednesday afternoons aren't you?"

"Yes, Wednesday will work fine."

He confirmed the time and place with her and left them. She hadn't told Alta about what happened on her date with Ernie or the band. So, Alta was anxious for news, and they found an excuse to work near each other for the rest of the afternoon.

With all of the excitement at Wakefield's Department Store, Ava completely forgot about her brother until they were back on the bus. The duty he charged her with came back to her mind, and she decided to go see Estelle as soon as she got home.

"Are you going to tell your parents about Douglas?" Rosemary asked.

"Oh, I don't know," Ava mused with new awareness. "Do you think they would make us quit if they knew?"

127

"I don't think so."

Rosemary had never been around colored people much, and she recalled the woman and her daughter who cleaned Dr. Green's house, Mrs. Green's domineering way with them, and the affectionate manner with which Jake always referred to them.

"We better not mention it just in case," Ava said and resumed her thoughts about visiting Estelle. Maybe telling her about the blind date would take her mind off James leaving.

Chapter 16

It had only been four days since James had left, and
Victoria Stilwell had already become the most patriotic woman
in Jacksonville, even surpassing the notorious Valencia Boozer
in enthusiasm. Ava and Estelle waited on the throng of garden
club, church, and neighbor women who Victoria had almost
threatened into attending her first Women Advancing the War
Efforts Committee meeting. The natural thing would have
been for her to involve herself with Red Cross work, but she
liked being in charge of her own doings, and, besides, she
couldn't tolerate Valencia calling her "Toria" for hours on end
and assigning her frivolous tasks. To begin her meeting she
had called for a rations swap, which all of the women eagerly
engaged in. Myrtle smiled down at her extra meat rations as
Victoria silenced the chattering group.

"Now, for more important matters," she announced
gravely, as lips all around her began to close shut.

"War bonds," she began, surveying her words' affect
on them. "Everyone has been selling them, but you all know as
well as I do that people have become tight wadded on the
subject."

Several heads began to bob around her, and she
continued bravely.

"So, that is why I am proposing a war bonds drive like
this town has never seen before, and, as a farmer's wife, I think

that this drive should begin with us farmers." She revealed a small pamphlet from behind her back.

"Twelve Facts for American Farmers About Defense Saving Bonds and Stamps from the U.S. Treasury Department," she read aloud.

"I want each of you to take two and read over one with your husbands tonight and give the other to a friend." She nodded at Ava, and Ava located the extra pamphlets on the kitchen table and began passing them out.

"My family is going to start the drive by buying a $37.50 bond and will try to buy more as we can."

The women began to consider their pamphlets.

"We must help this war succeed if we want our sons back," she pleaded, eyeing Sarah Gunter, Alice Johnson, and Mildred Waters, who all had sons in the service.

A tap at the screen door drew Ava's attention away from her mother, and she went to see about it.

"Is Mom's dang meeting about over?" Carson asked, peeking past her into the crowded room.

"Who knows?"

She was almost as ready as he was for it to be.

"I'm ready for bed."

"It's not even 8:30. Why don't you go over to Cousin Jude's like Dad and Grandpa?"

"Shucks, I've already been over there. All they want to talk about is the war, and they won't even turn on the radio." He scowled.

"What's the matter?" her father's voice called behind them.

"Oh nothing, just seeing how Mom's meeting's going, that's all," Carson said, softening his tone. "I'm going to go check on the mules."

Sheffield watched his son stalk away.

For the first couple of days after James left, Carson barely noticed his brother's absence because of the car. He drove it recklessly about their property when no one was watching and volunteered to pick things up in town, but he now believed James about the scarcity of gas, and the front left tire was getting low. It would be next to impossible to replace with the war going on, since rubber had become a priceless commodity. He passed the old barn housing their mules and sunk down by the base of an oak tree.

The newly pledged members of the Advancing the War Efforts Committee were finally leaving, and Estelle looked at Ava with tired eyes. Her love for James had not transformed into the same wild energy that her mother-in-law's had.

"Do you think we can leave now?" Ava asked, watching her mother usher the last two guests out the front door.

"You bet," Estelle said, following a long yawn.

Carson was now coming through the front door, and he marched past them without a word. Ava ran back to her room to gather her things.

Earlier that day, her parents had decided that she should stay with Estelle until her sister-in-law left for Texas. She picked up a few toiletries and her father's large, square suitcase full of her clothes. After what James had told her in private, she anticipated the stay being a long one.

They were excused after listening to her mother's critique of the meeting, and Ava followed Estelle to her house a short distance away. She felt like a grown-up as they walked, un-chaperoned, through the front door. The house was so different from her home. It wasn't cluttered with discarded

131

shoes and half-drunk glasses of sweet milk. Instead, its open space and small bouquets of cut flowers gave it a fresh amenity that made one want to spend long hours just sitting in it. Estelle's tiredness and already piercing loneliness from entering the house without James made her quiet, and Ava followed her to the home's only diminutive bedroom in silence.

"I cleaned you out part of our closet for your things." Estelle tried to smile, catching a glimpse of James's Sunday suit pushed far but neatly back into the closet.

"Thanks," Ava said, setting down her suitcase. "Guess what?"

"What?" Estelle played along as Ava bounced down on her knees on the bed.

"I have a blind date Friday night!"

"Really, tell me all about it." Estelle mustered up the most interested expression she could, but Ava noticed that it was somewhat forced, and she felt like she had just commented on the color of the sky at a funeral.

Chapter 17

Alta's house was the grandest house that Ava had ever been inside, and she marveled at its immensity, ornate fixtures, and many Tyler family portraits that lined the towering staircase and upstairs hallway. One picture of a bearded man with keen, confident eyes and a monstrous nose particularly caught her attention, because it appeared to be watching them as they passed and reminded her of haunted pictures from mystery radio programs. She laughed to herself thinking of what serious-faced portraits of her mother and father and Grandpa Chester would look like fixed upon their humble walls.

They were being picked up for their date here, and Alta wanted to get ready first. Her bedroom was on the second floor, and Ava was just as impressed with it as she was with the whole house. Her bed was the fluffiest bed she had ever seen with an assortment of various-shaped pillows resting on its deep purple coverlet.

"If you want to freshen up, Ava, my bathroom is right down the hall past my father's library or you can share my mirror," Alta said. She was sitting on a dainty stool in front of a large oval mirror sitting on her dresser.

"I just need to put on some more lipstick." Ava poked through her purse for the lipstick that Rosemary had given her and wondered at the need for a library in a house.

133

Her fingers found it, and she looked up at Alta's reflection in the mirror as her friend began to rearrange her hair.

"Sit here. I always have to be right up at the mirror when I put on lipstick." Alta rose from the stool with her hands still on her hair.

"Oh, no, I can see fine."

"Go ahead." Alta moved further away from the stool.

Ava sat down on it and began applying color to her lips.

"Why do you work?" she couldn't help but ask, still under the influence of the house's vastness.

"Because I want to," Alta answered and gave her a large, satisfied smile. "Of course, my mother hates me working. I'm only the second Tyler woman to work. A great aunt of mine once wrote scandalous stories for a social newspaper," she continued as her eyes flickered with their usual amusement, "but what can mother do?"

Ava looked away from her and back to her own reflection. She had never thought of herself as being bold to work.

"Any ideas now on who Sydney is bringing for me?" she changed the subject, somewhat embarrassed by her personal question.

"Nope," Alta replied, looking down at the tiny compact in her hand, and Ava wondered for the first time if she was being honest. "I'm sure whoever he is, though, he will be to your liking."

Alta now began to reapply her eye make-up. Ava watched as she framed her pale blue eyes with a more emboldening shade of gray. Just then the reflection of a dark complexioned woman appeared in the mirror, and Alta spun around to speak to her.

"Are they here?"

"Yes, Miss, they wait downstairs," the lady pronounced carefully in a thick accent.

"Thanks much, Margaret."

"Mom's house maid," she said when the woman had left.

"Where is she from?"

"Um, Guatemala, I think."

Alta took her time reexamining her appearance, and Ava wondered how long she would keep their dates waiting. A mixture of fear and excitement pervaded her now, and she was ready to run back down the stairs and meet whoever was there to get rid of the sick feeling.

"Ready?" Alta asked, noticing the look of frightful anticipation on her friend's face.

Ava nodded.

"You'll like him. I promise."

Alta ushered her out the door and down the hall. Passing the picture of the bearded man again, Ava imagined the Tyler patriarch as the man waiting for her, and the thought almost made her laugh. On the steps, she could already hear Sydney's infectious laughter, and she strained her ears for another male voice. They were now at the lower part of the staircase, and she could see the top of Sydney's sandy-brown head and the broad, muscular back of another uniformed man.

"Ladies," Sydney greeted.

The man with him turned, and Ava breathed in when she recognized Edwin. She could tell that he was just as surprised to see her by the way his blue eyes changed from cool to livid to cool once again in quick succession. His face was freshly shaven but still carried the traces of rough masculinity that she had noticed at the dance. He held his hat in his hand, and she noticed the shininess of his shoes and the neatness of his dress. Now over her own initial surprise, she was resolved to have the same confidence with him that she did before, despite the always defensive and searching nature of his gaze.

"Edwin, this is Ava Stilwell, the best little singer in Alabama." Sydney laughed as they continued to look at each other. "Alta, this is Edwin Livingston, the best shot in the United States Army."

"Nice to meet you, Edwin, right?" Ava smiled up at him and extended her hand, going along with the joke.

He met her hand with his own and felt his blood surge unnaturally through his body. It was a feeling like he had never known before, and he felt as if his whole face was burning.

"Yep, and you're Ann, or Ava?" he said, trying also to be at ease as he crumpled the hat in his hand.

He wasn't as adept as Sydney and Barry at thinking up witty remarks, but they all laughed, and he was pleased with himself.

"Some joke, Saunders."

"What do you mean?" Sydney threw up his hands and grinned.

"You're not disappointed are you?" Ava asked, amazed again by her boldness with him.

It was how she would act with Jimmy or Pete, not a man whom she barely knew. Suddenly realizing that it was her way of dealing with her nervousness, the thought almost broke her confidence. The creeping look of boyish embarrassment that stole over his face, however, reinforced her easiness with him, and she noticed how ruggedly handsome he was. When

136

he was shaken from his subdued behavior, he was almost as good looking as Percy.

"No…I mean, of course not," Edwin said, pleased by her flirting and embarrassed by the honesty of feeling that he could hear in his own voice.

"How are you, Alta?" He looked away from her to her friend.

"Good. Are you boys ready to go? I don't think that either of you want to meet my batty mother."

"Let's go." Sydney clapped his hands together and began hurrying them out the door.

As they stepped onto the house's long front porch, Ava felt the wind lift her hair away from her temples. The swift breeze had made the summer night cooler than normal, and she was glad of this. They were going to the Cotton Carnival at Oxford Lake, and she had been dreading the sticky feeling of being outside in the humid air for a long period of time. Edwin escorted her from a distance but was more of a gentleman about opening doors and letting her walk on the inside of the sidewalk than any man she had ever witnessed. Sydney teased him about his expression when he found out that Ava was his blind date as they walked to the bus stop, and she felt sorry for him and pleased by it all at the same time. If anything, it was keeping him the vulnerable soldier that she had grown to like at Wakefield's when he had tried to save her from Mrs. Crockett's wrath.

On the bus, he sat as far away from her as possible on the narrow seat, but his shoulder kept knocking hers, and he felt again as if his blood was racing dangerously through his body. Ava looked out the window to hide her amusement at his efforts to keep away from her.

"Have you been to a carnival before?"

Alta and Sydney were sitting two seats in front of them, so they would have to talk to each other.

"My father took us a few times when I was a boy."

They sat for a moment in silence, gazing at the tops of the heads in front of them.

"When I was a kid my grandparents took me to a big one in Birmingham where they live," Ava said, and he was embarrassed that she had to offer this information without him returning the question.

"What all did you do there?"

"Let me remember. Oh, I rode a white pony, and I won the cake walk!" she said with the enthusiasm that he admired. "But, it was the worst pineapple cake you ever put in your mouth." She laughed and screwed up her nose as if she had just tasted the cake again.

He laughed with her.

"Do you like pineapple cake?"

"Yep. My mom makes a really good one." He glanced down at her, and she noticed the strained way that he referred to his mother.

"You're lucky your mother bakes them. My mother doesn't think that fruit belongs in cakes."

Edwin laughed again, and she liked the way his laugh sounded merry, yet not too boisterous.

"What do your parents think about you being in the Army?"

"My mom I reckon is fine with it."

"But your dad isn't?" she asked, thinking of the battle of pride and uneasiness that she saw in her father's eyes daily since James left.

"My dad is dead," he replied as his face grew cool once again, and she regretted the question.

138

"I'm so sorry," Without thinking, she touched his arm. He winced, and she withdrew her hand.

"I'm sure he would be very proud of you," she said when he didn't say anything. "My oldest brother James just left for the Army this week, and my father is really proud of him going, even if he is somewhat scared by it."

"Where did they send him?"

"Texas," she said as if her brother had been sent to some exotic, far-off location.

"Is he leaving a wife or kids behind?" He remembered from the revival what her banjo-playing brothers looked like, and he recalled a woman with one of them.

"No kids, but he does have the sweetest wife alive. Estelle is going to be with him in Texas in a couple of weeks or so. I'm living with her until then."

Without meaning to, she then began to relate everything about James leaving for the war, the conflict over Estelle joining him, and Carson getting turned down by the Army. His eyes turned more fully upon her with each story she told, and he was looking her in the face when the bus halted.

"Are you guys coming or what?" Sydney yelled, and Edwin jumped up from their seat.

Ava concealed a giggle at his bumping his head on the roof of the bus. They made their way to the front, and Edwin bounded down the stairs and turned back toward her, offering his arm. She smiled at his chivalry, braced herself with his arm, and descended the steps. Rosemary and she normally laughed at such ridiculousness. The wind was still swift, and she smoothed her skirt down as they caught up with Alta and Sydney.

"There's quite a crowd," Alta said as they walked to the ticket booth. "The line for the Ferris Wheel will be halfway around the lake."

Ava watched the large, circular contraption already spinning with dozens of dangling feet and noses appearing over colorful baskets. As the evening darkened, the wheel's lights were becoming more vivid. Edwin paid for their tickets, and they followed Alta and Sydney into the carnival surrounding Oxford Lake. School-aged kids with cotton candy, strolling adults, and soldiers and their dates could be seen in every direction.

"Food first," Sydney said, eyeing a hot dog stand.

"I don't see how you're not 300 pounds!" Alta exclaimed. "Can't we walk around a bit first?"

"Oh, all right. But Winn can tell you that it's been a long time since our last chow call."

"Win your girl a cuddly Teddy bear!" the booming voice of a small, suited man halted them.

"Come on man, you know it's rigged." Sydney laughed, looking over the makeshift shooting gallery.

"What do you mean, G.I.?" The man cocked his hat and smirked. "All you do is hit this here target." He pointed at a mechanical beaver that kept appearing and disappearing from behind a fake log. "With this here gun." He picked up a pellet gun and pushed it in front of Edwin's face.

"Really, that simple? Well, if Winn can't do it, then it's definitely rigged."

"Got ourselves a sharp shooter, do we?" The man smiled a toothy, challenging grin, still inviting Edwin to take the gun.

"Let's see you do it, Edwin," Alta said, curious to see the ability that Sydney ranted about.

140

"Show 'em how it's done." Sydney clapped a hand on Edwin's back and shoved the gun into his hand.

"I don't know." Edwin shook his head.

"I'll put in the first ten cents," Ava said, taking ten cents from her purse and making his decision for him.

He looked down at her and raised the gun, blushing at the thought of missing the beaver.

"Three shots now," the toothy man said, pocketing Ava's money.

As soon as he cocked the gun to shoot, the beaver started ducking and darting up from behind the log at three times the speed that it had been before. Edwin studied it and then shot. He missed. Ava watched his fixed concentration as he bit his lip hard and pulled the trigger again. This time, the pellet hit the dashy beaver square in the head, and he fell over with a funny "boinging" noise.

"Yea! You did it!" Ava and Alta both cheered.

The carnival worker quit smiling and stared at his fallen beaver in disbelief.

"I say you are a good shot, boy."

"You don't doubt the Army," Sydney said as if it were he who had made the shot.

"Do you want to try?" Alta asked him.

"Oh, no, Winn's already shown 'em how it's done."

"What color bear do you want, pretty lady?" The man looked at Ava and pointed at his previously undisturbed display.

The bears were loud colors of blue, pink, and red with happy brown eyes.

"I'll take the red one," Ava said, and the man gave her the bear.

141

"Thanks for not wasting my money." She laughed up at Edwin, hugging the bear to her as they walked on.

He was proud of himself no matter how silly it was. They were now close to the Ferris Wheel line, and Alta took Sydney's hand and pulled him into it.

Edwin gulped. Heights made him dreadfully sick.

"When we're up top, we can find my house," Alta said.

"We can also find Wakefield's." Ava peered up at the moving baskets of people above them.

Edwin looked up at the now top basket, and his stomach took an odd flip as he remembered once two years ago when he had ridden in a crop dusting plane with his father and vomited in his lap.

Just don't look down, he commanded himself. The line moved quickly, and they were now in the next group to board.

The wheel came to a stop as each basket was emptied and filled again. Edwin and Ava mounted the platform for their turn and sat together on the wooden seat as it was pushed underneath them.

"It's much nicer riding with you than my brothers," she told him when their basket began to slowly ascend.

"Why's that?" He gazed above rather than below them. They were almost level with the treetops.

"Carson insists on rattling the basket as hard as he can just to make you mad and scared. Last time, though, mom screamed so loud at him from the ground that he had to stop just to get her to be quiet."

Edwin laughed, but he could tell, without looking, that they were at the very top of the wheel. Sweat beads were popping out all over his forehead, and his face and palms felt clammy and cold.

"I think Alta found her house," Ava said. She could see Alta pointing at something below.

"It's too big not to spot."

Ava laughed.

"Yes, it is humongous. Did you know that her father has a library in the house?"

They were now at the bottom, and Edwin let out a sigh of relief, but then inhaled as the wheel started up again without stopping.

"Really, a library," he said and gripped the bar for another go around.

He didn't know if he could make it through a second time.

"I don't really understand why she works. I guess that she just wants to meet people and keep from getting bored. She wouldn't get bored at my house. My parents don't believe in doing nothing."

"There's too much to do on a farm not to do something." They were just over the treetops again, and he tried to converse with her as normally as possible.

"Exactly...Oh hey, I can sort of make out Noble Street and The Noble Theater and Wakefield's." She leaned over the bar.

They were at the top again.

"Look!" she shouted, not noticing his closed eyes.

He opened them slowly and looked down. His stomach jerked, and before he could stop himself, he was vomiting over the side of their basket.

"Edwin!" Ava gasped at his pallid face. "Are you o.k.?"

He vomited again and slumped down in their seat with his eyes shut as hard as he could get them.

"No, I should have told you that heights don't agree with me."

His face was as white as cotton.

"We're almost to the bottom," she said, just as their basket stopped for the first pair of riders to dismount below them.

He was too humiliated to say anything more. Two more sets of riders dismounted, including Sydney and Alta, and then it was their turn. The safety rail lifted, and she grasped his arm to help him off. Sydney was staring at his friend with a wide, disbelieving smirk.

"You sick, Winn? No wonder you didn't want to fly planes for Uncle Sam!"

"I need to sit down." Edwin moved toward a half-empty bench.

He sat down on it, and the mother and child sitting on the other half obligingly moved.

"Do you want something to drink?" Alta asked.

"No, ya'll go on, and I'll come find you in a little while." He was more embarrassed than he had ever felt in his whole life.

They all three continued to stare at him.

"Seriously, go on."

"You two go have fun, and I'll sit with Edwin," Ava said.

"You can go, too."

"No, I would rather wait until you feel better."

"All right then," Sydney said, realizing how embarrassed his friend must feel. "Come on, Alta, I can't wait any longer for a hot dog anyway."

"I guess we'll be eating somewhere when you feel better," Alta said, rolling her eyes as they left.

144

Edwin and Ava sat for sometime without speaking.

"I'm sorry," he spoke after he could feel blood returning to his face.

"For what?" she asked, trying not to make him even more uncomfortable by looking at him.

"What do you mean for what? For getting sick and making you feel like you have to sit here with me."

"Nonsense, I would rather sit here with you. Besides, I like watching people."   "Watching people?" He cocked his eyebrows as if he didn't believe her.

"Yea, people can be funny. Look at that couple over there." She pointed at them and then looked away.

"They're having a really good brawl, and he is begging her to forgive him for something or other." She laughed and stole another glance at the couple.

Edwin watched the girl and boy without even caring not to stare. The young, school-aged girl was marching around with folded arms and a pouty expression. The boy stalked behind, begging her through gritted teeth and offering her all sorts of fair treats. They both laughed and then looked away when the girl's enraged circle widened closer to where they were sitting.

"I hope she forgives him," Ava said. "He's been going on like that since we sat down. What do you suppose he did?"

Edwin didn't answer, surprised by her interest in people she didn't know.

"I bet he was flirting with another girl right in front of her. Or he could have been nasty to her mother when he picked her up for the fair."

He laughed at her imagination. He would have never thought about such a thing.

145

"Or it could've been because he kept her sitting on a bench for hours and didn't let her enjoy the carnival," he said, feeling much better.

She looked up at him.

"Could be," she said, realizing that his disposition had changed and his coolness with her had melted once again.

The color had returned to his face, and he looked incredibly handsome smiling down at her with his moody blue eyes.

Ava had to tolerate a slew of questions from her mother about her date before going to Estelle's house, and she could barely sit still before she was finally allowed to go. She couldn't wait to tell Estelle the real story about her evening. Her face was glowing, and her gray eyes were luminous when she walked into her sister-in-law's house. Estelle was engulfed in a sea of clothes that she had been folding to keep herself awake.

"I don't even have to ask if you had a good time." Estelle laughed at seeing her face.

"You wouldn't believe it. It was Sydney's friend Edwin, the one I told you about from Tennessee. The tall, good-looking one who you feel hates you one minute and can't get enough of you the next."

"I take it he couldn't get enough of you tonight, then."

"Oh, he's really sweet, just shy sometimes and not sure how to act around girls he likes."

"Your brother certainly didn't have a problem with shyness," Estelle said, her cheeks warming with memories. "What all did you do?"

"He won me a Teddy bear at a shooting gallery and then got sick," she went on trying to tell all about the date in one breath and displaying the red bear.

"He got sick?" Estelle laughed again at Ava's excitement and took the wide-eyed bear from her.

"It was the Ferris Wheel. He can't take heights. He threw up everywhere." Ava collapsed in James's armchair.

Estelle felt less lonely seeing a face that looked so much like her husband's in its usual place.

"Is he better?"

"Oh, yes, he recovered and we watched a singing trio, ate hot dogs, and talked all night."

They went to bed but lay there giggling about Ava's evening and talking about James well into the night. Ava listened to embarrassing, romantic stories about her brother that made her pound her pillow in laughter and feel closer to her sister-in-law than she had ever felt before. They finally decided that they must go to sleep, and Ava smiled to herself, realizing that she was fulfilling her brother's request.

Chapter 18

Florence Burnham and Geraldine Dallas had still not come back to work since Douglas was hired, and the store was busier than ever. Ava, Rosemary, and Alta ran in all directions helping customers make purchases as Mrs. Crockett looked on with satisfaction.

"We just sold the last pair of those shoes a couple of hours ago," Ava told a woman in a flowery dress who was admiring a pair of black pumps with bows in the store window.

"Can I have the ones in the window then? The tag says that they're my size."

"I'll go ask." She hadn't thought of disturbing the proud window display before.

Ava left the woman and walked straight for Mrs. Crockett, who was conversing with a regular customer. She waited for a lapse in their conversation and inquired about the shoes.

"Of course she can," Mrs. Crockett said with exasperation as if the question had been a needless one, but Ava knew that if she hadn't asked, she would have been ambushed on opening the display case. "Just make sure to replace the pair with another good seller."

Ava rushed back to her customer.

"Our store manager says that will be fine."

"Good!" The lady smiled.

Ava opened the glass door of the display box and reached in, careful not to disturb anything other than the shoes. Mrs. Crockett liked every piece of merchandise turned in just the right direction to best catch the on-looker's eye. She couldn't help but glance out at the street whenever given the chance, and her eyes scanned the crowded sidewalks and fell on the face of Edwin. He was standing outside the store's door, trying to decide whether or not to come in. Placing her hands on the shoes, she watched him start to open the door and then turn back, almost colliding with a large woman coming from behind him. She laughed to herself as she withdrew the shoes off their pedestal and out of the window.

"Here you are," she said, smiling at what she had just seen.

"Thank you. I'll just go try these on by the mirror." The lady clutched hold of the shoes and left her.

I hope he makes it through the door, she thought and hurried to the back to replace the empty display. Mrs. Crockett would be livid if it remained imperfect for longer than a minute. She pushed open the back room door and ran inside.

"Whoa!" Douglas rushed from behind the opening door.

"Sorry, Douglas," she said, already rummaging through the shoeboxes for an appropriate pair to showcase.

"You're running around like a chicken that knows it's about to be supper."

"I feel like one today."

Ava breathed in before running back out of the room with the shoes. She had to make it back before Edwin came in. She lessened her jog to a casual walk as she re-approached the window. The bells fastened to the front door of the store rang out, and her heart quickened. She took her time fixing the women's Navy slippers on the pedestal and left the display case. Edwin was standing a few feet away from her, crumpling his hat in his hand. She smiled at him, and he walked toward her and then held up a finger to indicate, "Wait a minute." He then picked up a long, brown tie without even looking at it and started back toward her, but it was too late. The lady with the shoes was back, and Ava pulled out a ticket booklet and began filling it out for her. He stopped and pretended to be surveying the tie rack again. Ava saw Mrs. Crockett ask if he needed any help, and she bit her lip to keep from laughing. She was touched by his thoughtfulness of not wanting to get her in trouble.

"Can I help you, mister?" Ava asked when the lady had left with the shoes. "You're not shopping for dresses again are you?"

A bashful smile broke out over his face.

"Oh, I don't know. I might see one that fancies me."

"This would look good on you."

She glanced around to ensure that she didn't have Mrs. Crockett's attention and then took the tie from him and held it up to his chest approvingly. His ears turned red, and he took the tie back.

"Would you go to supper with me tonight?" he asked with a pained expression as if it had taken all that was within him to get out the question and he couldn't bear to hear her answer. All he could think about was how he had thrown up in front of her the night before.

Ava smiled, about to answer yes, and then, horrified, remembered her date with Ernie. Why had she agreed to go out with him again? Her brain hurt as she thought fast of what to do. He would be mortified if she refused and perhaps never ask again. His eyes were growing graver with each second of her hesitation.

"Of course," she said, and his stoic expression softened in relief. She would have to think of someway to get rid of Ernie.

When Edwin left, she went to the dressing area to find Rosemary and found her re-hanging an assortment of rejected apparel that filled her arms.

"Rosemary," she started, relieving her of a few dresses and following her from rack to rack without putting up anything herself. "I have a big favor to ask."

Rosemary paused for a moment and looked intently at her.

"Like what?" There was already a look of disapproval on her face.

"Did you see Edwin in here a few minutes ago?"
"Yes."

Rosemary could guess what was coming. She had already heard the same elaborate story about the blind date as Estelle had.

"He wants to have supper with me, and I couldn't tell him no. I can't go out with Ernie tonight. Would you wait for him and tell him…that…I'm not feeling well?"

Rosemary stared at her with a look of disbelief.

"I can't lie for you," she answered, and Ava momentarily despised her staunch integrity.

In frustration, she followed her around thinking of what to do next.

"Will you just give him a note for me then? I really like Edwin, Rosemary, more than any other boy I've ever liked."

Rosemary stopped and looked at her again, softening. Could her cousin actually be serious? Could she like this soldier in the way that she liked Jake?

"All right, but I'm not saying anything to him, not a single word."

Rosemary stood outside the store with Ava's note, excoriating herself for having agreed to such a dishonest errand. She looked down both sides of the street for Ernie's boyish face and watched several groups of young men and women pass by her. She was angry at Ava, but not for the reason that her cousin thought she was. The sickening feeling of being alone was rushing over her again, and she somehow blamed Ava for it. If she didn't have to be like Alta and go out with a different soldier every night, she wouldn't be riding the bus home by herself again, dwelling on Jake's absence and her own unhappiness. She didn't want to go home, but she also didn't want to stand here any longer feeling foolish.

Ernie appeared, and she smiled feebly, remembering what she was about to do. She could tell that he was looking for Ava, and a frown was deepening over his face at not seeing her.

"Hi, Ernie."

"How are you, Rosemary?" he asked, still looking behind her for Ava.

"Good. Um, Ava asked me to give you this note." She held out the folded slip of paper.

He took it from her, and she stood beside him as he read. His face flushed pink, and she knew that he didn't believe what it said.

"Thanks. If you see her, tell her I hope she feels better soon."

"I will," she said, and he left her.

She felt cruel and turned to walk toward the bus stop but was curtailed by a recognizable face and outreached hand.

"Percy!" She jumped away from him, but she knew she was glad to see him.

He wasn't taunting her with his usual haughty smile but was gazing down at her.

"I was hoping I would catch you. I really need someone to talk to."

She returned the gaze that always made her feel angry and weak and searched for signs of mischief in his eyes. There was none that could be detected, and she realized that he was grasping her hand.

"Have you had dinner yet?"

"No," she said, and without another word, he was leading her by the hand through the crowded streets.

Her heart was racing, and she felt as though her feet were floating behind him rather than thumping the ground. His hand was hot and caressing against hers. Where was he taking her? They stopped outside the Sanitary Café, and he pulled her through the door to an empty table in the back, only letting go of her hand when they sat down. A waitress approached them and asked for their order. Percy ordered for himself and asked what she wanted.

"I'll have the turkey and dressing plate," she read the first item listed under the daily specials.

When the waitress left, he leaned forward, his brown eyes boring into hers.

"Thanks for coming. I have to talk to someone other than the guys. Men were not made to be listeners." He smiled but without any mirth.

"I'll listen if you need me too," she replied, secretly wanting to talk to someone herself.

"I got a letter from my father at the afternoon mail call. He was trying to sound casual, but no one has heard from my brother in a month and a half. They wanted to know if I'd heard from him." His eyes glistened with released emotion.

"Have you?" she asked, thinking of how she would feel if they hadn't heard from Jake or James in that long.

"No."

The waitress interrupted them with glasses of tea, and they sat in silence until she left.

"Where was he the last time you heard from him?"

"Sicily." He gulped down almost half of his tea at once. "My sister-in-law hasn't even heard from him."

"A friend of my family has a son who has been overseas for two years, and she told my mother that Charlie doesn't always have the time or supplies to write."

He smiled at her efforts to comfort him, ran his fingers through his russet hair, and leaned back.

"I mean I'm sure that it's hard for them to write letters when they are in…," she stopped, not wanting to allude to his dangerous situation.

"Yea, but it's been nearly two months."

The waitress came with their food and stopped her from having to answer.

"Enough depressing talk while we eat. What have you been up to since I saw you last? Writing long letters to your Navy boyfriend?" he asked, his sly smile returning as he cut into his fried trout.

She flushed and looked down at her food.

"Yes," she replied, concentrating on putting a bite of turkey, dressing, and cranberry sauce all onto her fork at once.

"And what else? That can't take up all 24 hours of your day."

"I saw my cousin off for the war this week, and I've been working, of course, and helping my mother make summer clothes for my sister who is growing a foot every day."

He laughed, pleased about something.

"You have a sister? Is she as pretty and stubborn as you?"

Rosemary smiled despite herself.

"I'm not stubborn."

"Oh, yea, you wouldn't even be here if I hadn't made you."

"Well, I haven't been sure of your intentions."

He laughed loudly and finished his trout. They talked about Judith and James for a while before the conversation turned back to his brother. He paid for their dinner despite her resistance and insisted on waiting with her for the next bus to Jacksonville. At times their conversation was serious, but other times she couldn't believe how much she could laugh with him. The bus was approaching, and she turned to tell him goodbye. He grabbed her before she had time to react.

"Thanks, Rosemary," he whispered in her ear, and his hand went from her neck to her back and pressed her against his chest.

She felt as though she couldn't move. It felt so good to be embraced by him. He let her go just as the bus halted beside them.

"You're welcome," she replied and stepped onto the bus.

"I hope to see you next week at the dance," he shouted as the door closed behind her.

She found her usual seat and could see him looking up at her as the bus started off. When he couldn't see her anymore, she leaned back still feeling his arms encompassing her.

Sometime later, she sat on her bed staring down at a single sheet of paper. She had written the words "Dear Jake" and stopped. What could she possibly tell him about her day?

Chapter 19

Ava slid forward and pushed off the porch with her bare feet to send the swing higher. She was attempting to read *Nicholas Nickelby*, one of the many books her father had bought her in town, but she kept rereading the same sentences as her mind went back again and again to her date with Edwin. A stomping noise disrupted her happy thoughts, and she looked up to see Carson slouch half way up the porch stairs, retrace his steps, and fall with a loud thump on the bottom step. He didn't look up at her, but she could see the long, crooked cut across his face. It was more of an oozy gash now than a cut, and it pointed at his nose and jutted down toward his ear. He had been fighting with Edgar Gunter again, and it looked as though something sharp had caught hold of his face. According to Floraline, Edgar, who was still not over Carson beating him up in their first confrontation, called Carson a "conscientious objector," and Carson went after him just as he did at Jake's send-off party. She had heard the term "conscientious objector" before on the radio and remembered it referring to boys who disagreed with fighting in the war and who were instead sent off to work camps or even prison. Carson refused to say anything about the altercation, and she thought of how to ask him about the fight again without arousing his fast anger. He had already demanded once at lunch that she stop staring at him. She watched him over her book as he picked up a handful of rocks and threw them like baseballs out in front of him as hard and far as possible.

"Does Edgar's face look worse than yours?"

"Mind your own business."

"You really need to change your attitude and quit being so nasty to everyone."

Instead of yelling back at her, he threw the rock in his hand even harder than he threw the ones before it. It hit the ground several feet in front of the porch and sent a swirl of dry dust up in the air. The porch screen opened, and their mother poked her head through it.

"Still no sign of your father?" Victoria asked and gazed down the dirt road.

It had been three hours since Sheffield left to take Brother Whatley back to the bus stop, and it was now past their usual suppertime.

"No, ma'am," Ava answered her mother.

"You don't suppose the car broke down somewhere do you, Carson?"

"I don't see why it would have," Carson said, gripping the rocks still in his hand.

He didn't want to throw them in front of his mother in case she accused him of aiming for her flowerbeds.

"I hope he's not long. The cornbread's getting cold, and your Grandpa's lunch has already gotten away from him."

She stuck her head back in the house and let the screen door fall shut behind her. They always had pinto beans with cornbread and milk for Sunday night supper after feasting with the preacher at lunch.

Ava went back to reading but still couldn't concentrate. She had read the part about Nicholas going to work at the counting house four times when the roar of

James's car announced her father's return. She closed her book and went inside to tell her mother he was home. Estelle was eating at her own mother's house tonight, so it would just be the five of them for supper.

Grandpa Chester was already relishing his bowl of corn bread and milk when the rest of the family joined him at the table. He didn't believe that it was good for the stomach to wait for meals.

"Brother Whatley give you a second dose of preaching?" he said when Sheffield appeared.

Carson squeezed in his stomach and scooted past his grandfather to his place at the table.

"Nope, I've been chatting with Phil Boozer." Sheffield dipped his spoon hungrily into the bowl of mushy cornbread that his wife had just set in front of him.

Victoria stopped with Carson's bowl in her hand, arched her black eyebrows, and gave her husband a significant look that neither of her children failed to miss.

"I hope that you didn't make him late for his supper, too."

When everyone had a bowl of cornbread, milk, and beans, Sheffield cleared his throat and looked up at his son.

"Carson, you won't be needed tomorrow morning in the fields."

Carson looked back at his father dumbfounded and let his spoon slip with a clatter back into its bowl. Grandpa Chester looked just as stupefied as his grandson as he too paused between mouthfuls of cornbread. Victoria clasped her hands in front of her mouth and hid a smile behind them. Ava looked from the corners of her mother's mouth, which poked out from behind her hands, to her father, waiting for something else to be said. It didn't concern her, so she knew she wouldn't be allowed to ask questions.

"What do you mean?" Carson asked for her in the respectful manner with which he always addressed their parents.

"Because, you've got a job." Sheffield now smiled and casually loaded his spoon with another bite of beans.

"You been looking for a job, son?" Grandpa Chester peered at his grandson.

"I don't think so."

"Carson is going to do some farm work on Pelham Range up at the fort for the officers," Sheffield explained.

"Pelham Range!" Victoria gasped, her hidden smile vanishing. "You didn't say anything about Pelham Range. Isn't that where they shoot their guns?"

"Yes, blossom, but Carson's a smart boy. He won't go plowing and picking while there's a gun pointed at him."

"What are you two talking about?" Carson asked, forgetting his supper.

"The officers have been looking for someone to do a bit of farming for them, and Phil Boozer recommended you."

"My, my, Pelham Range." Grandpa Chester grinned. "Why, when I was a boy, we used to do some rabbit hunting up there. I can tell you all about it."

"Me?" Carson said, ignoring his grandpa's offer as a look of understanding spread over his beat-up face. "But what about you, Grandpa, and Cousin Jude?"

"We'll manage. Besides, we get along without you half the time as it is." Sheffield smiled, referring to Carson's stealthy fishing trips with his friends.

Grandpa Chester sighed and shut his mouth tight. He hadn't thought of the possibility of extra work yet.

160

"You can make yourself some money like your brother did and help out with the war effort at the same time. They've agreed to give you fifty cents an hour."

Ava watched her brother's eager face and understood her parents all at once. Carson would be working for the Army even though he couldn't join it. Her father was certainly clever.

"You had better eat up, Carson, if you're going to work in the morning," Victoria said, reminding everyone of their supper.

The next morning, Carson appeared at Fort McClellan's Post Headquarters well before the given time and waited on a wooden bench for the officer who would be overseeing him.

Gosh, you're not meeting a girl or anything, he told his nerves, patting his unruly hair once again without thinking.

He had never gotten this fixed up before to work in the field. He was wearing a pair of James's work pants and boots instead of his usual overalls and bare feet and had bathed, shaved, and tried to manage his thick, black hair. The woman at the typewriter paused in her typing, glanced at the clock, and smiled at him sympathetically again.

Why on earth did I get here so early? He sighed and looked out the window over the woman's head.

He could see the grassy, open area in the center of the officer's quarters and the post command buildings. It was wet and glossy with dew, and he wondered if they would allow him to eat his lunches there.

"Carson Stilwell." A man opened the door next to him and read from the paper in his hands.

"That's me." Carson stood up from his chair and faced the uniformed man, wondering if he should salute or something.

"So, you're the one who's going to attend to our little victory garden here," the soldier said and extended his hand. Carson met it with his own.

"I suppose so."

The older man was about his height, wore thick glasses, and was slim. He looked more like a banker than a soldier and didn't match any of Carson's preconceived notions about what men in the Army should look like.

"Major Frank Thunderstrom," he announced in a loud voice that seemed as if it should come from a much larger man. "Let's go. I'll take you straight to the area we've marked off for our little garden."

He waved for Carson to follow and then stopped to let the typist know of his intended whereabouts. They walked out of the building and down to a jeep parked on the side of a circular drive. Carson felt strange and out of place as he walked in civilian clothing past soldiers and listened to Major Thunderstrom exchange familiar greetings.

"Phil said that you tried to get into the Army but couldn't pass the eye exam."

"That's right." Carson felt his face burn with new embarrassment.

He thought he had gotten over the disappointment and was angry to feel it fresh again.

"That's a shame, but count yourself lucky. There are young men like you dying every day to this war."

Lucky?, Carson thought with surprise as he climbed into the passenger side of the jeep.

He had heard of great numbers of men dying in the war, but their glorified deaths and unfamiliar names made them seem unreal and his rejection sorely undignified.

The major pointed out various buildings to him as they rode, and Carson studied with interest each place that was drawn to his attention. He thought it odd to see so many Spanish-looking buildings with their flat, red-tile roofs in Anniston, Alabama. When they passed a long, different sort of building with several awnings, the Major stalled the jeep and pointed at its newly painted sign. Carson read, "Prisoner of War Camp Headquarters."

"If you need me, that's where you can find me in about two weeks," Major Thunderstrom's voice bellowed over the jeep's motor.

Carson nodded without speaking. He was still thinking about the unpleasant fact that he was "lucky."

They came to the outskirts of an open area, and Major Thunderstrom stopped the jeep. Carson could see men doing drills in the distance, but all around them was still and quiet. Before the major could point out the field, he had spotted it. It was almost as big as his grandpa's largest field and was hardly a "little victory garden."

"Some of the men tried planting a little corn, squash, and other things in the spring, but no one attended to them, and I'm afraid it was almost a waste."

"I'll see what I can do." Carson looked down the untidy rows of grass, weeds, and stubbles.

There was so much grass growing that almost all of what was planted had to be choked out.

"You know that it's too late to plant much of anything else, except for peas," Carson said with confidence now that he was back in familiar surroundings. "Well, I could plant some more corn, but corn planted this late usually gets eaten by the worms."

"Anything is better than nothing." The major followed his gaze from row to row. "We had intended to do a better job, but time got away from us. The other officers and I are pleased to hire you to grow something fresh for us for supper."

Major Thunderstorm's belief in him grew Carson's heart to the challenge. It would be a more difficult job than he imagined.

"All the tools you need you can find in that shed over there. You'll find a Ford 9N sitting inside there, too." The major pointed toward the shed, and Carson's eyes grew round at the idea of finding a tractor inside it. "If you need anything else, just let me know. The Army has a way of getting what it needs."

As soon as the major left, Carson almost ran to the shed and threw open its large double doors. There was a wide array of basic farming tools lying around and hanging from large nails protruding from the walls and, sitting right in the middle of them, was a real Ford 9N. He couldn't believe his eyes. It was the very tractor that he and his dad had looked at in Birmingham last year and wanted to buy if they could ever afford it. Forgetting the grassy field, he ran his hands over the tractor's large rubber tires and shiny metal body and wished with all his heart that his dad and grandpa were there to see it too. Not even Willis Ponder's old Fordson was as nice as this one.

Ava wasn't wearing a glamorous white dress and gloves like the girl at Lloyd's Crystal Ballroom and Banquet Hall, but she was wearing a loose-fitting white cotton gown that fell to her ankles, and the moonlight creeping through the barn doors enveloped her bare arms and served as a spotlight.

"O.k., Dixie, here goes again," she spoke to the mule.

She reread the first verse of the song in her hands and looked up into the mule's friendly eyes.

"I had the craziest dream last...night," she sang out.

"No, no, no." She stopped herself. "There must be a longer pause before night."

She was embarrassed during her last practice with the Willie Harold Band when she couldn't get the timing of the song's first line correct, and she was determined to be perfect during their practice this week. She was also determined to have all the words of her songs memorized and had been rehearsing them every night. At first, she practiced in her bedroom, but the main song she was singing talked about kissing, and she was afraid that her mother would overhear.

"I had the craziest dream last......night." She smiled, pleased with her timing. "I never dreamt it could be. Yet there you were in love with me."

She let the words of the song fall to the ground and clasped her hands in front of her bosom as her voice escalated.

"I felt your lips close to mine. I kissed you. You didn't mind." she paused at the sound of snickering, followed by Carson's outlandish singing.

"Your lips were close to mine," he sang in a high-pitched voice as he came dancing through the doors of the barn.

"Oh, you, shut up!" Ava picked up a clump of hay and threw it at him.

He was beside himself with laughter, and she resorted to pushing him as hard as she could back through the barn door.

165

"You get out of here!"

"Does Mom know you're out here singing love songs to Dixie?" He laughed, not budging any closer to the door.

"Out! Out! Out!"

Ava picked up a handful of small rocks and began throwing them at his backside, and he ran out the door still roaring at her clandestine performance. She picked up her music, but she couldn't concentrate, afraid that Carson was somewhere listening and ready to make fun of her again.

"Mean Carson," she said, petting Dixie. "He is certainly back to his old self. Maybe, dad shouldn't have got him that job after all."

Chapter 20

"I never dreamt it could be. Yet, there you were in love with me," Ava's voice rang out over the band's brassy ballad and filled the room.

The words of the song were coming out effortlessly and impeccably now as the presence of an audience shattered her inhibitions and provoked her talent. Her white night gown had been replaced with a solid green dress, but her arms were still bare as she gripped the microphone in front of her.

Edwin stood alone at the back of the room, concentrating on her every gesture over the bobbing heads of his dancing peers. This time he felt no reserve. He would watch her and not be embarrassed. After last Saturday, the week had been never ending without her, and he wanted a hundred remembrances to carry him through the next one. Her gray eyes looked in his direction, and he felt his heart surge. Everyone else seemed to disappear. It was as if she were singing to him alone. Out of instinct, his eyes began to flash in the opposite direction, but he held them steady under her flirtatious gaze. She was singing to him, and his blood was racing under her attention.

"Say it and make my craziest dreams come true," her voice called to him across the room.

He loved the way it rippled with emotion. It wasn't smooth and unfeeling, but always dripping with a fresh, unchecked passion that drew him to her. It was the first thing he had ever noticed about her and how he liked her best. The song ended, and the band immediately began the next one without her. He watched her make her way through the dancing couples to where he was standing. It seemed unreal that she was coming to him.

"Come on, soldier." Ava smiled under his brooding gaze. "If you're going to be my date, you have to dance."

He grasped her offered hand and followed her out to the dance floor. She could feel him letting go of himself as he held her around the waist and their feet fell in with the quick tempo of the music.

"How are you so brave up there on that stage?" he asked, almost shouting over the music.

"How are you so brave getting ready to go to war?" she shouted back. "I've been singing since I was born. I guess it's just a part of who I am."

He smiled. Really, his question would have been more accurate if he would have asked how she could bear to show so much emotion in front of the world. It was a quality that he had never known in his family.

The song ended, and a slower song took its place. Ava looked around the crowded room as their bodies swayed now rather than stepped and bounced to the music. Her eyes fell on the back of a uniformed man who was slowly turning a girl in her direction. The girl with long, wavy hair was her cousin, and she almost stopped moving at the recognition. It wasn't that she hadn't expected to see Rosemary or even to see Rosemary dancing with Percy. After all, he had succeeded in getting her to dance with him before. Rather, it was the way she was looking at him that surprised her. He was holding her extremely close and whispering something palpably funny in her ear by the way she was half dancing and half laughing out loud as she gazed up at him. She seemed free and familiar with him in a way that she had never seemed with Jake. Percy's back was now facing her again, and another couple had moved into her view. She bit her lip in contemplation. *Could Rosemary be falling for Percy?* She had thought it odd when Rosemary didn't remonstrate or even question whether or not she should go to the dance with her this time.

Maybe, she just feels comfortable with him because he has a fiancée back home, she speculated and, convinced of it, smiled up at Edwin.

"Wait, this song is my cue!" She separated herself from him. "My next song is right after this!"

"Good luck," he said as she hurried away from him.

She almost ran into Sydney and his dance partner as she made her way back to the stage. He smiled at her and pretended to be having a splendid time, but she knew he was miserable. Alta was out with someone else and not at the dance, and he was obviously trying to dance with as many girls as possible in her absence. Ava smiled back, tacitly promising to do her utmost to arouse her co-worker's jealousy.

Percy wanted to get away from the noise. So, they were drinking punch alone outside, and Rosemary hoped that Ava hadn't noticed their departure.

"I haven't danced like that in ages. You wore me out." He laughed, drinking half his punch in one thirsty gulp.

Rosemary smiled. She had never in her life danced that much.

"You are a better dancer than Anna."

The mention of his fiancée's name startled her, and she frowned without thinking and looked down at the glass in her hand.

"Do you not like me talking about her?" he asked with his charming, half-vexing smile.

She looked back up at him and shook her head.

"Oh, no, why would I mind. Her name is Anna then."

"Yes, it is. Anna Granberry." He looked away himself now and set his cup down on the railing in front of them.

"The truth is, Rosemary, I don't like to hear you talk about Jake or whatever his name is either." His hands were reaching for her, and she felt breathless. "You're the most real, most beautiful person I have ever known, and I like you whether I should or not."

His brown eyes were now inches from her own, and, before she could think about what he was saying, he was kissing her. His kisses were not shy, sincere kisses like Jake's, but needy, blood-rushing ones. She knew she was kissing him back, and she couldn't and didn't want to stop.

Rosemary's hands were shaking, and she felt feverish, excited, and worried all at once.

What happened? What have I done? Am I in love with him? she kept asking herself as she and Ava walked back to her house from the bus stop.

"When do you sing next?" Rosemary said, not intending to even listen to her cousin's answer.

She had staved off Ava's attention all the way home by asking her questions about the band and Edwin and pretending to listen. But she couldn't do it much longer. She was bursting inside, and soon it would all spill over. They were almost to her house.

170

"Wait," she stopped and blurted out.

"What's the matter?" Ava was agitated at being interrupted, but what she could discern of her cousin's face in the darkness curtailed her and recalled her earlier suspicions.

"I kissed Percy," Rosemary answered, relieved to have said it to someone.

Ava stared at the outline of her face, stunned by what she had just been told.

"You actually kissed him?"

"Well, he kissed me, and I kissed him back." Rosemary fell unladylike on the ground like she always chided Judith for doing.

"Do you like him?" Ava sat down just as unladylike beside her, her knees separated by green folds of dress.

"Yes, I think I've been falling in love with him for some time."

"What about Jake?"

"I don't know. I feel so awful about him." Rosemary felt sick to her stomach at the mention of his name.

She had never hurt someone like this before, and it nauseated her to think about what she was doing.

"Which one do you like more?"

Rosemary held her stomach, thinking of the right answer.

"I thought I loved Jake, but I don't see how I can if I feel like this about Percy. When Percy kissed me tonight," she paused, wondering if she was sharing too much, but went on since she had already started, "I never wanted him to stop. He makes me feel so different."

"He is very handsome."

"Yes, he is," Rosemary said, recalling the way his eyes always mocked and caressed her at the same time. "But it's his confidence, his manners, his maturity, his…."

She stopped not able to describe any more of what she felt toward him. Instead, she told Ava about eating supper with him the weekend before and about their conversations both then and tonight. As she let it all out, she knew she loved him. She could feel it in her heart. It was the strongest emotion she had ever felt for anyone, and it made her feelings for Jake seem petty and immature.

"What are you going to do about Jake?" Ava asked when she had finished.

"I don't know yet. I can't think about that tonight." Rosemary stood up and dusted off her skirt, and Ava did the same.

"You just have to decide if you would rather be with the Navy or the Army, run away with Clark Gable to Savannah or be a doctor's wife in Jacksonville, Alabama."

They both laughed, and Ava put her arm through her cousin's as they walked again toward Rosemary's house.

"If you want to be the esteemed Mrs. Percy Bledsoe or Jacksonville's next Mrs. Dr. Jake Patterson Green."

"That was mean!" Rosemary laughed at the reference to Jake's mother.

By the time they reached the house, Ava had succeeded in lightening her cousin's mood. But when Rosemary waved goodnight and closed the front door, the joy of kissing Percy and the pain of hurting Jake instantly filled her heart again.

Chapter 21

Carson threw off his sweaty work boots and socks and let the grass creep up between his toes. He hated wearing shoes in the summer. He slid down under the shade of a dogwood and opened his lunch of leftover biscuits and ham. Looking out at the field before him, he was pleased with himself and his work. Of the close to ten-acre field, he had already hoed and uprooted grass from almost a third of it. After the hoeing was finished, he would plant whatever he still could. As the first bite of buttery biscuit filled his stomach, the now familiar roar of a jeep interrupted his rest.

"Carson Stilwell," the driver yelled out over the motor.

"That's me."

"First Lieutenant Rouen. Major Thunderstrom would like a word with you."

"All right."

Carson put his lunch back in its bag. If his grandpa had been there, he would have insisted on eating first. He reluctantly pulled his socks and boots back on and climbed into the jeep.

They traveled toward the major's new office, and he paid more attention to his surroundings than he did the first time when he was reminded of his ineligibility for the service. The P.O.W. Headquarters lay on a hill to the west of the main post. They were now driving into the first of its three compounds, and Carson was drawn to a small, serene chapel surrounded by flowers and shrubbery. As they drove through the compound, he was amazed at the rows of barracks that lined each side of the dirt road and the buildings for kitchens, company orderly rooms, dispensaries, and reading rooms. The Prisoner of War Camp seemed more like a retreat than a punishment.

Just before they reached the camp's headquarters, a shout drew his attention away from the buildings to a uniformed man marching with a phalanx of prisoners just ahead. A surreal feeling of curiosity overcame him as he realized that he was face to face with the very enemy. Members of the odious German Army were only seconds from him. He leaned forward in his seat, expecting to see the cartooned images of severe German men leap into real life before him. Instead, he was shocked to see lines of young, haggard men, many younger than himself, march past him listlessly. Their faces seemed homesick and tired, and they looked more like overworked school boys than superior German war machines.

"You'll get used to seeing them around," the lieutenant said, and Carson realized with embarrassment that he was half hanging out of the jeep to look at them. "We'll have at least 3,000 of them before the month is up."

His brain swam trying to think of 3,000 Germans incarcerated so close to him. He looked once more at the lines of prisoners, and the stern, brown eyes of one met his own. The young man had prickly, unshaven cheeks, ears that stood out on both sides of his fair face, and curly, brown hair that overlapped his wind-chapped forehead. Carson smiled without thinking, and the young man looked away at the marching head in front of him.

"Are you ready, Carson?" Lieutenant Rouen called from outside the jeep.

Carson lumbered out of the passenger seat and followed the officer into the P.O.W. Headquarters building. The major was talking on the telephone but waved for them to enter anyway. With another nod of his head, the lieutenant left, and Carson waited for his turn with the major.

"Correct, sir, I'll see you at 19:00." Major Thunderstrom clicked the phone back onto its cradle and turned to Carson.

"How's the victory garden coming, son?"

"Fine, just fine, sir." Carson sat in the chair that the major motioned for him to take.

"Good. We've got some help for you. We're about to have 3,000 prisoners we need to keep busy, so I want to send at least twenty to you tomorrow. I don't care what you have them do. Just treat them with some respect and keep them working."

Carson looked back at him trying to hide his bewilderment. What was he to do with twenty Germans? The major confirmed a time with him and then dismissed him back to his work. He walked back to the field, thinking of the rows and rows of German men and the stoic face of the one who he had smiled at. He knew he was supposed to hate them, but seeing them face-to-face made hatred seem somehow impossible.

Carson dug his hands in his overall pockets and watched the prisoners carrying out his instructions. They understood more English than he expected, which made it easier to communicate with them. It felt strange huddling them up into a circle around him and explaining his plans for the

175

field and what he needed them to do. The major brought over more hoes and various tools for them to use early that morning, so everyone was able to work at the same time.

"We'll see what kind of workers they make," Private Tom Perry said and then grinned. He was the guard on duty, and he stood at the end of the field holding his gun futilely by his side.

Even if the prisoners wanted to escape, where would they go in Alabama?

"They look pretty darn good to me so far," Carson replied and returned the private's grin.

He could tell by the prisoners ease that many of them had done farm work before. A song broke out, and he looked at the men who started it. One of them was the German soldier who he had noticed the day before, and Carson watched as he sang, swung, and dug all at the same time. Other prisoners joined in, and, even though he couldn't comprehend the words of their song, he somehow knew that it was about home and love. It had a fast-moving chorus that transported them away from the present, and several even laughed as they sang. If he had just met the prisoners in town, without hearing their voices, he would have thought they were local boys just like him.

Chapter 22

It had been three weeks and three days since James left, and the mustard suitcase with its burgundy trim and handle, which had sat poised by the front door since the morning her brother left, was finally about to be moved. Ava sighed as Estelle alighted on it like a butterfly again and dropped a handkerchief into its corner. For over three weeks, she watched her sister-in-law fastidiously pack and repack the always-ready suitcase. If she had to wear something inside it, the garment was soon rewashed, refolded, and returned to its assigned place. This, however, would be the last time she would pack it. She received a letter from James yesterday telling her to leave for Texas in the morning. His letter stated that he found nothing fancy but something comfortable enough for her, which delighted Estelle and worried everyone else. Regardless of what her living arrangements would be, she was actually leaving in the morning, and Ava was almost more depressed over her leaving than she was when her brother left. She knew it was self-centered, but she didn't want to leave the quaint house. Her father's old brown suitcase also sat by the door now but was still void of any of her belongings. She looked back at Estelle who was whistling as she found another empty nook for a hairbrush. Her cheeks were pink as if James had been jesting with her, and her brown eyes were merry, dancing before her every move.

"Ava, I'll tell your mother that she should let you and Rosemary have a sleep over here while I'm away," Rosemary said, and Ava's cheeks crimsoned.

She wondered if Estelle could perceive her selfish despondency.

"It wouldn't be the same without you," Ava replied, growing hopeful despite herself.

She doubted that her mother would agree to the idea. Victoria didn't believe that young, unmarried girls should be left unsupervised overnight.

"It would make me feel better to know that someone was sleeping under our roof every so often while we're away. Houses are like people, they get lonely when left to themselves."

Ava smiled at Estelle's explanation. It seemed silly to her, but maybe her mother would fall for it out of loneliness for her son and daughter-in-law.

Early the next morning, Sheffield and Victoria arrived in James's Ford to take Estelle to the Anniston train station. Sheffield carried the mustard suitcase away from the door and to the car as his wife explained all the provisions she was sending James in a separate bag.

"I've wrapped the cake as tight as old rubber. It should still be moist when you finally get to eat it. There are also the clothes hangers he requested and a new pen and some tobacco inside. Goodness, I hope I'm not forgetting anything." Victoria indicated with the tip of her finger where each item was lodged in the bag.

"I'm sure you're not." Estelle took in one last look around her little house with all its belongings.

"Ava, keep it in order for me," she said loudly with a sly wink.

"I promise." Ava smiled, and her sister-in-law embraced her. Estelle was so happy that it seemed impossible to be sad at the moment.

Her father came back inside to usher them all out and picked up her bag in passing.

"I'll put your bag in the trunk to carry home," he said, holding the door open for the three of them.

Later that night, after her now usual Friday night date with Edwin, Ava passed by the empty house. It did indeed look lonely with no lamps lit and no sign of Estelle. Suddenly, her sister-in-law's absence stung her heart, and she stood staring up at the house and imagining Estelle fluttering about it. She then imagined James running after her, and she realized that she would miss her brother more. Without Estelle, he would seem farther and farther away.

She turned reluctantly toward her own house and could see a muffled light seeping through the curtains. Her mother was probably dosing under it as she waited up for her. Her throat grew thick with tears as she thought about not being able to recount her date to Estelle. Instead, she would have to answer all of her mother's questions and then go to bed without telling anyone what had developed in her heart that night. She unwillingly opened the front door and was surprised not to find her mother perched under the light. She peered about the room as if her absence were a bad omen.

"Ava, I'm in here," Victoria called, and Ava was startled to hear her mother's voice coming from her bedroom.

The lamp in her room was also lit, and she could hear the airy song of the music box that was her birthday present.

179

Her mother was bent over her father's suitcase, removing a cloth bag of hair clips, the last thing left in the now empty box. Ava looked around the room and could see that all of her clothes and the few things she took with her were put back in their place.

"Mom, you didn't have to," Ava said as her mother put the bag of hair clips in the first drawer of her dresser.

"I know I didn't have to. I wanted to. I've missed you being in this room."

Ava smiled. Her mother was obviously in a sentimental mood.

"Did you have a good time with Edwin again tonight?" Victoria sat down on her bed rather than leaving.

"Of course," Ava replied, not sure if sitting down herself would prolong the interview.

She decided to stand and breathed in, expecting the next question.

"I've been thinking. Since you like this boy so much and insist on seeing him every weekend, it's probably about time for your father and me to meet him."

Victoria smiled at her daughter's bulging eyes and thought how much she looked like herself but acted like her father.

"I'm sure he would like to meet you also," Ava said with uncertainty.

She knew that Edwin would fit in with her family since he came from a southern farming family himself, and she wanted them to meet, but she was afraid what would happen if they didn't like each other.

"That settles it then." Her mother stood up and pinched her cheek. "Bring him over for supper tomorrow night, and I'll cook him a Stilwell feast."

180

Ava stood stupefied trying to manage a smile. Had her mother really just asked a boy whom she was seeing over for supper? She had never had a man over for dinner before, and the suggestion of it seemed so grown-up.

"Good night," her mother said through a yawn. "I'm so glad you're back and so sad that Estelle's gone all at the same time."

Victoria shut the door behind her as her daughter always insisted. Having brothers made privacy a necessity.

Ava collapsed on her bed imagining Edwin's response when she told him they were eating supper with her parents. It was out of the question for him to refuse if he wanted to see her any longer.

Chapter 23

When her mother promised a feast, she wasn't exaggerating. Edwin was served cube steak, white gravy, biscuits, and three vegetables rather than their normal two. Ava glanced at his red ears, which had remained strawberry-colored since he was first introduced to her parents, and forced back a giggle. Everything was going much better than even she expected. So far, her mother had been charming, her father had been friendly and accommodating, her grandpa had been himself, and Carson had kept his mouth shut.

"Next week, we start training on the infiltration courses," Edwin said after swallowing another bite of steak as fast as he could.

He was having trouble eating and answering all their questions about his basic training at the same time.

"What kind of training is that?" Victoria asked, interested in everything he said.

She had been pleading with James to go into more detail about exactly what he was doing in the Army for the past two weeks. His letters home were frequent but short and told little beyond what day of the week it was, that Texas was hot and dry, and that he was well. She was glad at least that Estelle would be writing home now too.

"It's where we'll have to crawl and maneuver under live ammunition."

Victoria's face changed to one of horrification.

"They really make you do that? Won't you get enough of that in the actual war?" she said, forgetting to offer him another biscuit just as he finished his second one.

"They have to get their nerves used to the noise and the pressure," Sheffield explained for Edwin, which saved him from having to swallow another bite whole.

"You wouldn't want 'em put out there like fresh chickens, would you?" Grandpa Chester raised his thin eyebrows at his daughter.

"Does anyone ever get hurt?" Victoria ignored her father's comment.

Edwin thought of a story about a private getting his scalp grazed but said, "Nope, I haven't heard of any," instead, remembering Ava's brother James.

There was silence while everyone imagined the infiltration course, and Edwin gladly took it to finish his steak. He liked Ava's family. He could see sparks of her personality in each of them, and they had a warm affection for each other, even when they were joking, that his family lacked.

"Have you seen any of the German prisoners?" Carson broke the silence of chewing and clanging forks.

It was the first direct thing he had said to Edwin besides a casual greeting. He was acting how an older brother should always act when he first met a man who was courting his sister.

"Just in passing. We saw a bunch yesterday draining ditches and doing clearing operations at the main post."

"Major Thunderstrom sent a crew of them out to me this week to help out in the field."

Carson hadn't yet mentioned this to his family, and their reaction confirmed their surprise. His mother arched her eyebrows almost to her hairline, his grandpa and father both looked impressed, and Ava couldn't care less with Edwin at her kitchen table.

"How did they work for you?" Edwin continued his first conversation with Ava's brother, conscious of the approval he was receiving.

"Really well. They're actually decent fellows," Carson said, looking down at his plate.

"Decent fellows!" Victoria gasped. "How can they be decent fellows and be a part of all that evil Hitler man does?"

Carson just shrugged his shoulders.

"Blossom, do you have anything sweet? It's about that time for me to go fetch Brother Whatley," Sheffield reminded his wife of their supper and guest.

They all ate sweet potato pie, and the conversation reverted back to Edwin's basic training.

"How many of you can they house in one barrack?" Grandpa Chester asked.

"Oh, some five, some fifteen," Edwin said, now trying to eat pie and answer questions all at once.

"Remind me," Victoria looked at her husband, "to ask James in our next letter what sort of boys he is living with. Your mother and father are lucky to have a son who shares so much. Do you write them often?"

Ava gulped. Her mother had just raised the one subject she most dreaded, Edwin's parents. She studied his ears, which paled a little and then changed from strawberry-colored to an even deeper, tomato color.

"I try to, ma'am." Edwin cringed at the lie he was telling. In truth he wrote his mother and sister as little as possible. "Well, that is I write my mother when I can. My father has passed on."

"Oh, I'm so sorry to hear that," Victoria said, as everyone else gave him uncomfortable and sympathetic looks. "I lost my mother when I was just thirteen to Bright's disease."

Ava kicked herself under the table for not asking her parents to refrain from mentioning Edwin's father, but what good would it have done? It would have only kept the subject fresh on their minds and bound to come out one way or the other.

"Welp, I'm gone to get the preacher man." Sheffield clapped his hands on the table and stood up, signaling the end of their dinner and, gratefully, the end of their discussion about Edwin's father.

As they usually did, they listened to the radio while Sheffield went to get the preacher. When Brother Whatley arrived, he greeted Edwin as exuberantly as a prospective church member and insisted that he remembered him from the tent revival.

"You should come to church sometime with Ava."

Ava's heart sang. Now, she would see Edwin three days a week instead of two!

When Edwin left and Ava chanced a moment alone with her mother, she expected to hear her mother's favorable opinion of him. It was easy to tell that her parents liked him. Her mother was not good at hiding her feelings, and her father wouldn't have talked to him so much if he didn't like him. Instead, she was surprised when her mother asked her about Rosemary.

"Who's this older man Rosemary's been seeing?" Victoria asked with a tone of palpable disapproval.

So Rosemary did explain everything to her mother.

They had been so busy at work that she forgot to ask Rosemary how the conversation went. Her mother was scrutinizing her face, and she collected herself.

"He's a nice guy, Mom. He's a handsome lieutenant from Savannah, Georgia." She wished she had left out the word "handsome."

She was sure that Myrtle was deep in discussion with her mother about Rosemary's romantic affairs, and she wanted to be cautious what she said for her cousin's sake. Rosemary's parents were hopeful about Jake, and she didn't blame them, but she hoped their disappointment wouldn't make things difficult for her cousin.

Rosemary wiped the smile of her blissful night with Percy off her face as she entered the house. Her mother was reading the newspaper to her father as he reclined on the floor with his feet propped up in her lap, which was their usual late-night custom.

"The New York Cotton Exchange Service points out that in the last eight months the parity price of cotton has advanced," Myrtle read the Cotton Notes article, which was her father's favorite.

"Did you stay out of trouble and have a good day?" her father asked, half sitting up and offering her a cheek to kiss.

Rosemary leaned over and kissed it.

"Of course."

Her father winked his good brown eye at her.

"There's another letter for you on your bed," her mother said, also offering her a cheek to kiss.

Rosemary was angry with her mother for bringing up the letter and Jake almost as soon as she walked through the

186

door, but she kissed her on the cheek anyway. What difference did it matter to them whom she chose to love? They chose to love each other.

"Goodnight." She smiled to hide her temper.

"Goodnight," her father called, and her mother resumed the article.

Rosemary slipped into her bedroom and saw Judith's blonde ringlets peeking out from under the covers. Judith didn't have a bed of her own, and she either slept with their parents or her sister, depending on her disposition.

The letter was lying on her pillow. She peered at Jake's neat handwriting and decided to dress for bed first, knowing she couldn't ignore him much longer. She sighed at her dim reflection in the mirror and then touched the back of her neck. It was still warm from where Percy had brushed back her hair and kissed it. Thinking with all her fixed concentration on Percy, she took her time undressing and then turned back toward the letter. If she could just keep Percy's smile and words in her mind, it would make what she was about to do easier. He had already broken off things with Anna, and now she had to do the same with Jake. Deciding not to read his letter first, she took out a piece of stationary and a pen from under her bed and sat by the door. Reading his letter would only make things more difficult. In fact, she wouldn't read it at all tonight. The light from her mother's lamp fell through the crack in the door and into her lap.

"Dearest Jake," she wrote.

Feeling her heart start to panic, she quickly touched the back of her neck again and recalled Percy. She had to choose.

Chapter 24

The small, wooden bench Edwin was sitting on was as
uncomfortable as he felt. He hadn't been in church, besides the
tent revival which he didn't really count, since shortly after his
father died. He couldn't handle the way members of his church
all tried to console him after the funeral by saying things like,
"It was just God's will to take your father, son" or "God just
had to have your pa early." It made him sick just remembering
all their poor attempts at comfort. If it was God's will for his
father to die, then he didn't understand or like God. He was
also angry at their church for supporting his mother's marriage
to Davis Mathers. It was like they too forgot about his father
just days after he was laid in the ground.

"Edwin, are you not going to stand up?" Ava
whispered down to him.

He looked into her limpid eyes and remembered why
he was there. It was unreal the way a look or a word from her
could make him forget all his anger. He stood up and grabbed
hold of the half of the songbook she offered him. It was worth
coming just to stand beside her and hear her sing.

"Oh, victory in Jesus, my Savior forever," she sang.

When he didn't join her, she smiled up at him, and
when he still didn't sing, she whispered, "Can't Tennessee boys
sing?"

"I'm afraid they can't." He whispered back, and she laughed.

He never sang. In fact, he never even hummed or whistled to himself. The song ended, and they all sat down again. Victoria emerged from the side of the piano and her rich, euphonious voice split the early morning air.

"Rock of Ages, cleft for me," she sang out without any music, "let me hide myself in thee."

Her voice rang with a raw tremor as if a dozen trumpets were accompanying her, and Edwin understood Ava better. She could sing the way she did because she had been taught that way. She had been shown all her life how to fearlessly put herself and what she was feeling into every word her lips formed.

There was silence when Victoria finished the hymn, and Brother Whatley bolted up from his seat and bounded up to the pulpit. He laid his large Kings James Bible on the stand and peered out at his audience with green, fiery eyes.

"Rock of Ages, the song goes," he began, studying them for a response. "David found God to be his rock, and we, our family, and our country need Him to be our rock now more than ever."

But what if that Rock has already failed us? Edwin argued tacitly.

"The great Psalmist wrote in Psalms 18:2 'The Lord is my rock, my fortress and my deliverer'," Brother Whatley recited without opening his Bible.

Carson, who was on Edwin's other side, began flipping through his Bible, and Ava held out half of hers for Edwin to read along. He accepted it and read, although Brother Whatley was already finished with that passage and on to a second and then a third in quick succession. Ava watched him as he read and listened. She knew he wanted to be there with her, but she could feel his struggle.

After the service, they talked for a while with Rosemary's family and other church members and then went back to Ava's house for the usual Sunday afternoon meal with the preacher. When they could get away, Ava grabbed a quilt from her room and told Edwin to follow. He looked back at Sheffield and Carson to make sure he was allowed to leave with her, but no one seemed to notice. He had won their trust by going to church and eating at their table with them.

It was a sunny, cloudless day. At the door, Ava kicked off her shoes and gestured for him to do the same.

"You can't enjoy a day like this with your shoes on." She laughed, and he agreed by taking off his as well.

The grass felt crunchy and ticklish to their feet. He had to almost jog to keep up with her as they followed one of the many paths that led from the back of the house.

"After while, I'll introduce you to Dixie," Ava said.

They were passing the big barn.

"Who's Dixie?" He grabbed hold of her hand to slow her down.

Ava froze for a moment before pulling him along. It was the first time he had ever reached for her, except for when they were dancing.

"Just your biggest competition!"

"And why does your grandpa always call you Annie?" he asked, desperate to know everything about her.

"Because Mom named me after her Aunt Ava who he says was a 'despicable, intolerable old woman.' I don't believe him, though. Mom says that he just never liked her because she spoke her mind even more than he does."

190

Edwin laughed, and they stopped just behind the barn under a grove of pecan trees. The grove was on a hill, and, down below them, a creek gurgled as it poked along. She let go of his hand and motioned for him to help her spread out the blanket. He took two corners of the quilt, and they pulled it flat between them.

"This is my favorite spot," Ava said, sitting down on the sprawling blanket.

She wore a Navy dress with tiny white flowers that showed off the contrasts of her dark hair, light skin, and red mouth. Her hair wasn't black like her mother's, but it was a deep brown. He watched it fall away from her ears and neck as she reclined on her elbows and looked down at the creek.

"James and Carson used to try to fish in that creek, but there's nothing down there but tadpoles," Ava said, feeling his eyes on her.

He sat down beside her on the blanket.

"My Paw-Paw tried to fry tadpoles once."

"Yuck!"

"That's the same thing my dad said after he tried one." Edwin laughed.

"You miss your father terribly, don't you?" Ava asked without looking at him.

She was afraid she was going too far.

"Yeah, I guess I do," he answered, surprised at how easy it was to talk to her. "Things just aren't the same without him around."

"How so?"

"Well, my mother remarried for one thing, and the farm isn't doing that good, and I guess because he's just gone," he said, rolling a twig between his fingers.

191

He was struggling as he had at church, and she wanted so badly to help.

"Do you want to kiss me?" she asked, surprised at what came out of her mouth.

The twig fell from his hand, and he turned redder than she had ever seen him. The spectacle of his ears made her laugh.

"Did you know that your ears turn red when you're nervous or mad?"

"Is that so," he said, tickling her side. "And did you know that you talk when you're nervous and that you're the bravest...most beautiful girl I've ever seen?"

Edwin's face was inches from her own, and Ava didn't dare move or answer. He leaned down over her, and they kissed. His chest was touching hers, and she could feel his fast heartbeat through his clothes. She now knew what Rosemary meant when she said that she didn't want Percy to stop kissing her.

Chapter 25

The rain was lashing down and making mud holes out of the field as Carson sat dry in the shed with his work crew of prisoners. He screwed up his face, studying the checkerboard, and then relaxed it into an uncontrollable smile as he moved his red checker piece forward.

"Oh," moaned the German prisoner he was playing with when Carson's red chip leaped over and captured three of his black chips. "You play hard," he said in broken English, running both hands through his hair in frustration.

Carson laughed. The German would learn not to play checkers with a southern farmer. It was how they passed the time during rainstorms. The dark clouds that morning foretold rain, so he brought the checkerboard with him, believing their forecast. He imagined his dad and Cousin Jude were somewhere playing now also, and he wished that they were both as easy to beat as the German was.

"Start over," Albin said, beginning to pick up his remaining black chips.

"If you want." Carson laughed again, reassembling his red checker pieces into three neat rows on his side of the board. "You go first this time." He stretched out the crick in his neck from leaning over the makeshift table.

He saw his new German friend start to pick up one piece and then think better of it. It was the same young man who he had watched marching through the compound and singing in the field. Over the past couple of weeks, he had gotten to know Albin and some of the other Germans. At first, it seemed strange conversing with them, but now it didn't seem that much different from talking to Jimmy or Pete, except that the places they spoke of and the jokes they told were somewhat different from the ones he was used to. Albin reached out his hand again and slid his far left checker piece forward. Carson watched the hand that played more than the chip that was being played. Two scabbed over nubs were where two fingers should be on his right hand.

"Where did you lose those?"

"North Africa." Albin retracted his hand.

"How?" Carson couldn't help but ask, feeling as nosy as his sister was about his fights.

"Mortar wound."

Albin's answers were always short, possibly because his English wasn't perfect or possibly because he didn't care.

It was his turn, but Carson sat imagining what Albin had witnessed in Africa that he would never see. He absently moved his middle checker piece and watched Albin's nubs deliberate again.

"Do you hate being here?" he continued with some embarrassment.

"I'd rather be here than dead or had by the Russians," Albin replied without taking his eyes off the black checker piece he cautiously slid up the board.

Despite his inattention, Carson recognized the faulty move and jumped over and took two of Albin's checker pieces. The game was another short one. Albin gave up defeated and called for one of the other Germans to beat him.

"You play checkers too much," he said, lying down in the spot that Carson's new opponent had just vacated.

All of the other Germans were either asleep or smoking cigars that Carson and the now snoring guard had given them.

"Why don't you wipe that ridiculous grin off your face," Carson said to Ava later that night as he passed her on the porch.

She was reading again on the swing, but he knew that her mind was far away from nineteenth century London or wherever she was reading about this time. Ever since she had started seeing the Fort McClellan boy, she went around looking silly all the time.

"The only thing ridiculous around here is you," Ava shouted after him as he sauntered down the steps and disappeared.

It was his intention to read on the swing also, but Ava beat him to it so he walked out to the big barn and found a lumpy bed of hay to spread out on. The sun was starting to go down but was still sending slants of light through the cracks between the barn's boards. He opened up his Bible, which was his Grandpa Chester's old copy, and began to read. For some reason, he was drawn to reading it like he had never been before. He needed help sorting out his thoughts about what to do with his life now that he was a man and about his work at Fort McClellan. The Bible seemed like the logical place for him to search for clarity. His dad always read it for hours when he was making decisions or worried over the farm.

He read 1 Samuel 20, the chapter he had left off at the evening before. He liked reading about David because his life proved that God could do great things in an ordinary man's

195

life. It was the chapter about David and Jonathan's unlikely friendship, and it made him think about his own unlikely friendships with the German men he was working with. Was it wrong for him to befriend men his brother would be fighting against? He could feel something spiritual taking place within him, and it both frightened and excited him.

Chapter 26

Ava and Rosemary sat on the floor eating candy in front of James and Estelle's Emerson radio. They were in their nightgowns and surrounded by bags of coconut dips, fluffs, peanut candy, and caramels from W.T. Grant's 5, 10, and 25-cent store. Edwin and Percy were both on extended bivouac, and their mothers consented to let them look after Estelle's house for the night.

"Good evening, friends of the screeching door," came the eerie voice of the *Inner Sanctum Mysteries* host.

The slow creek of an opening door followed it. Ava giggled. The door always amused her more than anything else.

"Pass me the bag of coconut dips," Rosemary whispered.

Ava passed her the coconut candies and motioned for the bag of fluffs. They ate with their eyes fixed on the radio, even though it didn't move. They didn't want to miss a word of the horrifying tale of the "The Dead Walk at Night." The story was reaching its ghastly climax when Estelle's front door suddenly opened. They dropped their bags of candy, jumped to their feet, and faced the open door.

"Carson!" Ava screamed running to the door.

She was just in time to see his broad back vanish around the corner of the house.

"Mom said you better leave us alone!"

He was laughing now as he ran, and she slammed the door shut and walked back to the radio.

"What did I miss?"

Rosemary didn't answer as they both held their breath, and the fictional character Danny killed his fiancée with a cane.

"Until next week, good night, pleasant dreams," said the host's grisly voice when the mystery was concluded.

A news report immediately broke in, and Ava turned down the radio. She was tired now of hearing about the war. It only reminded her of the inevitability of Edwin's leaving.

"Are you going to show me the letter or not?" Ava asked, hugging her knees in expectation.

"All right," Rosemary gave in.

She reached for her bag of clothes and pulled out an envelope.

"Do you promise not to tell anyone what it says?" She held the letter back from her cousin's outreached hand.

Ava tightened her lips in exaggeration to prove her reticence on the subject and took the letter from her.

"Gosh, he responded fast. It's only been two weeks since you sent your letter."

"He had it air mailed." Rosemary sighed, watching Ava open the letter she had already opened and closed several times.

"My dear Rosemary," Ava read.

"Don't read it out loud. I already know what it says."

In truth, she was afraid that Carson might still be sneaking about thinking of another way to scare them.

Ava read on to herself.

My dear Rosemary,

I cannot begin to tell you how grieved I was to get your last letter. However, it was unfair of me to insinuate that you should remain faithful to me while I am gone. Who knows how long that will be and what will happen with this war? You must be as lonely as I am. I do not blame you, but I do hold this man accountable for his actions concerning you. You deserve only the best, Rosemary. No matter what happens, know that I remain yours and yours only.

Jake

"See! I wish he would have just balled me out or told me he never wanted to see me again rather than write that," Rosemary said when Ava stopped reading.

"I remain yours and yours only," Ava repeated.

"Stop it." Rosemary snatched the letter from her cousin's hand, folded it, and placed it back in her bag.

"How romantic he is though." Ava crossed her arms behind her head and imagined Jake's forlorn figure out in the ocean.

"To you maybe, but I feel guiltier now than I did before I wrote him."

"Well, don't be. Just think about Percy and forget about it."

Rosemary breathed in frustration. That was what she tried to do every day, but it didn't help that she wasn't getting to see Percy all weekend.

The news went off, and the Harry James Band began to play. Ava turned the radio back up and began lifting the ends of her gown and twirling in circles.

"You know Edwin's not a bad dancer," she said, collapsing again on the floor beside her downcast cousin.

"Quit thinking about that letter! Come on. Let's take a walk in the moonlight."

Ava jumped up and pulled on Rosemary's arm.

"In our night gowns?"

"Why not, it's only Carson out there, and maybe we can scare him back."

Ava bounded out the door, and Rosemary followed, her frown beginning to dissipate. Laughing in hushed whispers, they ran around the farm where Ava knew every hill, nook, and tree even in the dark. Unsuccessful in their search for Carson, they returned to the house and snuggled up under James and Estelle's covers. Ava felt strange to be in their house without Estelle. Even though it had only been for a few weeks, she still missed living with her sister-in-law.

The next morning, Ava and Rosemary got ready for work and walked over to Ava's house for breakfast. Their stomachs were still full of chocolate and caramel candies from the night before, but Ava knew that her mother wouldn't let them leave for work without a full breakfast. The scent of bacon welcomed them as they entered the front door, and its pungent smell tempted her hunger. No matter how full she was, bacon always made her ready to eat. They followed its smell into the kitchen where her father and grandfather were already eating thick pieces of it with biscuits and eggs.

"How'd you sleep?" her father asked.

"Good," Ava answered, handing Rosemary a plate.

"No bed bugs then?" Grandpa Chester said.

"Just one big one named Carson," Ava told on her brother, and Rosemary laughed as they selected two fat buttermilk biscuits from a black skillet on the wood stove and helped themselves to the bacon.

"If you want eggs, your mom said to holler. She's out back doing laundry," Sheffield said. "You have a letter from Estelle in your room."

"Just for me?"

"Just for you."

She ate a bite of biscuit and bacon and then left the table to find her letter. James's letters were always addressed to the whole family, but her father said that this one from Estelle was just to her. The letter was on her dresser, and her name was indeed alone on the envelope. Not able to wait until after breakfast, she tore it open and read.

Ava,

Here I am in the big state of Texas. It does seem as big as they claim it is with lots of open space and not very many trees. I already miss all of our trees. James found me a room to rent in a widow's house. I don't think she likes me very much, though, but the room is large and cozy enough. I don't have a place to do laundry or cook anything, which means I have to go out a lot by myself when James doesn't have a pass. I've learned to take books with me when I'm alone. There is a library nearby. Can you recommend any good books? You always were such a reader. Your brother is doing well, as I am sure you know from his letters. Believe it or not, he has actually gained a little weight. Well, I need to go to sleep. James should get a pass tomorrow, and we plan to take a long walk around town. Write when you have time. I've written my address down below. Mrs. Fletcher, the widow I am renting from, says to write my name big on the envelope where she won't open my mail by mistake.

Love,
Estelle

Ava frowned when she reached the end of the letter. Estelle sounded lonely, and she didn't understand how anyone couldn't like her sister-in-law. This old Mrs. Fletcher must be positively cold. She started to fold the letter back up, but noticed Estelle's postscript at the bottom.

P.S. I hope your mother is letting you look after the house every once in awhile.

Ava laughed and stuffed the now folded letter in the pocket of her skirt to show Rosemary on the bus. Estelle's furtive appeals to her mother had worked.

Estelle lay on her new, rented bed and tried not to look at the clock again. She could feel herself becoming desperate. Batting back tears, she tried to think brightly.

He's only an hour later than he should be if he's getting a pass, she told herself, but her fears told her otherwise.

If he wasn't there yet, he wasn't getting a pass, and she would be alone another night. Tears were now streaming down her face, and she patted them dry with her pillow. She didn't want to read again or try to make conversation with Mrs. Fletcher. The lady only glared at her as if she were encroaching on her space. She tried so hard not to touch anything in the house that wasn't in her room or make much noise.

She started a letter to her mother, but her fear of being alone again muddled her thoughts. She wished she could clean or can vegetables or do anything that would keep her busy.

After another long hour, there was a knock on her door. She sat up straight and wondered if either her crying had bothered Ms. Fletcher or her prayers had been answered. She held her breath as the door opened, and James walked in. She jumped off the bed and flung her arms around him, sobbing.

"Did you think I wasn't coming?" he asked, stroking her hair.

She nodded as joy flooded over her misery. This made it all worth it.

Chapter 27

Edwin kept his stomach and head as close to the ground as possible as he maneuvered over and under barbed wire and moved quickly across the open field. He ducked his head lower under the now steady whiz of machine gun bullets flying over him. Even with the bullets, he couldn't get the letter he just received from his sister out of his head. His stepfather was selling more of their land. He shuddered in anger, crawling even faster, and the sound of exploding dynamite jolted his body. It was night, and he could see the explosion's incandescent flames and feel their heat from where he was on the ground.

"Only a few more yards," he coached himself, and he raced on to the end of the course.

His anger was propelling him even faster than the bullets.

"Move it, Livingston," he heard Percy shouting at him.

More dynamite exploded nearby, and he dove past the finish point.

"Well done," Percy said as he held a lantern up to his watch. "You just might be the fastest one out here tonight."

Edwin smiled but said nothing. Barry was making his way through the infiltration course now, and all eyes were focused on the outline of his moving figure. Edwin didn't watch. He was breathing hard and bent over with his hands on his knees. He wanted to do it again. Even though he was tired, it felt good to push his body to its limits. He thought he would do terribly tonight. He was give out from bivouac, sleeping on the ground, and guard duty, but the anger he felt from his sister's news rejuvenated him, and he needed to let it out. Actually, he needed to see Ava. The weekend was miserable without her. He stood up and pictured her face the way he last remembered it. It was the way she looked after he kissed her for the first time. Her gray eyes were fastened on his, and she was smiling up at him as if she wanted to be kissed again.

"You were flying!" Barry clapped a hand on Edwin's back.

The picture of Ava in his mind faded, and he grinned at his friend.

"Was I?"

He could feel gratification over his performance swelling up inside of him alongside his anger at his family and passion for Ava.

The next morning, they were up at 6:30 for calisthenics, rifle inspection, and then rifle practice at Bandholtz Rifle Range. The last was what Edwin looked forward to more than anything else in his training. His dad had taught him how to shoot a gun, and he liked showing off what he knew best. Everything else about his father might be taken away from him, but no one could take away what was in his head.

He raised the Endfield close to his ear, like his father would have done, and shot. The bullet was dead on its target. Lowering his gun and relaxing his shoulders, he watched Sydney fire next to him. The bullet missed, and he laughed as Sydney cussed.

"What's so funny, Winn?" Sydney took aim again.

This time, his bullet hit the right side of the target. Edwin raised his gun again and fired. Sydney whistled as his friend's bullet hit the target dead on for the second time in a row.

"What a lousy shot," Sydney said and then laughed. "Let me show you how it's done."

Edwin watched as Sydney's bullet grazed the target. They both laughed.

"It takes more talent to barely hit the target than to hit it straight in the middle every time. Where's the talent in that?"

They finished their practice and started back for lunch. Percy caught up with them and asked Edwin to wait behind. Edwin obediently fell behind his squad. When they were at the fort, Percy made it clear that he wanted to be treated as their lieutenant and superior. Percy stopped, and Edwin stood by him at attention.

"Relax, Livingston." Percy smiled, dropping his commanding posture. "I just wanted you to know that I'm recommending you for corporal."

"What?" Edwin asked and relaxed his stance.

He was now talking to the Percy he knew on the weekends.

"You've out-shot and out-maneuvered everyone on your squad, so you're going to be a corporal."

Edwin could see the door of Wakefield's but not yet Ava. He couldn't wait to see her. He needed her to calm the frustration and excitement of his week with the more sweet excitement that she aroused within him. He could see her now. She had already spotted him and was smiling across the road at him. Her hair was even shorter, but he liked it. It made her neck and ears more visible. He waited for another car to pass and then ran across the street to her. He wanted to kiss her right there in public but grabbed her hand instead. Then, not able to resist, he touched her lips with his own.

"Edwin Livingston! We're in the middle of town!" Ava hit him playfully with her purse.

"I'm sorry, but I couldn't wait any longer," he said but threatened to kiss her again.

She had become the most important person in his life.

Chapter 28

"It seems to me I've heard that song before. It's from an old familiar score," Ava sang. "I know well that melody."

"I could look at you all night," Percy whispered in Rosemary's ear as he stood behind her and held her around the waist.

Rosemary's cheeks grew warm from his touch and admiration. They were listening to Ava sing, but she couldn't have repeated a word of her cousin's song.

"You like my new dress, then?" she asked and bit her lip.

The question sounded too forward once it was out, and her face grew hot with embarrassment. She was wearing her first store-bought dress. The plum-colored material of the dress's skirt fell lightly over her hips and bunched into a thick waistband that was high and tight across her stomach. The dress's sleeves were slightly puffed and made of the same light material, but the bodice was rayon and black with coordinating plum flowers. There was nothing inappropriate about the dress, but it flattered her figure in a way her other dresses didn't, and she was somewhat uncomfortable in it. She thought more confident girls, like Alta or Ava, should be wearing it, not her.

"It's very becoming on you, but I like the girl in the dress better," he told her, and her stomach took the familiar and giddy turn it always did when he was close to her.

"You didn't go out with anybody else in this dress last weekend when I wasn't around, did you?"

"Maybe not, but you shouldn't stay away too long or I might."

He laughed, and his cheek brushed against hers as he held her tighter. She closed her eyes as he held it there but opened them up when the band suddenly stopped playing. Shouting could be heard near the stage. Percy let her go. She could see glimpses of her cousin crying out for help and what looked like Edwin and a very clumsy-fisted soldier fighting it out. She turned toward Percy, but he was no longer next to her, and the crowd surrounding the fighting men was now too dense to see anything more. Moments later, Percy and another officer were escorting Edwin and the soldier he had been fighting with out the door. Ava found her. She was shaking all over, but her eyes were livid with excitement.

"What happened?" Rosemary asked.

"I finished my song and was walking back to Edwin when this drunken soldier asked me to dance. I told him I couldn't, but he grabbed me from behind anyway and started dancing. The next thing I saw was Edwin knocking him to the floor." Ava clasped her trembling hands and smiled irresistibly.

She knew it was terrible to feel so happy, but it was the most romantic thing anyone had ever done for her. He had fought for her, and she was in love with him now more than ever. Alta and Sydney appeared on her other side, and Ava repeated her story. She couldn't help but enjoy telling Alta, the girl who every man fell in love with, that a man had actually fought for her.

"He'll certainly get a balling out and extra KP duty for this," Sydney said. "I don't think you'll be seeing Winn tomorrow."

Ava's smile vanished. She was looking forward to another Sunday afternoon with Edwin. In her romanticism, she hadn't thought about him being punished. He rescued her from an inebriated beast which was, to her, not a reason to be reprimanded.

Even though she might have to endure a Sunday without him, Ava's heart soared when she thought of what Edwin had done for her. When she returned home that night, she couldn't resist telling her mother about it.

"This soldier who tried to dance with you was drunk?" Victoria's eyes peered at her daughter underneath raised eyebrows.

Ava's countenance fell. Her mother was focusing on the morality of the situation not the feelings Edwin demonstrated for her and how he had protected her.

"I think so."

"Someone needs to talk to Valencia Boozer about the kind of boys that are coming to these events. I thought she said they were all 'nice young men'," Victoria mocked her friend.

"They are," Ava said in exasperation, wondering why she ever tried to talk to her mother about this. "Well, most of them are. It's not her fault that some choose to misbehave before they come."

"She's in charge, though."

Ava stretched and made ready for bed. She wanted to escape the conversation. Her hand was on the door to her room when her mother called after her.

"Your Edwin is a nice boy."

Ava smiled. Maybe her mother did remember what it was like to be young and in love.

Chapter 29

Carson filled up a brown paper bag with tomatoes, peas, and corn. He wanted to present the first successful fruits of his crop to Major Thunderstrom. He was proud of his work. With the help of the German prisoners, he managed to save most of the corn and have an exceptional crop of peas. It was a hot day, but he was used to working in the heat. He rolled up his sleeves, gathered up the bag, and walked to the major's office, hoping the vegetables would prove himself to the officer. He would remember to mention how hard the prisoners worked with him.

Major Thunderstrom wasn't in, but his secretary said he could find him at Remington Hall. Carson shifted the bag to his other arm and followed the soldier's directions to the officer's club. It was located on Buckner Circle, directly across from post headquarters. The hall had the same red-tile roof as other buildings at the fort, but there was something ornate and distinguished about it that differentiated it from all the other buildings. Three tall arches accented the entrance, and a vertical sundial hung high over its doors.

Carson walked into a large room with a vaulted ceiling and dark wooden beams. On each side of the room were unlit fireplaces, and several officers were standing around talking and smoking. One was leaving, and Carson inquired about Major Thunderstrom's whereabouts.

"He's in there." The officer pointed to an adjoining room to their left

"Thanks," Carson said, and he tried to walk inconspicuously past the talking men.

Maybe he should have waited until the major was back in his office, but it was too late now. A large wooden bar jutted out into the center of the room, and tables and chairs surrounded it and lined the windows looking out onto Buckner Circle. What arrested Carson's attention, though, were the half-finished murals running across the top five feet of each wall. A man with his back turned away from him was holding a paintbrush and contemplating the wall in front of him.

"Carson," Major Thunderstrom called out.

The major was sitting alone at a table drinking coffee and working through a stack of legal-size paper.

"Do you have something from our humble victory garden?"

Carson put the bag on the table in the space that the major cleared of papers. Major Thunderstrom stood and rummaged through the vegetables. Carson shifted his weight uneasily as the outcome of his labor was examined.

"Now, we can have some real home cooking around here." The major grinned.

Carson smiled under his praise.

"You were able to save the corn?"

"Most of it. The prisoners you sent were very helpful."

"I'm glad they could be of service. Did you notice what they're doing to this place?"

Carson followed his eyes to the murals.

"It seems that three of them are artists, so we're letting them keep their paintbrushes wet."

213

The man painting turned at the mention of his work, and Carson was surprised to see Albin. His German friend nodded at him, and he nodded back.

"You know him?"

"Yes, he's one of the men you sent out to me for awhile."

"Get him to tell you about his work, then. It's interesting."

When Carson finished his conversation with the major, he followed his advice and walked over to Albin. He watched him work without saying anything at first. He was painting with his injured hand and held his brush awkwardly with three fingers instead of five. The picture was of a young woman with dark hair, and he was beginning to paint her hat and add slender shoulders to her delicate neck.

"You see what I do while you play checkers." Albin laughed, and Carson laughed with him.

"Do you like my paintings?" he asked without turning around.

"Yes, they're good," Carson replied, amazed by his ability to paint with a maimed hand.

"My wife," Albin told him as he concentrated on the curve of the lady's hat.

"She's pretty." Carson looked at the unfinished lady and at the pictures already finished on different parts of the wall.

The woman was sitting with a man wearing a hat, plume, and fancy clothing, and, surrounding the door, a pair of old soldiers in helmets held a goose and peered across at a another woman with long hair. The outline of a battle scene and a man holding a rock high over his head was on another part of the wall.

"The pictures look Spanish, like buildings here," Albin explained. "They will tell a soldier's life."

Carson looked back at the woman. Even unfinished, she was the best part of the murals so far.

"You like my wife? I like her too. Come back and see her beauty when she's finished," Albin said, dipping his paintbrush in a small pool of red egg and clay mixture.

Victoria ran her fingers through Carson's bag of peas.

"They look mighty tasty," she said.

"Major Thunderstrom insisted that I bring home a mess of 'em." Carson now enjoyed his mother's approval.

"I think we'll have some for supper," Victoria decided.

Ava walked in from work and sat down at the table.

"My feet are so sore. I had to stand all day today." She groaned and rubbed her tender right foot.

"They wouldn't hurt that bad if you wouldn't wear those ridiculously high heels everyday like I told you. Ava, I need you to shell some of Carson's peas for supper tonight."

Ava rolled her eyes at her brother when their mother turned away, and Carson laughed inaudibly and pointed his finger at her. He knew she hated shelling as much as he hated shoveling manure. Victoria turned back around, and Ava went to the wash pan to wash her hands as Carson started out the door.

"Carson, help your sister. I need them quick if they're going to be supper."

Carson slouched back to the table, and, when their mother moved back to the stove, it was Ava's turn to laugh. Now his peas weren't so much fun.

215

Later that night, Carson lay on his bed thinking of Albin's maimed hand painting a picture of his wife. He would have to go back to the officer's club and see the mural when it was finished. It was still strange to discover the everyday passions of the German prisoners. Before he knew them, he imagined them as cold, unfeeling human beings, but now he knew that their hearts beat in a common rhythm. His wife was remarkably pretty. He got up out of bed, lit his lantern, and took his Bible down from his shelf. As was his habit now, he would have to read before he could stop his mind from working and go to sleep.

Chapter 30

"Will you write to me when I leave?" Edwin asked Ava as they sat together by the creek on another Sunday afternoon.

"Will you remember me when you leave, Corporal Livingston?"

She loved calling him corporal. He tried to act like it was of no importance to him, but his face shone every time she referred to him in that way.

"I might remember that I knew a girl from Alabama once." Edwin laughed and drew her to his chest. "Now, how could I ever forget you?"

"Just to make sure, you need to write to me everyday," she said more seriously than she intended.

Something in her gravity silenced them both for a moment and provoked him into telling her what he told very few.

"I'm afraid I'm not the best writer." He turned his eyes from her gaze to the cooing creek.

"You just have to improve then, don't you?" Ava laughed, patting his coarse cheek and then running her fingers back over it.

He smiled and then kissed her, loving the way she challenged, rather than pitied him.

"You should start writing me every day now to practice," she said with her earlier hint of seriousness.

They were both beginning to realize that his time at Fort McClellan was coming to a swift end.

"You won't make fun of my letters?"

"Only if you misspell my name."

He kissed her again.

"You'll just have to teach me how to spell it, songbird."

"What did you just call me?" she asked, sitting up straight and tucking her bare feet underneath her.

"Ugh, songbird," he replied as his ears grew red.

It was what he called her in his private thoughts.

"I like it."

She smiled, leaned over, and kissed him herself this time.

Someone was at the front door, but Rosemary didn't bother to see who it was. It was probably Sheffield or one of the Gunter boys to talk to her father. Besides, she was snuggled up with Judith reading *Jack and Beanstalk*, her sister's favorite fairytale.

"Rosemary," she heard her mother calling her.

Her voice sounded unnatural, and she wondered what could be the matter. She took one of Judith's fat little fingers and placed it where she was leaving off.

"Now, don't you lose our spot," she said and left her with the open book.

As soon as she left her room, her eyes were locked in Percy's. He was standing at their front door with his hat in his hands. They weren't the proud, spiteful brown eyes she was used to encountering. Instead, they looked troubled. He smiled, and she blushed, realizing that her parents had never even seen him before. She looked to her mother and then to her father. Her mother looked back at her uneasily as her father examined the man who had just entered his front door. He wasn't used to being around men of distinction, and Percy was wearing his uniform with his lieutenant's markings.

"Hi, Rosemary," he broke the silence. "I just apologized to your parents for coming so late, but I...I...got an unexpected pass and had to see you."

He was never unnerved, and it alarmed her.

"Thank you, Mr. and Mrs. Bonds, for letting me come in," he spoke more politely to her parents than he even spoke to his superior officers.

"It's nice to finally meet you. We've heard so much about you," Myrtle said and an anxious giggle escaped her lips.

She looked sternly at her husband, who still hadn't said anything to the young man. Jude cleared his throat and focused his good eye on Percy as his glass one wandered around the room.

"Yes, our daughter talks about you often," he said.

"I think we'll take a walk," Rosemary announced.

She knew he wasn't there to meet her parents tonight. Judith was now in the room, and Percy smiled down at her.

"You must be Judith. I've been wanting to meet you," Percy said, and the little girl stared back up him and giggled much like her mother.

Rosemary led him out the door. Something was wrong. She was never able to see him on a Sunday. He had too much work to do. It was dark, and they walked away from the house. She didn't know where she was leading him. He gripped her hand, and she turned toward him.

"Percy, what's wrong? What's happened?" she asked as he sank to his knees in the grass.

He was crying too much to answer at first.

"My brother Robert is dead."

She cradled his head to her chest and ran her fingers through his hair.

"When did you find out?"

She couldn't see his tears, but she could feel them against her skin, and they made her hurt for him.

"This afternoon, my father sent me an urgent telegraph. I had to see you."

She touched his face and kissed his eyes, his cheeks, and then his mouth, wishing her caresses were magic water. His arms encircled her waist, and he pulled her down to him. She kissed him fervently as he cried, her heart beating with his and sharing his pain.

Chapter 31

The next morning at Wakefield's, Alta met them at the door with a flash of her hand. Ava and Rosemary both stood aghast looking down at the thin gold band that adorned her left hand.

"Sydney and I got married!" Alta said before they could respond.

"You didn't!" Ava grabbed her friend's hand and took a closer look at the wedding ring. "When did you decide to get married?"

The news was stunning considering their turbulent relationship and Alta's romantic fickleness.

"Yesterday. It was so sweet. We were having a picnic, and he just got on his knees and asked. He said he couldn't wait until he got back, and I couldn't think of a good reason why he should have to."

Ava could have given her several reasons, but she just smiled at her friend's impulsive happiness.

"Where did you get married?" Rosemary asked as Alta's ring finger moved from Ava's hand to her own.

"We went to my pastor's house right away and just did it."

"How did your parents take the news?" Ava said, thinking of the prestigious Tyler family and their protective esteem for their only child.

"Oh, they were angry all right, but they'll get over it. As a matter of fact, mother is already planning a reception for Saturday night, which you are both invited to. She wouldn't dare let her daughter get hitched without some sort of public acknowledgement. I think she always wanted me to get married in a big, fancy ceremony, where she and dad could throw their money around. Boy, did I surprise them!"

Mrs. Crockett gave them a warning look as she passed to turn the sign around from "closed" to "open," and they reluctantly got to work. Douglas humored them all morning by calling Alta "Mrs. Alta," and Mrs. Crockett even took a break to examine the new ring.

Finally, at lunch, they could continue their conversation.

"I still can't believe you're married," Ava said, mesmerized by the glint of gold that ascended and descended from the table as they ate.

"It's true all right." Alta smiled

"Why didn't you want to wait?" Rosemary asked, also watching the ring as the hand that wore it reached for a glass of water.

"Why not? I love Sydney, and married girls have more fun, if you know what I mean." Alta winked, and Rosemary's cheeks flushed to the color of the red-checkered tablecloth.

Ava laughed but noticed the fleeting look of degradation on her cousin's face. There was something strange about her behavior today. They spent the rest of the lunch break listening to Alta's honeymoon plans for the furlough that all the soldiers were hoping to get before going overseas. The plans made it hard for Ava to swallow the rest of her sandwich. She couldn't believe that it was almost time for Edwin to leave Anniston and enter the war.

"I didn't think we would ever be here again," Edwin whispered as he escorted Ava through the front doors of the Tyler mansion for the second time.

Ava glanced back at Rosemary and laughed. Her cousin's eyes were growing round at the prodigious house. Percy, however, looked unimpressed and nonplussed in the Tylers' environment.

White orchids with pink centers covered the banisters and doorways and sat in clusters on tables, sending out their sweet fragrance in all directions. Candles were lit in every window and cast a soft glow upon the house. Waiters wandered about with trays of cheeses, fruits, and tall wine glasses held high.

Sydney and his new wife stood together in the center of the large foyer. Alta's short blonde hair was arranged in tight ringlets around her head, and she wore a white suit and white pearls around her neck and on her ears. Her cheeks and mouth were pink like the centers of the flowers that filled the room, and she looked like the queen of the orchids. Sydney was by her side in his best uniform. His cheeks were smooth, his hair was trimmed, and his captivating smile, that Ava once thought she was in love with, never left his tanned face as he greeted person after person. Even the Tylers' immense dwelling looked full, as family members, business associates, and Anniston nobility streamed into the house.

"Have you seen Mrs. Crockett yet?" Alta whispered to Ava and Rosemary when they reached the front of the receiving line.

"No," Rosemary whispered back, and she and Ava both peered around the room for their boss.

"She's wearing that silk blue dress that was in the window last week." Alta giggled, and they laughed with her.

"You look stunning," Ava said.

"Why, thank you." Alta patted her blonde curls like the movie star Ava thought she was.

"What wedding song are you singing for us tonight?" Sydney smiled down at Ava after talking with Percy and Edwin.

Even if he didn't choose to love her, he was still enamored with her voice.

"I don't think I'm singing," Ava answered.

"Oh! You have to, Ava. I've already told mother you would. There's a pianist. Just tell him a song, and he'll play anything," Alta said as they moved down the line toward her parents.

Edwin and Ava stood near the piano waiting for her cue. She bit her lip and glanced around the room. Singing for the genteel class of Anniston would be different from singing for rowdy soldiers or easy-to-please church members.

"Quit fretting. You always sound beautiful when you sing," Edwin said to comfort her unusually excited nerves.

She smiled at his faith in her but continued to look around the room, imagining what various persons would think of her.

"You're not nervous because you're singing for Sydney are you?" he asked, silencing her apprehensions with his awkwardly jealous question.

"What?" She laughed and forgot for a moment about her impromptu performance.

"I used to think you cared for him."

"I never seriously liked him. I just," she looked away embarrassed, "thought I did because he paid me such attention, more than you did when we first met."

Edwin didn't have time to respond. Alta was calling for Ava to sing. The pianist was as talented as promised. He effortlessly accompanied Ava on the new song she was learning with the band. Edwin's innocent question occupied her mind as she sang "Sentimental Journey" for the wedded couple. Returning the groom's smile at that moment, she believed herself. She was never comfortable at first with any man with whom there existed a possibility of romance, and Sydney had overcome that part of her with his assiduous attention. That was it. It was how he made her feel that she once liked. The song ended with garish applause, and the toasts began.

Percy made fun of Mr. Tyler's old-fashioned whiskers as the father of the bride saluted the newlyweds.

"I think he believes it's still Civil War times," he whispered in Rosemary's ear, and she suppressed a giggle. "Sydney's going to have a time with those in-laws."

He put his arm around her waist, and she placed her fingers over his. Her hazel eyes, which looked almost emerald tonight next to her green dress, watched as Alta accepted her father's well wishes.

"To my beloved daughter and her new husband, who is serving our country so valiantly." Mr. Tyler raised his Champagne glass high.

He and his wife were consoling their anger at their daughter's sudden marriage with artificial patriotism over her marrying a soldier. Rosemary watched Percy raise his glass with

225

a hundred others all across the room and then swallow its contents. He felt her eyes on him, and he smiled down at her.

"Here, try just one harmless sip."

She shook her head, but he persisted until she took the glass from him and sampled the champagne. It burned as it went down her throat, and he laughed as she screwed up her nose, gave him back his glass, and quickly sipped her punch to rid her mouth of the foul taste.

"How do you drink that stuff?"

"I guess I'm used to it." He shrugged, charmed by her innocence. "I wish I could kiss you right now."

His smile and attraction to her emboldened her, and she whispered what she had been thinking all night.

"I would do for you what Alta did for Sydney." She looked up at him, her whole heart shining in her veracious eyes.

His smile began to fade and then broadened into one of arrogance as he took another thirsty gulp. She could feel her heart beginning to break under the small gesture, and she looked away from him, despising her unaccustomed boldness.

"I couldn't let you do that," he said softly, turning her chin back in his direction.

"Why not?" she asked, as he brushed a strand of hair away from her flustered face.

"What would happen to Alta if Sydney didn't come back? She shouldn't be a widow at eighteen."

Rosemary looked away and saw Sydney and Alta dancing. His swarthy cheeks were glowing, and his body, which moved with youthful energy and agility, was lean from weeks of hard physical training. She couldn't imagine him without life.

226

"When I think about what it must be like now for Irene…," he started and then stopped, emotion thick in his voice at the thought of his dead brother and widowed sister-in-law.

Rosemary grasped both of his hands in hers and gazed up at him.

"I'm so sorry," she said, and while everyone was watching the bride and groom, he wrapped his arms around her.

The reception festivities ended, and Ava and Rosemary both embraced the new bride in farewell. The house was as luminous and enchanting when they were leaving as when they entered, and Ava felt as though she were leaving a fairyland never to be seen again. She would never have a party like this when she got married. She inhaled the fresh aroma of the orchids once more and closed her eyes, absorbing the soft piano music.

Rosemary was leaving without a second thought to the house. Instead, her cheeks colored every time she thought about the temerity of suggesting that she would marry Percy. She knew he felt her discomfort by the way he kept making jokes and caressing her hand. They had almost reached the door when a well-known face stopped her cold in her step. It was Jake's mother. Though her hair was wispy and thin, it had the same blonde hue as her son's, and her eyes, which could look so haughty, were the same supple green. She was conversing with some of Atla's relatives, but her eyes were fixed upon Rosemary and Percy. There was something accusatory in the way she smiled and turned away, and Rosemary felt mortified. She should have remembered that the

Greens know everyone in north Alabama and would probably be at any event of this social magnitude.

"It's o.k.," Percy said where only she could hear. "I want to be with you just as much. Our time will come."

She smiled up at him. She wouldn't tell him who was in the room with them and who had unexpectedly come to her mind.

Chapter 32

Victoria gathered the family around to read their latest letter from James. She smiled as she broke the letter's seal, which she had been impatiently waiting to do all afternoon. Because James's letters were for the entire family, the entire family had to read them together, and she was aggravated at her daughter for practicing longer than usual with the band.

Ava sighed when her mother read her brother's customary greeting of, "Hi family." She preferred Estelle's personally addressed letters much more, because she could read them in private and whenever she liked.

"It's still all heat and sand out here. I've been sleeping with no covers," Victoria read on with a frown, and Ava stifled a giggle.

She knew her mother was tired of James's letters always beginning with a weather report. She wanted to know more about what he was eating, who he was befriending, and what sort of training he was engaging in.

"I passed the gunner's exam today." Victoria now smiled but looked puzzled. "What's that?" she asked looking up at her husband.

"Some sort of test for the mortars, I believe. Read on, though, he'll probably tell us if you keep reading."

"I scored a 96 out of a 100 and made first class gunner. We got a jeep stuck in the mud yesterday and had a swell time getting it out. By the way, how is the car, Carson?"

"He's always thinking about that car!" Victoria paused, frustrated that he didn't give more explanation about the test he did so well on. What would she tell the garden club?

"Tomorrow, we are going on a fifteen mile hike, which sure won't be fun. In answer to your questions, we mainly eat meat, potatoes, carrots, and pudding. I have made several friends. There is a guy in my company named Wilson who is from Moultrie, Alabama. Tell everyone else hello for me. Love always, James. P.S. I am enclosing letters from Estelle. Since G.I.s get postage free, I had her give me all of her letters to mail," Victoria finished reading.

"First class gunner, is that what he said?" Grandpa Chester asked as his daughter handed him the letter on top, which was his from Estelle.

"Sure did," Sheffield answered.

"Doesn't Bernadette Dempsey have cousins in Moultrie?" Victoria said.

"I believe so," Sheffield replied, receiving his letter.

"I'll have to see if she knows a Wilson. A last name would have been helpful, though." She made a mental note to ask for Wilson's surname in her next letter to Texas. "Carson, you better write your brother about that car before he goes bananas."

She handed her son his letter.

"I will." He was ashamed at his lack of writing to his brother. In truth, he had barely thought about the car or writing letters since going to work at the fort.

They each went their separate ways with their letters from Estelle.

Ava finished her letter and fell back on her pillow thinking about her sister-in-law. She was convinced that Estelle enjoyed writing her the most because, to her, she could share herself. She wrote Sheffield and Victoria about all the things they wanted to know that James left out of his letters. She wrote Grandpa Chester and Carson about all the funny and unusual happenings on an Army base. She wrote her own mother and sisters an always overly sunny report about her living arrangements and life as a soldier's wife. But, to Ava, she wrote more of what she was doing and feeling. Ava felt honored to be her confidante, and, without being asked, she knew what things she could tell her mother and what things Estelle would want left untold. Ava looked back over part of the letter and smiled. Estelle was happier, and she was glad. She attended a dinner for soldiers' wives provided by the Y.M.C.A. and met another wife living near the base. The woman's name was Opal, and she was from Vermont.

How exciting to meet people from so far away.

She smiled thinking of Barry's jokes and northern accent and wondered if Opal talked like Barry. Estelle was also working for the Red Cross making bandages and boxes of medical supplies. Ava was relieved that she wasn't stuck in the house all day anymore with that reproachful Mrs. Fletcher. She got up and tucked the folded letter in her lingerie drawer with all the other letters she had received from Estelle. Beside it was a new pile of letters, tied carefully together with a red bow. It was the first of her letters from Edwin. The ones she was making him write her for practice. She laughed thinking about his rudimentary language and dry correspondence. She would have to ask him to let her be his confidante too and write more about what was going on in his heart and head than about his day-to-day activities. Of course, she wanted to know the other, but she wanted to know the man more. She laughed again, remembering his confession of it taking him twenty minutes to write her two lines. She pulled out the stack of letters and kissed the top one. She didn't care how short they were. She loved every misspelled word and awkward sentence.

"Want me to beat you at checkers again?" Carson ducked his head in her doorway.

She placed the letters back in her drawer. She certainly didn't want him of all people knowing about them.

"I suppose I could beat you again," she said, leaving the room and letters behind.

Chapter 33

Edwin hadn't stopped smiling since they met, and Ava couldn't help but laugh at his anomalous demonstration of emotion. It was nice to see his usually firm face contorted by helpless smiles. He looked carefree and handsome in his uniform as he leaned across the table and took her hand. It was evident that he had something important to tell her.

"Now that our basic training is finished," he began.

Her face changed from one of expectancy to apprehension, and her hand fell limp in his.

"Don't give me that face." He laughed, caressing her palm. "It's not about that. I'm getting a three-day furlough!"

She looked back at him blankly, still thinking about the nearness of his leaving for the war.

"I'm sure your mother and sister will be glad to see you," she said, trying to smile with him.

"Nope, because I'm going to spend it here with you!"

A smile as big as his now upturned Ava's ruby lips, and she pressed his hands with hers.

"Won't they be mad?" she asked out of politeness for the mother she had never met.

"Why should they be? I'm not telling them. I don't care about seeing them. I just want to be with you."

His ears turned red from the revelation. It was still difficult for him to tell her what he felt for her.

"Edwin," she paused, trying to eradicate the look of pleasure from her eyes. "You can't hide from your family forever. You'll have to face them again."

"I know." He sighed, gripping her hands harder. "It's not about them. I just want to spend as much time with you as I can. Who knows when I won't have our weekends to get me through the week anymore."

He stopped. He was telling her too much. Her gray eyes were fastened to his, and he could feel his blood racing through his veins the way it always did when she was near.

They both barely touched the rest of their supper as they made plans for their extended time together. She wished he could stay at James and Estelle's house, but she knew her mother would never hear of it. He paid their ticket, and they walked to the Alabama Hotel.

"It'll be too expensive. Couldn't you just stay at the fort?" Ava pulled him back.

"Then it wouldn't be a furlough. They would find someway to put me to work," he said, still clasping her hands in excitement. "I don't care about the money. It'll be worth it."

He pulled her toward the door, and she pulled him back again.

"I can't go in there with you." She laughed. "We're not married."

He flushed, realizing what she was telling him.

"Oh." He grinned, running his free hand though his auburn hair. It was the longest Ava had ever seen it.

"Go on. I'll wait for you here," she told him, withdrawing her hand.

He kissed her forehead and almost ran inside the door, and she waited behind, laughing at his enthusiasm. When a family passed, she moved to the side of the walkway. Then,

realizing her situation as an unmarried woman in front of a
hotel, she began looking with disinterest at the window
displays of the surrounding stores. Bored, she fidgeted with her
purse, wondering what was taking him so long. The door
opened, and she looked up to see a porter with his arms full of
luggage exiting the hotel. A pale, depressed young woman and
her mother were following him. She fell to imagining what
could have saddened the girl until the door swung open again.
This time it was Edwin. He was looking for her, and she waved
to him. His face was beaming, and her heart beat as his eyes
told her what his lips still couldn't.

Percy laughed at Mickey Rooney's harebrained
onscreen character. Rosemary tried to laugh along, but the
sound of her voice was hollow and hypocritical. She could not
concentrate on the movie. She glanced at Percy's face to be
sure that he hadn't ascertained her true mood. She didn't want
to ruin what could be their last night together. Now that his
training was complete, she was afraid of what would happen
next. He was leaving for furlough tomorrow, but what if he
came back only to be shipped immediately overseas? She was
jealous of Ava and wished Percy was spending his furlough
with her as Edwin was spending his with Ava. She knew it was
selfish of her, so she wouldn't dare ask it of him. What would
his family think of her if she should ever meet them? He had
already made plans to go home. Ever since he came to her
after learning of his brother's death, she felt increasingly
desperate over him. Her eyes stung as they filled with
frustrated tears, and she tried unsuccessfully to laugh at the
movie again. It seemed absurd to her to be sitting next to him
without talking when she might not be able to talk to him for
so long. She couldn't make him stay with her, but she could

235

make him give her his attention. She squeezed his hand and then pretended to be immersed in the movie when he looked down at her. Blood rose to her guilty face as she felt his eyes on her.

"Let's go," he whispered close to her ear.

He pulled her up from her chair, and she followed him down the aisle and out the door of the theater. The lights of the advertisements flashed mockingly bright, and the air was thick. They walked down Noble Street and out to Zinn Park. They had never walked in this park together, and she wondered when he had been there before.

"You didn't want to see the end of the movie?" she asked with false cheerfulness.

"I would rather see you," he said, laughing in such a conceited manner that she knew her acting hadn't fooled him.

"Would you?" She refused to look at him.

They both understood that she was talking about more than just the movie or the furlough.

"Rosemary, it pains me every time I think about not seeing you." He stopped walking and forced her to look at him.

She could see the confident sparks of his brown eyes in the moonlight, and she knew that if anyone survived the war, it would be him. He was too proud and self-assured not to, but it wasn't his inviolable vulnerability that somehow frightened her. He kissed her with a longing that proved his words, and she felt like her heart was collapsing under her attachment to him.

"I'll come home early the last day of my furlough and see you," he promised, and she felt a relief that she didn't understand.

236

With the tension between them now resolved, she could laugh with him, and they walked back and forth through the park until the last bus call of the night.

Edwin sat next to Ava at his now usual place at the Stilwell table. All of the dishes were still passed to him first, except in the presence of Brother Whatley, and he took liberally from each one to fit in with the men of Ava's family and please her mother. Victoria believed that men should eat as heartily as women should eat sparingly, and she smiled at Edwin every time he filled his plate with a second helping.

"Do you believe that every person who comes to faith has a 'Road to Damascus' type experience?" Carson asked without turning his eyes from the turnip greens and tomatoes that he was mixing together with his fork.

He didn't want to see the pleased smiles his parents were undoubtedly sending his way over him asking such a serious question. Ava held in a sigh of exasperation and looked across the table at her brother. She couldn't believe that after all their mutual jokes about the pastor's never-ending sermonizing that he would actually encourage him in it.

"Well, son," Brother Whatley settled back in his chair and balanced his fork in the air thoughtfully. "I believe they do. Not as dramatic of course, even though a man over in Talladega once told me God struck him dumb, but I do think the Holy Spirit prods at each person's heart."

After answering Carson's question, the pastor dove into his sermon once again, and they all ate faster. Ava was embarrassed that their mealtime conversation wasn't more entertaining for her guest, and she kept trying to catch Carson's eye to serve him a stern look.

Finally, Grandpa Chester, who cared as little for the second dose of preaching than his granddaughter did, shifted Brother Whatley's focus.

"All the papers are saying that Italy will be in the bag any day now," he said as his daughter set a large slice of sweet potato pie in front him.

No matter who was at the table, he was still the first one to get dessert.

"I've been reading the same thing," Brother Whatley returned, easily changing his course of conversation from spiritual matters to war matters.

They talked about the probable events of the war till the meal was finished, and Ava was pleased that her parents asked for Edwin's opinion more than once on the subject.

After lunch, Ava and Edwin walked through the fields, listened to the radio, and played checkers with Carson until her mother began hinting that he leave for the night. When Victoria yawned and muttered what a long day it had been for the third time, Ava reminded her brother of his promise to drive Edwin back to Anniston. Carson gladly got ready to leave. Even though he wasn't as interested as he once was in the car, it still made him proud to show off his brother's prize possession. Ava wanted to sit in the back with Edwin but took the front seat by her brother instead.

"Nice set of wheels," Edwin said, stretching out in the back seat.

"They belong to James," Carson replied as he turned the car onto Pelham Road, the dirt road connecting Jacksonville to Anniston.

The exchange started a conversation about motor vehicles that Ava was as bored with as she had been with the table talk. She was happy that Carson and Edwin were getting

238

along, but she was glad that the rest of her time with Edwin during his furlough would be without her family. She wondered what James and Estelle would think about him, and the thought occupied her mind until they were almost in Anniston.

"How much longer will you be at McClellan?" Edwin asked when they passed the fort's main entrance off Pelham Road.

"Just a couple of more weeks. I want to be back in time for the cotton."

Ava turned up her nose and wrinkled her forehead at the word "cotton." Was it already September? She didn't want to leave her job and independence for school and afternoons stooping over prickly patches of cotton. The car stopped outside the Alabama Hotel.

"Thanks for the ride." Edwin opened his door.

"No problem."

Carson turned his head, and Ava also got out of the car. He didn't want to witness anything romantic involving his sister.

"I'll see you tomorrow at the Palace Drug Store," she said, touching Edwin's hand.

"I won't be late."

Even with her brother so close, it was difficult for him not to kiss her.

"You better not be." She laughed and got back in the car.

"I wouldn't risk it."

Carson pulled back onto the road, and they left him.

Alta was in Atlanta on a short honeymoon with Sydney, and, for the third day in a row, Edwin took her place with Ava and Rosemary at their usual lunch table. Today was easier for Rosemary. She wasn't jealous listening to all their plans for Edwin's last night of furlough, and she even laughed at Ava's retelling of the movie they had seen the night before. Percy had promised to come back early today to see her, and she expected him anytime that afternoon. He didn't tell her when specifically he would come or where he would see her, but she believed it would be soon. She couldn't help but glance at the drug store's door to see whether or not he had already found her.

"I'm going to tell Willie that you sing too so that he'll insist that you do a duet with me," Ava said and then laughed.

It was Wednesday, so the store was closing early, and Edwin was accompanying her to her band practice.

"And I'll tell him you're a devilish liar."

They joked for a while about the practice, and then Ava asked how he would amuse himself until then.

"I'll knock about somewhere to kill time." He shrugged, not caring what he did.

"I heard the museum has a new animal exhibition," Rosemary said.

It was where she thought she and Percy might go when he came back. It was a quiet place where they could talk and be undisturbed. They finished their lunch and headed back to Wakefield's for another hour and a half of work.

Rosemary felt like Ava as she continuously looked out the windows for Percy and forgot what she was fetching for a customer or whether or not she had already written a ticket for the item in question. Every time the door rang open, she looked up expectantly and was disappointed when she didn't see Percy.

The store closed, and Edwin met them at the door.

240

"You still haven't seen Percy?" Ava asked.

"Not yet, but I'm sure he won't be long." Rosemary forced a smile and then told them goodbye.

Not knowing whether to go home or stay in Anniston, she pretended to window shop for a while. Finally, she took the next bus home. He came to her before at her house. He would do it again. Her body ached remembering the night she had comforted him after he learned of his brother's death.

She was silent as she ate her supper with her parents. Judith was telling about the pig their father killed that day, but she heard nothing. All she could think about was where he was and how much longer she would have to wait. She could feel anger beginning to kindle within her. He should have been back hours ago.

Supper was now over, and she helped her mother clean up the kitchen. She was drying dishes with infuriated tears stinging her eyes when the sound of a car motor was heard. She knew it was him, and her heart felt like it was bursting with built up anticipation.

"Rosemary!" her father called from the porch. "It looks like your beau is here again."

She kept drying the pot in her hand even though it was dry. If he wasn't in a hurry to see her, then she wouldn't be in a hurry to see him.

"Were you expecting Percy?" her mother asked, going to the window.

"Not really."

In truth, she had expected him much earlier that afternoon, not tonight. She heard the car door open and close and then the polite voice Percy always used with her parents speaking to her father.

"Rosemary!" Jude called again.

241

"Here, I'll finish up." Myrtle took the pot from her hands.

"Good to hear Uncle Sam gave you some rest," her father was saying when she walked out.

Percy smiled up at her, and Jude left them.

"I couldn't wait to see you," he said, reaching for her hand.

His familiar smile and touch were already mollifying her anger, but she said nothing as she walked down the steps to him.

"Don't be mad, Rosemary. I flew to you as fast as I could. You don't know what it's like to get away from a mother who hasn't seen her son in months."

"I'm just glad you're here," she replied, the mention of his mother completely defeating her resentment.

He always turned their disagreements back in her direction.

"I borrowed a car from another officer at the fort, and your father said I could take you for a ride."

He opened the passenger door of the Ford Cabriolet. It was a beautiful black convertible with a soft, plush interior.

"It's gorgeous," she said.

He closed the door after her.

"I have a newer model just like it at home."

He circled back around the car to the driver's side and started the engine.

"Did you have a good time with your family?" she asked more happily as they drove away from her house.

It didn't matter what time it was. What mattered was that he was here, and she would enjoy herself.

"Mom was a great fuss, and poor Irene was a mess, but it was fine. I would have had a better time here with you," he said, patting the seat for her to sit nearer to him.

She moved closer, and they rode through the countryside with their shoulders touching. Rosemary had never ridden in a car without a top before, and she loved the carefree way the night air whipped her hair back. He placed the left hand he was holding on the wheel and motioned for her other hand.

"What are you doing?" she screamed, gripping the wheel.

"Teaching you to drive." He laughed and let go.

"Percy!"

She wouldn't dare drive James's car like Ava, and she had never even touched a wheel before.

"You got it." He grinned and crossed his arms behind his head.

"I'm going to kill us!"

Percy stepped on the gas and then the brake, suddenly stopping the car, and Rosemary fell back on his chest.

"You're impossible," she said.

"Come on. You know it was fun. We had to siphon gas off an Army jeep just to get her to crank."

He leaned down and kissed her and then pulled her away.

"I can't make you wait any longer?"

"For what?"

"For this," he said, reaching inside his pocket and pulling out a small box.

She started to take it, and he stopped her, kissing her again before relinquishing it to her. It was a black velvet box, and she couldn't help but remember their conversation at

Alta's reception. She looked up at him before opening its delicate lid. Inside was a silver necklace with an emerald heart setting. She had never seen anything more exquisite, and she couldn't think of anything to say.

"Do you like it?" he asked.

She nodded, and he took it out of the box and brushed her long hair to one side. He clasped the necklace around her and then kissed her neck. A rush of energy swept through her, and she turned toward him.

"That's just what the necklace reminded me of," he said.

"Of what?" She looked down at the emerald heart on her chest.

"It's the way your eyes change color when you're excited or mad or want something."

"Really, well, what do I want now?" she asked, her eyes becoming more of what he had described.

He laughed, turned the car lights off, and held her to himself.

On the way back to her house, she kept looking down at the heart necklace. What would her mother say? It was so expensive.

"Do you really think you'll be leaving soon?" The night was almost over and uncertainty was beginning to fill her mind again.

"Of course we will. They've already had us turn in our dog tags and send all sorts of stuff back home."

She felt sick and gripped his arm tightly.

"What will happen to us after the war?"

"I suppose, I'll come home to find that you've ran off with your Navy man." He laughed.

"You're cruel," she said, waiting for a serious answer.

"Oh, I'll be a beat-up war veteran coming back for you."

She smiled to herself in the dark. That is what she wanted more than kisses or necklaces or time during his furlough, just to know that he was coming back to her.

"Let me see your hands," he said.

"Oh, no! I'm not driving again. You're taking me home like a gentleman!"

Chapter 34

"Ava," Mrs. Crockett called out on the Friday afternoon after Edwin's furlough, "would you please fix the mannequin again."

"Sure," Ava replied, dropping the package she was wrapping.

"Is Lana's dress falling off again?" Alta laughed when Ava passed by her on the way to the window display.

Lana was the nickname they gave the store's tall, blond model, which looked like a stoic Lana Turner.

"She's not very modest." Ava laughed back.

Rosemary was replenishing the rack of men's shirts in front of the display, and she made room for her cousin behind the rack. Ava slipped her hand into the display box and hung the dress back properly on the mannequin's bare shoulder. Out of habit, she looked down busy Noble Street at a family getting out of a car and then at two soldiers entering Hudson's Department Store across the way. Looking down further, another group of soldiers was munching on ice cream cones. She closed the display box and made her way back around Rosemary, wondering how they could be away from the fort so early in the day. It was barely 4:00. Alta was humming the song that Douglas had been whistling all afternoon, and Ava joined her as she passed back by her for the half-wrapped dress box. She sighed at the rectangular box. Her packages were always so ruffled while Rosemary's were neat and pulled together tight at the edges. She was placing the finishing bow when the door burst open. Sydney came running into the store followed by Edwin and then Barry.

"Alta!" Sydney shouted and ran for his wife. "We're leaving in four hours!"

Alta said something in reply, but Ava didn't hear her as Edwin was excitedly telling her the same information.

"We're taking a night train out," he explained in rushed sentences.

"To where?"

The package slid off the counter and hit the floor. He picked it up for her.

"To our point of embarkation. I don't know where. It's confidential."

"My guess is I'm going home," Barry said.

"We all got afternoon passes and have to be back at the fort at 6:30 for final inspections and to be transported to the train station," Edwin said to both her and Rosemary now.

Alta and Sydney were behind them informing Mrs. Crockett of the abrupt departure.

"I have to leave," Alta was saying, untying her tape measure.

"I understand," Mrs. Crockett replied surprisingly.

Even she was susceptible to the raptures of young love.

"Oh, thank you." Alta hugged the stiff older woman.

Sydney embraced her too, which overcame her calm demeanor.

"You can both leave too. It's not that far to closing," she now addressed Ava and Rosemary, who also thanked her before running to the storage room to retrieve their purses and tell Douglas goodbye.

"If you all don't mind, I need some private time with Mrs. Saunders." Sydney grinned when they were all outside the door. "I'll see you two back at the fort. Oh, I almost forgot."

He pulled a letter out from one of his front pockets and handed it to Rosemary.

"Percy asked me to give you this," he said with the grimmest expression Ava had ever seen on his face.

In the confusion, it was the first time she realized that Percy hadn't come, and she felt horrible for her cousin. Rosemary turned away from them to read Percy's letter while Barry continued guessing at their point of embarkation. Ava watched Rosemary's back for signs of what the letter might say. When she finally turned back around, her eyes were wet.

"He has special duties. He can't get away. He told me goodbye," she said, clasping the emerald heart that hung underneath her blouse.

"I thought he had family...," Barry spoke then stopped as Rosemary's eyes turned upon him. "I guess I was wrong. A lot of officers are busy making final preparations."

"Let's go for an early supper," Edwin said.

All of the men wanted to feed their appetites before being condemned to endless C-rations.

"And ice cream. I heard you don't get much of that in Europe." Barry said.

Rosemary wanted to go home, but Ava wouldn't let her.

"Stay. Edwin and Barry want you to, and we could go to the loading depot afterward and watch them leave."

Rosemary's eyes sparked. Ava didn't have to say anything more. Percy would certainly be at the train station, with or without special duties.

Vic's café was full of uniformed men all having a last supper before departure, and the dinner was hasty and loud as men from different tables shouted and joked back and forth about leaving for the war. The atmosphere was contagiously exhilarating even for women who were losing their lovers. They were a part of world history, right there in their small chair in a small restaurant in a small southern town.

After supper and dessert, Barry and Edwin squeezed in among what looked like another hundred well-fed soldiers onto a bus for the fort, and Ava promised to see them at the train station. Even though it was over an hour before they would leave, she and Rosemary hurried to the loading depot and joined the other numerous mothers, fathers, wives, girlfriends, and children who were gathering for the send-off. The Army band was already in place playing "The Beer Barrel Polka," and red and blue stripes were flapping in every direction. Alta soon found them. She was out of breath and worried that Sydney might have been late.

The Army trucks full of men finally began to appear, and cheers broke out as family members found their loved ones for final embraces. Sydney and Edwin were on the fourth truck to arrive, and Rosemary stood behind as Ava and Alta ran for them. She strained her eyes looking for Percy, smiling at how surprised he would be to see her. She watched two more trucks unload and then walked through the crowd to be sure she hadn't missed him. More trucks came, and she still couldn't find him. Then she saw him. He was turned away from her, but she knew it was him, and she made her way to where he was standing. He was holding something. As she got closer, she saw it was a small child. Percy turned and the toddler's brown eyes met hers. With their bold clearness, they were so much like the man's who held him. Her heart stung and then collapsed when she noticed the small, jaunty brunette fixing the youngster's collar and hanging on Percy's arm. A poised, older woman stood with them, and Rosemary knew in an instant that his family had come. He was with his mother, his wife, and his child. An officer yelled for soldiers to begin boarding, and Rosemary watched as Percy kissed the woman on his arm. The train whistled, and Percy looked up and into Rosemary's eyes. His proud eyes flinched at the sight of her. She turned pale, and her eyes flared greener than the heart which was now hanging against her white blouse. Her pulse was beating furiously, but her dignity kept her head high and her gait calm as he watched her walk away from him. She had to get out of the station.

Outside, the air felt like it was choking her. She could now drop her head in disbelief. Even though she was shaking all over, she couldn't cry. Her anguish was beyond tears. She held her stomach tight and sank down in the dark, impervious shadows of the wall.

Inside the station, Ava watched Edwin's face and waving hand. The train rumbled and jerked forward.

"I love you," he mouthed to her, and even in the clamor and noise, she caught the words she had been waiting to hear.

She mouthed back the same words to him, and he looked into her eyes until her face blurred and then disappeared. No matter what lay ahead, it was the one image he would take with him wherever he went.

The instant the train departed, the music stopped, and the crowd's enthusiasm died. Whimpers could be heard throughout the station, and, as Ava became conscious of those around her, she saw many faces she didn't recognize. They were people from all across the United States come to visit and say farewell to their men. Suddenly, Edwin's leaving hit her heart, and a feeling of unrelenting coldness filled her. Even though there were people all around, she felt as though she were alone. Now, she could understand how Estelle felt when James left and how her presence in their house didn't dispel her loneliness. Alta was comforting another soldier's wife, and Ava began to look for Rosemary. She walked across the station back and forth, and, when she still couldn't find her, she began to worry. She walked outside and stood looking up and down the surrounding streets.

"Ava," she heard her name called out.

She turned in its direction but saw nothing.

"I'm over here," Rosemary called out again, reaching her hand into the streetlight.

Ava saw her hand and then the opaque outline of her figure sitting in the shadows. She sat down next to her, and neither of them spoke. They just listened to the various footsteps of the people leaving the station.

"I miss Edwin already too," Ava said.

Rosemary gasped loudly, and Ava looked at her bewildered face in the darkness.

"Percy is…is…," Rosemary tried to speak, but the words were too horrible to communicate.

"What?" Ava asked, realizing that something greater than loneliness was disturbing her cousin.

"He's married." The tears that wouldn't come began flowing down her cheeks and neck.

Ava couldn't believe what she heard. She stared down at Rosemary's downcast eyes.

"I'm sure you're mistaken."

"No, I saw him with his wife…and his child."

Rosemary was gasping harder. She leaned up on her hands and vomited. Ava held her around the waist until she stopped.

"Promise me you'll never tell anyone," Rosemary said. "Promise me."

"I promise," Ava vowed in the engulfing darkness.

Chapter 35

It was supposed to be Ava and Rosemary's last day at Wakefield's before the school year began, but Rosemary stayed home sick. Ava and Alta worked quietly side-by-side, thinking about those who had recently departed. To Ava, Anniston felt like the lonely train station of the night before. Even though the sun blazed through the windows, the day was dry and mirthless. Fewer people seemed to meander down the streets, and those who did venture into the store looked and bought little. In her own heart, she was miserable. There was nothing to look forward to that night, and no one was meeting her at the store door at closing. Also, every time she pictured her cousin's sick, grievous face in the darkness, her own stomach lurched uneasily. She shuddered in anger, not understanding how anyone could deceive someone as good as Rosemary. Alta reached over her for a coat hanger, and Ava wondered if she knew the truth about Percy. Recalling Sydney's remorseful face when he delivered Percy's letter, she was convinced that at least he knew. She longed to speak what was on her mind and ask Alta but decided not to break her oath to Rosemary. At closing, Mrs. Crockett gave her their last pay vouchers and earnings, and Alta made her promise to come visit on the weekends.

"We'll both need dinner dates now that Edwin and Sydney are gone." Alta embraced her.

253

"If you want to work some during your Christmas break, I'm certain we could use some extra hands," Mrs. Crockett said.

Now that the store was closed, Douglas could leave the back room, and he found them at the door.

"It's mighty not gonna be the same without your sweet face around here." He smiled down at her.

Ava smiled back, already missing him, Alta, and even Mrs. Crockett. When she finished all her goodbyes, she boarded the bus, thinking about why one week had to be full of so many endings. She pulled out her week's wages from its envelope.

"Twenty-one dollars and sixty three cents," she read.

She would also miss having her own money and the ability to take care of herself. Buying her own clothes and food had given her much personal satisfaction.

Off the bus, she walked straight to Rosemary's house with her cousin's check in her hand. Myrtle met her at the door as if she were expecting her and ushered her back outside.

"Is she feeling better?" Ava asked more brightly than she felt.

"Maybe, a little. I've given her Black Draught and some castor oil with orange juice your mother brought over, but she's still rather poorly," Myrtle reported with a tired sigh. "Ava, are you sure nothing else is bothering her besides Percy leaving?"

"Unless she picked up a bug at the store, I can't think of anything," Ava replied with the most innocent face she could muster, purposely misconstruing the question.

"No, I mean nothing else happened to her last night," Myrtle explained unnecessarily, looking back through the screen door toward her daughter's bedroom.

254

Ava shook her head, and guilt colored her cheeks to the shade of her lips.

"I just wish she wasn't so sensitive. She's just like her Aunt Ethel. My sister still gets sick every time she has to raise her voice at anything. Well, go on in. I'm sure she'll want to see you."

Ava tiptoed into the bedroom as if walking into a death room. Rosemary was lying on her stomach with her hands tucked under her head. Her face wasn't as pale as it was the night before, but puffy and blotched from where she had been crying. She opened her eyes and then moved over to the other side of the bed. Ava lay down next to her, asked how she was feeling, and then gave her the envelope with her week's wages.

"I'm not going back to school," Rosemary said and put the envelope unopened on her night table.

"You're not?"

"No, I told Mom and Dad today. I want to keep working."

Ava stared at her resolved face in disbelief.

"They don't care?"

"Probably a little but not as much as your parents would. Mom only went through the eighth grade herself."

"Then I'm not either," Ava said, enjoying the thought of retaining the independence she could already feel slipping away.

Rosemary smiled at her feebly. She didn't believe her, but she didn't feel like saying so.

Ava left after awhile, neither of them mentioning Percy, Edwin, or what had happened the night before. Rosemary roused herself up for supper when her mother brought a wash pan to her room, and she doused her face with its cool, transparent water. She picked up a hand mirror and looked down at her reflection. To her, what she had done was written in every crease and expression of her face.

"How can people not see?" she whispered.

Her lips trembled, and she studied her now dull eyes. So much had changed within her since last week, and, yet somehow, she knew that she always felt the truth. She recalled her walk with Percy in Zinn Park, the night he returned from his furlough, and, as always, the night he came to her after learning of his brother's death. She touched her lips and then recoiled with shame as her body still longed for the man who cruelly beguiled her. She lay down the mirror, unable to bear the image of herself any longer. She felt dirty and soiled. She closed her eyes, and the little boy's lucid brown eyes met hers again. Quivering with disgust, she splashed her face once more with water. She could never go back to school and pretend to be the person she was before.

School was the one subject Ava always knew to go to her father about first. His education was important to him, and he was determined that all of his children would have the same opportunities and values for books and learning as he did. Even though he didn't finish his degree at Howard College for the love of Victoria Carson, he regarded his two years there as one of the chief events that shaped his life and one of the most important things he ever did. He was always encouraging Ava in her schoolwork and bringing home new books for her from town. One of his favorite evening pastimes was assisting her in her algebraic homework, which she hated worse than shelling peas. The arithmetic problems were intriguing puzzles to him rather than complicated, pointless nonsense as Ava saw them.

She much preferred history and literature with their tragic and heroic stories about great people's lives.

She found her father early Sunday morning in the barn feeding Dixie and the other mules. When she entered, he dropped the heavy bucket of corn meal in his hand and smiled at her.

"You're up early," he said, leaning against Dixie's stall.

Ava gulped. It was going to be hard to tell him that she wasn't going back to school. She stroked Dixie's ears, avoiding what she had come to say.

"You always were his favorite." He patted the animal's portly side. "Has your momma started breakfast yet?"

Ava nodded. She knew he was wondering why she was out in the barn with him instead of helping her mother in the kitchen.

"I wanted to ask you something," she said without taking her eyes off Dixie.

"Anything." He smiled.

"I ...," she began, looking up now.

She swallowed hard, realizing that she couldn't do it. Her not going back to school would disappoint him too much.

"What?" he asked, beginning to grow uneasy with her undeclared question.

"I wanted to ask if I could work at Wakefield's during my Christmas break from school?"

"I don't see why not." He shrugged more at ease, thankful that her question didn't have anything to do with more singing engagements, boys, or living at James's house. "But that's a ways off."

"I know. Mrs. Crockett just mentioned it to me yesterday. All right then, I'm going to go help with breakfast. Brother Whatley will be up soon."

"It looks like we might be getting some rain. If it's messy in the morning, I'll drive you and Rosemary to school."

"You can take me, but Rosemary has decided to keep working and not go back."

Her father looked up at her with a face of disapproval, but she left before he could ask any questions.

Even though the morning sky was gray and moist, there had been no rain yet. Ava trudged off to school feeling as depressed as the sky above her. It felt strange going to school without Rosemary. She stopped where she would normally turn for the Bonds' house and then walked on. It was the first time she had ever been to school without her cousin, and she hated the way everything had changed over the last week. Edwin was gone. Her job in Anniston was over, and Rosemary was working without her. Last night, she cajoled herself by thinking that school might be a comforting change to help her not miss Edwin so badly. Leaving work on Saturday without him waiting for her by the door was painful, but, now that she was actually facing the reality of not going back, it was difficult to bear.

Nearing the school building, she spotted Aggie's freckled face and Floraline's hand waving at her in the distance, and she ran in their direction. She knew they would want to hear all about her summer and Edwin, and she couldn't wait to tell them everything.

Chapter 36

Carson closed the shed's doors, crossed his arms behind his head, and gazed out on the field he had sweated over for more than two months now. A feeling of self-satisfaction filled him, and, while no one else was looking, he smiled at his work. It might not be on the European or Pacific battlefront, but he accomplished something, no matter how small it might seem to other men.

He was leaving Fort McClellan. His family's cotton was almost ready for picking, and he was needed at home. He put his blistery hands in his pockets and thought about how glad his father was that he was coming back. It was harder without him than they ever let on.

There was one more thing he had to do before leaving. He turned his back on the field and started walking toward Remington Hall. He would see Albin's finished painting of his wife. Just last week, he ran into the German on his way to Major Thunderstrom's office, and the imprisoned painter had reminded him of his promise to come back and look at the mural. When he was alone and thinking to himself, he often thought of Albin's crippled hand and the dark-haired woman it painted.

When he got to Remington Hall, the building seemed almost deserted. The whole fort was quieter as a large number of soldiers had recently left and another group was trickling in.

He opened the building's thick wooden doors and then entered the room he had visited once before. The lights were off and no one was there, but the sun cast an ephemeral glow on the still unfinished murals. He moved toward the now complete woman and stood gazing up at her olive face and bright, brown eyes, which flirted with the Spanish soldier by her side.

Albin is certainly lonely for home, he thought and pictured the woman sitting in the same manner with his German friend.

He smiled. He would be lonely too if a woman like her was waiting for him. He thought of Aggie. She didn't compare to the soft, attractive woman in the picture. He hadn't seen her since Jake's party, and sometime that summer, he had stopped caring for her.

After gazing at the mural for a while, he turned to leave but then decided to try and find Albin instead. He walked out of the room's back entrance and looked down the hallway. A man carrying a large stack of plates was approaching. Carson could tell by his hardened jaw line that he was another prisoner.

"Excuse me, do you know where Albin the painter is?"

"Kitchen today," the German replied, eyeing him up and down.

It was evident to the man that he wasn't a soldier, and Carson knew he was trying to place his purpose at the fort and why he was asking for a specific prisoner.

"I'll get him," the man said.

Carson waited to see if the German had been sincere and could find his unlikely friend. He stepped farther into the hallway and looked into a large banquet hall. Long tables were arranged throughout the stately, pristine room, and he assumed it was where the officers dined and where they more than likely enjoyed the corn, peas, squash, and tomatoes from his crop.

"Carson," he heard his name pronounced in a thick European accent behind him.

"No painting today?" Carson smiled at Albin.

"Not today. I can only paint when my spirit is moved. Cook's work today."

"Your wife doesn't move your spirit everyday?"

They both laughed.

"Love is not the only passion that moves a man," Albin replied, a touch of sadness in his voice.

"Your wife greatly improves the look of these walls."

"You've looked at her then." Albin grinned with obvious appreciation.

"Yes, I wanted to see her before I left. I'm leaving today. I'm needed back at home."

"You have beat everyone at checkers then." Albin laughed, extending his hand.

Carson laughed with him and shook his outstretched hand. It was a handshake very much like the ones he shared with both Jimmy and Pete before they left him for the war.

When Carson buckled his overalls the next morning, he realized that it felt good to be working at home again. He missed solving problems with his father, listening to his grandpa retell the same stories, and talking about sports and fishing with Jude. He stepped out onto the porch and inhaled the crisp morning air. It was the first day he could feel fall's approach. His sister came out of the door behind him and passed him on her way to school. He would miss playing football this year but not classes and homework.

"You're back here now," Ava said. "You have to do actual work again."

Carson just frowned at her, fighting back the proclivity to retaliate with sarcasm.

Be nice to her. He remembered his mother's request that he be kind since Edwin left and she was no longer at Wakefield's.

Ava looked back with a provoking smile when he didn't respond. He bit his lip hard, the promise becoming difficult to keep, and ran off in the direction of where he knew his father would already be hard at work.

Chapter 37

Ava ripped open the letter as fast as her fingers would move. It was her first letter from Edwin since he left a week ago. She smiled, recognizing the starch, ivory stationary that she gave him the night he left. The letter unfolded in her lap, and her eyes devoured its contents.

"Deer Songbird," she began and giggled out loud at his obvious misspelling.

I still can't beleeve that we left and on our way to war. we feel like we will never lieve this train though and get to POE. we still don't know where the heck we're going. Could be Alaska. it very crowded. I can't sleep. Barry keps trying to play cards. its too cramped. I saw his cards 2 times by mistak. everyone say we will be there soon but I don't think so. I miss you already. did you hear what I said when we left?

Edwin.

Ava read back over the brief letter several times and then pulled out a matching sheet of stationary.

"Dear Edwin," she started and then paused, placing her pen over her lips. "I did hear what you said. Did you hear what I said back to you?"

A short distance away, Rosemary also received a letter. She took it to her room, and her mother's concerned eyes

263

followed her. She stared at the long, black letters of her name and address, her heart beating violently at the thought of the man who wrote them. How could Percy write to her? She thought about destroying the letter, but her curiosity compelled her to read it first. What could he possibly say in defense of his actions? The letter smelled like tobacco, and she felt as though he had just walked into the room and was gazing down her neck.

Dearest Rosemary,

When you get this letter, I will be far away from you, probably where you want me forever now. Please believe that I never meant to hurt you. I just wanted to be your friend, but I couldn't help but fall in love with you. You are the kindest and the gentlest woman I have ever known. I will never forget the way you comforted me after Robert's death. Please forgive me. No bullet or knife could ever injure me the way your sad eyes did the night I left. If I live through this war, I will make things right between us. I have been terrible and do not merit your affection, but please forgive me.

The letter continued, but she couldn't read the rest. Fresh tears streamed down her face and choked her throat. A soft tap announced her mother's presence. She could hear Judith singing *Ring Around the Roses* as the door opened.

"Is everything all right?" her mother asked behind her.

Rosemary gulped down stinging tears and without turning her head, answered, "Yes, everything is fine."

Myrtle stood in silence watching her daughter's back and then closed the door.

Later that night, when both of her children were asleep, she whispered to her husband in their bed, "Are you awake, Jude?"

There was no answer, so she spoke a little louder, sure that he couldn't have gone to sleep that fast. He wasn't even snoring yet.

"Jude, are you awake?"

"I am now," he said and turned his good eye on his wife.

"I'm worried about Rosemary."

"You're always worried about something." He sighed.

"No, I'm serious. She's so melancholy and barely eating anything."

"I'm sure she'll be back to her old self soon," Jude said more softly, thinking of his daughter. "Remember how she was when Jake left? This boy just seems to have made a little more of an impression on her, that's all."

He turned over on his side and closed his eyes again. Myrtle didn't reply. She wasn't as confident as her husband. Maybe it was a mother's discerning nature, but she knew there was something more bothering her daughter than a boy leaving. She did remember how Rosemary was when Jake left, and she also remembered how quickly the rosy floridness returned to her cheeks and her joy and hope at getting letters from him in the mail. She was certain that this boy, or man as he really was, had not only left her daughter but broken her heart as well. The realization angered her and made her ache with impotence. If this man had never come, Rosemary would still be happily waiting for Jake Green to return home. She once had so much hope for the two of them. Jake was such a fine boy who was sure to make something of his life. She closed her own eyes now but didn't sleep. Through the noise of her husband's rumbling snore, she muttered a quiet prayer for her daughter's happiness and for Jake Green, wherever he was.

Chapter 38

There was one thing that hadn't changed in Ava's life, and that was the band. She still went to practice every Wednesday after school, and, now that Edwin was gone, it was the event she looked forward to the most each week. She gazed down with excitement at the new pages of music in her lap.

"*Merriest* and *Santa Came in the Spring*," she read to herself as Willie Harold explained the need to begin practicing for Christmas now.

Christmas songs in September? Her luminous eyes flew over the notes and words of the songs she would begin learning today.

"Let's try *Santa Came in the Spring* first," Willie decided. "Ava, there is a fairly long musical interlude before you come in."

She flipped to the page where she would begin singing and nodded up at him.

"I'm going to sing this one with you. It sounds really good as a duet."

Ava nodded again, smiling at the thought of singing with another person besides her parents, cousin, and brothers. She had heard that Willie had an exceptional tenor voice but had never heard him sing before.

"I'll cue you when we come in," he said and turned back to the band.

"O.k., here goes." He raised his baton, it fell through the air, and the band played on command.

Ava waited for her cue, trying to follow along through the pages of music. Willie stopped the song, gave out more directions, and the song started a second time and then a third time and then a fourth time before it finally came to her part. The bandleader waved his free hand at her now, and they both begin singing.

"Santa Claus came in the spring. Santa Claus came when the skies were blue. I heard his sleigh bells jing-a-ling the day that I met you."

Willie's voice was fine-turned, yet melodically playful as it leaped and dipped through the notes, and Ava was impressed. Their duet was brief, and the band climaxed in a crescendo that ended the song.

"Not bad." Willie smiled, first at the band and then at her. "Ava, sing a little softer, and, you guys, pick up the tempo just a hair."

Ava was still practicing the song the next day but in a less pleasant environment. It was the time of year she dreaded more than all others – the harvesting of their foremost crop. Picking cotton was not just men's work. It was the whole family's job. School would be out all next week solely for that purpose, but, until then, she was told to come to the fields straight from class every day but Wednesday. It was vital that they get it all picked before any bad weather could threaten or destroy it.

"Santa Claus came in the spring," she sang more softly as Willie directed, stooping over another cotton plant.

Her back and fingers were already sore from the repetitive motion, and she stood up for a moment, let go of her half-full sack, and straightened and twisted her tight lower back. She sighed as she looked down at her fingers which were already red and dry. She heard a high-pitched laugh and looked back several rows. Even Judith was helping, and Ava watched Myrtle show her how to pluck the plant carefully without pricking her plump fingers.

"Ava, there's no time for dawdling!" Victoria called out from another row just ahead of her.

Ava scowled under her breath at her intrepid mother and picked back up her bag of cotton, envying her cousin. Rosemary would get out of most of the cotton picking this year. She was still expected to help after work, but there would only be enough sunlight for her to pick a short time.

"Santa Claus came with the daffodils," she sang on as she made her way down the row.

Her aching hands were in cotton, but her mind was far away, walking through daffodils with Edwin. The afternoon finally passed, and the evening approached bringing Rosemary with it.

The sun was blinding before it bowed goodnight, and Ava, Rosemary, and Carson all brought their full sacks of cotton to the already overloaded wagon. Ava dumped her bag first and stood back as Carson did the same. He gave her a sly smile which she instantly interpreted. As soon as Rosemary's bag was emptied, they leapt past her into the mounds of white substance. It was as much a family tradition as Santa Claus and chocolate birthday cakes. They laughed and looked back at Rosemary, waiting for her join them. Her lusterless face smiled, but she shook her head no.

"I'm too tired."

"Nonsense," Carson said, and he bounded back down, picked his cousin up, and tossed her into the wagon.

Even Rosemary was laughing now as the three of them rolled around and jumped in the soft, fresh cotton from which their family's livelihood would come.

Ava sat motionless, her chin and hands propped on the back of her chair. The band was performing a song without her, and she was listening from the floor below. *Sleepy Lagoon* didn't need a vocalist. The bombastic trumpeter was its soloist. This was her first U.S.O. dance without Edwin, and the experience was entirely different for her. The lively faces of new boys on the dance floor held no appeal for her. Instead, it was the glossy, gold instruments and the notes that oozed and boomed from them that filled her consciousness. She closed her eyes and let them overpower her senses. The undulating song rippled with sound and emotion, and a thousand, tessellated images and hopes of Edwin filled her dazzled head. A tap on her shoulder called her out of her stupor. She looked up into the bold face of a boy only slightly older than herself.

"Would you like to dance?" he asked, leaning over her chair.

"Thanks, but I'm working," Ava said, pointing at the band. "I have to sing the next number."

A sudden rush of loss filled her when she uttered her truthful excuse. If Edwin were there, she would have danced up until the last beat of the song before singing. The boy left her, and she closed her eyes again. The music refilled her head and carried her back to the soldier who left her. A husky voice interrupted her dreamy cogitation once again.

"Let's dance, baby."

Ava turned in her chair, not wanting to make another excuse for sitting alone. She would have to sit behind the band after her next number. Instead of another soldier, she laughed when she recognized Alta.

"Why you look so blue, sweet cakes?" Alta laughed, lowering her voice again.

"What are you doing here?" Ava asked, thankful to see a familiar face.

"Rosemary told me you would be here, and I thought you might enjoy some company."

The music was stopping, and Ava promised to be back soon. As she sang, it was the first time all night that she was ready for a song to end. She missed her long conversations with Alta and was jealous of Rosemary's continued friendship with her. The song finished, and she met Alta back at the table.

"Beautiful as always." Alta clapped.

She was sitting in one chair with her high-heeled feet crossed and propped in another.

"Have you heard from Edwin?"

"Yesterday," Ava said, "and Sydney?"

"Yesterday too. I guess we all got letters on the same day."

Ava nodded, wondering who "all" was supposed to insinuate. Did Rosemary get a letter from Percy? She doubted that her cousin would talk about Percy's deception with anyone, but maybe she did confess to receiving a letter.

"How's work?" Ava asked and turned her thoughts away from Rosemary.

"Same old, same old. We all miss you. The window display doesn't look half as good this week without you, and Mrs. Crockett got pretty huffy about it."

Ava laughed. That was the part of her job she enjoyed the most.

"It doesn't seem right that the last time we were here, they were with us, and now they're gone," Alta spoke, and as she did, a graveness passed over her face that Ava had never seen before.

Ava looked over at a couple dancing behind them and agreed. They talked awhile longer before she was needed on stage again. She was performing *I Had the Craziest Dream Last Night* for the second time, but there was no one to sing to, and her eyes and passion were directed upward to a man not present. This time when she finished her song, she found Alta smoking and talking with a couple of soldiers at their table. Ava watched her sultry smile and the way her eyes sparked as she laughed at a joke one of the men was telling. She didn't understand Alta's insatiable gaiety, but she couldn't picture her friend any other way. Alta lived to be admired and loved.

Chapter 39

With all the cotton now picked and taken to the gin and with the days becoming increasingly shorter, their suppers were eaten earlier, and they had more leisure time at night. Ava always enjoyed this time of year, because she got to spend more time with her father. Just then, she was telling him about Edwin's latest letter while Carson mulled over his next game move. She had just captured two of his checker pieces, and he was strategizing about how best to re-level the playing board. She could hear him huffing as he imagined what would be the denouement of each projected move.

"He says the blackout restrictions on their ship are strictly enforced," Ava told her father with an air of divulging secret information.

She liked it when he talked to her as an adult about worldly affairs.

"You don't say," her father replied, pretending that she was giving him novel information.

"You can't even smoke on deck at night," Ava went on, and Carson huffed louder.

The conversation was breaking his concentration. If he was winning, he wouldn't care if she was screaming and jumping on one leg.

"The soldiers have to endure much for their own safety," Sheffield said, digging for a cigar in his shirt pocket.

Their conversation was over. He was going outside to smoke with her grandpa. Victoria hated the smell of tobacco, and she wouldn't allow it in the house. Ava watched him leave, wishing he wanted to hear more about Edwin and what she knew of the war. She sighed thinking of what her father had said and remembered Edwin's description of the complete blackness of night on a ship, the never ceasing sound of separating water, and the numbing, yet exhilarating feeling of not knowing where you are going or what you will find once you get there. Closing her eyes, she imagined the darkness he described and how it must feel to not be able to see what you are traveling toward. She tried to never think about the danger he might face in war, but just then, the unhappy thought struck her in the face. She wished he didn't have to find out what lay ahead.

"It's your turn," Carson said, splintering her thoughts.

She opened up her eyes and looked down at the board and then at her brother. The way the corners of his mouth kept twitching in anticipation communicated that there was something to be watchful for. He was ready to pounce, and she had to stop him. The shuffle of footsteps outside roused their attention away from the game. Someone ran up the porch steps and was talking to their father and grandpa. She and Carson both sat up on their knees and listened, but they could catch only fragments of words.

"Germans...down at the Gunter's barn...Clyde Gunter and his son going down there with shotguns...everyone is...."

Carson jumped to his feet before they could hear anymore. Ava knew now that the voice belonged to Willis Ponder. Her brother was out the door in a second.

"They're going to do something stupid," Carson interjected as Ava listened behind him at the door. "You know they're not armed."

"We don't know that, but you're right about Clyde. That man would put a bullet through the president if he trespassed on his property," Sheffield replied.

"I'm going down there," Willis said, running back down the steps.

"And I'm getting the major," Carson told his father.

There was no time to debate what to do. He slammed the screen door open and headed for James's car keys.

"I'm going with you," Sheffield said.

"And I'm defending our house. Ain't no German stepping foot on Carson land," Grandpa Chester announced, going for his old muzzle-loading shotgun.

"Ava, tell your mother we've gone to the fort when she gets back from her sister's," Sheffield said.

"I will."

Carson and Sheffield roared away from the house, and Grandpa Chester reemerged from his bedroom, shotgun in hand.

"Stay inside, Annie."

Ava couldn't help but giggle at his heroic charade. She watched him plop down on the front step of the porch with his gun crossed over his upright chest. You would have thought that Hitler himself was about to come over the hill.

Carson sped as fast as he could toward the fort, glancing at the gas gauge every few seconds. He hoped they would have enough to get to the fort and back to the Gunter's. He knew that his father was also watching the gauge and thinking the same thing. Dust flew and swirled in every

275

direction as he maneuvered over the familiar curves and turns of the road. He had to get to the major before the Gunters did something terrible. He pictured Albin. What if the pretty girl in the mural didn't have a husband to wait for? Reason told him that, out of the 3,000 prisoners at Fort McClellan, it probably wasn't his German friend being held at gunpoint, but he raced on as if it was, the dark eyes of the painted woman beckoning him to drive even faster. His face reddened in anger at the thought of Edgar Gunter and his silly, crippled father. He never understood how Pete was so different from the two of them. The fort came into view, and he drove the car to the entrance of Baltzell gate. The guard on duty demanded his purpose, and Carson explained how he worked for Major Thunderstrom and must see him right away. Instead of allowing him through, the guard made him state his business and then radioed the major himself.

"Wait here," the guard ordered. "He's coming."

Only a couple of minutes passed before an Army jeep with the major and two members of the Military Police rode toward them. The major got out and walked to their car.

"Carson, good to see you. Where were they spotted?"

Carson told him everything he knew, and they followed him to the Gunters' land. The soldiers raided the barn as soon as they approached, and Carson and Sheffield watched from just outside their vehicle. Shouting could be heard from inside.

"Set your guns aside men! Don't Move!"

Soon after, two prisoners marched out, followed by the military policemen. Their faces were unfamiliar to Carson, neither one of them being Albin or anyone else who worked in the field for him. They were loaded in the jeep, and Major

Thunderstrom emerged from the barn with Willis Ponder, Edgar Gunter, Clyde Gunter, and Bo Dempsey.

"I apologize for the disturbance men, but, next time, notify us immediately before acting," the major said with a mixture of pleasantry and firmness.

Edgar's gun was lowered dastardly by his side, but, when he saw Carson, the arm that held it flinched, and he gazed at him. Carson stared back and breathed out in relief. He had stopped whatever they were about to do.

Chapter 40

Victoria's eyes grew round underneath elevated eyebrows at her daughter's latest news.

"Sheffield!" she shouted into the next room. "Write your mother. We're going to Birmingham."

Ava smiled as her mother embraced her and brushed her cheek with a kiss.

"What's going on?" Sheffield asked when he entered the kitchen.

"Ava's singing with the band in Birmingham, and the whole family's been invited to attend!" Victoria clapped her hands together.

"Well, I'll be dog." Sheffield laughed. "My daughter's singing for my home crowd. Where's the concert?"

"We're performing at Vulcan Park just before Christmas," Ava answered, flattered by her parents' partially unexpected enthusiasm.

"Your grandparents will be delighted."

"I'll just arrange for Brother Whatley to spend the weekend with Jude and Myrtle so we can all be there, even your grandpa," Victoria said, making all the necessary arrangements in her head.

She was tired of hearing from Valencia Boozer how well her daughter sang with the big band. Now, she would hear it for herself.

In just a few hours, the whole community knew that Ava was singing in Birmingham, but any excitement she felt over the concert dissipated with her next letter from Edwin. He was actually in the war now. For the first time, what happened across the world would directly affect her life, and the romantic notions she once had for all the war's events were crushed with just a few words. She could barely concentrate on her schoolwork or music for thinking about Edwin and what he had written. He was attached as a replacement to an outfit in the Mediterranean. Sydney was still with him, but Barry was assigned to another company.

It was during this time that she began joining her father in one of his favorite hobbies since James joined the Army, reading Ernie Pyle. His articles were not lengthy prognostications about the strength of the Luftwaffe versus the Allied Forces or news updates about the war's ongoing progression, but rather pungent, heart-felt stories about the men who made up the war. They told the story of the American soldier, and millions of people across the country ate up their words as if they were sweet letters from their own sons and lovers.

Out of habit now, Sheffield flipped past the front page of the newspaper and went straight for Pyle's article. He read slowly as he absorbed each word. When he finished, he passed it to his daughter's waiting hands. It was the most powerful article he had read by Pyle yet, and it was some time before he could attempt to focus on the next page of the newspaper. Instead, he sat admiring the men he read about.

Pyle's latest article was entitled "The Death of Captain Waskow," and Ava read slowly, like her father, looking for glimpses of Edwin in every word. It was about the retrieval of a captain's dead body and its effect on the men he commanded. The pictures Pyle's words painted were seductively somber and disturbingly real. Ava paused and closed her eyes after sentences such as "Soldiers made shadows as they walked" and "You don't cover up dead men on the combat zone. They just lie there in the shadows until somebody else comes after them." The helplessness of the fallen men touched her heart, but the almost reverent friendship of the brotherly soldiers soothed her sadness. She felt sorry for Edwin that Barry would not be with him anymore. The article ended with the lifeless soldiers lying quietly in the "shadow of the low stone wall," while the fighting men slept close by in the straw. Even in death, they were still unnatural brothers. The repeated word "shadow" resonated within her, provoking an ethereal image of death. Her heart began to mourn for the unknown Captain Waskow, but her father broke through her solace.

"Look here," he said, placing another page of the newspaper in her hands. "Betty Grable is auctioning off her stockings for the war effort. How much do you think we could get for your mother's?"

Chapter 41

The light from the fading sun fell through the window and onto her grandmother's white hair, making it seem to disappear in silvery strands around her long face. Ava loved to watch the way her grandmother did everything and, in particular, the way she moved her hands as she poured tea, fastened her glove buttons, or pointed at objects of conversation. It was as if her hands were the tools with which she effused elegance to the world.

Lavenia Stilwell was the apotheosis of Southern gentility. She carried her tall figure with graceful poise, and her manners and hospitality were impeccable. She hosted suppers for neighbors, organized charitable functions, and chaired a book club. She was also an unashamed erudite who desired and encouraged perfection.

"Ava dear, how many songs will you be singing tonight?" Lavenia asked as Ava observed her fingers stirring sugar in her tea with a spoon.

"At least six, right?" Victoria smiled over her own steaming cup.

"Yes, six," Ava answered, now noticing the heightened posture of her mother's back.

When her mother was with her grandmother, Ava always thought that she shone her brightest, proving that women from the country could be just as refined and that

Sheffield's choice in her was wisely made. That evening, Victoria was indeed resplendent. Her black, coarse hair, which she always kept up just behind her neck, was unloosed and hanging over her shoulders, and the long-sleeved, yellow dress she made for the concert dipped ever so slightly in the front and back to reveal her clear, olive complexion. Ava had smiled earlier at the way her father held the door open for her mother and touched the small of her back when he walked beside her.

"Goodness, so many! Have some lemon in your tea then. It is supposed to be good for the vocal chords." Lavenia set a crystal bowl of lemon wedges before her granddaughter. "Rosemary, would you care for some too?"

"No, thank you," Rosemary answered politely.

In her opinion, tea should always be served cold with the sugar already mixed in.

"The park will be a beautiful place to perform. I just wish they would get rid of that frightful iron vulcan. He's the ugliest thing ever made, and his bare backside is a city eyesore, but the Kiwanis Club wouldn't have it any other way until that thing was taken from the state fairgrounds and put on the top of Red Mountain for the world to see."

Ava glanced at her cousin who was also silently laughing at the statue's nudity, neither of them seeing the impropriety of the Roman god of the forge.

"Nevertheless, our next war bonds drive will be there, and, Victoria, I hope you don't mind, but I had a picture of James in his uniform put on some of our publicity posters."

"That's wonderful," Victoria said, truly honored that her son's picture might invoke generosity from others.

Victoria updated her mother-in-law on the progress of her Women Advancing the War Efforts Committee, and the two discussed and compared their energies until Carson,

Grandpa Chester, Sheffield, and Jack Stilwell returned from surveying the newest improvements to Stilwell Brothers' Grocery.

Jack Stilwell was a small man and shorter than his wife. As one of the city's most successful entrepreneurs, he represented the new Birmingham, unconnected with the city's great iron industry from which his wife came. Their marriage represented the union of the "Magic City's" past and future.

"I hope you all brought heavy coats. The temperature is dropping," Jack spoke with a shiver. "Ava, your father and I'll take you on down to the park. Carson, fix your grandpa and yourself something to drink and not that awful stuff your mother and sister are drinking."

"No, I'll get it," Lavenia interposed, her tall figure looming over the table of refreshments. "Lemonade, Chester?"

"Don't mind if I do," Grandpa Chester said and sprawled out his legs in the nearest chair.

Even though he admired their unreserved kindness and self-made wealth, the Stilwells never intimidated him.

As they drove through the streets of Birmingham, Ava rode between her grandfather and father. She alternated between listening to the exuberant greetings that her grandfather, who was known by everyone, was sending from his driver's window and her father's reminisces about all the places they were passing. Every spot reminded him of some adventure from his childhood, and Ava listened to his revelations of his younger self.

"See that house over yonder." Sheffield pointed out the window. "That's where old Mrs. Duncan who taught me how to play the violin lived. Boy, you sure better start playing

283

as soon as you enter her door or she won't offer you any cookies after practice."

Ava laughed. She had heard the story before, but she wouldn't tell him. She enjoyed imagining him as a young man with untidy hair and reckless energy like Carson.

The journey was a short one. They were soon at the park, and the band was already rehearsing for their big night. As the sun continued its descent, the numerous candles set about in brown paper bags came alive. They reminded Ava of Alta's wedding reception, but, this time, she was partly the reason everyone was coming.

The practice was a rushed one, and soon the crowd was in place for the concert. The audience was a motley ensemble of young families, older couples, teenage children, production workers recently let off work, and enlisted men. The soldiers were the guests of honor, and Ava watched from behind the low, wooden stage as they filled the front seats just in front of her family, who had been there some time. She was used to singing for strange men now. Her parents and grandparents were the ones who made her nervous; because it was their opinion she valued most. Singing for church and singing as she was about to were two totally different things to her, and she was afraid of shocking her family.

Soon the moment came, and she ascended the stage just as the band struck up its vibrant melody. She looked up at the 1904 World's Fair Winner and fifty-six foot-high iron symbol of Birmingham industrialization and smiled to herself. The Vulcan's backside was indeed uncovered, and the fact propitiated her developing nerves while the spearhead he brandished high in his right hand encouraged her. Willie Harold gave her a confident wink, and she began her song.

284

"I'd like to fix this bag of tricks and send them out with a fleeting greeting. Smiles for the frowners, salutes to the uppers, boos to the downers," she sang.

It was a cold night, and she was clad in her grandmother's red velvet jacket, but it wouldn't have mattered. She could have sung through a blizzard.

Song after song began and ended, some with her singing and some without her. Their last song was "Here Comes Santa Claus," and she was just beginning her solo when a soldier from the front row leaped up on stage and made it into an extemporaneous duet. The crowd applauded as he put his arm around her and sang out just as boldly. His voice didn't capture many of the notes, but his performance was hysterical, and Ava could barely sing for laughing. A camera flashed somewhere out in the distance, and, when the song ended, everyone was already standing for Santa Claus himself.

Even though Ava was completely exhausted, she couldn't fall asleep that night for thinking of her success. The band's performance enamored her parents, grandparents, and the city of Birmingham.

"Did you see the married couple dancing all night?" Ava asked Rosemary from her place on the large, oak bed.

The bed was so big that they could both lay with their arms and legs out and still not touch each other. She loved sleeping in the narrow, rectangular bedroom that made up her grandparent's third floor. A half moon window was just over their heads, and Ava rolled over on her stomach and looked out into the night sky.

"Your grandmother said that they were probably intoxicated." Rosemary laughed as she too turned and peered out the window.

285

"Nonsense, they just know you're not supposed to sit still while listening to that kind of music. I want to be like that when I'm married."

"There is no doubt you will be." Rosemary laughed again.

They both stared at the sky in silence, and Ava noted Rosemary's seeming happiness. She was thankful that Myrtle's suggestion of bringing her cousin with them might be lifting her spirits.

"Are you better now?" Ava decided to ask.

They hadn't spoken of Percy since the night at the train station.

"I mean about Percy and everything."

Rosemary's smile faded.

"Even though I despise him for what he did, I think about him all the time. I know I shouldn't, but I can't help it."

"It's hard to forget someone you once cared for," Ava said, even though she didn't know if what she was saying was true.

"I know, but everytime...," Rosemary closed her eyes and stopped, thinking of Percy's son's face.

"Since it's over, do you think there's any chance for Jake to...."

"No!" Rosemary almost shouted, sitting up.

Her eyes were blazing now, and Ava wished she wouldn't have mentioned Jake.

"I betrayed him, and I would never deserve his forgiveness. Besides, I couldn't have really loved him and done what I did to him."

"People break up and get back together all the time. Remember the time James broke up with Estelle because he kissed Lydia Green."

"That's different." Rosemary sighed and lay down. "I'm tired. I'm going to sleep."

Ava looked at her firmly closed eyes and said nothing. Underneath her silence was still a tormenting grief.

Chapter 42

Ava thumped her pen against the hardwood floor as she thought and then wrote at the bottom of the letter: "P.S. I'm enclosing an article and picture of myself singing at the concert in Birmingham. I wish you could have been there."

She looked again at the newspaper clipping before putting it into the envelope. Her grandmother had sent two copies of the article, which included a short description of her vocal capability and a picture of herself singing with the soldier who had invited himself on stage. His arm was around her waist, and she was laughing up at him as he howled out a false note.

She read the picture's caption: "Miss Ava Stilwell, granddaughter of Mr. and Mrs. Jack Stilwell, receives an unexpected singing partner."

She glanced back over the article's text and found her name again: "Ava Stilwell's precociously powerful voice mesmerized the City of Birmingham Saturday night."

"Precocious," she repeated out loud.

Her father said it meant that she had a mature voice, but she didn't exactly understand the compliment. What gave her voice the quality of maturity? She licked and closed the envelope, hoping Edwin would like the article and not be jealous about the soldier singing with her. It was too big of an event in her life not to share it with him. Besides, she wanted him to see her face again and be proud of her. She was beginning to worry that the war might change his affection for her.

"I'm going to meet Rosemary for supper and a show," Ava said and passed her mother in route to the door.

She hid the letter in her coat pocket, knowing that her mother would disapprove of her sending one of their only two copies of the newspaper article to Edwin. The garden club still hadn't seen the clipping.

"Have fun, dear," Victoria called out after her without looking up from the box of Christmas decorations she was rummaging through.

Ava hurried out the door and into the cool late afternoon air, thankful for the distraction of the holidays. A letter from James hinting at a Christmas furlough had sent her mother reeling with excitement. Victoria was desperate to have her family back together, and she was determined to make this year their most festive Christmas ever. They all tried not to think about the war in connection with James, but even she in her more solemn moments recognized the possible consequences to her family.

Ava mailed her letter and took the bus to Anniston. Rosemary was waiting for her at the Sanitary Café, and the two ate a quick supper before their movie.

"I should have brought a scarf," Ava said as they hurried down the street to the Noble Theater.

The wind had gained momentum, and she could feel its chilliness against her bare ears.

"Put your hands over your ears," Rosemary said, glad that her long hair was keeping hers warm.

"I can't. I forgot my gloves too."

Ava quickened her speed and then bumped into an unseen man coming from a side street. "I'm sorry miss," the man apologized, and the woman he was with squealed out in laughter.

Ava started to offer her own apology but stopped when she recognized the laugh and woman he was with.

"Alta!"

"Hey, girls." Alta giggled.

Her face looked florid and hot despite the December night air and the thin, uncovered dress she was wearing. Her blonde curls were scattered about her face, and she looked as though she would have blown over without the arm of the older man accompanying her.

"Are you feeling better? We missed you at work," Rosemary spoke, inhaling the strong sent of her co-worker's breath.

"I lied," Alta said and then laughed, letting go of the man's arm and almost falling on Rosemary. "I feel as fine as a hundred dollar bill!"

"Alta," the man leaned over, touching her face with his moustache, "I'll be in Vic's when you're finished talking to your girlfriends."

"Be with you in a second, honey."

"Go ahead. I know you want to know who the good-looking man is." She laughed when her date had left. "He's a filthy rich banker from Atlanta. Won't Mama and Daddy be proud?"

"How could you? What about Sydney?" Ava asked.

"What about him?" Alta stumbled backward in her high heels.

Ava and Rosemary both caught her arms.

"What about him? He's dead; time to move on."

290

"He's what?" Ava shouted, and she and Rosemary both looked at her in horror.

"He's dead," Alta answered more quietly, and as she did, the remark sobered her.

She sank to her knees and buried her face in the skirt of her dress.

"When? How do you know?" Ava asked, kneeling beside her with tears bubbling up in her eyes.

"I got...the...telegram....this morning," Alta mumbled in between escalating sobs.

Rosemary rocked her in her arms as Ava stared down at her in disbelief. Was it true? Could Edwin be dead too?

Despite the Christmas stockings hung in a neat row and the hope of James and Estelle coming home soon, Ava was cheerless. Sydney's death and her fear for Edwin never left her. She couldn't understand how someone so young could die. Death was for old and sick people, not healthy people just discovering life. Brother Whatley tried to help her understand by pointing out that Abel, Bathsheba's baby, and even Jesus died young by their standards, but it didn't comfort her. They were biblical people, not people from her life. For the first time, she believed in the frailty of life, and it stung her.

Instead of concentrating on her schoolwork and music, she thought about how many weeks since it happened she should expect a letter from Edwin. In his last letter, he wrote about how he and Sydney were sharing a foxhole and taking turns napping, and it seemed unreal to be reading about someone no longer breathing. Edwin's letters had become more irregular but she had learned to be patient. Now, she desperately wanted a letter from him more than anything she had ever wanted before.

291

A week passed, and her whole family shared her disconsolation. James and Estelle were not coming home for Christmas. He was denied a furlough pass. The Army wouldn't let any of the men leave because they were expected to be shipped out "any day," but that "any day" had already lingered for almost two months now. Even though James talked about his boredom with ongoing inspections and empty prognostications in his letters, he hid any actual restlessness to enter the war. After a sentence about the delays, Victoria would always comment that it was her prayers keeping his feet in Texas and away from Hitler.

Christmas was cold and quiet, and the New Year came uneventfully without the extra festivity Victoria desired. Letters from Edwin kept coming sporadically, all written before Sydney's death. Finally, the letter she anticipated came.

Deer Songbird

i dont know how to writ this. Sydney is dead. i saw it all it made no sense. we was in a ditch off a road he lifted his head to look out and a sniper hit him right betwen the eyes. it happen so fast. I lay beside him crying like baby. I was so afraid to move and then not to. tell Alta I wouldn't leeve him. I am sending for her his dog tags and last letter he writing to her.

Ava closed her eyes as the particulars of Sydney's death swirled unimaginably in her head. It all seemed so meaningless. If he wouldn't have lifted his head, everything could be different. Alta would still have a husband. It was unbelievable that a small, mundane movement of the body could result in so much pain. She finished the letter and folded it gently back together. Alta would want to know what really happened to her husband. All the war's victims did, no matter

292

how grotesque or unsavory the details proved to be. The knowledge provided a needed ending and stopped the imagination from its constant pursuit of guessing the truth.

When she went to see Alta, she couldn't tell her what she knew. Instead, she handed her the letter and waited close by. As she watched her friend read, she could tell that the facts of Sydney's death also seemed pointless to her by the way her eyes kept widening and narrowing in tacit questions.

"Tell Edwin thank you for me," Alta finally spoke, giving back the letter with moist eyes.

A slight smile curved her lips, and she clutched her husband's dog tags and the last letter he wrote to her. She knew the truth now, no matter what it meant.

Ava embraced her goodbye and left her with the last words she would ever receive from her husband. She couldn't help but wonder what Sydney's letter said. He couldn't have known that he was about to die. She paused at the door, but then went on. Words like that should be read alone.

Chapter 43

Ava hugged her knees to her chest and examined her red toenails as she listened to her mother recite another family letter from James. There were no individual letters from Estelle this time, and everyone was disappointed. All of their news would have to come from James's scant, routine correspondence.

"God is sending down a lot of rain on Texas right now. Being out in the field is miserable," Victoria read aloud. "Sleeping in half a tent on the wet ground is no picnic. I guess I better let you all know that Estelle has been feeling pretty puny. She is nauseous all the time and it's not the flu bug or the…"

Victoria's voice suddenly faltered, and Ava looked up at her mother. She was pressing one hand to her chest as her eyes expanded intuitively.

"Well, what is it?" Sheffield asked, folding up his long legs and sitting upright.

"I can't believe it!" Victoria looked from the letter to her husband. "Oh goodness!"

"Oh goodness what?" Grandpa Chester said, rubbing liniment on his dry elbows.

He was ready to hear the rest of his grandson's letter and retire for his after-supper nap.

"Estelle's expecting a baby!"

"Well, lordy mercy!" Sheffield jumped to his feet. "Are you sure?"

"What else does he write?" Ava asked.

"Let me see where I left off." Victoria narrowed her eyes, found her place in the letter, and began reading again, "She is nauseous all the time, and it's not the flu bug or the stomach ache. She is in the family way. The baby should arrive sometime in September."

"This certainly calls for a celebration. James is going to be a father, and we're going to be grandparents. Carson, go get us some cigars." Sheffield nudged his son's outstretched foot.

Carson, who hadn't moved from the floor throughout the letter, looked up at his father and then went for the cigars. Babies were mysterious anomalies to him, not something to celebrate.

"Another great-grandchild. Let's see that will make…um," Grandpa Chester thought out loud and looked up at the ceiling in calculation.

"I'm going to tell Jude and Myrtle," Victoria said, reaching for her shawl.

"I'll come. I want to tell Rosemary." Ava hurried back to her room for her coat.

"Aunt Ava," she whispered, catching sight of her reflection in the oval mirror sitting on her dresser.

She looked and felt much too young to be someone's aunt.

"Don't dawdle over it, scrub it." Victoria took the rag from Ava's hand to demonstrate the proper way to clean a window.

"I was scrubbing," Ava said when her mother bent over her and began stroking the window with all her might.

Ava leaned away. Her mother smelled like the homemade cleaner she was using to wipe down the kitchen -- a disagreeable mixture of lemon, vinegar, and dirty water.

"No, you weren't. This is a scrub, and this is what you were doing."

Ava frowned as her mother lightly brushed the window. She knew she was working harder than that.

"All right, I'm going back to the kitchen." Victoria put the soapy rag back in her daughter's hand. "Do a good job for Estelle. She isn't feeling her best."

"I will," Ava replied, trying hard to keep the frustration she felt out of her voice.

Another letter from James had revealed that he was sending Estelle home. He wrote that she was too sick in the afternoons to be alone most of the time, that he would definitely be leaving within the month, and that he hoped they would all help take care of her and the baby. Even though they were sorry for her daily discomfort, they were all thrilled she was coming home. Despite this, Ava couldn't understand why James's house needed a top to bottom cleaning. Everything was as neat as Estelle left it, but her mother insisted that every speck of dust and grime be wiped off the windows, the dishes, the tables, and the furniture. It was as if the smallest particle of dirt might contaminate the baby. Ava twisted her sore back, sighed at the spotless window, and vowed to herself that she would never wash windows when she had a home of her own. No matter how much she disliked it, though, having Estelle back would make it all worth it. Sheffield and Carson were picking her up from the Anniston train station that evening, and they would be waiting for her with a more than tidy house.

"Heavenly sunlight, heavenly sunlight," she heard her mother singing from the next room.

She dropped the rag, thinking about asking to stay with Estelle again, but decided to wait. Of course, they would want her to stay here. She just needed to be patient. A smile broke out over her face, and she picked back up the rag and began scrubbing the window as vigorously as her fingers would allow.

They cleaned all afternoon and then went home to cook a welcome back feast. Supper was fixed and sat cooling for over half an hour before James's car grunted up the driveway.

"She's here! Annie! Victoria!" Grandpa Chester yelled from the porch swing.

Ava ran out the door with her mother close behind. She still smelled like vinegar and lemon, despite the fried chicken and gravy she was cooking. Estelle emerged from the car smiling up at them. They all knew she didn't want to leave James, but she at least looked happy to see everyone again. She hurried for them as Sheffield closed the door behind her, and Carson carried her bags. Victoria scurried down the steps toward her daughter-in-law, and Ava followed and took in Estelle's appearance. Even though it was early, she naively expected Estelle's body to be softer and fuller with the pregnancy. Instead, she was gaunt and thin. Her floral dress fell loosely over her figure, and her cheekbones were painfully prominent under her dark skin.

"Looks like you need to be fed," Victoria said and embraced her.

"James said that was the first thing you would say to me." Estelle laughed.

Ava breathed easier, noticing how her cheeks still turned pink when she showed emotion, and how her amber eyes still shone with interested kindness at whomever she spoke to.

"I just can't keep anything down." She reached now for Ava.

Ava hugged her back, feeling her frail shoulder bones against her plumper arms. Something about it brought tears to her eyes, and she realized just how much she had missed her sister-in-law.

"We'll fix that." Victoria led her up the steps.

"Looking pretty as ever," Grandpa Chester said when it was his turn to be embraced.

The supper was more chatter than food as they caught up on all the things left out of James's letters. Ava couldn't wait to be alone with her sister-in-law. Estelle's inquisitive smiles hinted at her interest in all the things she could only speak of in private -- her letters from Edwin, Rosemary's heart break, and her music. After supper, Carson took Estelle to see her mother and sisters, and Ava was indeed allowed to pack her things and go on over and wait for her. As she waited, she wondered if Estelle would notice all their cleaning. Even though she wouldn't admit it to her mother, everything did have a crisper sparkle. It wasn't long before Estelle came back. She looked worn and tired, but her face lit up when she entered her house.

"Oh, it's so good to be back in my own house and away from that dismal room at Mrs. Fletcher's." Estelle sighed and collapsed in James's chair.

She looked fondly about the house at all the things she had been without the last several months. A cloud came over her face for a moment, and Ava knew she wished James was with her.

"Someone's been cleaning," Estelle said, and Ava confessed what they had been doing all afternoon.

"Any new letters from Edwin?"

Ava smiled and removed a letter from her father's old suitcase. There was so much to tell her that she had been unable to communicate in her letters. It seemed impossible to fully explain Rosemary's sadness, which she had promised not to relate the whole truth about, Sydney's death, and her worries over how it was affecting Edwin in a few dozen words. She needed expression and the passion of her voice to really tell it all, and it came pouring out of her like water rushing over a defeated dam.

Chapter 44

Ava stood to the far side of the bedroom window and lifted the lace curtain just enough to see outside. Her eyes searched in every direction until they found Estelle on her knees vomiting. She watched her sister-in-law's stomach lurch, and her hands grasp at the grass. Her afternoon spells were as bad as James described, and Ava felt miserable for her. Estelle covered the ground she stooped over with a thin layer of dirt, patted her face with her sleeve, and stood up. Ava ran back to her book, pretending not to have seen. When Estelle came back inside, she smiled, but her cheeks were sallow, and her forehead was spotted with beads of perspiration.

"I think I'm going to lie down a bit before supper."

"Are you sure there's nothing Mom or I can do?" Ava asked, closing her book.

"I'll be better. This baby just has to get used to me, that's all. No need to bother your mother," Estelle said and then lay down, clamping her teeth together and fighting another urge to vomit.

When she didn't get better over the next week and her vomiting grew more frequent and uncontrollable, Ava broke her promise and fetched her mother. Victoria hurried over and was soon bent over her daughter-in-law's body on the ground, soothing her with her fingers and words.

"It's o.k., Estelle," she whispered in the low, almost musical voice she always used with sick people.

Goose bumps went up Ava's spine. Her mother's voice had a way of healing and calming her like nothing else.

"Wipe your mouth on this." Victoria dabbed Estelle's mouth with a warm wet cloth and stroked back her hair.

Estelle pushed away the cloth and vomited again, but then obeyed and pressed it back to her quivering lips.

"Ava, help me get her inside."

Ava wrapped Estelle's right arm around her neck, and they carried her inside to the bed.

"Just rest. I'll bring supper to you," Victoria said.

"I'm so sorry." Tears streamed down Estelle's face.

"For what?"

"For worrying you when you already have so much to worry about," Estelle said as Victoria pressed the cloth to her wet cheeks. "I wasn't going to tell you until tonight, but…."

"But what?" Victoria asked, fearful of what she was about to hear but refusing to betray it in her voice.

"James is on his way to Europe. I have a letter I was going to bring you tonight."

"Shh…shh…," Victoria silenced her. "We'll talk about that later. Right now you need to rest. There is more to life than a man, Estelle, even if he is my son. You have a baby and yourself to take care of now. You have to leave James to God. You hear?"

Estelle nodded, and Ava stood back in awe of her mother's strength and composure. When Estelle finally closed her eyes, Victoria motioned for Ava to follow, and they left her.

"Just stay with her to supper, and I'll be over," Victoria spoke still in the same low manner.

Even though strength remained in her voice and eyes, Ava could see a new fear in the lines of her face.

With her mother-in-law's constant attention, Estelle's condition rapidly improved. Victoria made her lie down every afternoon around 2:00 and continually cooked and served her foods without strong smells and tastes to prevent nausea. A healthy shade of pink returned to her face, and her weight began to steadily increase.

"Do you think I shouldn't have sent that photograph to Edwin," Ava said, peering over the top of her letter at Estelle's prostrated figure.

"Of course you should have. Even though he doesn't like the soldier in the picture with you, he is proud to have a resemblance of you to look at and show to his buddies," Estelle replied, unconsciously placing a hand on her stomach.

Ava looked at Estelle's abdomen. It was hard to believe that another human being was growing inside such a small space.

"I suppose, but he keeps it folded in half to just see me, and it took a lot of convincing for him to believe that I don't even know the man."

Ava lifted the letter and hid a smile, secretly pleased by his jealousy.

"Do you know what you should do? You should have another picture made of yourself for him."

Ava's eyes widened with the idea. The only photographs she had ever had made of herself were her school pictures.

"Margaret used a photographer on Noble Street to take the children's picture," Estelle spoke of her older sister. "They were really good. You should go see him. If he can make three rowdy children appear pleasant and peaceful, he can do wonders with a beautiful girl."

Ava's eyes sparked with a new idea.

"Only if you go with me," she said.

"Me? James doesn't need a picture of me. He's seen me all his life."

"Yes, he does. We could go Saturday morning when you're feeling better and I don't have school. Please."

Estelle gazed at her thoughtfully and then consented with a gradual smile.

"All right, I guess a picture might help James remember his wife when he's surrounded by all those European girls."

Ava felt like a movie star. The photographer brushed back a strand of her hair and adjusted the black lace wrap around her bare shoulders.

"Perfect," he said, stepping back and approving her appearance.

The dark color of the wrap would stand out and show off her smooth, white skin even in a black and white photograph, and the way her hair curled away from her forehead and ears would help him focus the head shot on the luminosity of her face.

He walked back behind the camera, and Estelle winked at her and mouthed, "Gorgeous."

"Tilt your head slightly toward your right shoulder, Miss Stilwell," the photographer directed, and Ava obeyed.

She could feel the black beaded choker she was wearing strain against her neck as she turned. The camera began flashing, and she concentrated on keeping her burgundy lips fixed in a natural position. She wanted to manage a warm smile that wasn't too wide and friendly or closed and uninviting, and she hoped that the one she practiced in front of the mirror was being portrayed.

"All finished," the photographer said when the last flash penetrated the half-lit room. "You'll make a lovely photograph."

Ava thanked him and stepped down from the stool she had posed on.

"Mrs. Stilwell, it's your turn now." He turned to Estelle.

Even though Estelle insisted on wearing the simple, green dress she declared was James's favorite, she did allow Ava to curl back her straight hair and suggest a flattering shade of pink lip balm. While Ava was confident in front of the camera, Estelle was shy and embarrassed.

"For James," Ava whispered, and Estelle smiled on the photographer's cue.

The mention of his name lit up the gold in her amber eyes, and the look was just right, a mixture of love-inspired boldness and honesty. Ava was sure that it was the one James fell in love with.

Chapter 45

When Carson's knee nudged hers for the second time, Ava opened up one eye from her attitude of prayer and fastened it angrily on her brother's down-turned face. The look was powerless. He didn't even notice that he was hitting her. Their mother was playing, and their father was singing *Just As I Am* as Brother Whatley concluded the Sunday morning service.

"If you're struggling with sin, come on down to the altar," he pleaded in first a whisper and then as a loud command. "Don't turn your back on Jesus."

Ava glanced at her brother's bouncing knee again and then at his fingers which were fidgeting with first his Bible and then the back of his neck.

He's certainly convicted about something.

His eyes were shut tight, and he looked as if he was in pain.

"Don't let another day end without giving your cares to the Lord." Brother Whatley paced the aisles and peered at each humbled head as he passed. "We never know when today will be our last."

Ava closed her eyes when he neared their pew, but she reopened them when she felt Carson move from beside her. He met Brother Whatley in the center of the aisle, and they walked together back to the altar. Victoria's piano playing slowed as she concentrated more on her son than on the sheets of music before her, and Sheffield's voice halted for a moment to match the change in tempo. Brother Whatley bent over Carson's kneeling figure and prayed in fast, urgent whispers. Sheffield sang two more verses of song before the preacher finished his prayer and addressed the whole congregation again.

"Brethren, we have joyous tidings today. Brother Stilwell here has answered the call of preaching the Word."

Ava's mouth fell open at the unexpected news. Carson smiled sheepishly out at the congregation until his mother's arms landed around him.

The idea of Carson becoming a pastor was one that Ava would have to adjust to. As she listened to him explain his intentions to their family, she couldn't dissociate the conniving, temperamental side of her brother from his new religious one.

"It's something I've felt for the last several months. Actually, I started knowing that it was what God wanted me to do when I was up at the fort working with the prisoners."

"When God wants you to do something, son, he won't let you rest until you do it." Sheffield patted his son's back knowingly.

Carson nodded. Having mature conversations with his parents and being treated as an adult were new to him.

"Are you wanting to pastor a church nearby?" Victoria asked.

She had always longed for a son in the ministry.

"Actually, I...," Carson paused, "I want to be a chaplain at the P.O.W. camp first."

This news astonished Victoria as much as the first news surprised her daughter.

306

"What?" Her smile vanished, and her eyebrows raised themselves upward.

"They need a Baptist chaplain at the camp, and I've already talked to Major Thunderstrom about the possibility. He said after I was ordained, they could add me to the service rotation."

"That sounds fine, son," Sheffield said, placing a calming arm around his wife.

"Are you sure that's what you're supposed to do?" Victoria couldn't resist asking.

"Those prisoners need God too," Grandpa Chester entered the conversation on behalf of his grandson.

He believed that when a man made a decision it shouldn't be challenged.

"I know that. I just wanted to…," Victoria didn't finish her explanation, recognizing the weakness of her objection.

"Yes, I'm sure. As a matter of fact, I think that's why God didn't let me join the Army, and I know it sounds strange for James to be fighting the same men I'm helping, but that's what I think my role is supposed to be in this war. I know it must seem like it did when the apostle Paul preached to the Gentiles rather than the Jews, but that's what I have to do." Carson sighed. It felt good to release what he had been dealing with every day of his life recently.

No one spoke as they contemplated his words. There was nothing to discuss. He was a man now, and his decision was inviolable to their argument. Finally, Victoria rose from her chair and embraced her son.

Two weeks passed, and, as the congregation ordained James for war, they ordained Carson for the ministry. Once again, Ava sat still in her pew, watching the long of line of men lay hands on and pray over her brother. Estelle sat beside her as before, lifting up her own silent supplications for Carson and James too. Rosemary was on her other side, also observing the procession. Victoria's music wasn't as grave as it was for James but was merrily light and reverent all at once. Cousin Jude finished his turn with Carson and stepped aside. As he did, Ava caught a glimpse of her brother's bowed head and bent knees in the sawdust. She wondered what he was thinking. She didn't know that she could manage a straight face if all those men were breathing and sweating over her.

The Reverend Stilwell. She smiled at the sound of the words in her head.

She hoped the title wouldn't change him. She wanted him to remain the joke-playing and sometimes irascible brother she knew so well. In spite of her selfish misgivings and even though she would never tell him, she admired and respected him for his decision. The interminable service finally concluded, and they went home for a celebratory meal with yet another chocolate cake.

Chapter 46

Ava unfastened her high heels and stretched out on her stomach next to the creek. It was the first place Edwin kissed her and the ideal place to read his letters. It was also one of those rare, perfect May days. Not because it was neither unbearably hot nor cold, but because the mild, rejuvenating breeze whispered promises of new life and things to come. Orange, purple, and pink flowers that hadn't bloomed since last year were budding and popping out all over. The sounds of playful birds were plentiful, and the young grass was fresh and soft to the feet. She felt of the envelope again. It was thicker than usual, and she was eager to devour what lay inside. As she opened it, the events of the past year rippled like the creek through her mind. In less than two weeks, she would be eighteen and a high school graduate. She remembered her birthday last year and then the more important day after, the day she met Edwin. In a way, it seemed like she had just met him, and in another way, she couldn't remember not knowing him. His writing was quickly improving, and with every letter, she felt as though they were melting more and more into a shared existence. He was keeping his promise. He was writing to her about himself and not just about daily happenings full of customary and empty words. She smiled as she read the first line. He was finally spelling "dear" correctly.

Dear songbird,

I hate to open letter with more bad news I just saw Barry. he is hert with strapnul wounds to the chest. the doc say he will get beter. I've get a few more days of rest here before moving out. I've been staying with him chering him up. I writ Marg for him to tell her that he will be home soon. can you believe? I almost wish it was me wonded. I cant help it but all I can think about is you. I kep thinking about what if I don't I get to see you agein or kiss you agein. that thought is worse than tiredness, bad food, and war itself. just in case I don't I want to tell you how much I love you and ask you to mary me. just knowing you wont to mary me too and that I could maried you will be enough for me. I wish I could do things right and ask you dad and get down on my knee but I cant. Im jelous of Barry. at leest, he knows what it was like to marry the one he loves...

Disbelieving, Ava's eyes grew to the size of jar lids, and she reread the last few lines to assure herself.

"Did he really ask me to marry him?" she asked out loud.

As the letter confirmed it, she rolled over on her back and kicked her bare feet into the air.

"Yes, yes, yes," she shouted over and over again as if he could hear her.

She hurried to her feet, held his proposal to her chest, and ran all the way to Estelle's house. She had to tell someone that she was an engaged woman. Estelle wasn't at home, so she ran to her own house. Carson was loitering down the steps, and she almost knocked him over.

"Watch out!"

310

"Move it then, Reverend Dufus." Ava laughed.

She pushed open the screen door to find Estelle lying down as Victoria and Myrtle planned the next garden club meeting over her.

"What's the matter with you?" Victoria asked, seeing her daughter's face. "Has Jesus just come back?"

"I'm engaged!"

She didn't care this time how to best tell her parents. She just wanted to say it and keep saying it.

"Really? How? When?" Victoria, Estelle, and Myrtle all flooded her with questions, and she told them everything.

At the garden club meeting on Saturday, Ava was pleased to find herself the immediate topic of conversation.

"He wrote her the most romantic letter to propose," Victoria told Opal Gunter and Alice Fitzpatrick, the first two women, besides Myrtle, Estelle, and her daughter, to arrive.

Ava blushed with satisfaction and a hint of guilt, realizing that Edwin would not be happy to know that other eyes than hers had seen his passionate and imperfect declaration of love.

"Did your soldier propose to you in a letter?" Maris Ingram, who had just arrived, asked to catch up on the part of the conversation she had missed.

Ava nodded yes.

"How romantic to fall in love in the midst of such a perilous time," Alice sighed, and they all envied being young and receiving such a portentous love letter.

"Did you answer yes, dear?" Opal said, leaning in to Ava as if they were sharing secrets.

Ava didn't have time to answer as the arrival of Abigail Dempsey, Delores Waters, and her aunts Ingrid Carson and Elizabeth Parris each solicited a retelling of the story.

"Does James write such lovely letters?" Ingrid turned her fat chin and bulging blue eyes in Estelle's direction.

"No, no." Estelle laughed. "I'm afraid he's already too sure of me."

"Where is James now?" Abigail asked.

"He's billeted with a family in England," Estelle replied, and all the eyes that were on Ava were now observing her.

"Not for long, I'm afraid, if my nephew, who is also in England, is right," Delores spoke up. "He writes his mother that something big is about to happen over there."

Estelle's cheeks paled to the color of her white dress, but her lips and eyes stood steady.

"Pooh, something big is always about to happen," Ingrid said, throwing up two hands.

"I suppose," Delores muttered, aggravated to have her information belittled.

"How are you feeling, dear?" Opal now leaned in to Estelle. "Do you feel like a mother yet?"

Estelle's face regained its healthy color, and the yellow in her amber eyes glowed with the more agreeable subject.

"Ladies, I think we're all here, now, so let's get started," Victoria announced loudly over the several competing conversations that had broken out over love, war, and babies.

Her voice had an immediate effect, and they all grew quiet and turned their thoughts to the purpose of their gathering.

"Of course, this month we're talking about spring flowers. So when my daughter reads out your name, please respond with a spring flower."

"Myrtle Bonds," Ava called out from the official role call.

"Tulips." Myrtle giggled, and the meeting began.

Later that night, Ava sat up with Estelle as she ate a cold biscuit to keep from getting nauseous. They were both thinking about the garden club conversation.

"Does it still bother you to hear about the war?" Ava asked.

"Do you mean like what Delores Waters said today?" Estelle replied and lifted the first bite of dry, unwanted biscuit to her lips.

"Yea, that or just anything."

"I'd be a liar if I said it didn't, but I'm learning to be strong like your mother. I've changed the way I think about everything."

Ava looked into her sister-in-law's face, waiting for more.

"As long as God has a purpose for your life, he won't let anything harm you," she swallowed a sip of sweet milk and continued. "Now, James's life has the greatest purpose it could possibly have, so I try not to worry anymore."

Estelle rubbed her only slightly larger abdomen, and Ava realized that she was speaking of James being a father. She moved her hand from her stomach to Ava's hand lying on the table.

"Edwin also has a greater purpose now."

There was a tranquil, determined strength in her eyes. Ava smiled, both admiring and inwardly attempting the same

313

faith. However, the thought of Sydney's death always tested her confidence, and she was afraid that raised hopes would only accentuate her fear.

Chapter 47

Three weeks went by without another letter from Edwin, but Ava tried not to worry. His letters were often sporadic, and she romantically pictured him unable to write her another word until he knew that she had agreed to marry him. Her favorite daydream now was imagining him when he received her lengthy response. She could see his strong hands ripping open the letter's seal, his ears reddening with suspense, his forehead wrinkling as he concentrated on understanding her sprawling, cursive writing, his feral eyes first softening and then shining as he read, and finally, an indomitable smile breaking across his handsome, austere face. This is what she was thinking of as she walked into her house one Tuesday morning. School was over, but she wouldn't go back to work for another two weeks. Her mother was anxious to have her help with several annual cleaning projects.

The figures of her father and grandpa, sitting close by the radio, broke through her wistful thinking. She was surprised to see them. Normally, they would already be out feeding the animals. Her father's neck was bent forward over the black box, his elbows were upright on his knees, and his whole body was stiff. Grandpa Chester was more relaxed, but his arms were limp by his slouching sides, and his eyes were fixed on the ceiling above. Ava didn't dare move another step or say a word. Instead, she held her breath and listened to the clear, authoritative male voice coming through the box.

"Under the command of General Eisenhower, Allied naval forces, supported by strong air forces, began landing Allied armies this morning on the northern coast of France."

There was a long pause, and a more somber male voice spoke.

"You have just heard Colonel Ernest Dupuy, Eisenhower's press aide, confirm the invasion of Europe on June 6, 1944."

There was a loud sigh from her parents' bedroom, and Ava realized that her mother was also listening. They each knew that they had just been told where James was.

The workday was immediately defunct, and Ava spent part of the morning on her knees in prayer next to her mother and the other part of the morning checking on Estelle, whose newly inspired faith remained unyielding against the momentous news. By late morning, her head was pounding from having fasted breakfast, and she decided to escape her mother's prayer vigil and walk to town for ice cream. She scrounged up some pocket change from her quickly dwindling cup of work money and left without telling anyone where she was going. She would be ashamed if they knew. Ice cream seemed like a celebratory treat, not something to enjoy while her brother was in peril.

The day was both beautiful and surreal. She couldn't remember the last time she had a complete day of leisure, and the caressing sunshine was tempting happier thoughts again. She did fear for her brother, but she refused to fret in the face of Estelle's assurance. She was also certain that Edwin wasn't there. He was still in the Mediterranean, and her thoughts guiltily returned to his receiving her favorable letter.

316

As she entered the Jacksonville Square in route to the Westend Drug Store, the news of the day barraged her again. Instead of working, groups of farmers and tradesman stood in clusters guessing what the radio and papers didn't know and couldn't tell them. Church bells were ringing off the hour as if they were sounding an alarm, and car horns were answering back their call. She stood in the middle of the square listening to the diurnal noises that didn't compare to that of roaring planes, exploding shells, and shouting men that her brother was somewhere hearing. An abandoned paper blew to where she was standing, and she read it's screaming, bold headline – "INVASION!"

What does it all mean? Her head signaled her hunger again. *Will this one day decide the outcome of the war, James, and my family?*

She could feel the incendiary magnitude of the event setting a flame within her, and she wished with all the other people around her that she could see what was actually taking place on the vague, already infamous beachhead.

"Ava!" a girlish voice shouted beside her.

She looked up to see Aggie. Her strawberry blonde curls were scattered around her face, and her freckled cheeks were red from running.

"What are you doing here?" Aggie asked.

"Um, getting something to eat," Ava replied, still embarrassed of her selfish errand.

"Good, let's get some ice cream." Aggie smiled. "I'm starved. You know Jimmy's mother thinks he's there."

She accented the word "there," which didn't need defining.

"You think James is there?"

317

"We're sure he is," Ava said, and they crossed the street to the drug store.

"How's your other preacher brother?" Aggie giggled, and Ava looked at her crossly.

She could make fun of Carson, but she didn't want Aggie doing it, no matter how flirtatious it was intended.

"You girls want ice cream? Well, you better hurry. We're closing up." Clyde Ponder stuck his balding head through the door and hurried them inside.

"Closing?"

"Yep, that's right. Everywhere's closing up on account of D-day."

During the next few days, more and more reports began feeding the country's insatiable appetite for information, and everyone's vocabulary changed with place names like Utah Beach, Pointe du Hoc, and Omaha Beach. Ava still turned with her father to Ernie Pyle's articles for the personal, more human story. What he wrote gave one eyes to see the details of what was far away and unimaginable. He didn't attempt to illustrate the entire face of the battle. Instead, he gave readers the little pieces that made up and helped to understand the whole. In his latest article, the little pieces were "snapshots of families back home staring up at you from the sand," "bloody, abandoned shoes," "portable radios smashed beyond recognition," and "one youngster" who he thought was dead, but was "only sleeping." Ava paused over the dead soldier, who Ernie described as "young" and "tired" and holding a "large, smooth rock" as if "it were his last link with a vanishing world." Her imagination painted in first James's and then Edwin's face. Somehow, the image helped more than hurt, because it said they were all right even if the worst had happened. She sighed when the article ended, feeling as if someone had just turned off the only source of truthful illumination and all was darkness once again.

Several weeks passed and the best news that could ever be written about the war arrived. It was a letter from James, proving beyond every doubt that he had survived.

Hi family,

I guess you have heard by now that we snuck up on Jerry. I wasn't with the first wave to hit the beach, but we were soon after. You should have seen the waste and wreckage. I have never seen such a fireworks display in all my life. Bodies of soldiers were everywhere. It is numbing that so many men have to lose their lives. I guess that is something you have to figure out in church. I have barely slept since we hit the beaches. It seems like every few hours we are digging new foxholes or taking over ones left behind. Combat isn't exactly like I expected. It's a lot of hurry up and wait that can drive you mad. I was afraid I would forget everything I've been taught, but I surprised myself. I would tell you more, but it wouldn't make it past the censors. I love you all and hope to be home soon. But for now, I've got to chase Jerry through France.

Love always,
James

Chapter 48

Twelve weeks, the distressing thought erupted inside Ava again.

She looked out Wakefield's polished windows at the hot sidewalk and busy by-passers. Anniston had lost its charm.

"Where are you, Edwin?" she whispered as she searched the faces of those who passed but didn't enter.

It was a slow business day. People had staying cool on their minds, not spending money. The window display was her task alone today. Alta was in Mobile with her parents, and Rosemary was working the floor and unoccupied dressing rooms. She hung a red hat with a black feather on Lana the mannequin. In spite of her personal disappointment, it was still satisfying to create. The hat was tilted too much to one side, and she gently pushed its delicate brim in the other direction.

"Why did I ever tell Aggie and Floraline?" she asked the lifeless Lana.

She no longer considered herself engaged, and she was tired of running into them in town, smiling numbly, and confessing that she still hadn't received any more letters. They were too curious and cruel not to ask. Her mind had invented a dozen excuses for him, and with each one, her emotions fluctuated from anger to remorse to fear. He had changed his mind about marrying her. He never received her response and believed that she had refused him. He had written, but his mail wasn't getting through. He was captured, a prisoner of war. He was hurt. There was one thought she would never entertain, however, and that was that he was forever incapable of writing her again.

The bell on the front door greeted a new customer, but Ava didn't look up. She was smoothing down Lana's corn silk hair. Rosemary's surprised laughter and the voice of her mother drew her mind back into the store. She looked through the open display case at Rosemary introducing Victoria, Myrtle, and Estelle to Mrs. Crockett. Estelle looked in her direction. Her usually thin cheeks were puffed up, and her pink face was emanating the life within. Her cotton dress stretched tightly against her now round, overt belly, and all the church and garden club ladies were predicting a girl.

"Ava, take a break and help your mother do some shopping," Mrs. Crockett called out.

Ava left the window and joined their group. She couldn't believe that her mother was actually there. She had promised to come, but household duties always kept her away.

"I would like to have a look at some of those nylon stockings." Victoria winked at her daughter and clutched her Sunday purse to look as if shopping from stores, rather than peddlers, was routine instead of seldom.

"Give them a full tour of the store," Mrs. Crockett said to Rosemary and Ava and then turned toward their guests. "It's a pleasure to meet you. Both of your daughters are excellent workers."

The commendation in front of her mother and her mother's gratified smile pleased Ava more than she thought it would.

"This is of course our women's area," Rosemary began the tour. "We even have a few things for expectant mothers."

"Nonsense," Victoria whispered, "Estelle doesn't need to waste money on clothes she will only wear for a couple more months. We'll just keep letting out some of her old dresses and make news ones ourselves when we have to."

Estelle shared a secret smile with her sister-in-law, and they continued through the racks of women's apparel.

"Mom, you've never even tried on a store-bought dress. Why don't you pick out a couple to put on," Ava said, stopping at a rack of new arrivals.

She selected a periwinkle suit with a short jacket and lifted it up for her mother to see. Victoria took it from her and flipped up the skirt to examine the hem.

"I'm not sure about this hem. What do you think, Myrtle?"

Myrtle bent forward and squinted at the questionable garment.

"Oh, Mom, it's fine." Ava laughed. "This is one of our best brands."

They looked at numerous dresses and, with much prompting, even tried on a couple before each left with a pair of nylon hosiery. Stockings were one thing Victoria couldn't manufacture herself. The bell rang out as they left, and Ava returned to the window display. She was glad they had come. She pulled out a new pair of men's dress shoes from a box on the floor and contemplated where to showcase them. The thought of Edwin instantly provoked her good spirits again, and she went to laughing at her mother's thriftiness to alleviate the pain.

"Your mother went on and on all the way home about how you and Rosemary are so smart looking when you help costumers and about how Mrs. Crockett is so pleased with you," Estelle said as Ava cut a long piece of string over her bare belly.

"At least she liked us more than the clothes." Ava laughed and held out her hand. "Wedding ring."

Estelle nudged and then forced off the gold wedding band from her swollen finger.

"I may not be able to get this back on."

Ava took the ring from her, looped the string through it, and tied the ends of the string together.

"Now, let's see if it really is a girl." Ava dangled the string over her sister-in-law's abdomen and smiled mischievously.

She saw movement underneath Estelle's taut skin, and the unexpected sight stopped her for a moment. She had felt the baby kick but not seen it before. It was hard to believe that a part of James was so active and close.

"That was a hard one." Estelle laughed, and Ava refocused her attention on their superstitious endeavor.

Ava was glad her mother couldn't see them acting out her Aunt Elizabeth's advice. She would call it "playing with witchcraft." Ava moved her fingers from side to side and began swinging the ring. The tale went that if the string moved in a neat, up-and-down motion, the woman could expect a boy, but if the string moved in haphazard circles, the woman could expect a girl. They both watched as the gold ring wobbled and then cut through the air in wide, oblong circles.

"I guess we can write to James that it's a girl," Ava said, and they both fell to laughing at the nonsense of what they were doing.

"That's what he always wanted."

"Good, cause that's what he's getting." Ava stopped the gold ring in the palm of her hand. She looked down at it for a moment before untying the string.

"Edwin will come back," Estelle said, and Ava looked up at her, desperate for assurance.

"How do you know?" she asked as all the pain she felt crept into her eyes and voice.

"I can't explain it, but I just know that he will." Estelle smiled, and her calming clairvoyance brought a longed for peace to Ava's heart.

Chapter 49

Anniston ignited on September 15, 1944. News of the fire consumed Ava and Rosemary as soon as they stepped off the bus. Everyone's eyes were fixed upward at the continuous stream of dense, black smoke rushing up into the air and multiplying into unhealthy clouds.

"Where's it coming from?" Rosemary's eyes tried to follow the dark mass back to its root.

As if in response, the words "The Alabama Hotel" bounced back and forth from knowing persons returning from the scene.

"It's been burning since just before 5:00. They think everyone got out in time," a man in suspenders called to an approaching friend across the street.

"The whole building's coming down!" another man yelled.

They were early for work, and Ava and Rosemary hurried with the crowd toward the corner of Twelfth and Noble Streets to witness the culminating destruction. When they neared the smoldering building, whose first flames had already been extinguished, the fetid odor was suffocating, and they both covered their mouths and noses with their hands. Policeman forced the burgeoning crowd back. Firemen struggled to keep a constant flow of water concentrated on the hotel.

"I don't believe it," Ava said, watching the demise of the once grand building.

She looked first at the hotel's brass door which had turned black with the escaping smoke and thought of Edwin going through that very door to make a reservation for his furlough. Running her eyes up to the highest floor, which was disintegrating from within and crushing the floors below, she recalled when James and Estelle honeymooned there. Estelle had been delighted at sleeping above the city. The dazzling chandeliers, burgundy carpet, and suited bellboys absorbed her thoughts and sickened her heart. The waste was overpowering, and she could now understand how the wreckage of war stimulated Ernie Pyle's writing.

"They think a guest is still trapped inside," they overheard a woman who worked at the bank tell a co-worker who had just arrived.

"I thought everyone got out," Rosemary said. "Do they know who the person is?"

In such events, everything said was said to everyone. "No one knows."

A policeman was shouting, "Step back," and the crowd moved and pushed backward. The news that someone might or had lost their life lessened the importance of the structure and turned Ava's thoughts horrifically to the people affected. She looked back up at the top floor, her eyes scanning the windows of the rooms that still existed. Is someone still in there? Who could it be?

The newspapers the next day answered all the city's questions. Two people died, a man who attempted to lower himself to the ground with a chain of sheets and a Mrs. Violet Hemmert. Ava read and wept over the untimely obituary that interested many who never knew the young woman. She was a soldier's wife visiting her husband at Fort McClellan. The fire not only destroyed a prized landmark, but it also emblazed the name of an unknown woman into the memories of a whole town.

The conflagration that swept a corner of Anniston spread to the Stilwell household. Estelle was experiencing labor pains, and everyone was on alert. Grandpa Chester, Sheffield, and Carson stayed away as much as possible and tiptoed around the house without their boots on in fear of disturbing what they did not understand. Ava and Rosemary hurried home everyday expecting to encounter a crying baby, and Victoria, who remained controlled and lucid, conferred with Myrtle and Mott Dempsey, cared for Estelle, and waited for the impending moment.

Exactly two weeks after the fire and the death of Violet Hemmert, Ava and Rosemary left Wakefield's with pink and white wrapped packages. They eagerly watched Estelle's face as she unwrapped first the white, lacy infant's gown from Ava and then the matching bonnet and booties from Rosemary.

"They're adorable!" Estelle contorted her full face into an appreciative smile.

"I'm sure Mom can find a fault with them somewhere, but we thought she would look like a princess dressed in these," Ava said.

"She'll be the prettiest princess alive thanks to both of you."

The baby was always referred to as "she" now as everyone, including Victoria, believed the baby to be a girl. Grandpa Chester even called the unborn child "Little Estelle."

Ava and Rosemary spent the rest of the evening talking to keep Estelle's mind off the escalating pain in her abdomen. Later that night, when Rosemary had left and Ava was asleep, she felt a series of soft pushes on her shoulder and then heard her sister-in-law calling to her.

"Ava, my water's broke. Go get your mother," Estelle said when Ava's eyes were open and aware.

"She's coming?" Ava whispered in fright, looking down at the roundness underneath Estelle's ivory gown.

"Yes," Estelle heaved, and Ava realized that she was having difficulty breathing.

"If James could only be here," she heard her sister-in-law say when she ran out into the darkness that separated the two houses.

The screen door flung open and then slammed shut behind her, but, before she could get to her parents' bedroom, her mother was by her side, already dressed. For days, Victoria had listened for this exact moment.

"Her water broke!"

"I'll take care of things," Victoria said and gathered a bundle of items that had been laid out in preparation.

She was one of the best midwives in the community and had helped deliver dozens of babies.

"Carson!" she shouted, and the untidy head of her son appeared at his door, gazing at them with puffy, half-shut eyes.

"Go fetch Dr. Green. Ava, go get Myrtle." She was out the door.

Carson disappeared back into his room to find his boots, and Ava ran back out into the cool night. Her gown flapped in the chilly, late September breeze, but she didn't notice the shiver it produced. She was intent on following her mother's instructions as quickly as possible. She opened the door of her cousin's house and called out to her aunt, who was also listening for her.

"Is it time?" Myrtle asked, and Rosemary also appeared.

"Yes!"

"Rosemary, get dressed. You can help too," Myrtle said.

Minutes later, the three of them were on their way to join Victoria in the nocturnal delivery of her first grandchild. No sooner had they arrived, when headlights peeped then bounced through the trees before landing glaringly on the house. Carson turned off the engine, the lights vanished, and Dr. Green was out of the car and through the front door.

"Hello, Ava. Hello, Rosemary," he greeted before pushing open the door to Estelle's bedroom.

Rosemary's eyes fell underneath his brief, kind gaze, and her betrayal of his son slapped her in the face. She felt unworthy to be in his presence. The door closed behind him and then reopened.

"We need more pans of water," Victoria said.

More errands came throughout the night. Ava and Rosemary tirelessly fulfilled them all and waited outside the room listening to Estelle's screams and cries, Dr. Green's whispered instructions, and their mothers' movements. Finally, the cry of a baby was heard. Estelle was asking to see her little girl, but everything did not turn to calm. Urgent rustlings were overheard, followed by Dr. Green's louder directives.

"She's bleeding too much," he was saying more loudly than before.

Estelle was now quiet, and the baby's escalating screams and gasps of first air were all that could be heard. The next time Victoria came to the door, her composure was breaking, and her bottom lip trembled as she spoke.

"More sheets, towels, whatever you can find."

They ran throughout both houses finding what was needed, both terrified of what the silence and agitation behind the closed door might mean. Sheffield, Grandpa Chester, and Carson were all on the front porch waiting with ready cigars for the joyous news of the delivery. They said nothing as Ava and Rosemary passed, knowing that they were men and that, in such circumstances, they were not to interfere. Victoria reached out her arms for what they brought back, and the door closed again for what seemed like an interminable time, even though it was only half an hour. When the door reopened, Victoria emerged with a tiny, purplish baby in her arms. With its wrinkled face and oblong head, Ava thought it looked more like an alien than a little girl.

"This is your niece," Victoria said to her daughter, holding the baby out from her bosom.

She now looked up, and Ava and Rosemary saw something else and unexpected in her eyes. They were darker and full of both pain and joy.

"I need you to go get your father. I'm afraid Estelle is no longer with us. She didn't survive the birth of her daughter."

Ava felt like a crushing wind had knocked her over. Tears blurred her vision, and her body shook in disbelief. Myrtle was now with them, and she held Rosemary and Ava in her arms.

"I'll go talk to the Dempseys," Dr. Green said, his voice full of sincere sympathy.

Rosemary looked up at him over her mother's shoulder. He appeared tired and defeated, but his eyes were still tender like his son's.

Sheffield took the burden of writing to James. He shut himself up for hours in his bedroom, agonizing over and praying for the right words to send to his son. The irony of joy and sorrow was almost too painful to write and too painful for anyone in the family to bear. Victoria's impregnable strength rose up as in former days and carried the family. She took care of the baby, coordinated all the funeral arrangements, accepted baked goods of condolence from neighbors, and kept the household running. Carson was asked to preach his first funeral. At first, he refused, and Brother Whatley was called upon, but then, with tears streaking his ruddy cheeks, he declared he would do it.

The day of the funeral, Ava feared for her brother as he mounted the pulpit over Estelle's body. She didn't know how he would manage to speak through his grief, but she watched in awe as their mother's strength flared in his eyes, and as his voice stammered then rose in eloquent thanksgiving, praise, and supplication. To Ava, his first sentence was his bravest and the one she understood best.

"I don't know why God chose to take home such a kind, beautiful woman at such a young age," he spoke. "Maybe, he saw her as he did Enoch, a person who walked closely with the Lord and was ready for his eternal glory early. We'll never know in this lifetime, and we'll all miss her as a wife, a daughter, a granddaughter, a sister, a sister-in-law, a friend, and most recently…a mother."

Carson finished, and it was their father's turn to be strong. Sheffield's heavy voice broke the tension of low cries as he sang the first verse of *I'll Fly Away* without musical accompaniment. When the verse ended, there was a pause, and then he motioned for the congregation to join in.

"To a home on God's celestial shores, I'll fly away. I'll fly away, Oh Glory. I'll fly away, in the morning. When I die, hallelujah by and by. I'll fly away."

The church's song grew louder, and Ava was moved by the earnest conviction of their combined voices. They weren't just singing about the heaven they hoped for, but rather a real place where Estelle now was. The song ended with a swell of energy, and the pews of mourners took turns saying farewell to Estelle. Ava watched through the two rivers of tears that flowed down her face as Estelle's sisters and parents ceremoniously proceeded past the open casket. All four sisters had the same lofty cheekbones and slight figures, except for the oldest, who was beginning to emulate her mother's fleshy form. Mott Dempsey paused by her daughter's still body and screamed out in filial despair. Her husband placed an arm around her shoulders and pushed her forward.

It was now their turn, and Ava followed her mother, who was carrying James and Estelle's daughter. With her closed eyelids and sucked in bottom lip, her niece wasn't aware of the great lady she was being carried past and would forever wish she had known. Ava looked into Estelle's limpid face, and her heart ached for first her oldest brother and then selfishly for herself. Finally, the small, wooden casket was closed, lifted above the shoulders of the church men, and taken to the Carson family plot in the graveyard behind Rapid Brook Baptist Church.

Chapter 50

Not long after Estelle's death, another person left Ava's life. With her usual capricious habit of living, Alta decided to move in with her aunt in Mobile. Her eyes radiated with excitement as she explained to Ava and Rosemary her plans over supper.

"Daddy and Mother gave in because they think the move will help me deal with my widowhood."

"They could be right," Ava said, and the idea of unknown faces and surroundings brought a new longing for escape within her.

"Oh, it probably will. It will be nice to be near the water everyday anyhow."

Ava now jealously imagined soothing waves caressing the bottoms of Alta's feet as her friend strolled on a bright morning next to the ocean she had never seen.

"I'm sure your parents will miss you terribly," Rosemary spoke, her mind dwelling more on the home Alta would be giving up rather than on the ocean she also had never seen.

"Mother is so involved these days in her society club that she won't notice, and I'm sure they'll visit more than I or Aunt Memie prefer."

She sat up straighter in her chair, and her face broadened with a fresh idea.

"If you two want to visit, I can show you a good time. I met several good-looking 4-Fs working in the shipyard this summer."

They smiled in mock agreement, neither of their hearts capable of responding to the promise of strange men. Rosemary's unyielding asceticism after Percy's subterfuge ended any romantic dreams she had for herself, and Ava was trying to hold onto the hope of Edwin. She knew that Alta thought the relationship was over, and the realization hurt. To give up on Edwin was about more now than losing the man she loved, it was also about losing another part of Estelle. Her sister-in-law said Edwin would come back, and Ava wouldn't disbelieve her.

The days that followed were the loneliest Ava had ever known. It was as if the pain she felt after each person's departure ripped through her again with empowered brutality. She cried for her brother, agonized over Edwin, mourned for Estelle, and missed Alta. The only thing that effaced her sorrow was her music, because into it, she released herself. The effect was invigorating. Her voice improved, and the people who listened would stop dancing or talking and stare into her eyes and soul to empathize with her unhidden passions and discover their own. Exacerbating the effect was the fact that many of the band's new songs reflected the mood of the country and Ava's heart.

"Waiting in the depot by the railroad track. Looking for the choo-choo train that brings him back. I'm waiting for my life to begin. Waiting for the train to come in," Ava sang, looking into the dim space above the dancers as if an imaginary train depot existed there.

There was a brief musical interlude before her ending, and she gazed down at her audience for a moment. A young man with red hair caught her attention. His eyes were green rather than blue like Edwin's, and his hair was a more distinct red, but the resemblance stopped her heart.

"Waiting," her voice slid and fell, "Waiting, I'm waiting for the train to come in."

She ended the song and stepped down for the band's next number, which didn't include her. She knew the soldier would ask her to dance, and she started to turn for the back of the stage, but something stopped her. The young man was behind her. She could feel him trying to capture her attention again.

"Excuse me, would you like to dance?" he asked when she faced him.

He was smiling so hopefully that she couldn't say no. They began to dance, and Ava recalled how electrifying it was to move with the music. She closed her eyes and, imagining Edwin as her partner, let the thrill of movement fill her. From that night on, she never refused a dance, because she knew in her heart that, no matter who her partner was, she would never let go of Edwin until she knew that he had first let go of her.

Chapter 51

"Bye baby bunting, daddy's gone a hunting," Victoria's voice transcended the closed door and challenged Ava's concentration once again.

She sighed in renewed frustration, scratched through the sentence she had just written, and threw the sheet of stationary on top of a growing mound of rejects. Between her uncertainties of how to begin another letter to Edwin, which she didn't know would either get to him or be answered, and her niece's crying, she was having difficulty writing.

"Ava!" Victoria called, and Ava flung down her pen.

She knew better than to show her temper in front of her mother. She wished she could write outside, but the sun always went away too quickly during the winter months.

"I need you to watch Ella for a few minutes while I go out back to boil some dirty diapers," Victoria said once her daughter was by her side looking down at the disgruntled, undressed infant. "It's o.k…hush… hush…."

Ella's cries began to fade as the white gown was lowered over her head and the changing was complete.

"She's just like you and James when you were little. You both hated being messy, but hated me doing something about it even worse. Carson on the other hand could not have cared less which way I turned and tossed him."

Ava bit her tongue and said nothing as her mother placed the baby in a basket lined with clean blankets, picked up a brown sack of soiled cloths, and went out the back door. She crossed her arms over her chest and looked down at her niece, not sure what exactly she was watching for. The baby was wearing the lace gown she had purchased at Wakefield's, and the recognition brought back memories of her last night with her sister-in-law.

"Your mother thought you would be a princess in this dress."

It was the first time she had ever spoken to or even paid any prolonged attention to her niece. She knew it was wrong, but seeing the child made her think of Estelle's death, and she was secretly aggravated that her mother had become an unexpected mother once again. Ella Christine Stilwell opened her mouth in a wide yawn, stretched out her arms and legs as long as she could, and looked back at her aunt with broad, amber eyes. Ava winced in surprise. The baby was almost always sleeping, and she had never seen her full eyes before. With their brown and yellow swirls, it was as if Estelle was looking up at her.

"I'm so sorry I've ignored you," she said and took hold of one of the infant's diminutive hands.

It was amazing to her how tiny God could make fingers. She looked back into the baby's face, and this time looked for her brother. Before, she had always thought that all babies looked like fat, wrinkled bodies of rosy flesh. Now, she recognized that there were traces of hidden personalities and resemblances to be discovered if you only looked.

"Your daddy will certainly think of you as princess, because you have your mother in you." Ava smiled, wishing that the eyes looking back at her could comfort James.

Not long after Estelle's death, they had received a couple of frantic letters from him. He had traveled through a string of French towns and was on his way to Belgium. The first letter was one of shock, and the second asked for the details of his wife's funeral. Since then, they had barely heard from him, and Ava knew that he was being tormented by something far worse than German bombs and gunfire.

"You know," Victoria spoke from behind her, "it's natural to miss those who have gone, but to despair for them is to deny God's promise of heaven."

Ava looked up at her mother, realizing that she had been observing her.

"I know," she lied.

In honesty, Revelation's description of jeweled streets and multiple-eyed living creatures surrounding God's heavenly throne never interested her, and she didn't understand how God could not first allow Estelle to enjoy motherhood and growing old with James.

"She's happier there than anything on this earth could ever make her, including us, your brother, or Ella."

Ava nodded recalling the New Testament promise of a place without pain or sorrow. That was the only part that appealed to her, but she was just beginning to experience the earthly suffering needed to fully appreciate what it meant.

Chapter 52

Ava stood with her hands clasped behind the tall, black microphone reading "NBC" in white, prominent letters. She could hear Willie Harold and the program director whispering behind her as they anticipated the live air moment. They were at the WSGN radio station in Birmingham, and their music would be broadcast live for the first time all over northeast Alabama through the NBC Blue Network, including WHMA in Anniston. Ava breathed in as she listened to news reporter Walter Winchell's update on the war and tried to calm her anxiety. Allies bombed the Japanese capital of Tokyo for the first time, and a smiling image of Jake Green with her cousin at his send-off party filled her mind. She had heard he was in the Pacific. Was he near Tokyo? More bombings occurred in England. A German V-2 rocket hit a Woolworth's store in the town of Deptford, and 160 shoppers were killed. The burning and collapsing Alabama Hotel leaped into Ava's thoughts, followed by the innocent picture of Violet Hemmert in the newspaper. With the elation of D-Day, the capture of Rome, and Allied advancements, everyone hoped the war would be over by Christmas and that families would be reunited for holiday festivities, but each day brought stories of new battles in the Pacific, Italy, and northwestern Europe. The report ended, and Ava felt her nerves screaming within her before transforming into the adrenaline she needed to sing. She was performing for her largest audience ever, and, ironically, it was invisible.

"As a post-Thanksgiving treat, we have some special music tonight," the program director announced in a deep voice. "Our own local Willie Harold's Band is going to perform for us some of our favorite patriotic tunes."

"He's 1-A in the Army and A-1 in my heart. He's gone to help the country that helped give him a start. I love him so, because I know he wants to do his part. He's 1-A in the Army and A-1 in my heart," Ava sang into the microphone, and the band delivered the patriotic song requested.

"Marvelous," Lavenia Stilwell praised her granddaughter when the on-air concert was over. "You have made the Stilwell family proud once again."

She pinched Ava's chin with her long fingers, and her grandfather hugged her and congratulated the band members. They were picking her up from the station for the night and then taking her to the bus stop in the morning for her journey back home. She came alone this time, and it was nice to have her grandparents' full attention and to be in a place were her losses were not so keenly felt.

Ava knew her father had something on his mind by the way he kept staring up at the ceiling and biting his knuckles. Victoria was too busy feeding, burping, and bouncing the baby to notice. Carson was giving an evening chapel service at the fort, and Grandpa Chester was snoring through a Bob Hope radio program. Ava sat on the floor reading the latest book her father had bought for her.

"I ran into Hazel Wheeler in E.L.'s store the other day," Sheffield said once the program ended.

340

Victoria and Ava both looked at him, neither of them knowing who he was speaking of.

"You know, the music teacher at the State Teachers College in Jacksonville."

"Oh," was Victoria's only response, and Ava continued reading as if the conversation was just for her mother.

"Someone told her I was your father, Ava."

"Really?" Ava replied, looking back up at him with interest now.

"She thought you were wonderful on the radio last week."

"Of course she was," Victoria said and turned Ella over on her stomach and began patting her back.

"She would also love to have you as a student at the college." He smiled with conspicuous excitement.

Victoria raised her eyebrows as Ava sat trying to comprehend his meaning. Was it merely a compliment or something more? College always seemed like something rich girls from Anniston and Birmingham did, not girls like her.

"Sheffield, we would never have that kind of money," Victoria said.

"No, we wouldn't, but her grandparents would pay for it if she wanted to go." "You've already spoken to them about it?" Victoria asked, and Grandpa Chester grunted in his sleep before resuming his rhythmic snore.

"I know I should have talked to you first, but I didn't even want to mention it unless it was possible, especially with how busy you've become with the baby."

Ella began crying, and Victoria moved her from her knee to her shoulder.

"They really want to help, if Ava wants to go," he repeated the last part for his daughter's sake. "Your father has helped us out numerous times."

Victoria's eyes flashed, realizing that her husband knew the truth. Her difficult adolescence taught her more than hard work and sacrifice. It gave her a fierce independence, particularly when it came to earning one's own way in life. She diverted her eyes and sighed under her husband's gaze. She also didn't want to deny her daughter any chance at a better life.

"Would you want to go to college?" Victoria asked Ava, tacitly agreeing with her husband that the decision would be their daughter's.

"What's this? You going to college, Annie?" Grandpa Chester sat up and shook himself to consciousness.

As the greatest Allied battle of the war raged across the sea in heavy snow, Victoria tried to deliver a festive Christmas and raise her family's morale. She knew that the holiday season would make them all long for Estelle and James more, and she did everything in her power to ease their shared sorrow. She cooked the largest Christmas supper she had ever made and invited Jude, Myrtle, Rosemary, and Judith to celebrate with them. She gave the baby to Ava more often and sewed and made presents for every person in the family. Sheffield followed his wife's example, hung mistletoe above every door, and led the family in a never-ending string of carols on Christmas Eve. Despite their efforts, everyone felt the inexorable tinge of pain grip their hearts as they sang on full, content stomachs.

Another Christmas ended, and Ava left Wakefield's again. She was beginning 1945 with a new challenge. Standing

342

in a semi-circle of young girls in a choral room, she realized that her world had once again expanded. She emulated the perfect oval of Hazel Wheeler's mouth and sang in unison with the other girls.

"Guardian angels God will send thee, all through the night."

Everything she thought she knew about singing was decimated. Now, she focused on pronouncing consonants and breathing from a strange part of the body called the diaphragm. Her days were full of vocal lessons and academic classes, and her nights were full with studying and helping care for Ella.

Ella was growing faster than Ava thought possible. She hardly resembled the purplish infant of September. Her skin was now golden brown, matching her eyes, which widened in wonder as they discovered the world around them. Ava loved to point out novel things to her, like a cat or a bird, and watch her tiny face's candid reaction. The winter ended, and spring was passing with a mixture of musical notes and baby gurgles.

Chapter 53

Pete Gunter was the first one to come home. Ava's heart faltered one late afternoon when she neared the house and caught sight of a uniformed man sitting with Carson on the front porch. She had managed to push Edwin to the back of her thoughts, but not to the back of her heart. James's most recent letter confirmed that it wasn't him, but she still didn't know where Edwin was. For a moment, she wanted to run to the house, but then she had to force her legs to move forward in case the soldier wasn't him.

"Hey, Siren," she heard a familiar voice call, and she immediately recognized it to be Pete's.

Her heart fell in disappointment but then lifted in tardy elation at the return of her school friend.

"You mean they let you come back," she yelled, quickening her speed as her legs regained their strength.

Pete's face and body were palpably thinner, but he had the same carefree grin. She stooped down to hug him but then straightened, noticing the crutch reclined against the swing and the awkward, disjointed turn of his left leg.

"What's the matter? Never seen a cripple?" Pete laughed, and Ava reddened in embarrassment.

She leaned down and embraced him, trying not to look at the leg again.

"I just didn't know, that's all. Carson didn't tell me."

"You didn't ask," Carson said.

"It's all right. I surprised pretty much everyone. I reckon no one expected me back alive and cracked up like my old man." Pete laughed again, but Ava noticed that the mirth of his voice wasn't reflected in his eyes.

"When did you get back?" she asked to change the uncomfortable subject.

"Yester evening. Ma sent Edgar up to the train station to fetch me. Speaking of Edgar, I heard you two still ain't talking."

Carson's muscles flinched thinking of Edgar's ignorance and execrable behavior toward the escaped German prisoners.

"Aw, he's just scared to come around again." Carson shrugged his shoulders.

"Preachers are supposed to turn the other cheek, now."

Ava pretended to listen and laugh along with their conversation, but her attention was really focused on the changes to her friend. There was sadness in his face, despite his humor, and he looked and sounded like someone who had come home to the familiar only to find everything unfamiliar and displaced. His family made little over him, and he felt as useless now as his father. His friend Jimmy wasn't back, and his friend Carson had become a man of God. Ava tried to imagine what it must feel like to see that the world you once knew had flowed around and past you. Edwin came back to her thoughts, and she feared that maybe he already felt that way and that was why he hadn't written or come back to her. It was all useless guessing, and she shoved him back into the box she had built for him at the center of her heart.

Whatever acknowledgement and fuss Pete's family didn't make over him, Victoria made up for. Seeing Pete in her home gave her renewed hope that her son would also return alive and well, and she made him the honored guest at her next Women's Advancing the War Efforts Committee meeting. More women attended the extemporaneous meeting than the last three put together. A local hero had returned, and they all wanted to see and touch him.

Victoria's huffs became louder, however, when Emmylou Gunter didn't show. She couldn't comprehend how a mother could be so callous.

"Ava! Rosemary!" she called with the coolest smile she could produce. "Pour everyone more lemonade. I'm going to fetch Emmylou."

Ava watched her mother with heightened respect as she made her discreet exit in the direction of the Gunters' property. Her father would call it meddling, but, to her, it was necessary interference.

Several minutes later, Victoria ushered a shaken Emmylou Gunter to the front of the room and began the meeting. Pete wiped away cake crumbs from his mouth and stared at his mother.

"You are all by now aware of our honored guest tonight," Victoria paused and smiled at each person. "It's certainly an answer to prayer to have such a fine boy back in our midst."

All of the women turned admiring gazes upon Pete, and he realized that he was in a room surrounded by females.

"Pete, will you please tell us a little about your service to our country," Victoria said and moved to the side of the room.

All of the blood in Pete's face drained to his lower body, and, at first, it appeared that he couldn't speak.

"What did you do for the Army, son?" Alice Fitzpatrick asked.

"I ... I was part of the ordnance division in a tank maintenance company," Pete replied.

He was sure that they had all heard about Jimmy's daring flying exploits.

"My nephew Clive is always writing home about his tank," Delores Waters said. "Did you run into Clive, James, Jimmy, or Mel over yonder?" She whispered the last name. They all now knew that Mel Boozer would never return home.

"No, ma'am, I didn't. We were all pretty scattered. I did meet a nice feller from Opelika, Alabama, though."

Now that Pete's confidence had been boosted, a barrage of questions was aimed at him from every direction. He barely had time to finish one answer before the next one was demanded of him. Ava smiled at her friend, sensing that he was warming up to the prodigious female attention he was receiving. A misguided German flying bomb might have disfigured his leg, but his spirit was healing.

Chapter 54

A steady knock halted their song and sent Ms. Wheeler out of the choral room in a subdued fury. Her class was just beginning to sing the Italian selection correctly.

"I'm still not hearing our part in this piece," another mezzo-soprano named Rebekah told Ava after their teacher left the room.

"It's difficult," Ava replied, even though she was more concerned about holding and releasing her breath at the right moments during the lengthy chorus.

They looked back over their music, humming the questionable part together. The door to the choral room reopened, and Ms. Wheeler returned with a very different demeanor. Her cheeks were streaked with tears, and her hands and voice were shaky as she called for their attention.

"I have some unfortunate news to share with you ladies," she began. "President Roosevelt has just died in Warm Springs, Georgia."

Everyone was silent as they were called back to the reality of the world outside of music. Several girls began to cry, and Ava felt her own eyes swimming with tears. Their president and leader throughout the war had just died, and they each felt an ineffable sense of loss.

Classes and the U.S.O. event where Ava and the band were scheduled to perform were both canceled the next day, and the late President's body was ushered from Georgia to Washington, D.C. by railway. Eighteen days later, another infamous leader left the war and the world forever.

Ava listened with her brother, grandpa, and parents as a newsman reported over their radio, "The German radio has just announced that Hitler is dead. I repeat that the German radio has just announced that Hitler is dead."

While the country shared in a widespread mourning for President Roosevelt, they shared in a time of celebration over the death of the diabolical dictator who had taken so many of their loved ones' lives. The news was plastered over all the newspapers, and everyone waited for word of an inevitable German surrender. Final confirmation that the war in Europe was over came on May 8, 1945.

Newly sworn-in President Harry Truman declared in a quiet, rehearsed voice, "This is a solemn but a glorious hour. General Eisenhower informs me that the forces of Germany have surrendered to the United Nations. The flags of freedom fly over all Europe."

The news meant one thing to Victoria Stilwell.

"James can come home now!" She jumped up and down in front of the radio with Ella in her arms.

"There's still Japan to consider," Sheffield said, calming his wife's enthusiasm with his unwanted rationalism.

She raised her eyebrows and looked at him angrily. Like Sheffield, the country and soldiers everywhere now turned their eyes toward Japan. James's next letter both rejoiced over the possible end of C-ration stew and hash and contemplated his more than likely move to the Pacific front.

Chapter 55

Ava looked out from the U.S.O. stage at her audience of dancing and reveling soldiers and perceived the same light, relaxed mood that she had for the past month. Even though they had never seen combat, they were all eager to celebrate the end of the war in Europe and the likelihood that they might never see war if the conflict in Japan also ended soon. The way the men strutted and danced with their partners told that they felt invincible in their country's military dress, and Ava realized that her next song might never mean to them what it meant to her.

"Kiss me once, then kiss me twice, then kiss me once again. It's been a long, long time," Ava sang to the softer beat. "I haven't felt like this, my dear, since can't remember when. It's been a long, long time. You'll never know how many dreams I dreamed about you or just how empty they all seemed without you. So, kiss me once, then kiss me twice, then kiss me once again. It's been a long...."

She didn't get to the end of the verse because an often-wished-for face suddenly appeared in the back of the room where Edwin once stood. At first, she refused to believe her eyes. What if it was just another soldier who favored him? When he didn't vanish, she knew it was him. He was staring up at her with his familiar feral eyes, which told her that he would have to be broken by her boldness and his love for her once again. She smiled down at him, completely forgetting her song, and then watched in incredulous horror as he turned and walked back out the door. Her head and chest began to pound. He couldn't be leaving her again. She jumped down from the stage and pushed her way through a crowd of oblivious dancers. Panting in fear, she ran out the door that he had just vacated, and her eyes searched in all directions for the ghost of the man she loved.

"Edwin," she shouted again and again, and tears began to muffle her voice.

Just when she thought he was gone, a hand encircled her wrist, and she felt his mouth meet hers. He kissed her with a desperation that she also felt. When he finally released her, he pushed her away from him, and they both looked at each other in silence, not knowing what to say to someone you've wanted to say so much to for so long. His face and body were hardened and leaner than she remembered, and his auburn hair was almost past his ears.

"I was afraid you were never coming back," Ava finally spoke.

"I wasn't. I mean I'm not. I just had to see you one more time."

"What do you mean?" she asked, her own eyes becoming wild like his.

"It would never work. I'm different now. Things are different."

"What things? You still love me or you wouldn't be here. You wouldn't have proposed to me."

"Of course I love you," he shouted back, looking away from her.

He could never withstand the unbridled passion of her voice and expressive eyes.

"But I've seen too much now. I wouldn't make a fit husband. You were stupid to accept me."

"So, you did get my letters, but you just didn't respond."

"I was trying to make you stop caring, to move on. I've seen too many men die, Ava. Sydney is dead, and Barry is dead. Neither of them will ever be able to love again, and neither will I properly, the way you deserve. I'm dead inside."

"Barry's dead?" Ava said, suddenly recognizing his pain.

It was the same pain she had witnessed torturing him since he first told her about his father's death, only intensified.

"Yes, he died shortly after I wrote to you that last time. I watched him. It wasn't fair. The doctors all said he was one of the lucky ones, that he would get better and live a normal life."

"Just because they're dead, Edwin, and I mean your father, Sydney, Barry, and whatever friends you might have lost, doesn't mean you have to be too." She grasped his hands and felt them quiver before he pushed her away again.

"It's no use. It's over, Ava," he said with a harsh finality.

He turned to leave, and she attempted to reach out for him again, but the look he gave her stopped her. She was afraid that he would hit her if she tried once more, and she watched through a blur of tears as he walked away from her.

"Edwin, you were spared for a purpose," she yelled out, not caring who overheard and repeating Estelle's words that had comforted her and kept her sane so many times. "You're not meant to be dead. We're meant to love each other."

The words only seemed to bounce off him and echo back to her as his disappearing figure grew fainter. He was gone again.

By keeping her face diverted and her voice steady, Ava was able to hide from her mother what had just transpired. She couldn't admit to anyone, including herself just yet, what had happened. When she managed to close the door without raising suspicion, she collapsed in a broken heap on her bedroom floor. Inaudible sobs burned her throat and saturated her lap. She grasped her sides and realized for the first time how grief and disappointment could make her cousin sick. She felt as if her insides were exploding and as if a thousand tears were rushing to escape her. All of the hope she had held onto for so long had been dashed.

She didn't know when she fell asleep, but sometime the next morning, the sound of her mother's voice calling her father to breakfast aroused her. She was lying in the same helpless position, just inside the door, as she had been the night before after coming home from the dance. Trembling, she stood up and straightened her crumpled dress. Her pulsing temples confirmed that last night had been no dream.

She changed her clothes, washed her face, wound up the music box her parents had given her on her seventeenth birthday, and waited to its tune. The dreamy melody of *Midnight Serenade*, which often resonated within her, seemed to mock her sadness, but it kept her still. When she believed that she had waited long enough to avoid a leisurely breakfast and conversation with her mother, she rushed out of her room, grabbed a ham biscuit, and shouted good-bye behind her.

"Bye, mother. I woke up too late this morning!" The screen door slammed shut after her.

353

She was back at Wakefield's for the summer, and she hurried as usual to the place where she was to meet Rosemary. All last night, she had thought that Rosemary would be the one person she would tell everything to. She was the only one who would understand and not dismiss her feelings as youthful emotion, but, when she saw her cousin, something inside her tightened and wouldn't let her speak.

"Good Morning. How was the band last night?" Rosemary asked.

"Good, we sang a new number that everyone seemed to like," Ava said with a calmer face and tone than she thought possible, even though the mention of the song brought back the sensation of Edwin's painful kiss.

They took the bus to Anniston and began work as usual. Ava worked methodically and distractedly, going over every word that had been spoken between Edwin and her the night before. Rosemary was showing one of the store's summer arrivals to a customer, and Ava observed her for a moment. Her back was straight, and she carried herself with a new confidence as she explained the convenient position of the buttons on the dress's bodice. Something about her had changed. With Alta gone, she had assumed a more savant and prominent position in the store, and Ava realized that Mrs. Crockett rarely reprimanded or supervised her anymore. Rosemary had found a personal resolve and identity in her work that didn't include her family, her background, or a man. Her work was for her what music was for Ava, except that instead of it being primarily an outlet for her emotions, it was a vehicle of self-worth and importance. Ava breathed in and looked away, knowing that she, Rosemary, and the whole country would be all right after the war, but still, there was something inside her that wouldn't forget Edwin just yet.

Chapter 56

"In John 14:27, Jesus tells his followers, 'Peace I leave with you, my peace I give unto you; not as the world giveth, give I unto you. Let not your heart be troubled, neither let it be afraid'," Carson read from his King James Bible to the handful of Germans gathered in the chapel before him.

He wanted to bring them a comforting message of peace and hope, a hope that said that whatever the war had taken away from them – their dignity, their homes, their loved ones – the peace they had in Jesus Christ could never be taken away. Their faces had changed with recent events. He could see anguish in their contemplative eyes and vacate smiles. They were waking up at last from a grandiose dream of victory that Hitler and their political leaders had branded into them. Now, disillusioned, many were beginning to question whether or not they had been the real criminals of the war in which they had participated. The Army was forcing them to watch footage of the Jewish holocaust, and most of them claimed ignorance, while a few admitted to knowing of prison camps for criminals but nothing about the perverse torture and mass murders of innocent human lives. They were both ready and fearful of going home, afraid of what destruction and implacable changes they would find once there.

The front door of the chapel groaned open, but Carson didn't slow in his speech as a lone figure entered and slipped into the back pew. The German raised his lowered head, and Carson was surprised to see Albin. He had only come to one of his services before, preferring to attend those performed by the Catholic priest. Carson greeted him with a momentary smile and flipped to another passage in Philippians about the peace and reconciliation all believers share in Christ. After the reading and a prayer, he dismissed his small congregation and made his way to the back pew where his friend awaited him.

"I come to tell you bye," Albin spoke with the same complacent expression as the other prisoners.

"Will you be one of the first to leave then?" Carson asked.

"Yes, I believe it will be any time."

"You must be ready to get home to your wife."

"Of course. Be sure to look at her picture every once in awhile." Albin smiled.

"If they let chaplains in, I certainly will. Will you paint when you return home?"

Albin hesitated, narrowing his eyes as if he had never pondered the question before. Life now after the war and defeat was something the prisoners knew could not be planned, but rather faced. Everything had changed.

"Perhaps," he answered. "Perhaps I'll play checkers more also."

He then laughed, and the genuineness of the sound lightened both men's hearts.

"Farewell," Albin said, and the two shook hands for the last time.

As Carson watched him leave, the painting of the attractive, dark-haired woman filled his imagination and came alive as he pictured her embracing her husband after several years of separation. It was an inferior and different kind of peace from the one he preached about, but one that he almost envied.

Chapter 57

Ava and Rosemary worked longer than usual at Wakefield's one night to help Mrs. Crockett and Douglas complete a full, detailed report of the store's inventory. Mr. Wakefield had requested the report by mid-week, and it was nearly Wednesday. They were tired when they finally rattled the front door goodnight and stepped out onto Noble Street. The sun was just beginning to descend into darkness, and they hoped to eat something quick for supper and catch the next bus home. Once they rounded the corner toward the Sanitary Café, a man halted them. Ava felt her heart flitter and then resume a defiant steady beat.

"Edwin!" Rosemary gasped out loud.

"Hi, Rosemary," he replied without looking at her.

His eyes were focused on Ava, and she walked past him, neither of them saying a word. Rosemary watched them dumbfounded, and, when Edwin rushed forward and reached for Ava's arm, which she pulled back, she realized that something had happened between them that she didn't know about. The knowledge was astonishing considering how well she thought she knew everything that took place in her cousin's life. Realizing that they needed to be alone, she fell behind them.

Ava refused to stop walking or even look at the man bearing down on her. She wouldn't give in to him again so easily.

"Stop," he called and reached out for her swinging arms again.

This time she spun around and looked back up at him. He looked rough. His face was worn, his clothing was tousled, and the stubborn hair that grew on his chin was unshaven and curling about his mouth.

"I believe you've already made yourself clear," she said, taken aback by his appearance despite everything. "There's nothing left to be said between us."

She tried to free her arm for the second time, but he wouldn't let her go. He was holding her so tightly it hurt, but she didn't grimace as he pulled her to the side of the street.

"I don't want to be dead," he said, softening his voice and at the same time his grip.

"What do you mean?" She was glad that her words had not gone unheard or unremembered.

"What you said before," he began, "I mean after I left you the other night. I felt worse inside than I ever had, even worse than I did when...," but at this he paused.

"I tried to leave you, but I couldn't. I've been sleeping off the road every night since we last talked thinking about you and what you said to me."

Ava winced as pity lessened her anger.

"You've been sleeping out on the ground every night for more than two weeks?" she said, knowing that the question showed more sympathy than she was still ready to give.

"Ava, I've been in the Army. I'm used to sleeping in worse conditions."

She looked down at this statement, trying to resume her indifferent attitude toward him.

"I need you. You're right. I'm dead without you, and I don't want to be. I want you. I love you."

When she looked up, his eyes were watery with unused to passion. The sight of them broke her, and she flung her arms around him.

"I need you too," she said.

Now, she knew why she couldn't even tell Rosemary about his leaving her. She had believed Estelle. She knew he would come back.

The next few weeks were the happiest Ava had known since before Edwin left for the war. After discovering that he was camping out every night without even a tent for protection, Victoria offered to let him stay in James's unoccupied house. She still hoped that it would be filled once again by her son and his daughter any day, but, for the time being, she reasoned that an engagement made it more socially appropriate, that it would help out her future son-in-law, and that, most importantly, it would help make the house cheerful once again. No one had even breathed in the house since Estelle's body was removed, and she wanted to lift the feeling of despair confused with the place.

"Go let Edwin know that you're home and that supper will be early," Victoria said, poking at the bubbling okra in her iron skillet.

It was a Wednesday afternoon, and Willie Harold had released the band early on account of all their recent performances. Ava almost dropped the spoon she was stirring the cornbread with. Had she really just been given permission to be alone with Edwin for a few minutes at James's house?

"That boy is still scared to come over here when he thinks you're not home."

"I'll be right back," Ava said without looking up.

She didn't want her mother to see the glee in her eyes and send Carson after her fiancée instead. She left the kitchen, and then, as she ran her fingers through her tangled, thick hair, hurried across the short distance between the houses. She had counted on at least a few minutes to freshen up her appearance before Edwin arrived but was happier to have to forgo that time instead. At the door, she halted, suddenly remembering everything associated with the house before her. She had only entered it once since Estelle died, and that was only because her mother made her collect the things her sister-in-law had been accumulating for Ella's arrival. She knocked and forgot the horrible night of Estelle's death when Edwin opened the door. He wasn't expecting her, and she could tell that she had caught him in the middle of getting himself ready. He was barefoot, his hair was wet and slicked back with some sort of oil, and the white shirt he wore was completely open, revealing his work-hardened chest.

"You." He smiled in surprise and pulled her inside and to himself.

Ava felt her blood turn hot when his bare chest pressed against her, and he kissed her with the new, uninhibited passion he was beginning to exercise toward her.

"Supper's almost ready," she said in between kisses.

"I'm glad you came over, Songbird." He smiled and separated himself from her. "I have something that I can't wait any longer to give you."

"Then I can't wait to get it." She laughed, watching him fumble through both pockets of his pants.

361

He retrieved a small ivory box from his left pocket. Could it be what she thought it was?

"I know it's not as big as what you were probably hoping for, but...," he stopped talking and opened the box to reveal a thin, circular piece of gold supporting a small, oval diamond.

"Oh, it's more than I hoped for!" Ava held out her ready hand.

He carefully removed the ring from its box and placed it on the ring finger of her left hand.

"Now, we're officially engaged." His face and ears turned scarlet with his last word.

"It didn't take a ring for me to attach myself to you," Ava said, pulling his face toward hers and kissing him. "But, how did you afford it? Believe it or not, I wasn't expecting one."

"I wrote to my mother and told her to send all the money I saved while I was in the war."

Ava felt somewhat guilty at this news but not enough to argue with him.

"I love you," she replied.

"Then marry me this weekend."

"This weekend?"

She was ready to be married, but something about the suddenness of his request brought unaccustomed reason to her racing mind. She smiled slowly, not sure how to word her feelings. She didn't want to give up school and the band.

"I want to more than anything," she spoke, pressing his hands with her own, "but don't you need to figure things out for yourself first? We can't live on love alone."

As he listened, his eyes reverted to their protective habit of coldness.

"What's there to figure out? I'm back. We love each other."

"I know all that." Ava sighed, still caressing his hands. She didn't want to lose him again to his own emotional aloofness.

"I mean, what do you want for yourself now? Do you want to go back to Tennessee? Do you still want to farm?"

His eyes softened, but she could tell that he didn't expect this response. He was used to and admired her unrestrained passion, not clear-headedness. He let go of her hands and ran his fingers through his drying hair.

"I'm never going back to Tennessee. When I went back there after coming home from the war, it was even less like the place my dad had built than before," he answered, and the usual resentment he felt toward his mother and stepfather flared in his voice. "We can stay here with your family. I've enjoyed working with your father and grandpa the last few days. I don't think they'd mind, especially with Carson helping out less and less."

"I'm sure they wouldn't," she said gently, "and, if that's what you want, that's what I want, but why don't you give it all a few weeks to be sure."

There was silence as he considered her request.

"I'll go wherever you want once we're provided for," she said, secretly hoping it wouldn't mean giving up school. "But now, I want to reward you for my beautiful ring with a few more kisses before supper." She wanted to change the mood back to what it was before her reason had gotten the better of her.

He smiled down at her when she moved toward him and stretched out her arms. It was enough. He pulled her back

to his bare chest and kissed her with almost the same fervor as
before.

Chapter 58

"Your daddy's coming home!" Ava repeated over and over again to the bouncing infant in her arms.

Ella smiled unsuspectingly up at her aunt as her chestnut head bobbed up and down.

"I wanna ride." Judith giggled and plopped her chubby legs without invitation into Edwin's lap.

She still wasn't accustomed to or fond of not being the only small child. Ava laughed, and Edwin's body turned rigid. He didn't know what to do with little girls.

"Just take hold of her arms and give her a push with your knees," Ava explained, demonstrating with Ella.

"Judith, don't wear out our guests," Myrtle called from where she was placing a caramel and pecan cake in the center of the table.

It was Victoria's birthday and the one time of the year that Myrtle did all of the family cooking. Judith laughed when Edwin began to bounce her up into the air.

"Come on. You're going to be too wound up to eat cake," Rosemary said, removing her younger sister from Edwin's legs with an apologetic expression.

Ava stood up with Ella still in her arms, and the family gathered around the table where Victoria sat smiling behind the cake.

"This cake looks more delicious every year," Victoria said to Myrtle.

"Happy Birthday to you. Happy Birthday to you," Sheffield sang and invited everyone else to join in with his waving arms.

The song ended with Grandpa Chester's raspy howl, and Victoria blew out the candles, which were dull compared to the glow on her face. She was happier than she had been in months. President Truman had given her the greatest birthday present ever – her son back. They received the letter just yesterday. With the recent atomic bombings of Nagasaki and Hiroshima, for which no one could fully comprehend the destruction, and the subsequent surrender of Japan, James's company was no longer waiting for orders to head to the Pacific. Instead, they were boarding boats for home, and mothers all across the United States were relieved of new, unremitting worries.

When the cake eating was complete, the men went outside to smoke cigars while the women cleaned up. Edwin followed, this time not as uncomfortably as before. Working out in the fields with the men of the family had given him a new relationship with each of them, the type of masculine comradeship he had yearned for since the death of his father and leaving the Army. They settled into their customary places. Grandpa Chester and Jude shared the swing, Carson stretched out his full body on the other side of the porch, and Edwin joined Sheffield at the bottom of the steps. They smoked in silence for a time, each reflecting on whatever was occupying his mind. As Edwin watched the thick smoke from their cigars rise and separate in the air, he realized with surprise how content he had become. He was enjoying Ava's family more than he anticipated, and, for once, he didn't miss the world of his youth.

"I reckon we'll start in the bottom field tomorrow morning." Sheffield yawned.

Edwin nodded. It was the kind of casual statement his father would have made.

"We'll probably need to make a stop into town about mid-day too."

Edwin nodded again. He would help out in whatever way his soon-to-be father-in-law wanted.

There was silence again as smoke continued to climb and form sundry clouds around them. Jude began telling Grandpa Chester a fishing story he had heard the day before from Willis Ponder, but Edwin didn't listen.

"We've liked having you around the last few weeks," Sheffield spoke. "You like working with us?"

"Farming is all I've ever known, sir," Edwin said, hoping his answer was affirming enough.

He couldn't express how he really felt.

"Well, I'm going to tell you what I told both my boys." Sheffield lowered his voice. "Things are changing, son. We feel it a little more every year. I love the open fields. I gave up my family's grocery business for it, and I don't ever want to do anything else, but times are changing."

Edwin studied the speckled night sky trying to comprehend what Sheffield was saying. He felt privileged to be hearing what Carson and James had both already been told.

"What I'm trying to say is that a man's business may not always be in farming. It's getting harder for the average farmer to survive without all the fancy, new equipment being built everyday, and there's talk that the government may impose cotton allotment laws. I encouraged both my sons to look for and be open-minded for some other way to provide for their families, and I'm telling you the same."

Edwin felt as if he had just been punched in the stomach. What else was he supposed to do? What else was he good for?

"I don't think I'd be fit for anything else, sir," he replied, trying not to sound as though the air had just been knocked out of him.

"Sure you would. You're a smart, strong boy, and the world is full of opportunities now. The cotton mill and pipe shop are always hiring. The government keeps creating jobs, and I even read in the paper where they're going to make it possible for war veterans, like yourself, to go to college for free."

At the last suggestion, Edwin gulped. Obviously, Ava hadn't told her father about how poor his reading and writing skills were. He was grateful to have someone believe in him, but painfully realized that he had been hoping to continue farming with his future in-laws.

"Of course, you may decide to keep farming, and you can stay on with us as long as you like, but I just wanted to give you something to think about."

"Thank you, sir," Edwin said and was relieved to hear the door opening up behind them and Ava sprinting down the steps toward them.

"Mom wants to sing on her birthday!"

"We can certainly do that," Sheffield said and left them.

"Even you have to sing tonight," Ava said and then stopped, catching sight of Edwin's face in the moonlight. "Is everything all right?"

"Yep, just doing what you asked and thinking about the future." Edwin tried to smile as she pulled him back inside the house behind her.

They sang well into the night. Edwin was amazed at how many different songs they each knew by memory. As he listened to their merry music and tried to join in a few times at Ava's coaxing, his mind kept wandering to what Sheffield had told him, his past, and the last days he spent in the Army. Ava pressed his hand every time she noticed him slipping away, and the gesture confirmed to him that no matter how uncertain he felt about his future, he knew that his one place in the world was undoubtedly next to her.

Victoria finally grew tired and the music stopped. As everyone made ready to go home, Rosemary caught Edwin by himself for a moment on the porch.

She lowered her voice to almost a whisper and said, "I know I shouldn't ask, but what happened to Percy?"

The instant she said his name her face flushed as if she had spoken a forbidden word, and she looked away.

"I don't know," Edwin replied, and his own face grew red feeling her embarrassment.

Rosemary realized that he knew the truth, and it was degrading no matter how well he understood her position.

"The last I heard of him he had moved up in rank and was with a new company. I'm sorry."

"That's o.k. I shouldn't have…." She didn't have to finish because Ava appeared, and they all said goodnight.

Chapter 59

A few nights later, Ava said goodnight to Edwin and decided to take a walk. It had been weeks since she had been out walking alone, and Edwin needed his sleep. He had half-heartedly visited the cotton mill in Jacksonville that day to inquire about work and was planning to go to one of Anniston's several pipe shops in the morning. She wanted him to feel as fresh and confident as possible for what she knew he really didn't want to do but felt he must out of respect for her father.

Breathing in the familiar scent of grass, hay, and her mother's gardenia bushes, Ava felt at rest. There was something liberating and soothing about strolling through familiar paths in the darkness. She thought of Dixie and turned toward the old barn. Lately, she had ignored her favorite pet. There was light seeping through the barn's parallel doors, and she wondered if her father was checking on the animals before bedtime. Just as she was about to step inside, Carson's rising voice stopped her. She peeked through the partially open doors and saw her brother standing in the direct glow of a kerosene lamp with his Bible in hand. Ava stifled a laugh. He was taking after her and rehearsing his sermonizing in front of Dixie. She drew in her breath and listened.

"Brethren, we need to be like Paul and enjoy the freedom we have in Christ. There's no reason why we should ever be downcast," he shouted into the empty air. "With Christ, we have a power that is greater than anything in this world."

His voice did indeed sound compellingly powerful as he recited from Philippians, and Ava was reminded of God's voice speaking to Moses through the burning bush.

If he can speak like this Sunday morning, his new congregation will adore him.

She leaned her head against the rough wood of one of the open doors. She would have never imagined that her quiet and often temperamental brother could speak with such a forceful demeanor. With more prisoners of war leaving Fort McClellan every day, the number of chapel services had been cut in half, and Carson was now ready for a different kind of audience. Brother Whatley recommended him to a church in Heflin, Alabama, and he was speaking there for the first time on Sunday morning. Ava waited until he was winding down his practice sermon to plan an ambush. She couldn't let him go unnoticed, just as he wouldn't leave her alone to sing. At just the right moment, she burst through the doors.

"Quit telling Dixie he's going to hell." She laughed, and his voice faltered.

"What are you doing up?" He slammed his Bible shut and almost kicked over the lantern by his foot.

His preparatory sermon had come to an abrupt ending.

When Sunday morning came, Carson was indeed able to retain the authoritative voice he had captured in the barn. Ava sat between Edwin and her mother listening to the same words she heard by mistake earlier in the week. Victoria wouldn't think of the family not being present for Carson's first official sermon. It felt strange to be sitting next to her mother. Her parents always sat up front and in close proximity to the piano and pulpit at their church. Carson's eyes blazed, his voice swelled, and his legs ran down the aisle as he reached the climax of his speech. Instead of averting her eyes downward as she did when Brother Whatley came near, she watched her brother and was moved by his honest energy. It was apparent in his whole being that he was convinced and convicted of everything he said. Edwin bumped her elbow by accident, and she glanced up at his shaven face. His teeth were clenched tightly, and he was staring straight ahead and out the window at a group of cows lying on their fat sides. It was still evident that he was struggling with something beyond her, with an anger that her love was powerless to mollify. She sighed and closed her eyes just as Carson was calling for the congregation to stand in benediction. She couldn't help Edwin with her efforts, but she could help him with her prayers.

Victoria lay awake that night with a mixture of satisfaction and growing uneasiness. She was proud of Carson, certain that he would make a fine pastor, and she felt at peace about her daughter. Ava was back in college, something she would have never dreamed of for one of her children, and was engaged to a good man whom she believed would be a satisfactory provider. Her only source of discomfort now was her oldest son. It had been a little over a month since they had received the letter telling them that he was coming home, but still there was no sign or word from him.

"Where are you, James?" she whispered, staring up at the outline of the bedroom walls.

"Carson delivered a good, fiery sermon today, don't you think?" Sheffield asked.

Victoria blinked and looked over at her husband, who she thought was sleeping.

"Yes, I just wish James could have been there to hear it," she answered, allowing the uncertainty she felt to fill her voice.

If anyone could calm her fears, it was her husband, who had nerves of steel. He reached out and placed a hand on her slender abdomen.

"Yes, that would have made it even better."

"You do think he's coming home, don't you?"

"Everything takes a long time with the Army, blossom. He'll come home when he's able."

Victoria bit her lips together and moved her body up against her husband's. He draped his arms around her, and they fell asleep, both thinking of James.

Chapter 60

Ava reclined by the creek with her history book reading about Queen Elizabeth and her religious hatred for her Catholic cousin Mary Queen of Scots. History was the one non-musical course, besides calisthenics, that she was taking at Jacksonville's State Teachers College that semester, and it was more than indulging her fondness for learning about real-life, fascinating people.

"Whatcha reading, Songbird?" Edwin fell to his knees behind her and placed his chin on her shoulder.

"Queen Elizabeth," she answered and finished the sentence she was reading.

She then looked up into his face and noticed his unusually large smile. Placing a hand on his chin, she lowered his gruff face down to hers and kissed him.

"You're looking at an official Anniston Foundry employee," Edwin said.

Ava smiled at his happiness, somewhat surprised at his joy of actually being hired by the pipe shop to do something other than farming. She didn't want him to do anything just because her father suggested it.

"When do you start?" She pushed her book aside and invited him to sit beside her.

He sat down and took both of her hands in his own calloused palms.

"Monday, so that means we can get married this weekend. You said we could after I figured things out. Well, they're all figured."

Ava laughed and kissed him again, flattered by his eagerness to be with her.

"This weekend?" She sighed as his arms folded her into himself.

She loved being held by him, and the idea of being embraced by his bare body sent a fleeting sensation through her.

"I can't wait any longer. I can provide for us now, and your father said that James would want us to live in his house until we could find a place of our own."

Ava stood up and motioned for him to stand, her gray eyes vivid and her burgundy cheeks florid with mutual desire. He looked up at her, afraid of the meaning behind her sudden action and of being postponed once again.

"What are you doing?" he asked.

"If we're going to get hitched, we'll need a preacher. So, we better go find Carson!" she said and then raced away from him. He jumped up and ran after her.

Ava touched her white box hat to ensure its proper place in her dark, wavy hair and then ran her gloved hands over her hips and down the sleek, satin white dress her mother had somehow made in two days.

"You look radiant," Rosemary said. "Are you ready?"

Ava nodded and breathed in as Rosemary opened the door of Rapid Brook Baptist Church. Her eyes first met her brother's, who was suited and wearing his dignified preacher expression, and then Edwin's, whose hard, blue eyes softened at her appearance. It was the first time she had ever seen him wearing a suit, and he looked broader and handsomer. Even though they had chosen a small ceremony with her brother officiating and Rosemary acting as their only witness, Ava felt as if a hundred eyes were on her when she walked down the short aisle. Rosemary moved to the side of the altar, and Ava took Edwin's awaiting hand and stood before her brother. Carson's face fell as his relation of brother momentarily overshadowed his role as their spiritual leader.

"Ava, Edwin," he began, his voice thick with unexpected emotion, "I'm happy to have been asked to join you together as man and wife before God today. First, I would like to read two passages from Scripture about God's plan for marriage. 'Therefore shall a man leave his father and his mother, and shall cleave unto his wife: and they shall be one flesh.'"

His voice regained control as he read, and Ava tried to take in every word her brother spoke, but the heat of Edwin's hand and the reality of what was taking place between them were making her light-headed with happiness. Carson finished his biblical instructions and asked them to face one another.

"Do you, Edwin Paul Livingston, take Ava Lillian Stilwell to be your wife before God, in sickness and in health, in prosperity and in hardship, for better or for worse?"

"I do," Edwin replied.

"Do you, Ava Lillian Stilwell, take Edwin Paul Livingston to be your husband before God, in sickness and in health, in prosperity and in hardship, for better or for worse?"

"I do," Ava answered, and her eyes shone with the passion her new husband loved.

They exchanged small bands of gold, and Carson pronounced them man and wife. Rosemary alone blinked back tears at witnessing the intimate union. She felt more than ever the pain and humiliation of Percy's betrayal.

Chapter 61

Hi family,

I am writing to let you know that I will not be coming home for sometime. I decided to take a job at the Atlanta Municipal Airport with an Army buddy of mine from Atlanta. They need me to start right away, so I said I would. Tell Ava and Edwin congratulations and to stay in my house as long as they like. I hope everyone is as well as can be. I will write more later.

Love always,
James

Ava read and reread the letter, which had caused pandemonium in her family, as she fed Ella a warm bottle of milk. Her parents were still discussing the letter in hushed tones behind their bedroom door, and she could hear Grandpa Chester grumbling about it to Carson and Edwin behind her. Even though James opened and closed the letter with his familiar greetings, there was something distant in the tone of his writing.

"How can he avoid his own daughter?" she heard her mother's voice rise and demand, but her father's response was too low to make out.

"If you ask me, James is getting too many big-city notions. What's he want with a place like Atlanta anyway?" Grandpa Chester said.

He was angry that his celebrated grandson wasn't coming home to tell him all about the war and how he helped defeat Hitler.

"It could be a good job," Carson interjected on behalf of his absent brother. "One that could provide for him and Ella."

"There's a plenty of good jobs right here in Alabama," Grandpa Chester replied. "And what's more, doesn't he want to see his own family!"

That was the part that also stung Ava's heart. She missed her older brother terribly, and it was hard to understand how he could come so close to home without seeing any of them, even if he did get a high-paying job in Atlanta. Ella finished her milk, and Ava turned her over her shoulder and began patting her back. As she did, she met the child's Estelle-like eyes, and she knew that the recent news would have angered her sister-in-law as well. She agreed with her mother. How could James not be anxious to see his daughter? Her eyes then fell on the only other letter that had arrived that day and followed its formal, cursive writing. James wasn't coming home, but someone else was. Jake Green was returning at the end of the week, and his mother was throwing another elaborate party in the town square.

Jake Green's welcome home party was even grander than his send-off party. Francis Green filled the town square with patriotic balloons and ribbons and her guests' stomachs with fried chicken and every fixing imaginable. Once again, everyone in Jacksonville and beyond participated in the soiree, partly because of their shared esteem for Dr. Green and his son and partly because of the prodigious revelry and food to be enjoyed.

It was Ava's and Edwin's first event as a married couple, and Ava was eager to show off her new husband. Spotting Aggie Whorley and Floraline Dempsey in the crowd, she led Edwin to her school friends. They were already sitting in the grassy center of the square enjoying chicken and potato salad. Pete Gunter was also with them, and Ava noticed how close he was sitting next to Floraline and how her friend, who claimed to dislike Pete in the past, didn't seem to mind. Things had certainly changed, and Ava sighed at how the war gave confidence to and made heroes out of normal men and joined the most unlikely of individuals. She herself would never have met Edwin if it hadn't been for the war.

"This must be Edwin," Aggie said before any formal introductions could be made.

"Yes, this is him. Edwin, this is Aggie and Floraline, and you already know Pete," Ava introduced anyway, enjoying being married before her flirtatious friend.

"I so wish Bo could have met Edwin, but he had to work late at the cotton mill. You know he's a supervisor there and that we're planning to be married next month," Aggie said and invited them to sit down.

"Yes, Mother heard something about that at the last garden club meeting. Congratulations." Ava sat down and wondered to herself how Aggie could be attracted to such a whiskered and older man.

"Carson talked you into going fishing tomorrow evening just before dark yet?" Pete asked Edwin, and the two of them began their own conversation.

"I see you and Pete are getting along better," Ava whispered to her friend when she was sure the conversation about catfish was drowning their voices out.

Floraline's face reddened.

"I told you people would notice right away." Aggie laughed, her freckles dancing on her face.

"He's nicer now than he used to be. He doesn't make fun of me so much," Floraline explained, and Ava wondered if Pete had become more sensitive since becoming crippled.

"I'm happy for you. Pete's a great guy."

There was a loud shuffling in the crowd, and they all turned their attention toward it. Mrs. Green was ushering in the honored guest, closely followed by her husband, Mayor Ponder, and a throng of well-wishers. Ava could just make out the top of Jake's head as he was pushed up on the small platform that had been set up just for the occasion.

Mayor Ponder stepped forward and announced in his languid voice, "Join me in a round of welcome applause for one of our local heroes just returned from the war!"

Cheers and hoots came from every direction, and Jake stood on the platform with his mother still hanging on his arm. Ava watched him blush and recognized at once that he hadn't changed and that the attention still embarrassed him rather than honored him. His blond hair was almost white, and his skin was swarthy from working on a boat day after day. He smiled sheepishly out at the familiar faces of relatives and friends and waved in appreciation.

"Jake, as the Mayor of Jacksonville, we would like to bestow on you this medal of bravery, which we are proudly giving to all the boys from our city who have gone to serve our country most courageously."

Jake turned obligingly toward the mayor and was pinned with the medal as a new surge of cheers and hollers broke out. He whispered something to his mother, and she frowned and whispered to her husband.

Dr. Green stepped forward, silenced the crowd with his well-known hands, and then spoke as loudly as he could, "We don't want to keep you anymore from your supper. Please enjoy the food and music and be sure to stop by and see our son before leaving. Thank you all for coming."

Fervent harmonic music broke out, and the supper lines began filling up again. Ava and Edwin were making their way to the back of the food line when Jake managed to separate himself from his mother's friends and join them.

"Ava!" he shouted.

"Welcome back, Jake," Ava replied, embracing him. "You've certainly been missed around here."

"Oh, I couldn't have been too much."

"Did you not notice all the people out here?"

"You know these people are all here because of my mother and the food." He smiled and blushed again, eager to turn the attention away from himself. "Anyway, I hear you have a new last name."

"Yes, I do. Jake, this is my husband, Edwin Livingston," Ava said, relishing the sound of the word "husband" coming out of her mouth.

"Nice to meet you. You're a lucky man."

"Thank you." Edwin shook Jake's hand.

"How's James? Is he on his way home yet?"

"Yes and no." Ava frowned despite herself. "He's back in the U.S., but working in Atlanta."

"I'm just glad to know that he doesn't have occupational duty."

Ava smiled, wondering if that option would actually make her family happier and more at peace.

"Jake! Jake!" Mayor Ponder's wife, who was now standing with his mother, began calling out.

Jake smiled and waved in her direction but stayed where he was.

"I didn't see Rosemary here. Did she not come?"

Ava was too stunned at his asking about her cousin to answer for a moment.

"No, she couldn't make it," she lied and tried to smile.

"I'm sorry to hear that. Well, it's good to see you both again."

He started to leave them but then turned back.

"Is Rosemary happy? I hated the way things ended between us. I mean I understand that she was lonely. I should have never asked her to wait for me. Is he treating her right?"

Ava stood looking at him for a long minute, unsure of how to answer. There was her promise to Rosemary, but it was undeniable that Jake was still in love with her, and she decided to tell him everything. Jake's face fell and changed to one of outrage as Ava explained her cousin's unknowing affair with a married man over Mildred Ponder's persistent calling.

"Jake! Jake!" his own mother was now shouting and walking toward them.

"Thanks for telling me the truth, Ava," he said and grasped her hand in appreciation.

Another call and he was gone, coolly trying to converse with his mother and Mildred Ponder as his face pulsed with fresh anger.

Rosemary sat by herself listening to another episode of the *Inner Sanctum Mysteries.* Her parents and Judith had left over an hour ago to attend Jake's welcome home party. She had been surprised when they received the invitation in the mail but not surprised to find only her parents' names listed on the envelope. Of course, she wouldn't be wanted there, and she didn't want to confront Jake anyway. If he stayed in Jacksonville, she would eventually have to see him somewhere, but not tonight, and she was glad.

The mystery was still developing the plot behind another fictitious murder when there were first footsteps and then a knock on the door. She sat up, wondering if Ava had left the party early to console her. She didn't want consoling, and she thought about pretending to be out before walking warily to the door. She pushed open the door, and every muscle in her body tightened and her face turned white when her eyes met Jake Green's. His green eyes were fraught with pity as they stared at her through the screen door, and she knew at once that he somehow knew everything.

"Jake, how are you? It's so good to see you, but shouldn't you be at your party?" Rosemary managed to speak, and blood began to revive her cheeks.

"Can I come in?" he asked, and she realized that she was still holding the door only partially ajar.

"Of course."

He followed her back inside, and they sat down together, both unsure of where to begin.

"I was hoping to see you at the party," he started for them, breaking the silence.

"I'm sorry. Jake, I'm so sorry for everything. I wish…," she stopped unable to control the tears that were beginning to flood her eyes.

"I don't want your apologies," he hushed her, wanting so badly to quiet her with his arms as well as his voice. "I should have never asked you to wait for me. I should have known you would be lonely and need someone. I don't blame you for anything that man might have done to you."

"But, Jake, it was my fault. I made the decision. I betrayed you."

"But you wouldn't have if I would have been here," he replied, their eyes locked no longer in embarrassment but in hurtful honesty.

"I thought I loved him."

Her words bewildered him, and, for an instant, she saw a flash of hatred blaze in his gentle eyes.

"Thought, thought, you only thought you did!"

Rosemary dropped her head, and large tears began to roll down her face and into her lap. He reached for her hand, but she flung it away the moment their skin touched.

"Jake, I gave myself to him." She wept, and his silence confirmed to her that he understood her meaning and what she hadn't told anyone before.

He was now standing, looking down at her in incredulous amazement. Their eyes met once again, and the hatred she had witnessed in them just before now flared without control. He crossed the floor, slammed the door, and was gone.

Chapter 62

Ella's eyes widened as they followed the tip of Ava's outstretched finger to the silver, bulbous nose of a descending plane. The large plane seemed to grow in size as it roared closer and as its tires reached for the hard ground. Atlanta Municipal Airport was known for its record-breaking number of take-offs and landings in a single day, and Ava and Ella were witnessing their first landing together. Ava was in charge of entertaining her niece while her parents searched for James. After much private conversing, Sheffield and Victoria had decided to fill up the Ford Tudor with still precious fuel, drive to Atlanta, and find their eldest son. The plane was now rolling to a noisy stop, and Ava glanced back around for her parents. A series of questions filled her mind with the action. What would James look like now? How would he respond to her parents, to herself, and mostly to his daughter? How would he explain not coming home? Ella gurgled, and Ava looked back at the plane. A door had been slid open and a long ladder was emerging from its rotund belly. She watched the first of its passengers climb to the ground and wondered who they were and where they had been. The thought of returning through the sky from a far away destination was a romantic one, and she thought of all the places she would like to visit – England, France, New York City....

"Ava!" her mother's voice pulled her back to Atlanta, Georgia, and she spun around with Ella in her arms to see James walking toward them in between their parents.

He looked thin and pale, and the sight of him brought a stream of tears to Ava's eyes. She smiled, but he wasn't looking at her. He was surveying the child in her arms.

"Ella," Victoria called, and the little girl looked away from the plane and toward the sound of her name.

Her fat cheeks dimpled into a smile at recognizing her grandmother, and James's composure broke. His arms trembled, and his eyes grew watery as he saw his daughter for the first time.

"This is your daddy, Ella," Victoria said, taking the little girl from Ava's arms and moving her closer to her father.

James stood looking down at his child for a moment and then succumbed to irrepressible emotion. He was sobbing, and he turned away from them. Sheffield put an arm around his son and steadied his swaying figure.

"She's a beautiful girl. You should be proud."

"Her eyes are just like Estelle's. They're full of light," James said, trying to level his voice.

"I know. Aren't they gorgeous?" Victoria moved closer to her son, but he stepped away.

"I can't look at her, and I can't come home. I can't be around anything that reminds me of her or I won't be able to live. It was me that was supposed to die during this war, not her!"

"James, you have to give your grief to God. You have to be a father," Sheffield said. "It's what Estelle would have wanted."

James looked up at his parents and then Ava, avoiding Ella's eyes.

"I can't. I'm sorry, but I can't," he said before collapsing into his own father's arms.

"If he does come home, he doesn't ever want to live in this house again," Ava said to her husband as she slid a pink nightgown over her head and began brushing down her hair.

She looked at her reflection in the mirror and sighed at both the day with James and at how her hair was long enough to touch her shoulders once again. She met Edwin's eyes in the mirror and realized that he was watching her while he waited for her to come to bed. She improved her posture, and her cheeks crimsoned to the color of her lips. It was still awkward to undress in front of a man, but she loved the intimacy of marriage and the way her husband's desire for her made her feel beautiful.

"You don't think he'll come back?" Edwin asked.

Ava lifted the covers and lay down next to him. She placed her head on his broad chest and ran her fingers down his side before answering.

"I don't know. One day I guess he will, but I don't think it'll be as soon as Mom and Dad expect. He's terribly heart broken."

"But what about Ella?" he replied, wrapping his arms around her and stroking her hair.

He loved the softness and fresh smell of her hair and body whenever she was lying so close to him. The night was their favorite part of the day now. During it, they were undisturbed, and they enjoyed an emotional and physical freeness with someone that neither of them had ever experienced before.

"Hopefully, he'll come back before she's old enough to understand."

They lay in silence for some time thinking about each other as much as James and Ella.

"Anyway, he wants us to have the house," Ava said.

She had been saving this part for last, and she smiled as she felt his chest heave with the news.

"Ava, I could never just take a man's house." His fingers caught in her hair.

"What do you mean take? He's giving it to us. We're family." She sat up, astonished by his unfavorable response.

"I just wasn't raised to take things like that. James could change his mind, and your grandpa didn't give this house to us."

"Edwin, you're being silly. Everyone wants us to have it."

"Maybe for now, but probably not always. We can make our own home, just like my dad did and his dad did before that."

"Things are different now, Edwin. You need to quit worshiping your father and the past and live for yourself, for us," she said.

The minute she said the words she wished she could take them back. She could already feel him turning cold toward her.

"Goodnight," he said and kissed her on the cheek before rolling away from her.

Tears choked her throat, but she wouldn't cry. She meant what she said even if she wished she hadn't said it. Their night together had been ruined beyond immediate repair, and she turned in the opposite direction, stifling cries with her pillow. She was angry and tired of his constant fight and preoccupation with his own virility and purpose, which had been distorted by a kaleidoscopic mixture of his father's early death, his stepfather, the war, and his resentment of God.

It was difficult to sleep, but her body finally surrendered to its need for rest. Dreams took her mind away from their argument and to the stage. She was trying to sing, but no words would come out, and, as everyone watched, she was gripping her throat and motioning for first Willie Harold and then James to understand what was taking place. Suddenly, a blow to her side woke her up. She opened her eyes, thankful to find that her vocal ineptness had just been a dream. Another blow to the side made her writhe in lucid pain, and she looked at Edwin who was fighting with an imaginary opponent in his sleep. She screamed and ducked as his fist hit the bed frame directly over her head. Her yell and the pain of his knuckles woke him up, and he sat up trying to shake off the fictitious image that had attacked him. Ava shrank away from him, unsure if he was really awake, and the sight of her frightful eyes in the dim moonlight revealed to him what he had done.

"Did I hurt you?" he said, grasping first her head and then the rest of her body.

"No," she sobbed back.

"I'm so sorry." He kissed her face, mouth, and shoulders.

"I would kill myself if I ever hurt you."

The fight was over, the barrier was broken, and they were close once again.

Chapter 63

When the first of the year's yellow and gold leaves began to flee their trees and collect in wind-blown mounds on the cooler ground, members of the religious Jacksonville community gathered at Four Mile Baptist Church underneath the unneeded shade of a large tent for an all-night gospel singing. Local musical groups were invited to the event, and the Stilwells were always a part of the main entertainment. Ava, Edwin, Rosemary, Pete, and Floraline sat together on a large quilt listening to the Piedmont Quartet sing about the grace of God in melodic unison.

"The wedding will be on Christmas Day," Floraline told Ava and Rosemary as the three of them clapped along to the upbeat rhythm.

"You want a husband as a Christmas present." Ava laughed.

She liked spending time with Floraline more and more now that Estelle was gone. She wasn't as warm or funny as Estelle could be, but she had the same soft manners and easy nature that Ava missed so much.

"He should always remember your anniversary," Rosemary said. Her eyes bounced from the quartet to her friends to the people behind them. She couldn't help but look for Jake and dread another encounter with him.

"That is supposing I remember Christmas," Pete said, and they all laughed.

Ava looked down at his disfigured leg, which was lying sideways out in front of him, and felt happy that his old sense of humor was returning.

"If you don't remember, you may not make it through Christmas," Edwin joined the conversation, determined to be light-hearted with his new friends, which he knew his wife appreciated.

"That's some advice I'll remember. Hey, Jimmy's mother says that he might be home for a short stay around Christmas."

"Is she still upset about his decision to stay in the Army?" Rosemary asked, her eyes continuing to gaze about them. She didn't want to be there, but she knew that she couldn't stay locked up in her house forever.

"Yea, she's still crying off and on, but the idea of him coming home for Christmas is drying up her tears a little."

Ava was about to ask more about Jimmy when the quartet finished and Victoria waved for her to come up front to sing. She was eager to join her mother. No matter how much she loved the finer sounds of the big band and singing for Willie Harold, it still felt like home to perform with her family.

"I'll be back," she whispered and squeezed Edwin's hand.

"And I'll be here." He smiled.

Ever since the night of their argument, his temperament and actions had been nothing but endearing and apologetic. She smiled back at him and walked to her usual place between her father and Cousin Jude. The only one missing was James, but they had all been forced by now into accepting his absence.

At the thought of her elder brother, Ava looked down at Ella. She was sitting up front, sharing Myrtle's lap with Judith. Judith was playing with a bug on the ground as Ella pulled on her blonde ringlets. Ava laughed at the child. No matter what had happened; James and Estelle were still present, just in a different way. They were alive and joined together in their daughter.

So much has changed, yet so much is still the same, she thought, and her mother began playing the prelude to their first song.

A waving hand caught her attention, and she saw Grandpa Chester wink at her and mouth, "Good luck, Annie," just as she began the first verse.

Even though Rosemary clapped to the music and continued to discuss wedding plans with Floraline, she was still aware of everyone who moved around them, and, when someone sat down behind them, she knew it was Jake without even looking.

"Good to see you again, Edwin. Pete, how are you? Congratulations to you and Floraline on the engagement," he said in quick succession, addressing everyone but her.

Rosemary didn't say anything either. She sat with her back to him, pretending to be undisturbed by his presence and engrossed in her family's performance. When the song finished, Carson stood up from behind his banjo to address the crowd. Now that he was a full-fledged preacher of a legitimate Baptist church, Victoria and Sheffield let him do most of the speaking, and he didn't seem to mind his new position. Like

393

Brother Whatley and the prophet Jeremiah, he felt the word of God burning within him to escape.

"Our next song is one of our favorites, because it speaks of God's sustaining power. We've all experienced great changes to our communities, churches, and families over the last couple of years, but God has been faithful. While he hasn't shielded us from loss, death, and misfortune, he has kept us through it all. He has loved us through it all and blessed us in the midst of conflict. My own family has seen this and experienced great heartache, but today, we still stand together and are stronger as a result."

Rosemary's eyes moistened at her cousin's words, and, with Jake so close behind her, she felt the past year's humiliation, guilt, and forgiveness of God all flood her heart at once. It didn't matter what had happened, she would be a new person.

"I was standing by my window on a cold and cloudy day, when I saw the hearse come rollin'," Ava sang out with a mournful fervor that matched the words she articulated.

Rosemary closed her eyes, and a warm and familiar hand touched hers. Her body stiffened, and her heart quickened.

"How can you forgive me?" she whispered, but there was no answer.

Jake's hand remained on her hand, but this time she didn't move hers away.

"Well, I followed close behind. Tried to hold up and be brave," Ava sang, noticing Jake sitting close behind Rosemary and sympathizing with the misery her cousin must be feeling.

Her eyes moved to Edwin next. He wasn't looking at her. Instead, he was looking down, his head in an unnatural bowed position. Something about the way his strong shoulders were heaving up and down alarmed her, and she continued on to the next verse, unaware of everything but her husband.

"One by one the seats were empty, one by one they went away," her voice continued methodically as the love she felt for Edwin consumed her.

She wanted so desperately to help him, to feel whatever he was feeling, but she couldn't. Finally, he looked up, not at her, but up, as if to God. His blue eyes were wet, but they were eyes of peace, not of cold, hurtful stoicism. Ava felt her heart bursting. He had finally been broken by one far greater than she, by the only one who could ever make him a whole man and a whole husband.

"Will the circle be unbroken? By and by, Lord, by and by, there's a better home a-waitin' in the sky, Lord, in the sky," Ava, Victoria, Sheffield, Carson, and Jude sang out triumphantly together.

It's finally over, Ava thought when they sang the last note, and her voice swelled with more careless passion than ever before.

"The war is really over," she spoke to herself, and she looked from her parents, to Carson, to Jude, Grandpa Chester, Myrtle, Judith, Ella, Rosemary, and lastly, Edwin.

28419900R00240

Made in the USA
Charleston, SC
12 April 2014